Take a Christmas visit to two sets of sisters and see how festive sparkle and feeling can ch[illegible]

& MISTLETOE KISSES

Dreamy single mum Gwen McKenzie secretly longs for a happy-ever-after for herself and her adorable baby… Whereas her high-powered twin Gill craves success and has given up waiting for a Prince Charming to sweep her off her stilettos…

Amelia Hughes is a single mum whose five-year-old boy is trusting Santa to send him a daddy for Christmas… While Kelley gets more than a feast when a celebrity chef offers her his talents in the kitchen!

Praise for Susan Meier

"Ms Meier's smooth writing style, nice sense of humour and good pacing keep us well entertained indeed."
—*Romantic Times BOOKreviews*

Praise for Donna Alward

"Talented Donna Alward weaves a gorgeous secluded setting, an intense, suspenseful plot and well-developed characters into a most rewarding read…"
—*Cataromance.com*

Praise for Patricia Thayer

"…Patricia Thayer offers readers a rich reading experience with emotional power, fresh characters and passion."

Christmas Wishes
& MISTLETOE KISSES

SUSAN MEIER
BARBARA WALLACE
PATRICIA THAYER
DONNA ALWARD

Harlequin Mills & Boon Limited, Eton House,
18-24 Paradise Road, Richmond, Surrey TW9 1SR

ISBN: 978 0 263 88828 7

009-1210

Harlequin Mills & Boon policy is to use papers that are natural, renewable and recyclable products and made from wood grown in sustainable forests. The logging and manufacturing processes conform to the legal environmental regulations of the country of origin.

Printed and bound in Spain
by Litografia Rosés S.A., Barcelona

Baby Beneath the Christmas Tree

SUSAN MEIER

Dear Reader,

When I was offered the opportunity to write this anthology and asked if there was a new writer I'd like to work with, I didn't even hesitate. I instantly said Barbara Wallace!

I met Barbara at the Romance Writers of America National Conference. Not only was she pretty, but she was also sweet and kind. I knew those qualities would translate into a great story. And they did. Barbara created a wonderful twin sister for my heroine and put Gill in a romance readers will long remember.

It's always fun to write about Christmas. I believe it's a magical time of the year. I got a chance to really expand on that theme by setting *Baby Beneath the Christmas Tree* on a Christmas tree farm. Gwen and Drew are made for each other, but neither sees that because there are too many complications in their lives. Gwen is a young single mum, desperate to finish her degree and be able to support her child. CEO Drew's an absentee dad, getting a second chance with the sixteen-year-old son he barely knows.

They have an age difference, a class difference and even a totally different outlook on life. So it's more than magic when they realise each can solve the other's problem. But solving problems is one thing. Getting the courage to take another chance on love when each has been hurt before is quite another. And maybe, just maybe, they'll get some extra-special help from the spirit that permeates Teaberry Farms.

I hope you enjoy *Baby Beneath the Christmas Tree* as much as I enjoyed writing it! To an author every book is special, but for me this one truly is magic.

Susan Meier

PS Look out for an exciting new trilogy from Susan in spring 2011 –Ed.

To my friend Denise, who listens to every incarnation of every story long before I write it!

CHAPTER ONE

FOR as long as Gwendolyn McKenzie could remember the old timers in the tiny town of Towering Pines, West Virginia, had whispered that Teaberry Farms was enchanted. The rumor was that if you touched one of the Teaberry Christmas trees while wishing, your wish would come true.

Driving up the fir-lined mountain road that took her to the farm, Gwen glanced around in amazement, understanding why the legend had formed. Majestic evergreens punched into a vast indigo sky. Fat, fluffy white snowflakes pirouetted around the green pine branches, falling heavily, like frosting on sugar cookies, creating a magical world.

But when she reached the Teaberry mansion, Gwen's mouth dropped open in dismay. Two rows of tall windows with thin black shutters dominated the huge redbrick home, but the shutters tilted drunkenly from age and neglect. The Teaberry family hadn't even visited for at least a decade, so it didn't surprise her that the house was in disrepair. But she'd thought Andrew Teaberry, her new boss, would have called ahead to have the place prepared to be used. If the house was this bad on the outside, she feared it would be worse on the inside.

Still, a wisp of smoke rose from the redbrick chimney, disappearing into the inky sky, proof that the caretaker must have started a fire in preparation for the owner's return. At least she and her daughter wouldn't spend their time shivering while they waited for Andrew to arrive.

She got out of her beat-up little red car, opened the back door and reached in to unbuckle the car seat of her three-month-old baby. When she'd gotten pregnant by a boyfriend who'd bolted the very second she'd told him, Gwen and her twin sister Gill had both worried that she might fall into the same trap their mom had. Ginger McKenzie had married the man who had gotten *her* pregnant. But when twins were born he'd panicked, saying one baby was difficult enough to handle, two was impossible. He left town, leaving Ginger to raise the girls alone, watching out the window, longing for him to come home.

Six months after her mom's sudden death, finding herself in a position very close to Ginger's, Gwen had quickly shaped up. She didn't want to be one of those women who wasted her entire life pining after a man who didn't want her. She'd stopped believing in miracles. She'd stopped believing wishes came true. She'd packed away her dreamy side. And she now only dealt in facts.

Which was why she was at this rundown old house, about to start a job as the assistant to a man she'd never met. She had to pay her own way, support a child and finish her degree. This job might be temporary, but it paid enough money that if she watched how she spent she could keep herself and Claire through her last semester of university.

"Hey, Claire-bear," she said, lifting the little girl and rubbing noses. Bundled in her thick pink snowsuit, with the white fur of the hood framing her face, chubby, happy Claire really did look something like a stuffed pink bear.

Using the key sent to her by Andrew Teaberry, Gwen unlocked the front door and stepped inside. A huge curving mahogany staircase greeted her and Claire. But so did cobwebs. A layer of dust coated the banister and the stairs.

"Wow. We could be in big trouble, Claire-bear."

Walking from room to room, she felt her dismay grow. Though the lights worked, the sinks had water and the kitchen appliances had been plugged into electrical outlets and hummed with life, the house was filthy. Her boss might have instructed the caretaker to get the utilities turned on and the furnace working, but he'd forgotten about cleaning.

Discovering a suite in the back that had probably at one time been the maid's quarters, Gwen set Claire's baby carrier on the dusty bare mattress of the single bed, but then lifted it up again. She'd arrived an hour early, hoping to make a good impression, but Andrew hadn't yet arrived. If she hurried, she could race home for a vacuum cleaner, mop, broom, soap and dustcloths, and still have time to clean this suite enough that Claire could sleep here.

Two hours later, Andrew Teaberry pulled his shiny black SUV into the circular driveway in front of his family's old homestead and his face fell in disgust. Pressed for time on this spur-of-the-moment trip, he'd thought ahead enough to hire an assistant and have the caretaker open the place, but he hadn't considered that the Teaberry mansion might not be habitable.

"So this is the fabulous Teaberry Farms." In the passenger's seat of the SUV, Drew's sixteen-year-old son Brody glanced around and snorted with derision. "Looks like a rat-hole to me."

Drew nearly squeezed his eyes shut in frustration. As if it wasn't bad enough that he had to move into this old monstrosity while he negotiated the purchase of a local manufacturing company, his ex-wife had decided to get remarried, forcing Drew to keep their son for the entire month of her honeymoon. So while he negotiated to buy the business of crusty old Jimmy Lane, a West Virginia entrepreneur who only wanted to sell his business to someone who lived in West Virginia, he was saddled with a sassy sixteen-year-old.

Inserting the key into the back door lock, he glanced behind him at Brody, who was so engrossed in whatever he was doing with his cell phone that he didn't even watch where he walked. Wearing a black knit cap over his yellow hair, and a thick parka that seemed to swallow him whole, Brody was the complete opposite of his dark-haired, dark-eyed, always observant dad. The kid was going to step into traffic one day.

Brushing up against one of the pine trees beside the kitchen door as he pulled the key out of the door lock, Drew prayed that they both survived this month. He pushed open the door, stepped into a kitchen that looked like something out of a horror movie and froze.

"Mr. Teaberry!" The woman standing by the dusty kitchen counter winced. "I'd say welcome home, but I'm not sure that's exactly appropriate, given the condition of the place."

Drew blinked at yet another surprise this morning. Unless she was Max Peabody, the caretaker, this had to be his temporary administrative assistant, Gwen McKenzie. In their phone interview she'd told him she had one more semester of university to finish, so he'd pictured her as being a petite sprite, someone who'd look only a little older than his son. Instead he'd hired a classically beautiful woman with thick blond hair and catlike green eyes, who was built like every man's fantasy come to life. A bright red sweater accented her ample bosom. Dark, low-riding jeans caressed her perfect bottom. Her shoulder-length hair swung when she moved.

He slid his laptop onto an available counter, glancing around at the nightmare of a kitchen. The oak cabinets were solid, but coated in dust, as were the kitchen table and the four chairs around it. But, like the cabinets, the furniture and the ceramic floor tiles looked to be in good shape. The house wasn't really falling apart, just dirty.

"Good morning. Sorry we're late. We couldn't get on the road until hours after we'd planned."

She batted her hand in dismissal. "Not a problem."

Brody pushed into the kitchen behind his dad, not caring that he'd bumped into him. "Hey, babe, thought for sure you'd have muffins and coffee waiting."

Drew blanched at his son's disrespect. "Not only is Gwen not our cook, but we don't call employees *babe*."

"All right. Great. No babe." Brody pulled his sunglasses down his nose and peered over the rim at Gwen. "Sorry about that, sweetie."

"We don't call employees sweetie, either!" Drew said, his temperature rising. If he didn't know better, he'd think the kid was deliberately antagonizing him. "How about an apology?"

Brody glared at his dad. "Fine. I'm sorry. Why don't you just write a list of rules so I know what I can and can't say this next month?"

With that he stormed through the kitchen, all but knocking the swinging door off its hinges as he punched through it.

Though Drew knew he should go after him, he had no idea what to say to this new version of Brody. That was part of the problem. Sixteen years ago, when his ex had moved herself and their son to Colorado, two thousand miles away from Drew, he'd protested. But in the end she hadn't budged, and his visits with Brody had become something like two-week vacations, spent on tropical islands or at ski resorts.

They'd always gotten along well. Until this trip. Now, Brody was suddenly obnoxious. Drew had absolutely no idea what the heck he was going to do with him for the entire month of December. One-on-one in a house so far out in the country that it didn't get cable TV, they were going to be miserable. Especially since Drew wasn't even sure when or why Brody had turned into such a mouthy kid or where to start with discipline.

He did, however, know exactly what to say to an embarrassed employee. He turned to Gwen. "I apologize for my son's behavior."

"Not a big deal," she said with a laugh. "He's what? Fifteen? Sixteen? He's testing the water. All kids do it."

A steamroller of relief rumbled through Drew. At least the relationship with his temporary administrative assistant would be normal. Then she smiled at him, her pretty green eyes shining, her full lips winging upward, and everything male inside of Drew responded. Her thick, shiny blond hair framed a heart-shaped face with bright eyes, a pert nose, and generous lips made for kissing.

Involuntarily, his gaze once again swept down the red sweater and tight jeans. He rarely went out, and when he did the women he dated were nothing like Gwen. They were tall, cool sophisticates. Models. Starlets. But there was no denying that this gorgeous blonde made him wonder what it would be like to kiss her—

He groaned inwardly. He wanted a normal working relationship with this woman! Plus, even if he was the kind to dabble in affairs, she was too young for him, and an employee. If those weren't enough, he had responsibilities as Chairman of the Board of his grandfather's conglomerate. The pressure of holding top position in a global company left him no time for anything but work. That was why he'd only spent vacations with Brody. Why Brody had had time to change without Drew even realizing. Why he had to figure out how he'd handle him for the four long weeks of December.

"I think I'll grab Brody and get our bags."

She winked. "Good idea."

Her wink was cute. Not flirty, but happy. And for some reason or another that sent a sizzle through Drew when he'd already reminded himself he wasn't allowed to be interested. Eager to get away from this confusing situation, he headed for the door that Brody had stormed through, and found himself in a hall and then a foyer, where Brody was bounding up the dusty steps.

He glanced around in renewed disgust. Cobwebs hung from the ceiling and created feathery loops on the walls. The house wasn't even clean enough to sleep in, but they had to stay here. There wasn't a hotel in tiny Towering Pines, and they were too far away from a city to drive back and forth. Plus, Jimmy Lane loved the idea that Drew was one of the original Teaberrys. He wanted to visit the Christmas tree farm. He wanted to see the mansion. Somehow or another Drew was going to have to make this place sparkle before his visit.

But as Brody stormed away Drew knew he'd have to deal with that later. "Hey! Aren't you going to help me with the bags?"

"Don't you have people for that?"

"Not here!" Drew yelled, as Brody continued up the steps. "Except for Ms. McKenzie, who's *my* assistant and not yours, we're on our own."

"Oh, I get it. *You* can use *Ms. McKenzie* for personal things, but I can't."

Something in the way Brody said that stopped Drew cold. Not because he shouldn't have an assistant, but because he was attracted to her. The entire time he'd been in the kitchen he'd kept losing his train of thought and stealing inappropriate looks at her.

Brody huffed out a sigh and started down the stairs. When he reached the bottom, Drew led him out the front door.

Stepping into the falling snow again, Drew headed toward his black SUV. The six inches that had blanketed West Virginia that morning gave the farm the look of a Currier and Ives painting. Even in disrepair, the big redbrick house had a solid, steady feel to it. Huge pines wrapped it in a warm embrace. Snow covered the fence and outbuildings, making everything sparkle.

Brody glanced around. "What a dump."

A sting of guilt whipped through Drew as he popped the hatch of the car. "Just because it isn't our cup of tea, that doesn't mean the farm is a dump."

"Whatever." Brody reached in and dragged his duffle bag out of the rear compartment. It fell into the snow with a thud. Brody sighed heavily. "What good is it to be rich if you have to carry your own luggage?"

Anger surged through Drew. "Life isn't only about comfort."

Yanking his duffle from the snow, Brody looked up over the rim of his sunglasses at his dad. “Whatever.”

Drew knew he was in over his head with this kid, and he needed to fix this situation, fast.

CHAPTER TWO

GWEN heard Claire's soft cries through the small monitor she had on the kitchen counter. Without a second thought she turned and ran back into the hall, through the sitting room of the maid's quarters that she'd managed to clean before the Teaberrys arrived, and into the bedroom.

"Hey, Claire-bear. I'm here," she whispered, lifting her baby out of the portable crib. She kissed her warm cheek, changed her into a fresh one-piece sleeper and returned to the kitchen, fighting a funny feeling of confusion in the pit of her stomach.

For some reason or another she'd expected Andrew Teaberry to be older. Like sixty. Not thirty-five or so. She also hadn't expected fathomless dark eyes or gorgeous black hair. The hitch in her breath and the way her stomach had plummeted when she'd looked at him were also surprises.

Grabbing a bottle from the refrigerator, she told herself to stop thinking about how attractive her new employer was and get her baby fed and into her carrier before he returned from getting his bags. She wasn't sure how or where they'd work in this dusty house, but she wasn't assuming anything. From the way he'd instantly dealt with his son for calling her babe, it was clear he wasn't a man who took well to mistakes or assumptions. So she wouldn't make any.

She placed the bottle in the warmer she'd brought. As it

heated, Claire began to cry. Gwen tried to comfort her, but her crying only grew louder.

"Come on, sweetie. I know you're hungry, but it will only take a minute to warm your bottle."

Just then the swinging door swung open and Drew burst inside. His horrified gaze fell to Claire, then swung back to Gwen. "Is that a baby?"

She laughed nervously. "Well, it's not a Siamese cat." She rocked her sobbing child, trying to get her to settle down. This was no way for him to meet her baby! "This is my daughter Claire."

He gaped at her. "You brought your baby to work?"

This time the flip-flop of Gwen's stomach had nothing to do with the attractiveness of her boss and everything to do with fear. "I told you about Claire in my interview."

"You told me you had a child. You didn't say you were bringing her with you."

Drew's loud voice caused Claire's crying to rise in competition. Gwen desperately rocked her, but the baby filled the room with her wails.

Gwen had to shout to be heard. "I did say she was still a bit too young to go to daycare and I don't have a sitter yet. I thought the conclusion was obvious."

"I thought you said that to let me know you needed time to look for a sitter." He raked his fingers through his hair. "I'm sorry, but I hired you because I need help. Serious help. You're not going to have time to care for a baby *and* do your work."

Gwen's heart stopped. *He was firing her?* He couldn't! She needed this job. "She's only three months old! She sleeps a lot. I can handle it."

He looked at the screaming baby, then bestowed a look upon Gwen that sent a shiver through her. "Really?"

Mustering her courage, she said, "Yes!"

"That's not how it looks to me. I know how this baby thing goes. I had a crying baby. Brody screamed for three months straight. I failed that semester of university. My wife left me—"

Just then the swinging door bounced closed. Gwen hadn't even realized it had been opened again. With Claire's crying and their heated conversation she'd missed Brody walking through the room.

Drew's face paled, then he squeezed his eyes shut. "Perfect." Heading for the door, he yelled, "Brody!" Then he pushed out of the kitchen.

The light on the bottle warmer finally declared the milk was warm, and Gwen took her baby to a chair to feed her.

This was not going anything like she'd hoped it would. She fed Claire and then sat at the table, totally confused about what she should do. Technically, Drew hadn't fired her. And she needed this job. She was not leaving without a fight.

Drew ran into the hallway just in time to see the foyer door close. He grabbed his jacket from the newel post on the stairs where he'd stashed it and headed outside.

Brody bounded toward the SUV around the side of the house.

"What are you going to do?" Drew shouted after his son. "Leave?" He dangled the keys. "You'll need these. Unless you want to walk."

"What do you care? Mom's on her honeymoon. You're trying to buy some old guy's company. And I'm stuck here."

"Look, Brody, if I had a choice we'd be skiing right now."

Brody snorted.

"We would." The heavy snow had reduced itself to flurries but it was cold. Bitter cold. And he had work to do. Not knowing what else to say, Drew glanced longingly at the kitchen door. Because the top half of the door was glass, he could see Gwen McKenzie at the table with her baby. He nearly groaned. Could this day get any more complicated?

"I'm sorry you heard what you heard, but truthfully I would

have thought by now that you would have guessed your mom and I had a terrible marriage. We were only married for just under a year before we divorced."

Refusing to look at him, Brody said, "And I'm the cause."

"No!" He laughed miserably. "Lord, no. Your mom and I had lots of problems before you were born."

"But I added to them—"

"No!" Drew said again, this time stronger.

"I heard what you said about me screaming all the time."

"You were colicky. That happens. Babies do not destroy marriages. Adults do. Your mom and I never should have gotten married. But she got pregnant—"

Deliberately, she'd told him later. She'd taken out loans to attend her first semester at Harvard and had known four years' worth of borrowing that kind of money would put her too far in debt when she graduated. Drew's family was wealthy. He and Olivia had dated and liked each other. So she'd thought they'd be very happy raising a baby and attending university—all paid for by his parents. But his parents had been furious when Drew told them they had gotten married because she was pregnant, and they'd cut him off. The happy marriage that Olivia had envisioned had quickly become a nightmare.

Still, this wasn't the time or the way to tell Brody all that. And he wasn't even sure he should be the one to tell Brody. It seemed this story would be much better coming from his mother.

"How about if we talk later? Right now, I have a mini-crisis in the kitchen."

Brody sighed and raised his face to the snow. It looked to Drew as if the cool flakes were settling him down, so when he said, "Go," Drew headed back to the kitchen.

With a deep calming breath of his own, he opened the kitchen door and stepped inside. "I'm sorry you had to see that."

Gwen McKenzie slowly raised her gaze to his, her green eyes wary.

He knew she needed this job. He didn't have to glance at the now sleeping baby to remember that, but he did, and his heart stuttered in his chest. He'd told Brody he had been colicky, but that had been only half the problem. Neither Drew nor Olivia had had any experience caring for an infant, and they'd had nowhere to turn for help. He knew how loudly a baby could cry, how despondent a parent could feel…how one tiny life really could throw a monkey wrench into the best-laid plans. And his plans to buy Jimmy Lane's company were precarious at best. Despite the efforts of most of his staff, he knew nothing about the owner of Lane Works except that he was reclusive and demanding. That didn't give Drew much to go on by way of figuring out how to handle him. So his "plan" was more like a guess.

"I'm sorry, but you having a baby here doesn't work for me."

Instead of the tears he'd expected, Gwen McKenzie shook her head and said, "No kidding."

He gaped at her. Had she just sassed him? Yes, she had. He'd already had a lifetime share of sassing this morning. So his voice shivered with barely controlled anger when he said, "Get your things and leave."

She rose from the chair. "Fine, but I would think that a guy who can't get along with his son would like having another parent around for some help and advice."

An unexpected laugh escaped him. "You think *you're* going to straighten out Brody?"

"Nope." She headed for the door. "But I might have some ideas for how you could."

He snorted in derision. "Right. You've been a parent now… what? All of two months?"

She turned and smiled. "Three. But I was sixteen only a few years ago. I think I might remember a bit more about what it was like than you do."

Drew's eyes narrowed and Gwen's stomach shivered. She knew she should probably shut up, but he was in trouble with Brody and that seemed like her only angle to keep this job. Now that he'd shrugged out of the thick parka, she could not only see his expensive blue sweater, she could also see that the body he'd hidden beneath his jacket was incredible. Soft knit hugged his broad shoulders and flat tummy and stopped at trim hips encased in denim. He was handsome, rich, and he held her fate in his hands…

And she was taunting him? Was she crazy?

"Are you calling me old?"

She should be. She should think that a guy in his mid-thirties was way too old for her. She should think he was too grouchy for her. Instead, all she saw was a handsome, sexy guy who needed her help. And, strangely, even with as many problems as she had of her own, she actually thought she could provide it.

She lifted her chin. Caught his gaze. "No. I'm not calling you old."

Their gazes clung. Time seemed to be suspended. She had a feeling she didn't have to tell him she didn't think he was old because she found him attractive. It was probably written all over her reddening face.

"But you do need me."

He crossed his arms on his chest as his gaze rippled over her. Suddenly feeling like a downtrodden waif, brought to the castle for the king's pleasure, Gwen cuddled Claire to her chest.

"You're dusty."

That wasn't at all what she'd expected him to say. So nervous her voice shook, she said, "I cleaned the maid's quarters so Claire would have somewhere to sleep."

He said nothing, only narrowed his eyes at her, as if trying to figure out if she was lying. So she hastily added, "I brought my vacuum, cleaning solutions and a bucket and mop from home."

"You know how to clean?"

She frowned. "Of course I know how to clean." A thought struck her and she said, "You don't?"

He shook his head.

Her spirits lifted. "There's another thing I could help you with."

He raked his fingers through his hair and looked at sleeping Claire again. She could almost see the wheels turning in his head as he drew the obvious conclusions. Claire wasn't a bad baby. Gwen knew how to clean. And this place was filthy.

"I won't even ask for more money."

His mouth dropped open, then he snorted a laugh. "Right. As if you're in a position to bargain."

"Come on," Gwen said, a slight note of feminine pleading in her voice. She instantly regretted it when his gaze caught hers and that "thing" sprang up between them again. The air she breathed turned hot and shivery. Something like electricity arched between them.

It was another item in the laundry list of problems they had. His son was trouble. The house wasn't falling apart around them, but did need a good cleaning. She had a baby who might disrupt everything. And they were attracted to each other.

But he also had a business he was trying to buy. In their phone interview he'd told her he needed to be in West Virginia to be close to the seller. And now he needed somebody who could bring order to the chaos of this house.

"Maybe I *should* ask for more money?" Cheeky, perhaps even a tad over-confident, she strolled over to him. "You're stuck here. There is no cleaning service in Towering Pines. You're also lucky you found me—an administrative assistant who doesn't mind a temporary job and has time to work at your beck and call. You have what? Four weeks to negotiate this deal before Jimmy Lane loses interest and moves on?" She smiled. "I think you're the one who isn't in a position to negotiate."

He held her gaze. "So you're saying it wouldn't cause a

problem for you if I asked you to clean this kitchen while I left for a conference call?"

"Are you going to give me the raise?"

"How much?"

"Another two thousand."

His eyes narrowed, but they never left hers. "All right. But you'd better be worth it."

She strolled away, suddenly seeing that the best way to communicate with this man was as an equal. And maybe that was what Brody was doing wrong? Not quite sure where that thought had come from, she shook her head to dislodge it and went back to the negotiations at hand.

"Sure. I'll clean in between administrative assistant assignments. As long as you don't mind that I wear old jeans and ugly sweatshirts."

He crossed his arms on his chest. "Look around. There's nobody here to impress. And even if there were this house would ruin any chance we had of impressing them."

She couldn't help it. She laughed. "Yeah. Big-time."

"So we have a deal? You work as my administrative assistant when I need you and clean in your downtime. You can dress any way you want and bring your baby." He caught her gaze again. "As long as you keep her out of my way."

"Does 'out of your way' mean you don't want to see her? Because I was hoping I could keep her in the same room with me. I have a swing that will rock her to sleep and keep her sleeping for hours."

He groaned and squeezed his eyes shut, but in the end he sighed and said, "Fine. But if she cries you leave the room."

"Got it."

"Great. As long as we stick to our commitments, this should work out fine." He walked over and held out his hand to shake on the deal.

When Gwen took it, little sparkles of awareness danced up her arm. Their gazes caught and clung.

Now all they had to do was forget about their attraction.

CHAPTER THREE

DREW turned to leave the room, his hand tingling from just touching Gwen's. He told himself it was ridiculous to be attracted to somebody closer to Brody's age than his own—and with a *baby,* no less—but it didn't stop the tightness that had captured his chest.

"Um, Drew?"

He stopped. Half afraid she was about to say something about their attraction—maybe even tell him she didn't want her *old* boss hitting on her—he faced her.

"We still need supplies." She winced. "I brought my equipment from home, but no real cleaning supplies. To make the bathrooms usable I think we need some disinfectant cleanser." She caught his gaze. "I also noticed there are no sheets or towels or pillows. No laundry detergent, dishwashing detergent, dishes or silverware. Or even basic pots and pans. You could also probably use a coffee-maker—"

Relieved that she was focusing on the job, Drew reached for his wallet. "And food?"

"And food."

"Okay." He pulled out several hundred-dollar bills. "Can you take care of getting all of that?"

"I don't think we have a choice."

She glanced at the stack of bills then back up at him. "You do realize we don't have a Saks Fifth Avenue, right? I'm only going to the local discount department store."

"Are you telling me you have too much money or not enough?"

"I'm saying the sheets won't be silk."

He laughed.

A wonderful feeling filled her again. Her pulse scrambled. Her knees weakened. Her brain became fuzzy and dreamy. When he wasn't being angry with Brody, he was actually a fun, nice guy—

That had to be irrelevant! It would be insanity for a woman with a baby to find a man who obviously didn't like kids attractive. Especially a boss. A rich boss. A man so far out of her league she shouldn't even be looking at him.

Drew's cell phone rang in the silent kitchen. He clicked a button and said, "Teaberry." A pause. "Actually, I don't even have my laptop set up yet. The fax, printer and two boxes of files are still in my SUV."

He walked toward the kitchen door. "I pretty much know Jimmy Lane's biggest objection to the Teaberry Corporation buying his company is that I'm not a local, but I'm fixing that. I'm moving into my grandparents' old homestead," he said, shoving against the swinging door and then disappearing behind it, effectively shutting off his conversation to her.

Ignoring the unwanted sparkle still twinkling through her, Gwen glanced down at sleeping Claire. "Well, this is going to be different than what we'd expected, but not something we can't handle."

Once Claire was dressed in her snowsuit, Gwen left for the store. A few more inches of fresh snow had fallen on the road since her last trip, making the drive down the mountain slow. She spent an hour at the discount department store, and another hour at the grocery, trying to guess what two rich guys would be able to cook for breakfast, lunch and dinner.

With her shopping completed, she stopped at her house. Not only did she pack extra clothes for Claire, she packed extra clothes for herself. She'd leave at least two outfits of cleaning clothes and two outfits of administrative assistant clothes in the maid's quarters, just in case.

She also packed Claire's swing—a gift she'd gotten at her baby shower. Now she had Drew's full permission to have Claire at the house, there was no reason Claire couldn't be totally comfortable.

The drive back up the mountain was even slower than the drive down. When she entered the kitchen, carrying Claire in the baby carrier and three plastic bags of towels, Brody was sitting at the kitchen table, looking bored out of his mind.

"Help me bring in the things from my car, would you?" she said lightly as she dropped the bags on the kitchen floor. She tossed her keys to Brody. "I'll be out in two minutes. I just need to put Claire down for her nap."

She didn't know where Drew was, but she and Brody took so long carrying in the bags and putting the groceries into the kitchen pantry that Claire had awakened from her nap. After Gwen got Claire from the bedroom and fed her, she again found Brody in the kitchen.

"Blue towels and linens are yours," she said to Brody, who was remarkably cooperative. From the way he'd behaved with his father, she'd thought he'd throw a fit when she asked for his help. But he hadn't even flinched when she'd asked him to carry in the groceries and linens. She pointed at the bags that contained his linens. "Why don't you take them upstairs?"

He grabbed the bags. "Got it." He turned to leave the kitchen, but as he passed the table where Claire sat in her carrier he stopped and smiled at the baby. "She's cute."

"Yeah." Gwen smiled, too. Another surprise. She'd have thought rich, obviously spoiled Brody wouldn't care one way or another for a baby. "I adore her."

The swinging door opened and Drew walked in. "Hey." He glanced at the bags still on the floor and the cleaning supplies lined up on the kitchen counter and faced Gwen. "Thanks."

Brody turned away from Claire. Without a word, he headed out of the room.

Drew winced, but swung his gaze to Gwen. "I didn't expect you back so soon."

"I've been gone for hours."

"Really?" He looked at his watch. "Wow. That time certainly flew."

The temptation to remind him that he'd left Brody alone and bored the whole time she was gone was strong, but she resisted. Not only had he scoffed when she'd suggested she might be able to help with his son, but also he hadn't added "help with his son" to the list of things he wanted her to do when they were negotiating. It might not have been intentional, but Brody was his child. His responsibility. She was only an employee. If he wanted her help, he'd have to ask for it.

Still, she couldn't resist the urge to mention that Brody had carried in the bags—if only because the way Brody behaved had her thinking something was off in the relationship between Drew and his son. Maybe even unjustly off.

"Brody carried in most of the groceries and linens. I couldn't have done it without him."

He sighed. "Yeah, I figured that out. His mother's never complained about him. Deep down he's an okay kid. I'm getting the feeling he's just mad at me."

Drew's cell phone rang again.

He clicked the button. "Teaberry. Can you hold on a second, Hal?" He caught Gwen's gaze. "Two things. First, while you were gone I got a lot of the dust up in the office."

Her eyes widened in surprise. She couldn't imagine a man in a pale blue cashmere sweater dusting a filthy room, but now that he mentioned it she did see a fine coating of dust on his sweater and jeans.

"So I'm ready to start working. I'm going to have a list of people I want you to e-mail with the landline number for the phone. But while I'm gathering that list of names why don't you go check on Brody? Maybe take the vacuum cleaner upstairs and show him how to use it. I'd do it, but I have a feeling he'll listen better to you."

Gwen's heart turned over in her chest. Brody was a good kid, and Drew seemed like an okay guy, yet the two of them seemed to be at war. Still, she'd pushed her luck already, getting to keep this job. She wouldn't overstep any boundaries.

Tuesday morning she came prepared. Revved up. Ready to go. With a sloppy sweatshirt and jeans under her thick coat, she let herself into the kitchen and found Brody at the stove, making eggs—which were burning.

Choking as she entered the room, she used her free hand to wave the smoke around. "Step away from the stove."

He laughed. "My pleasure."

She set Claire's carrier on the table and immediately took the skillet off the gas burner. Before she could do anything else Drew burst into the room. "I'm getting e-mails from three lawyers, all of whom have looked at a different part of the agreement I want to send to Jimmy Lane. I need you in the office now!"

As quickly as he'd popped into the room he popped back out. Gwen glanced at the baby carrier, then at Brody.

He said, "Go. I'll make toast. I'm fine."

She quickly grabbed the baby carrier, put sleepy Claire into the portable crib, stashed the baby monitor in the big pocket in front of her sweatshirt and raced to the office. When she got there, Drew was on the phone. After two minutes of listening to him argue with an attorney, she glanced longingly at the door.

She could have made Brody's eggs by now. Maybe even the toast.

After five minutes she started to fume. She could have easily made Brody's eggs, put on a pot of coffee, squeezed some orange juice *and* set up Claire's swing in the office.

Just when she was ready to leave to do something productive, Drew ended his phone call.

"Okay. I've e-mailed all three lawyers' comments on the

agreement to the account I set up for you. All you have to do is print them."

She opened her mouth to lambast him for calling her in for such a simple assignment and then making her wait, but he added, "Your password is Claire."

Her anger deflated. He'd remembered her baby's name? Stupid, dreamy thoughts about how romantic that was popped into her head. But she stopped them. Mostly because they were ridiculous, schoolgirl stupidity. She wasn't a schoolgirl anymore. She was an adult. A woman with a baby. Someone who didn't build fantasies around offhand comments.

When she was done printing the legal assessments, Drew told her to clean the master bedroom. He pointed at the sofa. "I slept on that last night and it wasn't even a little comfortable."

She caught the giggle that nearly bubbled out. It wasn't funny that he'd been uncomfortable, but the look on his handsome face was priceless. Still, she only nodded her understanding and left the room.

She ran into Brody on the way to the maid's quarters to check on Claire before she went upstairs.

"What's up?"

"Nothing." She stopped in front of him. "I'm just on my way to clean the master suite."

"Need any help?"

She swallowed her surprise. "Well, yes and no. I am capable of cleaning that room myself. But a little help would make the job go faster."

"I'll get the vacuum."

The master suite was huge, but as dirty as everything else. While Brody sucked dust off the heavy drapes, the bare mattress, the walls and the carpeting, Gwen cleaned the bathroom. Brody put the sheets and pillows on the big bed. She placed towels in the bathroom. In two hours they had the room sparkling.

Brody said, "Now what?"

She shrugged. "I need to check in with your dad. See what he wants me to do."

His eyes darkened. "Okay."

"Hey, if it's housework, I'll happily share it with you."

"Might as well. There's nothing else to do in this dump."

With that Brody left the room, and Gwen stared after him. When he was busy he didn't call the place a dump. One word from her to Drew could get Brody something to do. But she was so afraid to say that word. She'd already pushed him by negotiating to keep Claire in his house, and she'd pushed it even further by demanding extra money for helping with the cleaning.

And Brody was his son. That was personal. She couldn't, absolutely couldn't, butt into that.

Unfortunately, when she reached Drew's office and he kept her waiting as he talked on the phone for forty-five minutes, stopping her every time she headed for the door, with a "just one more minute" signal with his index finger, she truly empathized with Brody's boredom.

In fact she'd got so bored by the time he disconnected his call that she said, "You do realize Brody is bored, right?"

His face scrunched in confusion. "What?"

"While you're back here working, Brody's rambling around this big house with nothing to do."

Obviously impatient, Drew glanced down at the notes he'd taken during his phone conversation.

Irritation crackled through her. "Don't you care?"

Drew looked up slowly, hooked her gaze and held it for several seconds without saying a word. Finally, he said, "He has a cell phone that connects him to his friends and probably hundreds of thousands of online games. He's fine. This is none of your business."

Because he had her on that, she answered honestly. "Maybe not. But I'm the one walking around the house, bumping into him, seeing how bored he is, and you're the one sitting back here so engrossed in your work that I'll bet you don't even know what time it is."

As if to confirm her suspicion, Drew's gaze fell to the clock on his desk. His face registered shock, but his voice was calm when he said, "Since it troubles you so much, you'll be glad to know I talked with Max, the farm's caretaker, this morning. I want to open up the Christmas tree farm, and he tells me that with a little help he could probably be ready Saturday after next. Once Max gets here this afternoon Brody's going to have plenty to do."

Her mouth fell open in dismay. She didn't know which part of his plan to address first. "You're going to make him work on the Christmas tree farm?"

Drew glanced up lazily. "I take it you have a problem with that, too?"

Embarrassment suffused her. Was she an idiot? Arguing with the man who literally held her future in his hands? The salary from this job would make it possible for her to finish her education, and once she finished her education she could get a teaching job to support herself and Claire. They wouldn't live in the lap of luxury, but they'd be fine. Especially since she and Gill had inherited her mom's house in Towering Pines. Gill didn't want it, but to Gwen it was home. Not having to pay rent meant she really could live comfortably.

If she got her degree.

Suddenly Claire's cry roared through the baby monitor in her sweatshirt pocket. Drew about jumped out of his seat. "What was that?"

She pulled the monitor from her pocket. "Baby monitor. Claire's awake." Without another word, she headed out of the office.

He stopped her. "I'm going to need an hour or two to review some new information I just got. It would be great if you could clean the kitchen."

"Okay." Great. That kept her and Claire out of his way, and gave her something to do—but not Brody. Of course, if he strolled into the kitchen again she could ask him to help her, but by now she was feeling like his taskmaster. Brody had already volunteered more than the normal sixteen-year-old. What he needed was something fun to do. Like snowboarding or skiing.

After changing and feeding Claire, Gwen set up the baby swing in the kitchen and started cleaning. Either Drew or Brody had cleaned enough that they could use the stove, sink, countertops and table. So she dusted the walls, wiped down the cabinets and scrubbed the floor.

When Drew arrived in the kitchen two hours later he looked around in amazement. "Wow. This place is actually nice."

Glad that he wasn't angry with her for her interference about Brody that morning, she panted in a breath and straightened up from the mop. "Cleaning doesn't have to take long."

"Yeah, but I don't think I could have made it look this good this quickly."

His unexpected praise filled her with warmth. But she reminded herself that he was her boss and he was supposed to praise good work. He hadn't told her she was pretty or sweet. He appreciated the work she was doing in his house. There was nothing more to the compliment than that. Besides, she probably looked like something the cat brought in after sweating over the dirty walls and cabinets.

"I'm making a sandwich for lunch. Care to join me?"

"Sure." She glanced at Claire, who had tired herself out in her swing and was ready to nod off. "But first I need to take Claire back to the bedroom for a nap."

She warmed a bottle while Drew gathered cold cuts and condiments from the refrigerator. When the bottle was ready, she slid Claire out of the swing and headed for the bedroom. Claire ate greedily and immediately fell asleep. Gwen returned to the kitchen and found Drew sitting alone at the table.

"Where's Brody?"

He finished the last bite of the sandwich on his plate, then said, "I called him. He should be here soon."

Brody slogged into the kitchen and flopped into a chair. Not wanting an argument to ensue, Gwen quickly prepared a sandwich for him and brought him a glass of milk.

Drew made himself another sandwich and took the seat beside Brody. Wanting everything to go well, Gwen poured some potato chips into a bowl and set them on the table, along with a bag of store-bought cookies.

As she sat, Drew said, "Gwen tells me you have nothing to do."

Her eyes widened and she gaped at him, but before she could say anything, he continued, "I know it's boring here. My dad told me stories about being so bored here before your grandfather moved to North Carolina that he thought he'd go nuts. So I've arranged for something to do for you."

Brightening, Brody sat up.

Gwen's chest tightened with fear. She might not have been a parent long, but she absolutely knew Drew was going about this all the wrong way.

"We're opening up the Christmas tree farm."

Brody said, "What?"

"The farm. We're opening it. Jimmy Lane used to come to Teaberry Farms for his tree when he was a young father. He's eager to see the place again. I thought it would be good for him if it was up and running. Sort of recreate that memory for him."

Brody just gaped at his dad.

Drew obliviously trotted on. "Max is coming over this afternoon to start harvesting the trees. He's already investigated how we should price them. We'll have bunches of pre-cut trees for people in a hurry, and let other people go into the fields to choose their own. It will be fun."

Brody's gape turned into a look of utter horror. *"Fun?"*

"Sure."

"And how much of this fun are *you* going to have?"

"Hey, I'll be plenty busy."

"Yeah," Brody said, shoving back his chair as he rose.

"Inside. In your warm office. While I'm outside freezing and lugging trees."

"Brody, you know I have to work—"

"Right. Work. That's all you think about. You didn't really come up with the Christmas tree farm idea for me. You need the farm open to impress the old guy, and you're using me as slave labor."

"That's not how it is!"

"Uh-huh? Sure. First Mom doesn't want me because she's got a new life, a new husband—" Brody's voice shook, and Gwen's heart squeezed with empathy for his pain. "Now you're using me to get a business deal."

He turned and strode to the back door, where he plucked his parka from a hook by the door.

Drew rose. "Brody, wait! Stop! I'm not using you for slave labor! And your mother isn't abandoning you just because she got married."

When Brody turned to face them, tears glistened on his eyelids. "Oh, that's right. She probably hasn't called you yet. But she will. I heard her telling Marc that she'd 'take care of it' after they got back from their honeymoon. She says you can't argue about keeping me now, since she's had me my whole life and you've barely seen me. So it's your turn."

With that he stormed out the door. Gwen sat stunned. Drew hovered by the table, obviously shell shocked. "I have absolutely no idea what to do."

She said nothing.

He glanced down. "You offered to give me advice. I need advice. So you can start talking anytime now."

"You scoffed at my advice, remember? And just this morning you told me that Brody was none of my concern."

"Well, I'm not so picky now."

She sucked in a breath. Sixteen-year-old boys didn't cry unless something was seriously wrong—horribly wrong. So wrong he felt totally out of control. But if she told Drew that he wouldn't sensitively delve until he got to the heart of the

you can go out with the customers who want to choose their own." He pointed at a rundown outbuilding. "There's a little stand stored in there. We used it as a checkout table where my wife Sunny used to take the money from customers." He sent his gaze back to Drew. "But if you're trying to impress somebody, we're probably going to have to spruce up these old outbuildings. It's too cold and wet to paint them, but it wouldn't hurt to replace the missing boards."

Brody glanced fearfully at Drew. Drew tried his damnedest to smile. He saw himself putting in eight-hour days on the farm and then eight hours in the office at night. And all of this was Gwen's fault.

The second he thought of her his blood heated. She held her ground with him like no one else in his world had ever even tried. And she was cute about it. Her nose wrinkled. Her eyes sparked with fire. He couldn't even imagine what kind of liberties she'd take with him if he wasn't her boss and she spoke freely.

His heart-rate spiked and the temperature of his blood rose another degree or two. He didn't know whether to laugh or groan. Thinking about her might be a way to keep from freezing to death while lugging trees in this frozen tundra of a farm. But thinking about her all afternoon while he tromped around might make it a little harder to be a good, objective boss when he came back inside to work at night.

Because they *would* be working together at night.

That would be her punishment for coming up with this hare-brained scheme. Opening the Christmas tree farm might have been his idea, but his sharing the labor had been hers. So she would suffer right along with him.

Gwen watched out the kitchen window as Max waved his hands around in the general direction of the vast expanse of trees beyond them. She saw Brody eating the sandwich she'd sent out and sighed with relief. But her sigh was short-lived when she saw Drew cast a narrow-eyed look in the direction of the house.

She dropped the curtain and jumped back from the window. Oh, he was going to make her pay for this.

Deciding the best defense was a good offense, Gwen took the roast she'd bought when she was at the grocery store the day before, cut it into cubes, and began preparing a hearty stew. She peeled potatoes and carrots, browned the meat, and made a rich gravy. When everything was on the burner to simmer, a thought occurred to her, and she went in search of the things she'd need to make homemade dinner rolls.

Once the dough was rising, she decided to also make homemade muffins. It was one of the skills her mom had taught her. She and Gill loved muffins, so at a very young age Ginger had shown her girls how to make their own.

By the time Drew and Brody stomped into the house five hours later the stew bubbled on the stove, fresh dinner rolls sat in a basket and the sweet scent of pumpkin muffins permeated the air.

Drew dropped his gloves on the counter and sniffed. "This has to be heaven."

"Anywhere would be heaven compared to that damn field."

Drew bit back a sigh. Brody hadn't really complained all day, for which Drew thanked God, but now that they were away from Max his son was back to saying damn and would probably be snotty for the rest of the night.

Deciding that ignoring Brody might be the thing to do, he focused on the obvious. "Everything smells great." Because that was the absolute truth, he closed his eyes in ecstasy. "I only hope I have the strength to eat it."

Brody snorted a laugh and headed for the swinging door. "I want to clean up."

When he was gone, Drew caught Gwen's gaze. All day long he'd thought about ways he'd punish her for her idea, but now that he had her alone, in a kitchen that smelled so good he could have eaten the table, he was suddenly tongue-tied.

"These are just a few things my mom taught me to make."

"Your mom must be an excellent cook."

"She was."

"Was?"

"She passed away. It was a year last September."

"I'm sorry."

She shrugged and grabbed plates from the cupboard. "It's okay. Gill and I have each other."

Feeling awkward about having her wait on him, Drew headed for the silverware drawer. "Gill is your sister?"

"Twin sister."

He stopped. Smiled stupidly. "You're a twin?"

"It doesn't make me a freak."

"No. I think it's kind of cute." He did. Damn it. Everything he heard about her made her special. And she'd fixed them dinner. She hadn't rested on her laurels while he was outside. She'd done the thing that most needed to be done: she'd made food, probably recognizing that they'd be starving.

They ate dinner in near silence. Not because they were tiptoeing around each other, but because the men didn't pause long enough between bites of food to converse. After he'd eaten Brody excused himself. Drew knew he was going upstairs to bed. He didn't stop him. Drew would have liked to drop into a warm bed himself right now. But everything he'd neglected while learning to cut and prune Christmas trees now had to be addressed.

"You *do* know we'll have to work tonight, right?"

She nodded. "Yes." She caught his gaze. "You *do* know that I'll have to have Claire in the office in her swing, right?"

"Yes."

"So we're set?"

He couldn't help it. He smiled at her. She didn't leave anything to chance, but more than that she negotiated with him like an equal. She wasn't afraid of anything. Not even him. She had so much spunk and intelligence that if she didn't live so far away from North Carolina he'd probably hire her for his corporate office.

Of course then he'd have to deal with being attracted to her and not being allowed to kiss her or touch her or sleep with her—

Sleep with her? Oh, Lord. Why had he let *that* thought form? The vision of having her warm and naked beside him shot an arrow of arousal through him. The images in his brain weren't just crystal-clear, they came with feelings that rumbled through him. *Feelings.* His attraction was morphing into something he didn't dare even name—because he didn't want it and neither should she.

He bounced from his seat. "Let's get to work."

They worked until ten. At ten, tired from his manual labor, Drew ran his hand down his face and said, "That's it. I'm done for the night."

She collapsed on her desk. "I'm so glad you said that."

He laughed. "Go home."

She immediately rose. "You don't have to tell me twice."

With that she left the room, and Drew chuckled again then caught himself. He liked her too much. Everything about her. He wasn't just attracted to her because she was gorgeous. She had given him good advice about Brody, had cooked a great supper, and hadn't complained when he'd told her she'd have to work late.

He rose from the desk and ambled into the kitchen, where he grabbed one of her homemade muffins and groaned in ecstasy when he bit into it. She really was too good to be true. *And too young for him.* He had to remember that. She was young and smart and had her whole life in front of her. What the hell would she want with a guy twelve years older than she was?

After finishing his muffin, he headed down the hall to the

foyer stairs. Unfortunately, when he rounded the corner, he nearly bumped into Gwen. He skidded to a stop. So did she.

"Sorry," automatically came out of his mouth, then his gaze collided with her baby carrier and he took a step back. "I forgot all about Claire. I thought you said she'd have to be in the office with us?"

She shrugged. "She was asleep when I got done with the kitchen so I let her sleep on." She laughed lightly. "I told you she was a good baby."

"Yes." But it was cold outside. Bitter cold. And not only had Gwen bundled herself to go home, but she'd had to bundle her baby. Now she'd drive fifteen or twenty minutes in the cold to get into town and to her house.

The urge to tell her to stay the night rose up in him like a tsunami. But when he met the gaze of her pretty green eyes his stomach plummeted. Damn, she was gorgeous. And he *was* attracted to her. If he asked her to stay, she might take it the wrong way. Worse, she might take it the right way and agree that sleeping at his house was smarter and safer. Then he'd probably lie in his bed thinking about how she was downstairs. How he was attracted to her and how he couldn't have her. And he wouldn't get any sleep.

Reminding himself that the roads were safe and she was a West Virginia girl, accustomed to driving in the snow, he reached for the doorknob and opened the door for her. "See you tomorrow."

She smiled her beautiful smile at him. "See you tomorrow."

She walked out into the cold, and as he watched her go he noticed the little puff of smoke coming from the exhaust pipe of her car. She'd already started it. At least he didn't have to worry about her and the baby being cold on the drive down.

When she was gone, he sucked in a breath.

It had been one hell of a two days. First he couldn't deal with Brody. Then he was attracted to the woman he'd hired to be his assistant, and if that wasn't bad enough she had a baby. Then he had to do manual labor to make his son feel he wasn't a slave. And now he couldn't even do the kindness of letting his secretary and her baby stay at his house because he was worried about his attraction to her.

Somehow, some way, he had to get control of something.

Gwen had breakfast ready when Brody and Drew woke up the next morning. She'd warmed the pumpkin muffins in the oven and made fresh coffee, eggs and bacon. She knew the scent of it greeted them as they pushed inside through the swinging door.

"I'm famished," Brody said without preamble.

Drew's gaze met hers. "Me, too."

She smiled to hide the shiver that raced through her. From the way he'd looked at her the night before when she left, she knew that he might be hungry for food, but he also felt something for her. Probably the same crazy thing that rose up in her every time she looked at him.

But she'd already sorted this out in her head. He was too old for her. He came from a different world than she did. A world she probably wouldn't fit in because she loved her small town. Plus, she had a baby. He didn't like babies, and even if he did she and Claire couldn't possibly fit into his life when Brody barely did.

That settled in her head once again, she joined the men when they sat at the table.

Drew peeked at her. "What time did you have to get up to be here and have all this ready by seven o'clock in the morning?"

"Four." She laughed. "But don't worry. Some days Claire gets me up at four. The days she doesn't want to go back to sleep, I'm happy to have something to do rather than sit in my dark living room."

The look he gave her tightened her chest. She wasn't sure what was going on in his brain, but something about her getting up in the middle of the night didn't sit well with him.

Before she could say anything, Max arrived. “Ready to work?”

Both men groaned. When they did, Gwen noticed the strange look Brody gave his dad. It seemed Drew had won Brody’s respect—not by being willing to work alongside him, but by hating the work as much as Brody did.

Drew rose. “Do you have things to do today?” he asked Gwen as he walked to the hooks by the back door to retrieve his coat.

“Plenty,” Gwen assured him.

He sucked in a breath, caught her gaze and said, “Then we’re off.”

Brody slapped him on the shoulder. “Don’t worry, Dad. You’ll get the hang of that saw eventually.”

With that they left, and Gwen stared at the door smiling. Brody had spoken normally to his dad. And he’d slapped his shoulder affectionately.

She really had given Drew the right advice.

Lunch was quickly eaten sandwiches, but when the Teaberry men stepped into the house for supper the scent of gingerbread greeted them.

Drew saw a baked chicken, mashed potatoes, stuffing and green beans all sitting on the stove waiting for them, but the gingerbread stole his attention.

“Did you make real gingerbread men? From scratch?”

“Yes. They’re one of my favorites.”

He met her gaze. A warm, syrupy feeling flooded him. He now understood how men in the old west had felt when they’d come home to a log cabin that smelled like supper. “They’re my favorites, too.”

She smiled. “Thanks. I really love to cook.”

And he really loved to eat. He nearly sighed. They complemented each other so well that it seemed impossible they weren’t allowed to have a relationship.

"Hey, I like gingerbread men, too," Brody said, grabbing one and stuffing it into his mouth. "Umm. They *are* good."

Gwen playfully slapped his hand. "You're going to spoil your dinner."

"No worry on that," Drew answered for Brody. "Max worked us so hard today we'll probably each need two dinners."

She laughed and told them to wash up. They left the kitchen, and when they entered the hall Drew saw rows of gold tinsel strung along the now clean walls. They spiraled up the banister of the stairway. Red bows with bright red and gold Christmas tree ornaments accented the tinsel.

Brody glanced around in awe. "Wow!"

Drew looked around, too. "Yeah, wow. I can't believe she did all this and made dinner."

Brody said, "I can't believe how cool this looks."

Drew peered at him. "Seriously?"

"Yeah. It's great."

Drew thought his son a little too old to be awed by a bit of tinsel, but he didn't mention that. He had noticed the calluses forming on Brody's hands, because he had corresponding calluses on his own hands, but that moment of camaraderie there in the foyer, looking at the Christmas decorations, made it all worth it. Two days ago Brody would have stormed by the decorations. He wouldn't have spoken to his dad. Today they'd talked like normal guys. A father and son.

Gwen had been right. Working together was changing Brody. Relaxing him. Bringing back the son Drew remembered.

They returned to the kitchen and Brody complimented Gwen profusely on the decorations. "My mom doesn't do anything like this," he said, then dug into his chicken with gusto. "She has these weird blue and pink decorations that don't look like Christmas at all. But these," he said, pointing at the hallway, "look like the things we had in elementary school. That was when Christmas really felt like Christmas."

Drew glanced up at Gwen, who nodded her head slightly in acknowledgement of the silent thanks he'd sent. He'd never thought of his son as deprived, and he certainly wasn't. But it was sad that his favorite Christmas memories were from so long ago. Maybe that was his fault? Maybe it was Brody's mom's? Maybe it was life changing as Brody grew older? But whatever the reason it troubled Drew that Brody believed his best Christmases were a decade behind him.

Fierce fatherly instinct rose up in him. He had three weeks until Christmas, and somehow, some way, he wanted to make this a Christmas Brody would never forget.

The only problem was…he wasn't sure how.

CHAPTER FIVE

THE next week, Drew and Brody worked feverishly with Max, removing the last of the debris and cutting trees for customers. But on the Friday before opening day Max called to let them know he couldn't come over until the afternoon because his wife Sunny had a doctor's appointment. After a hearty breakfast, Drew and Brody headed for the door.

"Max told us we'd need to replace the missing boards on the old shed," Drew explained to Gwen as they slid into their outdoor gear. "I think we can handle that on our own."

"Sure, and why not set up the stand, too?" Brody groused. "It's not like a morning off after nearly two weeks of slave labor would have been a good idea."

Seeing the look of confusion that came to Drew's handsome face, Gwen felt her chest swell with fear. He and his son had been getting along so well that it surprised her that Brody picked this morning to return to being a brat. She suspected Max probably acted like a buffer or referee for them, and worried that after two wonderful weeks of comradeship they'd get into a deal-breaker fight without someone to run interference.

Still, Drew headed to the door and Brody followed him outside. Then they were gone. Out of her sight. There was nothing she could do now about what happened between them. Fear scuttled through her again, and she knew she had to keep herself busy or she'd fret all morning.

She carted Claire and her baby swing into the living room. Though she'd vacuumed the furniture, walls and carpet of every room to get up the dust, this room had fallen to a place close to the bottom on the "real" cleaning list. Only the formal dining room and guest bedrooms were below it. But today was the day she had to dig in.

She vacuumed everything again, getting any stubborn dust that might have resisted during her initial vacuum, and then washed the windows, walls and woodwork. When the room was clean she glanced around. She'd brought the tinsel and ribbons and ornaments from home to decorate the hallway and make sure Jimmy Lane walked into a pretty entrance in case he made a surprise visit. But now that the room was clean, the fireplace screamed for some tinsel. Maybe stockings, too?

She'd only brought enough decorations for the hallway, and didn't have anything else at home she could spare. So she headed for the attic. People who didn't take their furniture usually also left behind the contents of attics and basements. Maybe she'd find some decorations there?

She went upstairs and found a virtual treasure trove. Sealed from the dust and grime of the attic in airtight boxes, the ornaments, lights, tinsel, stockings and Christmas tree star she found were like new. She carted them downstairs, but before she set about decorating she knew she had to put Claire down for a nap.

In the kitchen, making Claire's bottle, she saw the milk in the fridge and another idea struck her. She'd worried all morning about Drew and Brody, and it was only eleven o'clock. They'd be out there at least another hour before she'd get to see how they'd gotten along without Max. But if she took hot cocoa out to them she could not only give them a break, she could also see if they were fighting.

She fed Claire, put her down for her nap, made the chocolate and, as casually as she could, took a Thermos of hot cocoa and paper cups outside. Not seeing Drew or Brody anywhere, she peeked into the shed and there they were—standing over some boards so old they were black.

"I think we should carry these boards outside and rebuild the shed out there, rather than rebuild it in here and have to lug it outside."

Brody leaned negligently against a beam. "Whatever."

"Come on, Brody. We open tomorrow. We don't have time for this."

Deciding that this was a great moment to interrupt them, Gwen stepped into the shed. "Hey! How's it going? I brought hot chocolate."

Brody glanced gratefully in her direction. Drew slid off his gloves before he took the Thermos from her hands. "Great. I'm dying of thirst."

"Yeah, and it's not like the house isn't thirty feet away and we could stop for water or anything."

"If you're thirsty, all you have to do is go in the house and get a drink—"

"And get the third degree about why I'm leaving?"

Knowing that a real argument was about to ensue, Gwen pointed at the old steel-runner sled hanging on the wall and quickly said, "Hey, look! It's an old sled."

Her comment was just confusing enough to stop the men. Both glanced in the direction she pointed.

Drew smiled. "I haven't seen one of those in ages."

Gwen turned to Brody. "Do you sled-ride?"

"I snowboard and ski."

"You would love an old-fashioned sled ride," she said, then faced Drew. "Why don't you two take ten minutes and see if that old thing still works?"

Drew looked at Brody. Brody looked at Drew.

Drew shrugged. "We have to get this shed put together, but we could do that this afternoon, before we go out into the field with Max to cut the last of the trees we'll need for tomorrow."

Brody's eyes lit. "Really? We're going to take a break?"

"Until this afternoon when Max gets here." He pointed at the sled. "Pull that down. We'll see if it works."

Brody lifted the sled from the rack on the wall.

Drew opened the door for him as he carried it outside. "My dad told me stories about a hill behind the house where he rode a sled—probably this one. Let's walk back there and see if we can test it out."

Gwen merrily followed them. Baby monitor in her pocket, she knew she'd hear Claire if she awoke. Plus, they weren't going too far from the house. She could watch Brody and Drew sled-ride for a few minutes before she had to get back inside to start lunch.

They walked only twenty feet or so past the house before Brody stopped suddenly. "Whoa!"

Drew stopped, too. His laugh echoed down the mountain. "That's a hill!"

Brody grabbed the sled. "Me first."

"Absolutely," Drew said. "You be the guinea pig."

Brody laughed, threw the sled down and landed on top of it, sending it careening down the slope. His laughter echoed up to Gwen and Drew, who stood side-by-side at the top of the hill.

When Brody reached the bottom and began carrying the sled back Drew turned to Gwen. "Give me the baby monitor and you can go next."

She stepped back. "That's okay. I don't want a ride."

"Sure you do. I heard you laughing at Brody's fun."

She took another step back. "I know, but I'm kind of scared."

"Scared? Haven't you ever done this before?"

"When I was ten or twelve. But not lately."

"It's fun," Brody said, cresting the hill, obviously having heard their conversation. He offered the sled to her. "Go ahead."

She shook her head fiercely.

Drew took the sled from Brody with one hand and caught

her hand with the other. Before she knew what he was about to do, she was pushed down on the sled and Drew landed heavily on top of her. She didn't even have time to squeak out a protest. With the extra weight, the sled didn't fly down the hill the way it had with only Brody on top. Instead, it careered drunkenly. When they hit the bottom, it tilted. Drew rolled off and Gwen rolled on top of him, the breath knocked out of her.

She sucked in some air, then some more, then suddenly realized she was on top of Drew. He blinked up at her. She stared down at him. In that moment they weren't a boss and his assistant. He wasn't old. She wasn't young. They were just two people. Two people incredibly attracted to each other.

The air suddenly became heavy with promise. All she had to do would be to let her head fall a bit and she could kiss him. All he had to do would be to slide his hand a fraction of an inch and he could be touching her bottom.

"Hey! You guys aren't hurt, are you?" Brody's voice got closer with every word, and Gwen realized he was running down the hill. His boots stopped beside her and she raised her gaze to look at him.

"We're fine." But her voice came out as a croak. She'd been fighting this thing with Drew ever since she first saw him. He was too good-looking. Any woman would find him attractive. But lying on top of him as she was had somehow made it all real. Everything that had seemed vague and dreamlike about considering a relationship with him suddenly felt real.

Possible.

Brody held his hand out to her. "Here."

She glanced at Drew. Their eyes locked. And it didn't take a genius to know his thoughts had gone in the same direction hers had. *That* was why it all suddenly felt possible. They weren't merely attracted, they were becoming friends. Sort of. When they weren't arguing or negotiating.

Realizing she had lingered a little too long, she took Brody's hand. He hoisted her up and she brushed the snow off her jacket and jeans. Then she checked the baby monitor, breathing a sigh of relief when it was not only in one piece, but also silent.

She waved the monitor at the Teaberrys. "I better go check on Claire."

She didn't even wait to see Drew's reaction. She simply headed up the hill, walked into the house, checked on her sleeping baby and started lunch.

She refused to think about the possibility she'd felt at the bottom of that snowy hill. Though she did laugh. Damned if he hadn't gotten her on the sled.

She made lunch—soup and sandwiches—but didn't eat with the Teaberrys. As they laughed and talked about sledding, tingles of awareness pirouetted through her, so she excused herself and went back to work on decorating the living room. She liked Drew. She liked him a lot. Yes, they had their differences, but in some ways that was what made their relationship interesting.

She groaned in her head. Now she was calling what they had a *relationship?* She was getting too connected to him and his son, and when they left she was going to be hurt. She remembered very well how it had felt to be left behind by Nick when she'd told him she was pregnant. She remembered the pain. The chest-tightening sadness that the man she'd thought she loved didn't care enough about her to help her through a pregnancy. It had taken six months to get beyond her depression and another three to feel happy again. Did she really want to repeat all that pain when she had a chance to avoid it simply by keeping her distance from her boss?

Determined to forget about Drew, she lost herself in Christmas decorating. Stockings were hung on the marble fireplace mantel. Evergreen bows with red velvet ribbons were strung along the top of the tan brocade drapes that covered the two front windows. Santa and Mrs. Santa figurines were placed on the coffee table between the two green plaid sofas that flanked the fireplace. Elf figurines were scattered around the room, making the place look like Santa's workshop.

She was so engrossed in her work that she didn't hear Drew approach until he said, "Wow."

She spun to face him. "You like it?" Her face reddened when she realized how eager she sounded for his approval. She cleared her throat and toned down her enthusiasm. "I found these decorations upstairs. There are boxes of them."

He stepped into the room. "It's perfect." He glanced around, then pointed at the space in front of the side-by-side windows. "Except I think you need a tree."

She laughed. "Here I am at a Christmas tree farm and I don't have a tree."

He looked over at her. His dark eyes sparked with appreciation and something else. Something deeper. Something that made her tummy shimmy, her pulse scramble, and a wave of heat fall from her head to her toes. The feeling of promise she'd felt lying on top of him at the bottom of the hill returned full force.

"I'll get you one."

She swallowed and nodded, and then he was gone. Gwen collapsed on the sofa. She wasn't really sorry she'd taken cocoa out to him and Brody. She wasn't really sorry she'd suggested they sled-ride. She almost wasn't sorry they'd landed on top of each other at the bottom of a snowy hill.

But she had absolutely no idea how she'd handle the ramifications of any of it.

Drew walked straight through the kitchen, grabbed his coat, and went out into the snowy afternoon. He needed the drop in temperature to cool down. Gwen wasn't just cute and sweet. It was as if she read his mind. Everything he needed to have done, she did. Including decorate for Christmas for his son. If he weren't her boss, he wouldn't be able to resist her.

But he was her boss. He was also twelve years older. And he was a workaholic. And she—

He stopped. Snow fell heavily on his shoulders and caught on his eyelashes as he stood confused in the circular driveway of his family's first home. He really didn't know anything about Gwen. He knew she had a child. He knew she had a twin. She'd helped him with his son, cleaned this mess of a house so he could now live in it, cooked, and acted as his administrative assistant and he knew virtually nothing about her.

Was he selfish or was it self-preservation? After all, it wouldn't be smart for them to get involved. Not only were they wrong for each other, but he was leaving soon. And she would—

Damn. He had no idea what she'd do when he left. When he'd tried to fire her she'd told him she desperately needed this job, but he hadn't thought far enough ahead to realize she might not have a way to make money once he was gone.

A bubble of protectiveness formed in his chest. She'd negotiated a little more money from him than the original salary they'd agreed upon, but when he was gone he had no idea how she'd support herself and Claire.

He shook his head resolutely. He couldn't think about that. She was a smart, savvy adult who would be fine. If he meddled in her life they'd get closer, and he might not be able to pull away when the time came. And that would be a disaster. She was young enough and pretty enough that she'd probably forget about him two weeks after he was gone. And then where would he be? Alone in North Carolina, feeling hopeless and dejected, aching with hurt as he had when Olivia left him.

He headed for the shed, hoping Max had arrived so he could get his mind off Gwen. Instead he passed her beaten-up car, and saw that at least four inches of snow had accumulated since her arrival and the storm was just getting started. She'd be driving down a mountain road in a foot of snow tonight.

The protective bubble in his chest tightened. He had to at least offer her the opportunity to stay nights. If he intended to work her fourteen hours a day he had to for once forget about his own fears and think about hers.

Because Claire had taken an overly long nap that afternoon, Gwen brought her to the supper table that night. As she sat, Drew peered over at her precious baby. He let his gaze linger on the little girl, as if taking in every detail about her, maybe growing accustomed to her. Then he turned his attention to Brody, talking about the stand they'd helped Max rebuild.

Gwen happily let the conversation steer itself totally away from her. After the sled ride, then the look he'd given her over the Christmas tree conversation, she knew they'd be better off ignoring each other.

When dinner was eaten, she got up from the table and started the dishes. Brody excused himself for his room, and as he left for the office Drew reminded her that they again had to work that night.

After the dishes were done, she lifted Claire's carrier and headed off to join him. As she stepped inside the office Drew was deep in concentration, reading a document. She settled Claire in the swing.

"Will she be okay?"

His question startled her, but didn't surprise her. She'd caught him staring at Claire at dinner and knew he wasn't complaining as much as acknowledging that he was okay with her being here.

"As long as she can see me she's fine."

Drew set the contract he was reading back on his desk, scrubbed his hand across his face as if wrestling with himself about something, then said, "That's going to be hard when you get a real job."

She frowned. That was a weird comment. Especially since he'd barely ever asked her anything about herself. Their last discussion about something personal about her had been when she'd told him about Gill.

Still, she couldn't ignore him. "I'm not getting a real job

for a while. Once this assignment is over I'm taking the money I earn here and using it to support us while I finish my degree."

He sat forward on his chair. "You're that close?"

She nodded and smiled. It felt good to have a real plan, not just a dream or a hope or a wish. "I got pregnant the next-to-last semester of college. I finished that semester, but not the last. So I have to take some classes, but mostly I'll be student teaching."

His eyes lit. "You're going to be a teacher?"

"Yep. So for the next four months, when I'm not teaching or taking a class, I'll be with Claire. But I'll also be away from her enough that I'm hoping she'll adjust to daycare before she has to be there for eight-hour days."

He smiled. "You have it all thought out."

"I have to. I can't leave anything to chance."

"I guess." He fiddled with the pencil he was holding, then caught her gaze again. "Speaking of chance…is there any chance you'd consider sleeping here at nights?" His face reddened endearingly. "I said that wrong. Everything has changed since I decided to open the Christmas tree farm. You're working eight hours in the house during the day and four hours with me at night." He rubbed his hand along the back of his neck. "I worry about you driving down the mountain."

The warm, fuzzy feeling in the pit of her stomach returned. *He worried about her—*

She stopped her thoughts. To her dreamy schoolgirl side that might seem wonderful, but it wasn't smart for two attracted people who were beginning to care about each other to sleep in the same house. He had to know that as much as she did.

She peered over at him.

He held her gaze. "Okay, since the episode on the sled outed both of us, I think it's time for us to be honest." He paused, sucked in a breath. "We're very attracted to each other."

The air in her chest stuttered. She licked her suddenly dry

lips. He was right. Since the fall off the sled neither one of them could pretend indifference. Still, she hadn't expected him to come right out and talk about it.

"But our lives are totally different. I'm not going to start something that I know is wrong. So if you agree to stay nights you'll be perfectly safe with me."

His reassurance should have made her happy. After all, he was right about the drive down the mountain at night. Instead, her heart hurt. Her pride felt wounded. He might be attracted to her, but he absolutely, positively didn't want to be. He'd sent her that message every day in subtle, silent ways. And she'd caught it. That was why she held back her own feelings.

But she still had them, and spending more time with him, no matter how convenient and smart it might be, would only add fuel to the fire. She wasn't just attracted to him anymore. She had real feelings for him, and was getting a little too comfortable in this house.

She looked down, then back up at him. "How about if I think about it?"

He nodded, maybe a little too eagerly, as if happy to have the awkward conversation over. "Okay."

Her heart plummeted. It was one thing to decide herself to keep her distance, quite another to have him come right out and say he didn't want anything to do with her.

CHAPTER SIX

As if Mother Nature wanted Teaberry Farms opening day to be a grand success, the snow stopped the next morning. Gwen arrived at the Teaberry mansion to find Max, Drew and Brody sitting at the kitchen table. Jovial Max laughed like a kid at Christmas, Drew grinned—looking every bit as excited as Max—and Brody pouted.

"The three of us will have our work cut out for us this morning," Max said over the rim of his coffee mug. "It's two weeks till Christmas. People are going to be coming in droves. I think it will work best if two of us assist the customers and one mans the cash register."

Brody snorted derisively. Drew nodded. "I'll take the cash register." He glanced at Gwen, his eyes cool, emotionless, telling her with their lack of expression that she truly was safe with him. "I'm expecting a fax around eleven. If I stay in one place all morning, you'll know where to find me when it comes in."

Turning to get a cup from the cupboard, so he wouldn't see the hurt in her eyes, she said, "Okay."

With that, the men rose from the table. Max and Drew grabbed the coats they stored on the hooks by the kitchen door. Brody had to go upstairs for his. In a silent protest at the work he had to do, he'd stopped leaving his parka by the door, so he could delay going outside while he got it.

Seeing a flicker of apprehension race across Drew's face,

Gwen said a silent prayer that everything would go okay, and within seconds the men were outside and the Christmas tree farm was officially open.

Gwen carried Claire's swing into the dining room and went to work. She cleaned first, then began to decorate. She strung lights and tinsel through the arms of the chandelier above the long mahogany table, looped tinsel above the tan brocade drapes, and made a centerpiece of evergreens and Christmas tree ornaments for the table.

She longed to see if Drew and Max had any customers. She knew how much Drew was banking on the Christmas tree farm impressing Jimmy Lane. The old man was dragging his feet in negotiations, ignoring Drew's e-mails, and only corresponding enough that Drew knew he hadn't totally lost the possibility of buying Jimmy's company. So Gwen was too apprehensive to even let herself look out the window at their success or failure. It was ridiculous. Foolish. Caring too much about a man who clearly didn't want her was almost as bad as wishing a man would return to her life the way her mom had. She knew better than this.

When Drew's fax arrived at eleven-thirty, she put on her coat and walked out the front door into total chaos. Cars lined the lane that led to the Teaberry mansion. People milled about the groups of already cut trees that leaned against the wood fence for inspection and purchase. A glance past the outbuildings into the rows of uncut trees showed that even more customers were in the field, choosing their very own special tree.

Not even sure where to look for the cash register, Gwen wove through the customers. She saw Max and Brody first, hoisting trees to car roofs and securing them with twine, or shoving them into the backs of SUVs and pickups.

"They're all here because of the legend," she heard Max telling Brody. "Every year someone who buys one of these trees has a fantastic wish granted."

Brody snorted.

"Scoff if you want to," Max said, "but even though only one person gets a great wish, lots of people get little wishes granted. Family members show up unexpectedly for Christmas dinner, special presents arrive, money finds its way into bank accounts." He tapped Brody's shoulder. "And all because there's magic in our trees."

Brody rolled his eyes. "Right."

"And you've been touching them for two weeks now." Max's eyes twinkled. "Imagine how good of a wish you could be granted if you'd just believe."

Not wanting Brody to scoff again, and ruin Max's holiday cheer, Gwen rushed over to them. "Where's Drew?"

Max pointed to a crowded area. "He's at the back of that line, taking money."

Following the direction of Max's glove-covered finger, Gwen looped around the crowd and saw Drew.

A short woman in a worn blue coat walked up to the sales stand as his next customer. "How much?"

Drew examined her tree as Brody and Max approached. "Thirty… Um…" He looked down at the tattered wallet the woman produced from her coat pocket at the same time as Gwen noticed the big sign behind the makeshift checkout area. The sign said the trees were priced at five dollars a foot, and this customer had at least a six-foot tree.

She didn't expect Drew to realize that thirty dollars was a lot of money. In his world it probably wasn't. But in the world of the woman in the tattered coat it was a small fortune.

He glanced down at the cash register, then looked up with a beaming smile. "Guess what? Your tree is free. You're our one-hundredth customer."

The woman's face bloomed into a glowing expression of delight. "I am?"

Brody said, "She is?"

Max nudged Brody in the ribs to get him to hush.

Gwen stifled a giggle.

"She is." Drew waved away her money. "Merry Christmas from Teaberry Farms."

With a chuckle, Max wrapped his gloved hand around the trunk of the tree and angled his head to Brody, indicating that Brody should follow him. They loaded the woman's tree onto the roof of her beaten-up car. As she drove off Brody looked from the woman's car to his dad and back again, shaking his head.

Drew was smoother with the next customer, an elderly gentleman with two grandkids dancing around his legs.

Drew glanced at the tree, then the man, then the kids, and said, "Ten dollars."

The man happily paid, and Max and Brody loaded the tree. This time Brody didn't appear to be confused. He actually smiled.

Realizing there wasn't a break in the line of customers for her to pull Drew away, Gwen walked to the counter and handed his fax to him.

"Thanks."

"You're welcome."

She should have turned away and gone back to the house, but all she could do was stare at him. He'd given away the tree so kindly, so naturally, that only she, Max and Brody had recognized his generosity. She suddenly understood why she was so drawn to him. Deep down he was a good man. A very good man. Her instincts had known it all along. That was why she kept forgetting there were too many differences between them for them to have a relationship. That was why she'd gotten so depressed when he'd reminded her the night before that they should keep their distance. She *wanted* a relationship with him.

Drew nodded toward the house. "You should go back in. It's cold."

She might want a relationship with him, but he didn't want one with her. She had to accept that.

Without looking at him she said, "Okay," and walked to

the house. But at the front door she paused and glanced back at him, just in time to see him fold the fax and put it in his pocket so he could serve the next customer. He was putting his tree customers before his conglomerate.

She opened the front door and stepped inside the house. If he were hers, she'd tell him what a wonderful guy he was. But he wasn't hers. He would never be hers.

The tree farm didn't officially close for the day until after eight. Gwen took sandwiches and coffee out to the men at one for lunch, and again at six, but she had a real dinner waiting for them when they came in for the night.

Drew didn't even look at her when he said, "Thanks."

She smiled anyway. "You're welcome."

Brody snorted and kicked off his boots. "*Thanks. You're welcome.* You can stop the act. I get it."

Drew cast a horrified glance in his son's direction. "What are you talking about?"

"You're trying to teach me better manners. I get it. But you can stop now."

Obviously tired from the day's work, Drew looked like a man who had reached his limit. Gwen wasn't surprised when he exploded.

"Why are you so grouchy?"

Brody rounded on him. "Me? Grouchy? You bring me to the pit from hell, put me to work, then constantly act super-polite around me with Gwen, as if you're walking on eggshells."

Gwen's breath caught in her throat. He thought they were walking on eggshells because of *him?* She saw a corresponding look of horror come to Drew's face.

Luckily, he recovered quickly. "I'm sorry, but Gwen and I aren't walking on eggshells because of you. We're professionals. A boss and his assistant, trying to get our work done."

"Then why do I hear you talking nicer to each other when I'm not around and only being super-polite when I am?"

Gwen coughed uncomfortably.

Drew shook his head. "I don't know what to say, Brody—"

Neither did Gwen. Was it appropriate to tell Drew's sixteen-year-old son that they were fighting their attraction and that was why they were so stiff and polite with each other?

Brody blew his breath out. "Right. You don't know what to say. You never know what to say because I'm a pain in your butt. An extra person underfoot that you don't need right now. Why don't you just ship me off, like mom did?"

"Hey, look, Brody, this might not be convenient for you, but your mom is on her honeymoon. Give her a break."

Brody snorted. "You still think she's taking me back, don't you? I'll bet you never even called her to ask if what I'd told you was true." He shook his head. "You know, Dad, for a smart guy you can make it amazingly easy for someone to pull the wool over your eyes."

As he said that, Brody shoved his boots to the corner by the door and stormed out of the room.

In the silence that followed, Drew's gaze strayed over to Gwen. She smiled sympathetically, but embarrassment rose up in her. It was hard being attracted to someone and not being able to show it. They'd flubbed this deal royally.

Drew shook his head. "I don't even know where to start with the apologies."

"You don't need to apologize to me. But I do think you need to call Brody's mom. That's the second time he's said she doesn't want him back. The first time I thought he was just exaggerating to make himself look put upon, but now I'm not so sure."

Drew sighed. "Yeah. I'm going to have to call." He glanced at the table. "Sorry about ruining dinner."

She waved a hand in dismissal. "Everything will keep until you and Brody get this straightened out."

"And if we don't?"

"You'll eat it as leftovers tomorrow."

Drew couldn't help it; he burst out laughing. Was it any

wonder he found Gwen irresistible? In the face of all the trouble they'd had with Brody, she managed to not only give him good advice but also to make him laugh.

But when he dropped to the seat behind the desk and dialed the number for Olivia's cell phone, he forgot all about Gwen and braced himself for a difficult conversation—if only because his conversations with Olivia were always difficult. He didn't beat around the bush or waste time. He simply came right out and asked if she planned on taking Brody back after her honeymoon. She didn't mince words, either. Now that she had a new husband she wanted a new life. Brody was officially Drew's responsibility.

He spent ten minutes alone in the office after he disconnected the call. He didn't know whether to be angry because Olivia had handled this so poorly or scared to death because he now had the care of a sixteen-year-old who clearly didn't like him.

Gwen was still at the table when he returned to the kitchen.

She faced him eagerly. "Well?"

He took a seat across from her and blew his breath out on a heavy sigh. "She wants me to keep him."

Her face scrunched warily. "Is that good or bad?"

"Well, I work a lot—"

"You can fit Brody in. In the two weeks you've been here you've managed to find eight hours a day to run a Christmas tree farm, keep your conglomerate going, and continue to negotiate to buy a new business."

"Only because I pawned a lot of work off on my vice-presidents."

She laughed merrily. "So? Keep doing that."

Catching her gaze, he relaxed on his chair. "I guess I could."

"You hired those people for a reason. I'll bet they're thrilled to be getting more responsibility." She put her elbow on the table and her chin on her fist and smiled at him. "What else?"

He winced. "Now I have to tell Brody that he was right. He will be living with me." He blew his breath out. "I have no idea what to say."

Gwen glanced down at the table, thinking of her own dad, wondering how she would have felt if he'd suddenly gotten custody of her and Gill. Her mom would have had to have been deathly ill to give them up, and Gwen would have been terrified to live with the dad who hadn't wanted her.

Drew snorted a laugh. "How can I expect to be a good father when I don't even know how to tell him he's now living with me?"

She slowly raised her gaze to meet Drew's. "My dad left my mom when Gill and I were born."

Drew frowned, obviously not understanding why she'd said that.

She plugged on, talking about the most humiliating, most difficult situation in her life. "Mom said he was expecting one baby and got two." She shrugged. "It freaked him out. And—" She sucked in a breath. "If he had suddenly gotten custody of us, I would have been terrified."

"I suppose so. You didn't know him?"

She shook her head. "No. That isn't what would have frightened me. I would have been terrified because I knew he didn't want us. I don't know the guy, so I couldn't have said he would have beaten us or not fed us or anything like that. But can you imagine living with someone who ignored you? Or complained about having you around?"

Drew's eyes narrowed. "Are you saying Brody's acting out because he's afraid I don't want him?"

"I don't know. But think it through. How would you feel if the mother you loved suddenly didn't want you anymore and the dad you were sent to live with didn't really have time for you?"

Drew squeezed his eyes shut. Several seconds passed in

absolute silence. Then he rose from his seat and headed out of the kitchen.

Thinking she'd screwed up with her advice, since Drew wasn't really anything like her totally absent father, Gwen scrambled after him. But he was quicker than she was. By the time she got to Brody's room he was already inside.

"I want you."

Gwen skidded to a stop in front of the open door, just in time to see Brody glare up at his dad from his position on the bed. "Big whoop."

Drew sat on the bed beside Brody's long legs. "It is a big whoop. I missed your baby years. I missed elementary school. I missed middle school. But not by choice. Your mom moved you far away." He looked down, then back up at Brody again. "It's a blessing for me to get you. I may only have two years before you're off to university, but I want those years. I want every minute I can get with you to get to know you."

Brody's eyes narrowed. "Really?"

"Yes. I think the next two years with you might be the happiest of my life."

Brody unexpectedly bounced up and grabbed his father in a hug. Tears filled Gwen's eyes and she backed out of the room, leaving father and son to their personal moment.

But when Drew returned to the kitchen she didn't hesitate. She said, "That was the sweetest thing I've ever seen anybody do," caught the front of his shirt, pulled him to her, and kissed him.

CHAPTER SEVEN

SHE tasted his passion first. Surprised as he had been, he reacted instinctively and naturally fell into the kiss. All his pent-up desires rushed out in one fierce press of his mouth to hers. But as quickly as that registered for Gwen he shifted, changed. As if suddenly realizing he was finally getting what he'd been itching to take, he tempered his passion, and he smoothed his lips over hers gently, experimentally.

She rose to her tiptoes and kissed him back. She glided her hands up his arms to his shoulders. His arms slid around her waist as his tongue slipped into her mouth.

Sweet fire exploded in her veins, rocking her to her core. It took several seconds for the world to right itself, but when it did he twined his tongue with hers and the fire inside her roared with life and energy. No simple kiss had ever affected her as this one did, and when his hands slid up her back, tightening her more snugly against him, she suspected the kiss was as explosive for him as it was for her.

She knew why. They truly liked each other. All along they'd had sexual chemistry, but adding emotion to that chemistry had made them a fiery combination. She couldn't even begin to imagine what it would be like to actually make love to him if a kiss could reduce her to a simmering bundle of need.

But before she could take her thoughts any further he released her, stepped back and rubbed his hands down his face. "I'm sorry."

"Don't be sorry! That was great. Plus, I started it. What you did with Brody was fantastic. No woman could resist that."

Self-conscious, he took another step back. "It was still wrong. And we can't do that again. You're so young, Gwen. You have your whole life ahead of you. I'm settled with who I am and what I have, and now I have a sixteen-year-old son to raise. Hell, you're barely older than he is. I won't get involved with you."

With that he strode out of the kitchen, and Gwen fell despondently to one of the chairs around the table. She wasn't sorry she'd kissed him. But she was sorry about the age gap between them. How could she possibly fight that? Change that? She couldn't.

With the awkward way Drew treated her over the next few days Gwen was glad she hadn't started the practice of spending the night—though she had packed pajamas for herself and Claire, just in case the weather was truly too bad for her to drive in.

Drew was careful to be cheerful around Brody, so there was no doubt that he was wanted, but around her he was withdrawn, as if he were afraid that one kind word would cause her to kiss him again. She should have been embarrassed, but she wasn't. How could she be embarrassed about kissing a man she genuinely liked? Someone she knew liked her, too?

On Tuesday afternoon Drew brought in the Christmas tree he'd promised her, and set it up in the living room without a word. She'd found an old tree stand and he shoved it inside, but couldn't secure it. Not waiting to be asked, she rushed to help him. When they both reached for the same spot on the tree trunk their hands brushed.

Awareness twinkled from her hand to her heart. Her feelings for him were so strong that her chest swelled with longing. He caught her gaze, glanced at their hands, then slowly moved his fingers higher on the trunk.

This time her chest squeezed with pain. He clearly hadn't

changed his mind. She wanted a relationship. She had kissed him. He'd kissed her back, only to rebuff her. He didn't want her.

Maybe she should just accept that?

After that, she continued to cook for the Teaberrys, but she stopped eating with them and forgot all about staying overnight.

But on Friday night, when Max and Brody came into the house after their day's work, Max laughed at the fact that she was in her coat, ready to run out and start her car before she and Claire left for home.

"You might as well sit down and have some of that chicken you made for us," he said, shrugging out of his coat.

Avoiding even accidentally meeting Drew's gaze by looking at the floor, she said, "I can't stay tonight."

"You're going to have to." Brody laughed and pulled out a chair. "Last customer said the mountain road is blowing shut."

She lifted her head and gaped at Brody. "Blowing shut?"

Max chuckled as he also took a seat at the table. "That wind is fierce! Have you been so busy you haven't even heard the storm?"

Not busy. Preoccupied with making sure Drew didn't see how hurt she was by his not wanting her. She glanced down at her baby, happily cooing in the carrier, already dressed in her snowsuit.

Drew walked to the stove. "You take care of Claire. Get her settled for the night. I'll get the food on the table."

Appalled that she'd been so nervous all day she hadn't even noticed the storm moving in, she raced back to her bedroom, tossed Claire's diaper bag to the bed, shrugged out of her coat and undressed her baby, chastising herself for being an idiot.

Still, when she went back into the kitchen she pretended her staying the night was no big deal, asking Max and Brody about their days, enjoying their company. After dinner she persuaded Brody to help with the dishes, and he happily complied.

When Drew tried to join them she took the stack of cups from his hands. "Why don't you go back to the office and finish reading the most recent e-mail from Jimmy Lane?"

"Because it's Friday night and I'd already decided we weren't going to work."

She shook her head. "It's a big deal that he finally got back to you with a serious e-mail countering your last offer. You can't ignore it. Go. We'll be fine."

Then she turned away, faced the sink, and wouldn't even look back until she was absolutely positive he'd left the room.

After finishing reading the e-mail Gwen had all but demanded he read, Drew walked to the living room, where Max had laid a fire in the marble fireplace. Instead of finding the room empty, as he'd expected, he found Brody and Gwen decorating the Christmas tree. Little Claire sat in her carrier on the sofa.

"Hey, Dad!" Brody said, pointing at a box of ornaments. "Dig in. This tree is huge. We can use all the help we can get."

"That's okay, I'll—"

"Stay," Gwen said, her gaze drifting over to his before she nudged her head in Brody's direction, as if telling him his staying would be good for Brody.

He hesitated. She looked cute in a pair of Santa-covered flannel pajamas that matched the one-piece pajamas worn by Claire, whose eyes were glued to the lights twinkling on the tree. Brody had showered, and wore red and green plaid pajama pants and a red T-shirt. With the tree behind them, they could have been the picture on a Christmas card.

He stepped into the room. "I don't know how much help I'll be."

Gwen handed Brody an ornament to hang at the top of

the tree. "Haven't you ever done this before?" she asked jokingly.

But he replied seriously. "I go to my parents for Christmas dinner and spend twelve-hour days at the office. Not much point in having a tree in my condo."

"Then it's lucky you're learning how to decorate one," Brody said, teasing the way Gwen was. "Because I'll want a tree."

"And you'll want a tree now, too, Drew," Gwen said, handing Brody a colored ball to hang near the gold star at the top of the tree. She caught Drew's gaze, sending him another signal by glancing at Brody, then back at him. "Didn't you tell me that you were going to start delegating more of your work to your vice-presidents, so you could have more time at home?"

"Yes," Drew answered quickly, glad she'd brought that up because he hadn't really told Brody that part of the plan.

Not wanting his nervousness to show when he spoke, he grabbed an ornament and walked around the back of the tree, to the side in front of the window, away from both Gwen and Brody, and began decorating there.

"While I've been here, I've only really worked half-days." He peered around the tree at Brody. "Not that I'm going to cut my schedule in half now that you're living with me, but I *can* see that it would be possible to only work eight-hour days if I delegate."

Brody said, "All right!"

Drew sighed with relief. "I was also thinking we should get a house."

Gwen peered over at him. "A house?"

"Yeah." He avoided her gaze. He'd thought about moving out of the condo and into a real house because of her. She'd made this shabby old house into a home—something he didn't think his streamlined condo could ever be. And a family needed a house. He and Brody might not be a big family, but they were still a family.

Brody danced for joy. "A beach house?"

Drew cautiously said, "Would you want to live on the beach?"

"Hell, yeah!"

Both Drew and Gwen said, "Don't say hell."

Brody laughed. "This is great!" He pulled his cell phone from a pocket in his pajama pants. "I have to text my friends."

With that he zipped out of the room, and Drew froze. Except for when they worked together at night, this was the first time he'd been alone with Gwen since their kiss, and he absolutely didn't know what to say. He knew he'd hurt her. He'd hurt himself. Brushing her off after that kiss had been the hardest thing he'd ever done. He'd thought about it for days afterward. Mourned the decision he knew he had to make.

"A house sounds like a good idea."

"Yeah." He picked up another ornament for the tree and looped around to the back side, avoiding her. "A condo's no place for a kid. He'll need room to roam."

"On the ocean? Is he going to walk on water?"

Her comment made him laugh. Again. She always knew how to make him laugh. "No, he'll have miles of beach to walk on." He sucked in a breath. "I'm probably going to have to get him an ATV. A surfboard. A boogey board. Scuba gear."

"You're going to be busy."

He laughed. "It feels weird."

"But I'll bet it's a good weird."

It was. "Had you told me two weeks ago that I'd be looking forward to living with Brody I would have thought you were nuts."

She chuckled. "Haven't you *ever* thought about having Brody with you for longer than two weeks?"

Using the tree for protection, he answered honestly. "Yes. Because I was an only child I'd grown up thinking how much fun it would be to have a big family." He shrugged. "But a few years after Brody was born I settled to just have him with me for one holiday."

"Why didn't you try for more?"

"Because I knew Olivia would fight me. I didn't want Brody to see us fighting or risk losing the scant visitation I had."

"Sad."

"Yeah."

She walked around to his side of the tree. "So why didn't you find another wife? Have more kids?"

He busied himself hanging a candy cane and didn't answer.

After a minute or two of silence, Gwen said, "You're a natural Christmas tree decorator."

He laughed. "It's not exactly rocket science."

"I have some cocoa and cookies on the table if you want some."

Grateful that she hadn't pursued her question about another wife and kids, he walked around the other side of the tree, so he didn't accidentally brush against her. He didn't know how to answer her. What could he say? He'd been too busy? He had been, but tonight that reason seemed lame.

When he reached down to get a gingerbread man he found himself at eye-level with Claire.

She cooed at him.

His heart melted. It was the first time he'd been this close to her, so he'd never before noticed that her eyes were dark—not green, like her mom's, but almost black, like Drew's. Her hair was the same color as her mom's, though. Shiny, silky blond.

She cooed again.

He set the cookie back on the plate and inched over to her. He gingerly extended his index finger and ran it along the velvety skin of her hand. He couldn't stop his whispered, "Wow."

"I know," Gwen said from behind him. "She's adorable."

"And soft." He cautiously turned his head and caught Gwen's gaze. "I'd forgotten how soft babies are."

"It sounds like Brody's first months of life weren't easy for you—not something you wanted to remember."

He sucked in a breath. "No." And maybe that was why he'd never found another wife? The one he'd had had soured him on marriage. "Those years aren't something I like to remember."

She snagged a gingerbread man and eased over to the tree again. Picking up a striped ball, she said, "Have you ever stopped to think that maybe you're not opposed to us trying a relationship because of my age as much as because you're afraid?"

He spun around. "What?"

"Your first marriage sounds like it was pretty bad. I don't know your ex-wife, and I could be way off base, but from the way she handled giving you custody of Brody she seems like she might have been—" She sucked in a breath. "Self-centered."

He laughed at her choice of words. "She was worse than self-centered."

She waited until he looked over at her before she said, "Not all women are like her."

The truth of that shimmied through him, because Gwen was the living, breathing evidence of what she'd said. But it didn't change the fact that she was twelve years younger than he was.

"I get what you're saying. And I agree. My first marriage *was* abysmal. But this thing between us is wrong." He glanced at Claire, then back at Gwen. "How about if we just go back to decorating the tree and forget all about my first marriage?"

She smiled. "Okay."

He couldn't believe how easily she'd agreed, but then guessed the conversation had probably been difficult for her, too. They continued decorating the tree in silence. Gwen's baby cooed as Gwen's hands busily adjusted the ornaments so they were just perfect. Brody returned to the room and began happily chatting about his friends' reactions to Brody living at the beach.

And Drew's heart broke. For the first time in his life he was experiencing a glimpse of the life he'd always wanted. And it was with a woman he couldn't have.

CHAPTER EIGHT

THE next day was December twenty-second. Three days till Christmas. Customers formed a non-stop line on the tree-lined lane to Teaberry Farms, and Gwen bundled up twice that day to bring hot cocoa to grateful Drew, Max and Brody.

But on her second trip she looked up from handing Drew a cup of cocoa and saw the woman who had "won" the free tree. This time she wasn't wearing the tattered blue coat. She wore a black leather jacket, black boots, and carried a purse Gwen knew cost over a thousand dollars.

Her mouth fell open. After waiting for Drew to finish with his customer, she caught his arm and dragged him a few feet away from the stand. "Remember the woman you said was the one-hundredth customer so you could give her a tree?"

He nodded. "Yes."

"She's back. In line."

Drew peered at the trail of customers. "No, she's not."

"Yes, she is. She's wearing an expensive black coat and boots, and carrying a bag that costs more than I'll make in a month when I start teaching."

Drew glanced out at the line again. When he saw the woman Gwen referred to his eyes narrowed. "That *is* her." He swung his gaze back to Gwen. "I gave a rich woman a free tree."

Brody sidled over to them. "Maybe she just got a Christmas tree wish?"

Max growled, "Stop making fun of the legend," before he picked up the tree Drew had just sold and headed off with Brody to secure it on top of the car of the customer.

Drew said, "So what do we do?"

"Nothing. Unless you want to charge her double for the tree she's about to buy?"

Drew shook his head. "Nope. I was duped. My loss."

Gwen nodded, but stood at the cash box with him and helped him collect the money for the trees as the well-dressed woman approached. When it was her turn, Gwen stopped what she was doing and watched Drew.

Instead of being angry, or even annoyed, he pretended not to know her. "Merry Christmas," he said, the same way he had to the ten customers he'd handled before her. "That'll be thirty dollars."

She happily opened her wallet and handed him the money, but before he could take it she sighed. "Okay. I saw you guys pointing at me, and I'm guessing you remember me from the other day."

Drew crossed his arms on his chest. "We do. We gave you a free tree."

"And really impressed me." She extended her hand across the cash counter. "I'm Jimmy Lane."

Gwen's mouth fell open. All this time Drew had thought he was negotiating with a cranky old man, and instead "Jimmy" was a gorgeous young woman in a sexy leather coat and boots, with blond hair that fell past her shoulders and bright blue eyes.

When neither Drew nor Gwen spoke, she laughed. "I get it," she said, glancing from shell-shocked Drew to Gwen, then back to Drew again. "You thought you were dealing with my grandfather."

Drew was the first to find his voice. "Yes."

"Well, you were," Jimmy said. "I'm his namesake and his replacement. I was the one typing the e-mails, but he had the final say on everything that went into them. He sent me here to check up on you. You passed with flying colors when you gave the woman you thought was poor a free tree. My grandfather is now convinced you're the perfect person to own his company." She jostled her tree in Drew's direction. "By the way, I still want to buy this tree."

"You already have one," Gwen said sourly, then nearly bit her tongue, hardly believing she'd been so rude. She wasn't angry that the woman had finagled a tree. Jimmy had had her reasons for her ruse, and she hadn't asked Drew to give her a tree. So Gwen had no idea why she couldn't be nice to her.

"We have a big house. We put up six trees. My grandfather can't get enough of Christmas."

"Sounds like my grandfather," Drew said as he headed for the cash register. Gwen almost thought he'd give the tree to Jimmy as another gesture of good will, until she suddenly realized that this was a business transaction. Jimmy and Drew were business people. Equals. The Lanes weren't about to give him a discount on the company he was buying from them. He wasn't about to give them a discount on the tree they were buying from him. And Jimmy didn't expect one. She easily opened her wallet and pulled out the cash.

It was like she and Drew were on the same page.

Gwen's eyes narrowed. They *were* on the same page. About the same age. Raised in luxury. Groomed to take over the family holdings. Smart, educated, attractive.

She glanced down at her worn parka and boots. How the devil had she ever thought Drew might want *her?*

As Drew made change, Jimmy glanced around. "You know, I'm sort of sorry I won't be coming back. This place is gorgeous."

"Thanks."

"So where is your real home?"

"North Carolina."

"My family has a beach house in Charleston." She smiled. "Maybe we could get together some time?"

Drew inclined his head. "Why? Does your conglomerate have other companies you're looking to sell?"

Jimmy smiled at Max as he hoisted the tree to take it to her SUV. "Thanks."

But the smile she gave to Drew when she faced him again had nothing to do with business. "Yes, we do have other companies we could sell, but I also make a wicked lasagna and have a wine collection that will knock your socks off."

Gwen's breath shivered in her chest. Jimmy had blatantly flirted with Drew in front of Gwen. Why? Because Gwen was an employee. A servant. Jimmy had dismissed her as being unimportant.

Gwen had to fight the anger that welled up inside of her. Mostly because she didn't know who she was angry with. Jimmy for dismissing her? Drew for being the perfect match for Jimmy? Or herself for being an idiot, thinking she was made for somebody like Drew?

She turned in the snow and headed back into the house. The sound of Claire crying or even awakening hadn't come through the baby monitor, but right now Gwen needed to see her baby to feel loved, wanted. She slipped off her boots by the kitchen door and headed for the maid's quarters.

She shook her head. She was even staying in the maid's quarters. Like the servant she was. Yet she'd fallen in love with a man who didn't want her. Hell, he'd even told her that.

Seeing that Claire was still sound asleep, she headed out of the room to make dinner just as Drew stepped inside. Before Gwen could slip out of his way he caught her around the waist and danced her around the room.

"She approved our last version of the agreement."

Gwen pulled herself out of his arms. "Well, she did say her grandfather had already called you the perfect person to buy his company."

"I know! Isn't it fantastic? Honestly, I think I got one of Max's Christmas tree miracles."

Avoiding his gaze, she puttered around her bedroom,

feeling odd that he felt at ease being in her sleeping quarters until she realized that to him this wasn't a bedroom. It was the maid's quarters.

"Don't you feel like celebrating?"

She tried to smile, but couldn't. Fact upon fact bombarded her. What right did she have to celebrate Drew's purchase of a business? In just a few minutes in Jimmy's company Gwen had easily seen Jimmy was the kind of woman Drew belonged with. Even if he got carried away in the enthusiasm of the moment, told Gwen he loved her, asked her to marry him, they didn't belong together. He'd been right all along.

Tears stung her eyes. Stupidly, she'd fallen in love with a man who wouldn't ever love her.

She swallowed and turned away. "You know what? I just realized that with the agreement for the purchase finalized my work is done."

"Yeah. So now we celebrate." He tried to catch her, probably to turn her to face him, but she skittered away.

"It's three days till Christmas, Drew. I've been almost living here for weeks now. My house isn't cleaned for the holiday, or decorated."

He stepped back. "What?"

She pressed her hand to her chest. "I need to go home."

"Oh."

"It's Claire's first Christmas. She loves your tree, but I'd like to give her one of my own."

Watching Gwen's little red car disappear down the country road, Drew swallowed the lump in his throat. This was for the best. They weren't right for each other. No matter how much it hurt to see her drive away, he had to let her go.

With another six hours of selling trees to get through, he took his position at the cash register and lost himself in the crush of Christmas tree customers. Once word had circulated that the farm was open, people had come from miles around to get their trees. Most older customers had a story about a miracle that had happened in their lives after buying one of their trees. Drew shook his head sadly. He'd thought getting Jimmy Lane's company was his miracle, but now that Gwen was gone he had to admit the purchase of one more company for an already burgeoning conglomerate felt empty. Hollow.

The second they closed that night, as Max waved goodbye to go home, and Brody happily turned off the lights strung across the outbuildings and lit the cheery colored bulbs lighting the fir trees around the mansion, Drew's heart sank. It was the first night since they'd been here that Gwen wouldn't be there. There'd be no dinner. No gingerbread. No muffins. No warmth. No joy.

He followed Brody into the house, not saying a word when his son announced he was running upstairs for his shower.

Twenty minutes later, when Brody returned to the kitchen, his flushed cheeks made his bright blue eyes seem even brighter. Drew hadn't ever seen his son this youthfully excited over a holiday. Though he'd like to take the credit, he couldn't. Gwen had decorated the house. Gwen had made the place smell like heaven. Gwen had even given him the advice he'd needed to make Brody happy.

"Where is everybody?"

Drew pulled in a breath. "Gwen has gone home."

It hurt to even say the words, so he turned back to the stove, his grim mood becoming downright sour.

"What do you mean, she's gone home? They're staying here."

The grilled cheese sandwiches Drew was cooking to go with the canned vegetable soup heating on the pot beside the grill weren't very appetizing, especially compared to the wonderful meals Gwen had prepared for them, but they were warm and filling, and after all the work he'd done that day, Brody should be hungry enough to be grateful for it—not taking Drew to task for something that was none of his business.

"Son, the deal is done now, and Gwen needed to get herself ready for Christmas. I'm sure her sister will get time off for the holiday, and Gwen wants to spend time with her twin—her family."

Brody unexpectedly caught his dad's upper arm and spun him away from the stove. His eyes sparked with anger. His breaths came in short puffs. "She *was* with family. Us!"

Surprised by the strength Brody had acquired working only a few short weeks, Drew nonetheless didn't back down. "No. She wasn't. We're not her family."

Brody held his ground, too. "Yes, we are."

Suddenly tired, Drew faced the stove, snapped off the now bubbling soup and flipped the cheese sandwiches. "Brody, we came here for a month. I'd like to come back every Christmas, to open the tree farm, but Gwen McKenzie is a young woman who is just starting her life—"

"Is that what this is all about?" Brody asked, his voice dripping with so much surprise that Drew peered over his shoulder.

"What?"

"You're afraid."

"I'm not afraid," Drew blustered, annoyed because Gwen had suggested the same thing.

"Sure you are. You like Gwen, but you're afraid of getting married."

Drew's jaw dropped. "Brody, this is none of your business!"

"It is! Dad, just because your marriage to Mom didn't work out that doesn't mean you should stop trying!"

"I didn't stop trying."

"Really? Then why do you hardly even date?"

"I date."

"Okay, then why haven't you married any of those women?"

"Because we didn't click."

"You clicked with Gwen. I saw it. Yet I'll bet you never even kissed her."

Drew's face heated. He couldn't believe he was having this

conversation, and prayed he could figure out a way to get out of it.

"You *did* kiss her! You *do* like her! You do click with her but you're afraid."

"Brody, I'm so much older than she is!"

"That's an excuse. Come on, Dad. If you're going to let her leave, at least be honest with yourself about why."

With that Brody grabbed a sandwich and left the kitchen. Drew sat at the table and ran his hand down his face. One month ago he'd been a lonely single guy who could do what he wanted. Now he had custody of a sixteen-year-old who didn't hesitate to interfere in his life and his broken heart.

He stopped.

He did have a broken heart. A seriously broken heart. And Gwen did, too. One word from him—or maybe three words from him—could fix both their hearts, yet he couldn't say them.

He ran his hand down his face again. Was Brody right? Was Gwen right? Was he simply afraid?

CHAPTER NINE

GWEN got off the phone with Gill the next morning and wiped tears from her eyes. It was now official. Her life sucked. Not only had Andrew Teaberry let her go, as if she were any other employee, but now Gill couldn't come home for Christmas. She had time off, but had waited too long to make airline reservations and now couldn't get a flight home.

Gwen's baby's first Christmas would be a small, lonely event spent with only her mom.

But at least she'd have gifts and a tree and any kind of food she wanted—not that she could eat food—because Drew had wired her salary into her account and he'd added five thousand dollars more than what she'd negotiated when she'd agreed to help him clean the house.

Part of her wanted to call him and tell him she wouldn't take his charity. The other part absolutely refused to have any more contact with him. She loved him. He'd broken her heart. She'd keep the damn five thousand dollars before she'd risk seeing him again.

With Claire down for her morning nap, Gwen's house was eerily quiet. Even when she and Claire had been alone in Drew's house the hum of the wind through the mountain pass had kept her company. The knowledge that there were other people living in that house had made her feel secure, bonded, almost as if she were in a family.

But that was her problem. She'd grown accustomed to things that weren't hers and now she had to face the truth. Drew hadn't wanted her. She wasn't part of his family. She was alone.

She turned to go into her kitchen, but before she took two steps there was a quick rap at her door. Expecting it to be a delivery man with her gift from Gill, she pivoted and raced to the door. With one quick yank she opened it, and there stood Drew, holding a tree.

Her heart wanted her to believe he'd come because he'd realized that he was wrong. That their age difference didn't matter. That he was a young thirty-four and she was a mature twenty-two. That he could love her. That he *did* love her.

But her head remembered that he'd let her leave. That he'd given her extra money to salve his conscience. That he didn't want her.

"Hello, Drew."

With his fingers wrapped around the trunk of a blue spruce, Drew simply stared at her. Finally he cleared his throat and said, "I, um, thought it weird that you'd worked at a Christmas tree farm for an entire month and we never thought to get you a tree for your house."

Her heart sank again. He was only here to give her a tree. Worse, seeing him brought nothing but craziness and confusion for her. When she should be keeping her distance, caring for her own broken heart, all she could think of was that he looked tired, drawn, and fearful—as if he expected her to slam the door in his face.

Well, she wouldn't. He was right. She didn't have a tree. And getting one from Teaberry Farms seemed appropriate.

"Thank you." She averted her eyes and motioned for him to come in. "Bring it inside."

Drew stepped into her foyer. "Where do you want it?"

"The corner by the stairway is where my mom always had

it," Gwen said, then choked up as she remembered the happy Christmas Eves she and her sister had spent decorating the tree with their mom. This might be their second holiday without her, but the memories and pain were still fresh, like an open wound.

Gwen turned away. She missed her mom. She missed being a little girl who had enjoyed every magical Christmas. Though she loved Claire with her whole heart and soul, she'd screwed up by trusting a man who didn't really love her. And now she'd fallen in love—real love—with another man who didn't want her.

The living room suddenly became quiet. Gwen refused to turn around. With tears shimmering on her eyelids, she headed for the kitchen. "I'll make cocoa while you put the tree into the stand."

Not in any hurry, Gwen found the milk, powdered cocoa, sugar and vanilla, and slowly began her brew. By the time she returned to the living room Drew had installed the tree into the old tree stand.

As she entered the room he took the tray from her hands and set it on the coffee table. "Can we talk?"

"I think you've said everything that needs to be said."

He looked away, then back at her. "Sometimes I can be an ass."

His unexpected comment made her laugh. That was one of the things she loved about him. He had a serious job, a great deal of responsibilities, yet he had a sense of humor. Or maybe she'd helped him find his sense of humor?

"Okay."

A hopeful expression came to his face. "I'm sorry I let you go." He stopped. Sighed. "Actually, Brody was genuinely annoyed with me for that. But the point is I shouldn't have."

Gwen stared at him. *Was he offering her a job?* Damned if she knew. But there was no way in hell she was going to say anything and risk misinterpreting him. No way she'd embarrass herself. So she stayed silent, hoping against hope he was not trying to hire her back.

Especially since most of the work she'd done for him had been house-cleaning and he might want her back as his maid!

He rubbed his hand across the back of his neck. "I am so bad at this because I've never said anything like it. I screwed up by telling you our age difference should keep us apart."

Gwen's heart leaped with hope, but she still stayed silent. Unless or until he told her he loved her, she wasn't making any assumptions.

Struggling, Drew glanced around the room. His gaze landed on the tree.

"Okay, tree, I'm not much on magic or miracles or things like that, but right now I need some help." He drew a breath. "I wish Gwen would give me another chance. I screwed everything up by being afraid. I know I was wrong. That's why I need another chance."

Gwen blinked tears from her eyes. She knew how hard this was for him. Knew that he was putting himself out on a limb, trusting her, when the last time he'd trusted a woman he'd not only gotten his heart broken but that woman had taken his son away from him.

Now the ball was in her court. If she didn't trust him she'd hurt him more than he'd ever hurt her.

"You don't need magic to get a second chance," she whispered, praying she was making the right choice. "You only have to tell me you love me."

"I love you."

He held out his arms and she raced into them.

He kissed her hair. "Your life's not going to be easy with me."

She put her arms around his neck. Warmth suffused her. So did joy. "Do you think I haven't already figured that out?"

He slid his arms around her waist. "Oh, yeah? What have you figured out?"

"That you're accustomed to perfection. That you're intense about your family's business. That you want everything done right and well."

"I'll make room for you. I swear."

"Have you ever stopped to think you won't have to make room for me? That I'll fit? And maybe even having me around might ease your burden a bit?"

He smiled slowly. "Someone to come home to at night," he said as his head began to descend.

"Someone to have dinner waiting."

"Or be waiting at the door wearing nothing but a smile."

With that his lips met hers, and her giggle was swallowed up by his mouth.

Christmas morning, and Gwen was in the kitchen of the Teaberry mansion. She'd found all the ingredients for apple cinnamon muffins, and as her baby chewed on a rattle she set about to make the kitchen smell warm and sweet.

She was just pulling the last tin of muffins from the oven when Drew walked into the kitchen.

She smiled at him. "Hey."

He ambled over sleepily. "Hey. What are you doing up so early?"

"It's eight. Besides, Claire's been up since six-thirty. She didn't wake in the middle of the night, so I guess getting up early was her way to make up for that."

He stopped her words with a kiss.

When he pulled away, she smiled at him. "Merry Christmas."

"Merry Christmas." He laughed. "I have to say you're probably the best Christmas present I've ever gotten."

"I hope so, because I didn't have time to buy you anything."

"Which reminds me—" He turned toward the swinging door. "Wanna come in now?"

The kitchen door swung open slowly, and there stood Gill.

Gwen screamed with joy. Gill screamed with delight. They ran into each other's arms.

Drew said, "Claire didn't really sleep through the night. She woke when Gill got here." He laughed as the twins hugged each other. "But I got her a bottle."

Gwen pulled out of Gill's hug. "I don't know what shocks me more. That you somehow got Gill here—"

"Private plane," Drew supplied.

"Or that you took care of Claire."

"Hey, I've got to start sometime."

Gill laughed, walked to the counter and glanced at the muffins. "Are these apple cinnamon?"

Gwen nodded, "Yes."

"All right!" She headed for the refrigerator. "I'll make bacon."

Brody stepped into the room. He glanced at Gwen, then Gill, and laughed. "You must be the twin."

"Gill," Gwen supplied.

Gill said, "You must be Brody."

Brody nodded. "So, what are we making?"

"Apple cinnamon muffins and bacon," Gill said. "Then we open presents."

Brody's face brightened. "You got *me* something?"

Gill winced. "At the gift shop in the airport."

Brody laughed. "I am going to love having an aunt."

Drew leaned against the countertop, admiring his wife-to-be, loving his new *family.*

Brody was right. He had been afraid. Or maybe he'd simply been waiting for the right woman? Either way, he'd like to live on Teaberry Farms for the rest of his life—where wishes came true and families were formed.

But it wouldn't matter where he lived so long as Gwen was with him.

* * * * *

Magic Under the Mistletoe

BARBARA WALLACE

Dear Reader,

Imagine how excited I was to learn I would be making my Mills & Boon® debut with Susan Meier! Susan has long been one of my favourite authors and working with her made my first writing assignment a joy. As we fleshed out the McKenzie twins' stories we discovered we had a lot in common, including a mutual appreciation for the magic surrounding Christmas—the kind that comes from opening your heart to the season's beauty and possibilities.

Workaholic Gill McKenzie is so bent on success she's forgotten what real Christmas magic is. Fortunately Oliver Harrington and his charges are there to remind her. And maybe, just maybe, open Oliver's eyes a little too.

As for me, I'm enjoying the magic of being part of the Mills & Boon® family. I hope you enjoy reading Gill's story as much as I enjoyed writing it. Meanwhile, on behalf of my husband and son here in New England, I wish you all a very Merry Christmas.

Happy holidays!

Barbara Wallace

PS Look for new, full-length stories from Barbara in 2011 in our Cherish™ series. –Ed.

CHAPTER ONE

THE brightly painted silhouettes of children decorating the McNabb Community Center couldn't mask its surroundings. Broken windows and padlocked storefronts told the truth. Across the street a group of young men, too young to be out of school, congregated in a convenience store doorway. Gill McKenzie felt them eyeing her as she stepped from the cab. An elderly woman pulling a metal shopping cart with groceries approached on the sidewalk. She too cast Gill a look as she passed.

Welcome to wrong side of the tracks.

Pulling out her cell phone, she double-checked the meeting time on her calendar and noted she had, as usual, arrived early. Punctuality was something she prided herself on. It showed clients you considered their projects important and of high priority.

Except this wasn't supposed to be her project, was it? She was *supposed* to handle the Remaillard aftershave launch. Remaillard was Rosenthal Public Relations' biggest client and organizing a successful product launch would have virtually guaranteed Gill the new vice-president position.

Enter Stephanie DeWitt. Gill could still hear the mock apology Stephanie gave during this morning's meeting. "I suggested to Elliot that you were the best person for the job. What with your family owning a Christmas tree farm and all."

No, her brother-in-law owned the farm, Gill had wanted to scream. And Stephanie wanted the promotion as badly as she did. But Elliot Rosenthal had been right there, so she'd simply smiled graciously, seething inside.

So, while Stephanie took over the launch, with its big budget and luxury setting, Gill stood here, in the worst section of Boston, charged with throwing a kids' Christmas party. Not just any Christmas party. A magical, stunning, media-attention-generating party with less than a month's notice. Her only help was the center's director. Some guy named Oliver Harrington.

Across the street, the store owner chased the teenagers away, hollering what she was pretty sure were obscenities in Spanish. The kids swore back, and one of them tossed an empty can into the street. The rattle echoed in the frigid air. Gill sighed.

Stop feeling sorry for yourself, Gillian McKenzie. So Stephanie had got the project she wanted? Big deal. Since when did she let a setback get in her way of success? She hadn't become the youngest account supervisor in Rosenthal PR's history for nothing. If she wanted something in this world, she had to make it happen. Let Stephanie have her aftershave launch. Gill would throw the best damn charity party Boston ever saw and make sure Elliot Rosenthal would *have* to promote her.

Confidence renewed, she yanked open the door. Oliver Harrington, look out. Gill McKenzie was here to make some Christmas magic.

A watched water spot never grows.

Oliver Harrington stared at the spot on the ceiling in his office. It definitely looked bigger than when he'd left last night. Somewhere the center had a leaky pipe.

Another expense he didn't have money for. Along with a new van and replacement glass for the broken rear windows.

His list of expenses he couldn't afford was growing as fast as that leak.

He supposed he could always charge the plumber on his personal card and put in for reimbursement when the center had money. But at this rate his "get reimbursed later" list would be the longest list of all.

Saving the world wasn't supposed to be this expensive.

Sipping his cold coffee—everything in the center seemed to be cold these days—he turned away from the stain, back to the mish-mash of papers on his desk. Stacks of bills, receipts and forms warred for his attention.

Then there was Julia. The photo of his ex-fiancée beamed up at him from the newspaper. She certainly rebounded well after their break-up, or so it appeared by the way she clung to her current fiancé's arm. The heir to a pharmaceutical fortune or something like that. Wealthy, a corporate success, socially prominent. Basically everything Oliver refused to be. The guy looked happy enough.

Never was good enough for you, was I?

Sometimes he wondered what life would be like if he had caved to Julia's demands and taken a job with her father. He'd be senior vice president by now. He'd be driving a luxury sedan instead of a broken-down pickup.

He sure as hell wouldn't be worrying about water leaks. Crumpling the photo, he took aim for the wastebasket and shot, missing by a foot.

"Your girlfriend's here."

The pronouncement, short and sweet, kicked all thoughts of "what if?" aside.

"My what?" Since the disaster with Julia he had but one committed relationship, and that was with the center.

Maria Carrerra folded her arms across her body. Though only five foot one, the mother of six was by far the most formidable volunteer the center had. Her first day on the job, she'd stared down the surliest teenagers on the block with a look. Oliver knew because he'd been one of them. Her expression hadn't been unlike the one she was shooting him now. A look that said he should know what she was talking about.

"The woman from that public relations agency."

"Right." Now he remembered. "The party planner."

Peter McNabb, head of the McNabb Foundation and Oliver's chief donor, had had the misfortune of getting caught by a camera phone *in flagrante delicto* with his au pair, and so he was throwing a huge children's Christmas party at the center for damage control. Personally, Oliver hated seeing his center being used for some PR stunt, but he didn't have much choice. Not if he wanted a decent budget next year. He thought of the water stain that was no doubt expanding behind him as they spoke.

Maria, meanwhile, still stood in the doorway, giving him the look. As a volunteer she was terrific. As a secretary, not so much. "What's the matter? Go ahead and send McNabb's image-polisher in."

"I can't. She's not here."

"You just said—"

"I said she was here, meaning at the center. She went straight to the community room. Right after telling me you need to bring a tape measure with you. She's kinda bossy." A frown marred her petite features. "We're not going to have to run around doing all sorts of errands for her, are we?"

"Don't worry. I'll make sure she understands we've got other work to do besides throw this party." He might not have a choice about hosting the party, but he refused to let Peter McNabb's PR stunt take over his center.

"Good," Maria replied. "Because right now I don't think she realizes that."

The community room was in the back of the building. A refurbished cafetorium left over from when the building had been an elementary school in the 1950s, it now served as the center's main gathering space. Overall, it wasn't much. There was a stage at the far end of the room, and a battered piano tucked in the corner that Oliver had paid to have tuned last month. Several large tables were pushed against the walls, along with boxes of toys and balls of various sizes. Two of the windows had boards in them thanks to broken glass. The walls, he noticed, were looking pretty dingy, too. They could stand fresh paint. Another item for his list.

At the moment, the room played host to the preschool playgroup. Mothers gathered in folding chairs, chatting and nursing babies, while toddlers wreaked their usual havoc on the toys and snacks. Oliver spotted his appointment immediately. The willowy blond pacing the perimeter looked as out of place as a cellist at a rap competition.

He watched as her coat swayed in cadence with her steps. Cell phone stuck to her ear. Cashmere scarf. Faux-fur-trimmed hood. Stiletto-heeled boots that cost more than his paycheck. Visions of society photos danced in his head. Uptown all the way, wasn't she?

No sooner did he step toward her than a particularly havoc-wreaking boy, slightly older than the others, ran up, his mouth filled with cookies. He held out the box for Oliver to see. "Mr. Oliver! We got animal crackers!" At least that was what Oliver *thought* he said.

"Jamarcus, you get back here!" His mother, a very pregnant young woman, gestured at the boy to return. "Leave Mr. Oliver alone."

Oliver smiled. "You better listen to your mother, Jamarcus."

Realizing he was outnumbered, Jamarcus did as he was told, racing back across the room at top speed and nearly taking out the PR woman in the process.

"Whoa, pal, save the speed for the Olympics," she said, ducking out of his path. "Someone needs to cut back on the caffeine."

She moved in, hand extended. "Oliver Harrington? I'm Gill McKenzie from Rosenthal Public Relations."

For a second, Oliver lost the ability to speak. Uptown, downtown—the woman was an absolute knockout. That blond hair framed the face of an angel. A very sexy angel. With sparkling green eyes and an incredibly perfect bow of a mouth. A guy could spend hours exploring that mouth...

"Did you bring the tape measure?" he heard her ask. "I can't stay long, and I wanted to get some layout measurements. This space looks like the best area. A little dingy, but what the heck? That's what decorations are for, right?"

Had she said *dingy?* That snapped him back to reality. In a flash, everything he'd come to loathe about uptown came flying back. Gone were the longing and melancholy thoughts, wiped away by an angel-faced interloper. Didn't matter how gorgeous she was. Who did she think she was, coming here slinging insults as *his* center?

"About the space. You're going to have to move that piano, along with those tables. The toys, too. Are the kids using this room all the time? Because I'm going to need a couple days to—"

"Whoa—slow down, angel." He finally found his voice. "I'm not moving anything yet."

She blinked. A slow, deliberate action that no doubt usually had men begging to do her bidding. That it made his own insides twitch didn't help.

"Gill," she said. "My name is Gill, not Angel."

Then maybe she should *look* like a Gill. Wasn't that a man's name anyway? "My mistake, *Gill.*" His annoyance was growing with each passing second. This woman was too sexy, too good-looking, too much like a society-page photo for his comfort. "But I'm still not moving a thing without knowing what's going on."

She took a moment before nodding in concession. "Sorry. I tend to get ahead of myself." Her voice had a Southern twang that didn't match her appearance. "I was thinking this room would be the best space for Mr. McNabb's Christmas party."

"You mean the center's party."

She gave him another one of those slow motion blinks.

"I was under the impression you were here to plan a Christmas party to promote the center."

"True. Mr. McNabb does want to see the McNabb Center get some well-deserved media attention, among other things."

"Among other things? Is that PR speak for creating a distraction?"

To her credit, Angel's—Gill's—expression didn't slip. "With the right message you can parlay this party into donations. People always look for causes to support come the holiday."

Which was the only reason he wasn't fighting McNabb about the event. He hated charity events, hated working them even more, but he'd sell his soul to the devil if it meant a better budget. Right now, the devil looked suspiciously angelic.

"Now," Gill continued, "about the party. Like I said, this room makes the most sense, but we're going to have to clear the space. Do you think you can have your people move the furniture?"

"I don't know. I'll have to check with my *people*."

She was trying not to roll her eyes; he could tell. He also knew he was being over the top with his attitude. He couldn't help himself. Gill, here, was pushing his buttons. He knew her type—oh, he knew her type very well. It was all about image and success. They saw his center as merely a building. They didn't see the people. Feel the connection he felt. Once they got what they needed, they walked away.

Well, if he had to court their vanity for donations, so be it. But that didn't mean he would be her lap dog, bowing to her wishes. As far as he was concerned, the people at the center were his family. And he'd never let his family be taken advantage of. His green-eyed angel had better learn the ground rules from the start.

CHAPTER TWO

GROUND rules? Gill was trying to keep her patience—really she was—but this director was making it difficult. Bad enough they were having this meeting with kids running amok, but now he wanted ground rules?

What was with all the attitude anyway? Why act as if she was the enemy? It wasn't as if she'd begged to be here.

Focus on the promotion. She took a deep breath. "What kind of ground rules?"

"First, this is a community center, not some hotel ballroom. Our job is to serve the community—which means, yes, the kids *will* be using this space right up to the party. You'll have to work around our schedule. Second, I don't have *people.* I have volunteers. They're here on their own time because they want to help the neighborhood. They aren't here to do your bidding. You want them to do something, you ask me first. If they aren't busy volunteering with the kids, then we'll see."

In other words, no help from him. She was *so* going to kill Stephanie when she got back to the office. "Anything else?"

"Yeah. I want the kids involved."

Okay, that one she could manage. "Already done. Little hard to highlight the center's work without them here."

"Not invited," he said. "Involved. There's a difference." He gestured at a group of toddlers playing some random running game that only little kids could understand. "For a lot of these kids, this is the only real Christmas celebration they'll get. I'm not going to let their holiday be hijacked, no matter how many donations this party attracts. If they get shoved aside, I won't cooperate."

Because he was the picture of cooperation at the moment. "The kids will be involved. I promise."

Gill waited while Oliver studied her face. Assessing her sincerity, no doubt. She stood her ground, even though the scrutiny made her insides jumble.

At last he nodded, apparently satisfied with what he saw. "Okay, then, why don't I show you the facilities?"

"Officially, our mission is to provide a safe alternative to life on the streets."

"And unofficially?" Gill asked. They were walking along the rear corridor of the center. She could tell from Oliver's tone of voice there were a lot of "unofficial" duties.

"Unofficially we're whatever people need us to be. Different day, different challenge."

"Sounds a lot like public relations work."

Her attempt at camaraderie didn't raise so much as a smile. "Except in this case, instead of the bottom line, people are worried about simply surviving."

"For some of my clients the bottom line *is* about survival."

"Trust me," Oliver replied with a soft snort, "it's not the same thing."

Gill said nothing. Arguing would only waste time she didn't have. Still, she didn't appreciate his dismissiveness. She worked every bit as hard as the next person, maybe harder, and just because she didn't work for a nonprofit organization, it didn't mean her work didn't count for something. It counted for a lot. It was who she was. Gill McKenzie, youngest account supervisor in Rosenthal PR's history. She'd worked hard for that title. *To become someone worth noticing.*

They rounded the corner and stopped at a set of double doors. "This is the gym," Oliver said, holding the door open.

Gill peered in, recognizing the age-old smell of sneakers and dust. Handmade posters taped to the cement wall chanted "Go Panthers!" and "Panthers Rule!"

She arched her brow. "Panthers?"

"Center's basketball team. Some of the kids are pretty good."

Pride shone in his brown eyes. It was the first time she'd seen his face show any kind of enthusiasm, and Gill had to admit the change was amazing. When she'd first met him, she'd considered Oliver Harrington handsome, but now those good-looks went deeper. His enthusiasm seemed to come from the inside and shine out, like a glow. It took what were sharp, patrician features and softened them, turning his expression youthful and engaging.

"Sounds like you all take the community part of your name seriously." That was good. She could do a lot with that line. In the back of her mind she began drafting press releases.

Oliver seemed less impressed. "We do what we can. 'Course we could always do more."

"Then Peter McNabb took the right time to get caught with his pants down, didn't he?" At Oliver's sidelong look, she added, "You get this party."

"I'm sure Mrs. McNabb feels the same way."

Actually, Gill doubted Mrs. McNabb was as upset as the board of directors, but she kept that to herself. "Seriously, if we do this party right, the center will get a ton of donations." She purposely emphasized the word *we*. Anything to buy a little cooperation.

Oliver closed the gymnasium door. "What do you mean by 'right'?"

"Go all out. Create an event so extraordinary the media and public will have to pay attention. Give major donors a reason to attend."

"In other words, put this party on the society pages?"

Exactly. Although the way he ground out the word *society* made her regret the suggestion. "People's generosity increases after a few drinks," she reminded him. Suddenly an idea popped into her head. "We could turn the center into a Winter Wonderland, complete with snow, trees and all the rest of the holiday trimmings."

She could already picture the idea.

"Every room can focus on a different theme, with themed refreshments. Gingerbread martinis in the gymnasium, candy cane cocktails in the community room. We'll say 'The McNabb Community Center—Where Magic Happens Everywhere. Every day.' We'll be knee-deep in media coverage."

"How do the kids factor into this society wonderland?"

"Kids?"

"Yeah, the kids." He shoved his hands in his pockets, giving her a look that said she should already know what he was talking about. "You promised the kids would be involved, remember? What are they going to do? Serve the martinis?"

Ground rule number three. In her enthusiasm she had forgotten; she'd been too busy imagining decorating concepts.

It wasn't that she didn't *want* to include the kids, she simply wasn't used to kid events. That was her sister Gwen's territory. She was the maternal one in the family. Gill had always been busy working.

The scowl on Oliver's face told her that excuse wouldn't fly. "I promise the event will be kid-friendly, too," she said.

"I hope so. I was dead serious earlier. I'm not letting you shove my kids aside so a bunch of socialites can get their photo in the paper. There are plenty of other parties where they can accomplish that."

His kids? Bit possessive, wasn't he? "Even if those socialites end the night by writing you a big fat check?"

"I'd rather they write a check after walking a mile in these kids' shoes, not after sipping designer drinks. Maybe if they experienced the hardships these kids experience they'd be a little less interested in publicity."

And maybe if someone lost the chip on his shoulder he'd get a few more donations. Man, but he was difficult. Originally she'd thought putting him in a tuxedo and unleashing those good-looks on a room of society matrons would have the money rolling in. Now she wasn't so sure. With that attitude, it was a wonder he charmed any donors at all.

She glanced at her cell. The meeting was almost over. Thank goodness. She wasn't sure how much more of Oliver Harrington she could take. "Can I please see the kitchen facilities?"

"This way."

They re-entered the community room where the preschoolers were still playing their running game, although they'd broken off into smaller groups at this point. Oliver led her to a set of swinging doors. "The kitchen is right off the community room. Left over from the cafeteria days. We use it more for storage than anything. Any gatherings we host are pizza parties or pot luck."

She could tell. To call the room dated would be generous. The painted cupboards were cracked and in some cases missing hinges. Opening one, Gill found juice boxes and bulk snack packages.

"I'm sure your big-time donors would go for potato chips and apple juice," Oliver said. "I hear they're all the rage on the charity circuit these days."

"So are caterers," Gill replied, closing the refrigerator. She was starting to get seriously sick of the comments. There were charities out there that would kill for the kind of event she could provide. He could be a little more appreciative. "I'll call a couple of services I've worked with before and have them work up numbers. If that's okay with you," she added.

Oliver shrugged. "Long as my *people* aren't inconvenienced, knock yourself out."

For the first time since they'd met, Gill didn't bother disguising her eye-roll.

* * *

It was after nine o'clock when Gill finally walked through her front door. She tossed her keys in the bowl with an exhausted groan. Could today be any longer? First Stephanie's blindside this morning, followed by back-to-back meetings all day long.

Then there was Oliver Harrington and his ground rules. How was she supposed to plan a Christmas party to beat all Christmas parties with that chip he carried blocking her progress?

She was wiped. Too tired even to boil water. Thank goodness for microwave popcorn, dinner of champions.

While she waited for the kernels to pop, she unpacked her briefcase, spreading the contents across her desk. Being home didn't mean work stopped. Not if she wanted that vice presidency.

Outside, the lights on the Boston Commons sparkled and swayed like colored stars. There was a glow in the distance from the Frog Pond Pavilion. She'd heard the music from the rink when the cab dropped her off.

She loved this view. It was one of the best in the city. The first day she'd arrived in Boston, she'd walked the edge of the Common from the State House to the Central Burial Ground and fell in love with every inch. When she saw the line of brick row houses on Beacon Street—once the homes of Boston Brahmin—she knew immediately she had to live in one. It had taken eighteen months of scrimping, saving and burning the midnight oil, but she'd managed to check that goal off her list six months ago.

You've come a long way from Towering Pines and the little house on Jensen Street, she thought proudly. She wasn't poor little abandoned Gill McKenzie anymore. She was a success. Someone the world couldn't pretend didn't exist. And once she got that promotion… Well, the sky was the limit.

Of course that all depended on getting Oliver Harrington to play ball.

A beep announced dinner. How could she win the man

over? she wondered as she padded back to the kitchen. There was something about the man she couldn't put her finger on—beyond the chip on his shoulder. At first glance he was arrogant and stubborn. Dedicated, though. You could see that from the way his face had lit up talking about the basketball team. You had to admire his loyalty.

Maybe that was what was throwing her. The look in his eye when he talked about the kids. The way he glowed from the inside out.

If only she could find a way to make him look that way at *her.* That was, get him to see how a successful, mind-blowing party would help his kids.

Her eyes traveled to the tabletop tree on her dining room table. Gwen had laughed when she'd sent her a photo of the tree. "Oh, my God, it's a mini-tree! How'd you get it away from its mother?" her twin had teased. Then she'd offered to send Gill what she called a "real" tree.

That was it! A tree! Gill nearly dropped the popcorn bag. Why hadn't she thought of the solution earlier? A tree was the perfect goodwill gesture. The kids would be thrilled, Oliver would see she wanted to do right by the center with this party, and maybe—just maybe—he'd give her a little more cooperation.

Grabbing her cell, she dialed Gwen's number, hoping she wasn't calling too late.

On the third ring, a familiar voice answered. "Teaberry Farms."

Warm feelings washed over her. "Hey, any idea where a girl can get a good Christmas tree?"

"Gill!" Her sister squealed with delight, making Gill smile. Gwen always sounded as if her phone calls were a lottery jackpot, even though they talked every few days. "I was just thinking of calling you."

"At this hour? I figured you and Drew would be all cozy and romantic. Don't tell me the honeymoon's over?"

"No, it's definitely still in full swing," her sister replied, almost dreamily. “Drew’s at the airport getting Brody. He’s in for Christmas break.”

“I can’t believe you have a college-age stepson. How is Mr. UCLA doing, anyway? Still planning to be the next big movie director?”

“Depends on who you ask. He says great. His father thinks he spends too much time enjoying himself and not enough time in the library.”

“Typical student.”

“And he’s been talking a lot about some girl named Susan.”

“Is it serious?”

“Doubt it. Last month it was Jessica.”

“Don’t worry, he’ll settle down eventually. Look at his father.” Drew Teaberry had been quite the playboy until he’d met Gwen. Now he was a doting father and husband.

“True. Drew just hopes he doesn’t take as long as he did to smarten up. How about you? Any irons in the fire?”

Gill, who was emptying the popcorn into a bowl, laughed. She knew what kind of irons Gwen meant. They had this same conversation at least once a month. The problem with her twin was that Gwen had an incurable romantic streak, and marriage to the man of her dreams had only made it worse.

“When would I have time to meet anyone? Between meetings? I’ve been working nonstop.”

“But it’s Christmas.”

“Like that makes a difference in the PR industry.”

“Don’t you want someone to cuddle up with under the Christmas tree? Or to get trapped under the mistletoe with?”

“The only thing I want for Christmas is promotion to vice president. Which,” she tossed a kernel in the air and caught it in her mouth “got a little harder, thanks to Stephanie DeWitt.”

Briefly she explained how she’d lost the Remaillard account and ended up working on the Christmas party.

"Talk about passive-aggressive," Gwen said when she was done. "I can't believe your boss buys her act."

"Worse, the guy I'm supposed to work with, Oliver Harrington, has major attitude issues. He absolutely hates the idea of throwing this party and refuses to cooperate."

"Sounds like a piece of work."

"Oh, he is." Gill flopped on the sofa. "Sad thing is, without the superiority complex he'd probably be a nice guy. He's certainly dedicated to the center. I'm not certain, but I think he might actually live there."

"A workaholic? Sounds like you two have something in common."

"Hardy, har-har." She wasn't that big a workaholic. Just goal-oriented. "I just wish I knew what made him so angry. I mean, I get the whole frustrated nonprofit thing, but his attitude goes a lot deeper."

"Maybe he got burned once upon a time by some big bad donor?"

"He did say they were having budget issues. And Peter McNabb hasn't exactly been paying attention to the center the past few years." She tossed another piece of popcorn in the air. "Except for a little while, he acted more like he was mad at me personally, and for the life of me I don't know what I did."

"Maybe you look like his ex-wife?"

"You're a laugh riot tonight, sis. Maybe you ought to chuck the Christmas tree business for standup comedy."

"And *you* need some sleep. You always get cranky when you're tired. Sounds like this guy's gotten under your skin."

"More like *on* my skin, like a big old rash. I can tell right now he's going to give me a hard time with this whole project."

"You can always quit and join us down here, selling Christmas trees."

"I'm sure Drew would love that."

"Seriously, why not visit for the weekend? Claire would

love to see her Aunt Gilly. Lord knows we could use the help. From the buzz in town, this might be our busiest year yet."

"Everyone's looking for a piece of Teaberry magic," Gill joked. "Hoping to have their Christmas wish granted."

"Why not? It worked for me and Drew," Gill replied.

No, thought Gwen, love, timing and effort had worked for them. Whatever magic Gwen and Drew had found, they'd made it for themselves. They still made magic. Gill didn't think she'd ever seen two people more in love or more happy. As if they'd been waiting their whole lives to find each other.

Suddenly a heavy feeling settled in the pit of her stomach. Guess popcorn for dinner wasn't a good idea after all.

"I'd love to see you guys, but with this last-minute project I'm swamped. Plus, if I have any hope of getting this promotion...."

"Say no more. I understand," Gwen replied. "That's the price I pay for having a high-powered executive for a sister."

"I'm not a high-powered executive yet."

"You will be. You always succeed when you put your mind to something. Remember when Mr. Delphino said he didn't think you could handle advanced chemistry?"

"I remember studying my butt off day and night."

"Finishing with the highest grade in the class. You make things happen, Gill."

Yes, she did. That was how it had always been. Gwen was the romantic dreamer; Gill was the doer. Not that she'd had much of choice, what with their mother working day and night, and dear old Dad... Well, better to take a page from his book and wipe him from her memory.

Her stomach got a little heavier.

"Too bad you won't put that mind to making something happen in your personal life," Gwen continued.

Back to that, were they? Her sister could be a real broken record sometimes. Gill told her as much.

"Can't help it. I want you to be as happy as Drew and I are."

"I *am* happy. I have the career I always wanted, a great apartment, you guys... What more could I want?"

"You want the long or the short list?"

"Neither, thank you. What I really need is a favor." Clearing her throat, she set down the popcorn and sat up a little straighter. "I need you to ship a little Teaberry magic up north."

"You need a Christmas tree?"

"Not *just* a Christmas tree. The most amazing Christmas tree you've got." She started explaining, and Gwen quickly caught on to her plan. Score one for the twin connection. By the time the call ended they'd come up with one amazing tree.

Gill hung up feeling a little better. Talking to Gwen never failed to cheer her up.

But as she lay back and studied the Christmas lights on her mini-tree it wasn't her sister she was thinking about. It was Oliver Harrington. No way he'd be able to keep that chip on his shoulder now. He was going to be blown away.

She couldn't wait.

CHAPTER THREE

"WE'RE low on lights."

Gill squinted up at the decorator standing on the scaffolding.

"Are you sure this is all we can use?" he asked.

"Positive. I don't want to take a chance on blowing any circuits." Further incurring Oliver's wrath. "Lord knows when they last upgraded their electrical system."

Gill had expected quite a different reaction from him when he came in today. She'd been disappointed to find him out this morning, but Maria had said he'd spent the last two days dealing with a plumbing crisis and was home catching some much needed sleep.

It surprised her how *off* the center felt without him. There was an emptiness in the air. Not that she missed him. She was simply aware of his absence.

On the other hand, having him gone made installing the tree easier. She'd be able to surprise him with it fully decorated. Why impressing him had become so important she wasn't sure, other than knowing his cooperation would make her job easier. His disapproval was so damn frustrating. The way he glared at her, as if she was the enemy in high heels.

"Done!" the decorator hollered down. "I still think we need more lights…"

"No, it's perfect."

Gwen and Drew had outdone themselves. Decked from

trunk to tip with ribbons and poinsettias, the tree was a magnificent sight of red and gold. And even without a lot of lights the tree sparkled. The crystal decorations caught the light from the windows, creating their own twinkling reflection. Gill got a giddy shiver. She couldn't wait for the rest of the center to see it. *For Oliver to see it.*

Gwen's note was clipped to her clipboard.

Here's your tree, Sis. May you get the Christmas magic you deserve.

Leave it to her sister to turn a business transaction whimsical. Still, if by "magic" she meant the tree would bring Oliver's goodwill and cooperation, then Gill would take it.

"Wow!" Maria's voice sounded behind her. "So this is why you needed to get in here at the crack of dawn. That thing looks bigger than the one at City Hall."

"Being inside makes it look bigger."

"Maybe. It looks huge. Smells good, too."

"Doesn't it?" A fresh pine scent filled the community room. If Gill closed her eyes she could picture Christmas morning. Claire, her niece, tearing open presents with toddler enthusiasm. Brody engrossed in the latest video game. Gwen and Drew cuddling on the sofa. Her sitting by the fire.

Alone.

A sudden wave of longing swept over her, not unlike the emptiness that filled the center. Gill frowned. This was because of Gwen's note and her romanticism. They'd put weird thoughts into her head.

"Looks like they'll finish decorating before Oliver returns. Do you think he'll be surprised?" she asked Maria.

Odd how he was her next thought. On the other hand, why wouldn't he be? She'd gotten this tree for him. That was, to win him over.

"He'll be something, that's for sure," the volunteer replied.

"There are matching decorations for the foyer and the rest of the building, too. Enough to deck out the whole place."

"Wow."

Maria sounded blown away. Exactly the reaction Gill had hoped for. Now just let Oliver have the same reaction when he arrived later. Absentmindedly she played with the end of a branch. "Christmas magic, do your stuff," she murmured.

"What the hell—?"

At the sound of Oliver's voice, she whirled around with a grin. "Surprise!"

Oliver stood like a guardian sentinel in the doorway. The atmosphere, she noticed, had returned to normal with his arrival. "What is *that?*" he asked.

She grinned wider. "The center's Christmas tree. What do you think?"

He set down the bags of supplies he'd been carrying and stepped closer. Unlike their last meeting, when he'd been in corduroys and a sweater, today he was dressed for hard labor. His jeans were paint-splattered and worn, as was his heavy zippered sweatshirt and a flannel shirt. A faded Red Sox cap topped his head. Normally Gill didn't get the whole construction worker fascination, but now seeing Oliver, she kind of understood better.

"I thought you went home to sleep," Maria commented.

"I did. Then I went to the hardware store for paint. Thought I'd paint the storage room while the center was slow." While he talked, his eyes took in everything. The ladders, the decorators, the piles of garlands waiting to be hung. Gill was practically bouncing in her shoes, waiting for his response. "This tree looks like it came from a decorating magazine."

"Isn't it fantastic?" She had to fight to keep from giggling with enthusiasm. "The same decorators did the tree at the Governor's house." She cradled one of the glass globes. "Look! Lalique."

"Lalique crystal?"

"I know what you're thinking." She'd already anticipated the argument. "But this won't impact the budget a bit. Everything you see has been donated by Teaberry Farms—finest Christmas trees in West Virginia." She let the globe rest among the branches. "Originally Gwen and I discussed just the tree, but then Drew got involved and insisted on the decorations and the trimmings, too."

"Drew?" Oliver repeated. "As in Drew Teaberry? From Teaberry Industries?"

"Uh-huh. He's married to my sister Gwen. I had the tree shipped up earlier this week And before you ask, yes, I got the necessary permits. Everything is legal and to code."

"I'm sure it is," he said.

"So what do you think?"

Thus far he hadn't shown any reaction all, other than to stare and walk back and forth. Gill tried studying his profile, but his handsome features were unreadable. She glanced at Maria, only to get an equally cryptic shrug.

"Twenty feet of blue spruce," she continued, filling the silence. "I wasn't sure of the exact ceiling measurements, so I erred on the side of caution. From the looks of things…" she craned her neck upward "…I could have gone another five or six feet."

Still nothing. Her spirits flagged. What now? She'd just presented him with a stunning, one-of-kind designer tree and trimmings free of charge. Where was the happiness? The gratitude? The appreciation?

"Usually we get our tree from the vendor up the street," he replied finally.

"If you're concerned about taking business away from the neighborhood, we can make a donation."

"What about the kids? They were supposed to make decorations today. What happened to keeping them involved?"

"They can be involved in something else. Trust me, when they see this tree they won't mind."

"That's another thing. How am I supposed to explain

where all this came from?" He waved his arm across the decorations.

"How about Santa's workshop?"

"I'm serious."

So was she. Not to mention increasingly frustrated. "For goodness' sake, it's a Christmas tree. Why are you acting like I kicked a puppy?"

He turned, giving her full view of his annoyed expression. "A lot of these kids will be lucky if they get a handful of gifts, and most of those will be donated. What are they going to think when they see a tree with decorations that cost more than their parents will make in a year?"

Gill bit her lip. She hadn't thought about that point, although the solution seemed simple enough. "Tell them the truth. The tree was a generous donation."

"Sure. Right after I tell them I had to spend the money for the new ping-pong table on plumbing supplies. I'll say 'Hey, kids, no ping-pong, but good news—we got a tree.'"

Oh, for crying out loud. Was there no pleasing this guy? "You know," she said, crossing her arms, "Most people in your shoes would say thank you when presented with a gift like this."

"Really? And what would you know about what people 'in my shoes' would say?"

More than you know, Gill wanted to reply. She knew exactly what it felt like to look in someone's window and see the Christmas you couldn't have. "I'm only trying to give the kids something special."

"Don't you mean show off? Is that what people in *your shoes* do?"

How dared—? She turned so Oliver couldn't see the hurt and anger in her eyes. Since the moment they'd met, Oliver had acted as if she was the enemy. All she wanted was to do a good job. What had she done to make this man dislike her so much?

Well, she was done trying to win him over. The tree was

amazing, and if he was too stubborn to appreciate her efforts, or even to show a modicum of gratitude—well, then he could simply go to blazes. She didn't care anymore.

"We're done!" the decorator called down. "Do you want to light her up and see what she looks like?"

"Ask Mr. Harrington," she called back. "It's his electrical system."

She gathered her coat and belongings, no longer able to stand the stiff, unfriendly atmosphere. "Tell you what," she snapped. "If you don't like the tree, take it down. Better yet, why don't you stick it—?"

Her voice cracked, preventing her from finishing the sentence. Didn't matter; he'd get the idea. "It can keep the other stick that's up there company."

CHAPTER FOUR

"SELF-RIGHTEOUS, stubborn, obnoxious…" Gill ran out of adjectives before she reached the sidewalk. What was this man's problem? She got him a one-of-a-kind tree half the city—strike that, the *whole* city—would kill for, and he was insulted? Did he hate Christmas?

Or just hate her?

She stomped down the front steps, blaming the harsh December air for the moisture rimming her eyes. She'd been so certain he'd like the tree; so excited to show him.

"Stupid Christmas party," she muttered, swiping at her cheeks. Stupid Oliver Harrington and his stupid brown eyes and broad shoulders. She wished she'd never met the man.

Oliver and Maria stood listening to the silence left in the wake of Gill's door slam. "You know," Maria said, "sometimes you can be a real jerk."

He certainly felt like one right now.

"She thought she was doing something nice," Maria continued. "And you come in here acting like she stole all your money or something. What's wrong with you?"

He wished he knew. He'd overreacted for sure. When he saw the tree, big and beautiful, unlike anything he could ever afford, and Gill standing by its branches, her angelic face all excited, looking like a magazine advertisement, he'd lost it. Big-time.

He thought of the way Gill's face had crumpled at his reaction. Like a five-year-old being told there was no Santa Claus. She'd tried to hide it, but he'd caught the moisture in her eyes. The way her lower lip had trembled with disappointment.

Maria was right. He was a jerk.

She might as well kiss that promotion goodbye right now. If she couldn't handle a simple Christmas party, how on earth was Elliot going to see her as vice president material? So much for Teaberry magic. Stupid tree blew up in her face.

The look on Oliver's face… She couldn't shake the image. He'd looked so…angry. No, not angry. Horrified. *Face it, Gillian. The guy simply doesn't like you.*

Her breath made a white puff as she sighed. She'd had it all planned. She'd create this magical tree, unlike anything the kids at the center had ever seen, beautiful and breathtaking and beyond their wildest imaginations. Oliver would see how much she wanted to help the center and, impressed, he'd be thrilled to work with her. Instead, she was now more on his bad side than ever.

Okay, so maybe she *was* showing off a little, like Oliver had said. Maybe she *could* have toned things down a bit. Then again, why? The tree was absolutely gorgeous. Leave it to Oliver Harrington to prefer paper chain garlands and popsicle stick ornaments over Lalique crystal.

For the life of her, she didn't know why his disapproval bothered her so much. In the larger scheme of things, whether he liked the tree or not didn't matter. Neither did his cooperation. As long as she made Peter McNabb look good in the press.

So why was she so determined to dazzle Oliver?

You're jealous of a tree. It was true. In a million years Oliver couldn't give the center a tree like this, and Gill McKenzie had done it with one simple phone call. To her millionaire brother-in-law to boot.

"So what are you going to do?" Maria asked.

"I don't know."

"Here's an idea. How about you apologize?"

Yeah, he owed Gill at least that. How would she know the tree would hit such a strong nerve?

Or that her appearance would be part of the problem?

Therein lay the crux of the matter. Gill McKenzie was uptown, upscale, and everything else he wasn't. Would never be.

She's not Julia.

No, but she was a walking reminder of everything Julia had chosen when she'd walked out on him.

Still, that was no reason to take his frustration out on the woman.

On the other hand, there was no reason for him to be so worried about her feelings, either. It wasn't as if they would have a relationship beyond this party, right? In fact, *relationship* wasn't even the right word, since that implied something long-lasting. Once this party debacle was over she would head back uptown, never to be seen again.

Still… Those trembling lips flashed in front of his eyes.

He should definitely apologize.

Her surroundings began to change, morphing from slightly rundown to the bland brick buildings of a housing project. So intent had Gill been on fuming, she hadn't realized she'd walked to the center of the neighborhood. Because it was the middle of a work day, the area was quiet. A pair of women bundled in heavy coats waited at the bus stop. One held the hand of a little boy, his face hidden by his bulky hood. He had some type of plastic toy in his hand.

Glancing up at the apartment windows, she saw collections of lights and various decorations. Nothing fancy. Certainly nothing like her tree. One window toward the end of the building was covered with paper snowflakes. Despite her bad mood, Gill couldn't help smiling, thinking how she and Gwen had used to do the same thing. They hadn't had a lot as kids. They hadn't been as badly off as some of these families, but they'd done their fair share of going without. Every Christmas she and Gwen would deck their house with pictures and cut-out snowflakes. Their mother would hang up each and every one as if they were precious works of art. Same with those God-awful decorations they'd made at school. Their tree would be literally covered with sparkly pieces of cardboard and popsicle sticks. It wouldn't have won any decorating awards, but it had been erected with love.

Her smile faded.

Like the tree Oliver had planned for the center.

"Wow!"

"It's got to be like a hundred feet tall!"

"Is it real?"

"Can we touch it?"

The kids in the after-school program peppered Oliver with question after question, barely waiting for an answer before asking another. They loved the tree—couldn't stop talking about how awesome and amazing it was. Every comment was a little "I told you so" kick to the stomach.

"Looks like Gill was right," Maria said, adding to the attack. "The kids are blown away."

"I noticed." Guilt made his stomach ache worse.

"Did you call her and apologize?"

"Her office said she was out." Twice. He'd tried calling her cell phone, too, with no luck. She had either turned it off or she was ignoring his calls. He told himself the unsettled feeling in his stomach was simply eagerness to clear the air, nothing more. "I'll try again later, after the kids settle down."

"Did Santa bring the tree?"

Looking down, he saw Becky, one of the younger girls in the program, her brown eyes wide with curiosity.

"How'd he fit it in the sleigh?"

"You'd be surprised at what those elves can do," a familiar voice replied.

Like a dancer hearing her cue, in waltzed Gill, carrying a tabletop tree. Her cheeks were bright pink, her hair tussled and windblown. She wore a smile so bright that Oliver's first thought was that she outshone the tree.

"Hey," she continued, "they pack for an entire Christmas Eve in one trip. A tree is nothing."

"What's that?" Becky asked, pointing to the tree in Gill's hand.

"Oh, this? This is a mini-tree. You can't have an enchanted forest without a lot of trees, right?"

"What's enchanted mean?"

"It means magical," Gill replied.

Carlos DeGarza, the boy standing behind Becky, scoffed. "There's no such thing as a magical Christmas tree."

Gill eyed him. "You sure?"

"I ain't seen one."

"You've never seen an elephant in your backyard, either. Doesn't mean they don't exist."

"I saw an elephant at the zoo," Becky said.

"Well, this tree is from where I grew up," Gill said. "And in my hometown people believe in magical trees all the time."

"They do?"

"Uh-huh."

She glanced at Oliver, hesitation in her eyes, and Oliver felt a stab of guilt, knowing it was his attitude that had put it there. With a nod, he encouraged her to continue. He had to admit he was as curious as the kids to hear what she was going to say. This young woman in front of him, talking about magical Christmas trees, was barely recognizable as the glossy Gill McKenzie of this morning.

Gill moved over to the tree and plucked a couple of pine needles. "This isn't just *any* tree. This is a Teaberry tree."

"So?" Carlos asked.

"So," she answered, "for as long as I can remember people

have believed if you touch the branch of a Teaberry tree and make a wish, the wish will come true."

Carlos, junior cynic that he was, frowned. "No way. That's stupid."

Clearly Becky didn't think so. Her eyes, impossible to believe, were larger than ever. "Do they?"

"Sometimes," Gill replied, casting a quick glance in Oliver's direction. "But only if the person really *wants* the wish to come true."

Squatting down to the kids' eye level, she held out the needles, drawing Oliver and the kids further into her orbit. "See, I have a theory. I think the real magic is inside us. It's not the tree or the actual wishing, it's what we do with the wish. I think the tree knows this and rewards the people who do the work."

"Like doing your homework so you do good in school?" Becky piped in.

"Exactly. Or practicing your hook shot so you make the high school basketball team."

"I have a hook shot," Carlos said. He'd been won over.

"But what are the little trees for?" Becky asked.

"Like I said, this tree is part of an enchanted forest."

"But it doesn't have any decorations," said a voice from the back. Oliver recognized it as Dontrell, one of the older boys.

Gill smiled. Her eyes grew almost as wide as Becky's. "Then I guess we better do something about that. Oliver said you guys were going to make Christmas decorations today, right?"

The little girl looked at Oliver, as if to ask. He nodded. "If you want to."

"You better make a lot, then," Gill told them. "I've got a few dozen more mini-trees on their way. Enough for everyone to have their own to decorate."

She might as well have announced Santa had arrived. The

center erupted with murmurs of enthusiasm. "Cool. Do we get to keep them?" someone asked.

Gill smiled. "Absolutely. You can bring them home Christmas Eve."

"Will they be magical, too?" Becky asked.

"Maybe," she replied, giving the girl's braids a tug. "Maybe…"

Oliver watched as the kids gathered around Gill, peppering her with the same excited questions they'd asked him a short time before. To her credit, she fielded each and every one with an enthusiasm to match. It was impressive to see. For an uptown girl she was more comfortable with kids than he'd expected.

"Looks like you owe her more than a simple apology," he heard Maria murmur in his ear.

Unable to tear his gaze away from Gill's enthusiastic face, he nodded. "Yeah," he replied. "I think I do."

CHAPTER FIVE

AS PROMISED, the trees arrived, and the kids had a blast bickering over which tree would be "theirs." Gill watched the chaos, feeling pretty darn good about her problem-solving skills. The kids were happy. Peter McNabb would be happy.

And Oliver was happy. She looked over at how he was smiling at the kids and felt a surge of satisfaction.

He must have felt her stare, for he suddenly turned his smile in her direction. Gill's insides tumbled. She'd never noticed before, but his eyes had green-gold flecks in them. And dimples. He had dimples. Made her wonder what else she missed.

Picking up one of the leftover mini-trees, she headed in his direction.

"That a peace offering?" he asked, seeing what she carried.

"Santa had room for one more. Looks like it might be the runt of the litter, though."

"It's not such a bad little tree."

Her insides jumbled a wee bit more. Maybe he wasn't such an ogre after all.

Turning to the craziness on the other side of the room, she said, "Looks like the kids liked my idea." She couldn't help the smug smile tugging the corners of her mouth. "Not to mention my tree."

"Yeah, about that… I, um…" With his free hand, he rubbed

the back of his neck. From his sheepish expression, and the way he suddenly averted his eyes, Gill suspected admitting a mistake wasn't something he did much of. "I might have overreacted a bit."

Gill couldn't help herself. "A bit?"

"Maybe more than a bit. I saw the tree and the decorations and I… Well, it's complicated."

"I understand."

"You do?"

Gill nodded. "Took me a few minutes—or blocks, as the case may be—but, yeah, I do. You were looking out for the kids. You didn't want them to get the wrong idea. And maybe…"

She brushed her hand over the bottom branch of Oliver's tree, studying the needles that stuck to her palm. Admitting she was wrong wasn't something *she* did well, either. "Maybe I got a bit carried away, too."

"A bit?"

"Point taken. Though you've got to admit the tree *is* pretty amazing."

"Breathtaking," Oliver replied, catching her gaze.

All of sudden the air in the center grew close, and for a moment it was as if he meant her, not the tree. A heat rose up inside her, starting somewhere low and feminine, and moving through her limbs and chest until she was warm and melty all over.

Oliver turned his attention back to the kids, and the sensation vanished as quickly as it appeared. "So," he said clearing his throat, "magical Teaberry trees, huh?"

She'd surprised herself with the tale. Normally she wasn't the gather-round-for a-story type, but for some reason the words had seemed to pour out easily today. "What can I say? I'm from the South. We're full of rural legends. I grew up on that one. My sister Gwen believes it wholeheartedly." Too wholeheartedly, maybe, she added, thinking about the note in her pocket.

"But you don't."

A statement rather than a question. Gill appreciated the understanding. "I believe what I told the kids—people make their own magic. You want something in this life, you have to make it happen."

She realized Oliver was looking at her again, with an odd glint in his eye. "Is that experience talking?"

"You bet."

"Hmmm." In his response, Gill found a kind of kinship, a bond they'd missed during their other meetings. "Yet here you are surrounded by Teaberry trees and talking magic. Funny how home has a way of pulling people back."

"A onetime occurrence, I assure you." Perhaps it was the way Oliver said it, but hearing the word *home* brought on a restlessness she couldn't identify. As if something was eating away at the periphery of her life's plan. She'd felt the same feeling earlier in the day, when setting up the tree. "I made up my mind a long time ago to get as far away from Towering Pines as possible. If Gwen wasn't there, I'd never go back."

"Onward and upward, huh?" There was an edge to his voice she couldn't identify.

"Something like that."

Carlos, Becky and a few other kids were rooting around the greenery still on the floor, picking up the scraps of bunting the decorators had left behind. Gill watched, marveling at their enthusiasm. Did kids always find fun in everything?

"You didn't let the decorators do the windows and the other decorations," she noted to Oliver. "Is that because you don't want to?"

"No, I told them I'd do the decorating myself. After our little..." he cleared his throat "...discussion, I got the impression they weren't keen on sticking around with a guy who had a stick up his..." He looked away, but not before Gill caught the color flooding his cheeks.

She felt her own cheeks growing warm, too. "I probably

overstepped a little there. Though you have to admit you have had a bit of a—"

"Stick?"

"I was going to say chip."

Their eyes met, and in spite of themselves they both grinned. "Think we can start over?" Gill asked. "Call a truce?"

Oliver looked at the kids, who were still laughing and scrounging among the pine boughs. "We could try."

With that, he slipped his fingers around hers to seal the deal. Their hands, Gill couldn't but notice, fit together perfectly. The melty sensation began anew.

"What's this?" Carlos hollered.

He ran up holding a sprig of green and white berries he'd dug from amid the branches. The stem had a red bow tied to it. The minute she saw what he had in his hand, Gill felt her cheeks grow red again. *Gwen, I'm going to kill you….*

"Can you eat the berries?"

Oliver was the first of them to recover, releasing Gill's hand and snatching the twig from the boy. "You do and you'll get sick. This is mistletoe."

"If you don't eat it, what *do* you do?"

"You hang it," Gill explained. "Then, if you're standing under it with a girl at Christmas time, you're supposed to kiss her."

"And she can't slap you?"

"No," Oliver chuckled. "She can't."

"Sweet! Where you gonna hang it?" Carlos asked. You could see from the glint in his eye he was already making plans to drag some unsuspecting girl or girls underneath.

"We'll see, Carlos. Maria's passing out art supplies. You better go get yours." He waited until the boy had sprinted back to the crowd before holding the sprig up for review. "Mistletoe? Let me guess. Your sister believes in its magical powers, too. Or is this your doing?"

Her cheeks hotter than Hades, Gill shook her head. And not because when Oliver held it up she thought about getting stuck beneath the branch with him. "She must have slipped it into the order as her way of creating more Christmas magic."

"Well, from the sounds of things Carlos is thinking of making his own."

"Are you going to hang it up?"

Oliver shrugged. "I don't know," he replied, catching her eye. "What do you think?"

Again came the melting sensation. What was wrong with her? Ever since she'd returned to the center she'd been having completely uncharacteristic reactions. Since when did she get all weak-kneed around a male colleague? Men didn't fit into her eighty-hour work week—at least not in traditional, dating members of the opposite sex terms. So why was she reacting like a teenage girl every time Oliver so much as looked in her direction this afternoon?

Figuring the best solution would be distance, she snatched a bough from the ground. "What I think is that I should get this garland hung before the kids trample everything."

For the next few hours she immersed herself in hanging greenery and draping bunting. Her conscience nagged that she should be back at the office tending to other clients. Except, she argued with herself, she was already dressed for manual labor, so it made sense to do all the decorating in one day rather than make a second trip. Besides, the enchanted forest was her vision. She didn't want to trust the decorations to someone else.

At least that was the argument she made to herself. It was about doing this party right.

It had nothing to do with the man painting the supply room nearby.

She was tacking up the last piece of garland around the community room door when the alarm on her cell rang, indicating it was time for her Pilates class. It couldn't be six o'clock already, could it?

Sure enough, checking the screen, she saw she'd shot the entire day.

"Time has a way of getting away from you at this place, doesn't it?" Oliver remarked, wiping his hands on a cloth in the doorway. Flecks of white decorated his hat brim and the shoulders of his flannel shirt. His face was flushed, no doubt from working in a small space. Manual labor looked good on him, thought Gill. Really good.

So much for distance curing her fixation.

"Happens to me all the time," he continued. "Some days I wonder if I wouldn't be better off setting up a cot in my office."

"Some days I wonder why you haven't," Maria remarked, shrugging into her coat. "I've got to go home and remind my teenagers what I look like. The decorations look amazing, Gill. For what it's worth, I told Grinchy here there was nothing wrong with your original tree."

Red crept into Oliver's cheeks. "I've already apologized for my behavior."

"Well, it wouldn't hurt for you to apologize again," she called over her shoulder. "You could use the practice." With that, the front door shut, leaving Gill and Oliver.

Alone.

CHAPTER SIX

OLIVER immediately ducked his head, rubbing the back of his neck. "She, uh, doesn't cut me a lot of slack."

"She certainly speaks her mind," Gill replied.

"That she does."

They stood in awkward silence, with each smiling at the other like mute statues. Something between them had shifted since this morning's shouting match. Sure, Oliver had apologized, but there was more. Gill felt as if she was seeing him in a different light. He was in his element. That was it. She'd spent the afternoon watching him interact with the kids. No wonder he seemed so appealing.

The kids weren't here now, though. And the atmosphere still felt charged between them.

"I should head back downtown," she said, aware that she'd made the same comment three hours earlier.

"Back to the grind?"

"I think I've already blown the day. I'll probably go home and catch up on some e-mails from there." She headed toward the piano where she'd draped her coat and portfolio. The mistletoe lay next to her belongings. With a chuckle, she held it up. "Decided against Carlos' plan after all?"

"No, I'm going to hang the branch; I just thought I'd wait until Carlos and the girls were gone to keep the kissing to a minimum. Something tells me I'm going to have to keep an eye on him."

“Boys will be boys.” She twirled Gwen’s surprise between her fingers, mentally shaking her head at her sister’s romanticism.

“Although nothing says I can’t make carrying out his plans a little more difficult.” Near the stage there was a display board, filled with notices and announcements. Oliver crossed the room and removed a pushpin from one of the flyers.

“Come here,” he said.

Gill obeyed, joining him under the main entrance. Wordlessly, he slipped the mistletoe branch from her hand and, using the pin, suspended the ribbon from the top of the frame.

“There,” he said with a satisfied voice. “Now I can watch the action from all angles.”

“Smart,” Gill remarked, her eyes on the tiny green branch. “If Operation Mistletoe gets out of hand—”

“I can nip it in the bud.”

They lowered their gazes at the same time, coming eye to eye.

The air stilled. Or maybe just Gill’s breathing. Either way, she was suddenly overwhelmed by how silent and close the room felt. Oliver’s gaze lowered to her mouth and then moved back. The flannel of his shirt brushed against the edge of her jacket. Had they always been standing so close?

Neither moved. There was paint in Oliver’s hair, Gill noticed. And on his face. Freckle-size white spots splattered across the bridge of his nose. She had the sudden urge to wipe them away with her hand. Then comb her fingers through his light brown hair…

Suddenly Oliver was speaking, “Let me lock up and I’ll walk you to your car. You shouldn’t be walking the streets alone in the dark.”

“That’s all right.” In the back of her mind she wanted to note that he’d let Maria walk alone, but couldn’t. “I’ll call a cab.”

"A taxi will take forever at rush hour—if it bothers to come to this neighborhood at all. Why don't I drive you?"

"I—I—" With him standing so near, her brain had trouble working right. Of course she could step back, but, as twice before, her feet simply wouldn't move. "I don't want to put you out," she finally managed to say.

"Consider the ride my second apology."

If she hadn't been standing a hair's width from the man she'd have told him no, a ride wasn't necessary. But he *was* standing that close, and the idea of trading that proximity for a ride in a cold, dark cab all of a sudden seemed quite foolish. "If you don't mind…"

He smiled. "I'll get my jacket and keys."

"Meanwhile, while I'm spending all this effort selling the magazine on an article, the client decides she needs to 'liven up' her image, and so when the photographer arrives at her office she's wearing a leather suit and lace bustier."

"Wait—I thought you said the client was in her early sixties?"

"I did."

"Whoa!"

"Whoa, indeed," Gill replied. "Worse yet, the article was highlighting her conservative family values."

Oliver coughed. "Nice. After that, Peter McNabb must be a piece of cake."

"Believe me, he is."

She watched as Oliver topped off her green tea. What was she doing? This was supposed to be a simple ride home. How had she ended up in a hole-in-the-wall Chinese restaurant in an area of Chinatown she'd never known existed?

It had all started when they'd got into Oliver's truck. The last time she'd been in a pickup truck was in high school, when Bill Travers had driven her to homecoming. As she'd slid into the passenger seat of Oliver's vehicle she'd been struck by how small and dark the space was. She didn't remember Billy's truck feeling so…so…intimate. She'd been in the middle of buckling her seat belt, and hoping the cold would kill the weird sensation, when her stomach had chosen that moment to growl. Loudly.

Oliver had heard, and asked when she'd last eaten.

"Breakfast," she'd confessed. After that, she'd been too preoccupied for food.

"Me, too," Oliver had replied as he'd started the engine. "I meant to go out and grab a bite, but I kept getting distracted."

By her and her trees.

Gill had assumed the exchange marked the end of the conversation, but then her stomach had continued to rumble. About a block into the drive, during which her stomach had growled at least three or four times, Oliver had turned and looked at her. "You like Chinese?"

Gill had nodded. Chinese was her favorite.

"There's a place not far from here that serves a mean Kung Pao Chicken. How about we grab some?"

Common sense had told her to say no. Her phone was full of e-mails waiting for her answer. Plus she should call Gwen, to let her know how the kids had loved the tree.

But she'd been sitting in Oliver's dimly lit truck, still in close enough proximity that the mistletoe's spell hadn't worn off, and she'd said yes instead. It would be like a meeting, she'd rationalized. They could talk about the party and what she envisioned for publicity.

Now, an hour later, they were sitting in the back of a half-filled restaurant, having talked about everything *but* Peter McNabb's party until now, and Gill was wondering once again how and when things between them had shifted so dramatically.

She sipped her tea, noticing Oliver was studying her mouth again. Her mind flashed to that moment under the mistletoe. The spell continued to linger in the air between them, making every action seem slow-eyed and deliberate. Gwen, if she were here, would be having a field-day with the knowledge.

Gill tried to think of the last time she'd found a man so attractive. The answer failed her. Then again, who had time for dating when building a career? Going solo was the trade-off you made for success. Besides, she wasn't interested in dating.

Not that this was a date anyway. Even if the restaurant's dim lighting and soft music *were* made for romance.

"Hey, where'd you go?" Oliver called to her from thc other side of the table. "You faded off there for a moment," he said.

"Sorry. I was thinking about work." The answer was half-true, anyway. "I'm going to have a lot of work to make up tomorrow."

"That your hint that you want to leave?"

"No, not yet." What was she doing? He'd given her the perfect out, and she was dragging her feet. "I'm enjoying myself."

"Me, too," he replied, spearing a piece of broccoli as he spoke. "Nice change of pace, eating Chinese food that's not from a carton."

"Tell me about it. The take-out guy in my neighborhood knows me by name."

"I hear that's a hazard of being a workaholic."

"Says the man who stayed up late repairing drywall," she remarked, accepting the plate of pork fried rice he was handing her.

"Point taken," he replied. "Though in my case I kind of have to. The center's budget doesn't exactly allow for delegating. Or hiring a repairman, for that matter." He took a bite of chicken, chewing it thoughtfully. "What's your excuse?"

"Love of hard work. I like my job. I like making things happen."

"Do you? Make things happen?"

She returned his grin. "All the time."

Before either of them could continue the waitress arrived with the bill and customary fortune cookies. Oliver reached into his back pocket for his wallet. “Let me,” she said. “We’ll call it a business expense.”

He regarded her with a tilt of his head. “Is that what this was? Business?”

“Everything’s business in my life,” she replied.

The answer earned her a strangely shadowed look that she couldn’t decipher. Surely he wasn’t disappointed by her response? Did he think this dinner was something more? Or was that wishful thinking on her part?

No, not wishful thinking. She wasn’t looking for more in her life than what she already had, thank you very much.

Cutting off her circular thoughts, she proffered the plate of cookies instead. “Go ahead—you choose first. You have to share what fortune you get, though.”

“Very well.” He broke the cookie open, revealing the thin white strip. “‘What you’ve been looking for will soon be yours.’ Hope that means I’m getting a new van.”

“Or a plumbing credit,” Gill said.

“Now, *that* would be a good fortune,” he replied, popping half the cookie in his mouth. When Gill didn’t crack hers open, he gestured with his head. “Your turn. Unless you’re afraid the magic tree will get jealous?”

“Very funny. I think the tree will understand.” Sending him a quick smirk, she broke open her cookie. “Aw,” she said, frowning, “it’s the same one. That’s no fun.”

“The restaurant must be at the bottom of the box or something. Either that or we’re looking for the same thing.”

“Well, in a way we are, aren’t we?” Gill offered.

“Really?”

She met his eyes across the table. How on earth could one set of eyes have so many different hues? she asked herself, her breath catching. In the restaurant lighting, the gold and green combined to create a new shade of amber. She swore they flickered, too, like a candle.

"Isn't it obvious? We both want a successful party."

"Right. The party."

"Of course. If it's a hit, we both get what we want."

"I hope you're right."

Sitting back in his seat, he'd lowered his gaze. No longer able to see their color, Gill got a strange feeling the dancing amber in his eyes had disappeared. She didn't know why, but the idea bothered her.

Shaking off the notion, she raised her half-finished teacup. "Why don't we seal our good fortune with a toast? To a successful event."

"And—" he tapped his cup to hers "—to getting what we're looking for."

CHAPTER SEVEN

It was snowing when they left the restaurant. The flakes sparkled in the streetlights, like tiny white lights falling from the sky, and landed on Gill's hair and face. Oliver studied their sparkle. Moisture kissed her cheeks and eyelids, and when she smiled the drops shone from the glow on her face.

"First snow of the season. Pretty, isn't it?" She was referring to the snow.

"Gorgeous," Oliver replied. He wasn't. Surely she knew how good snow looked on her? Those perfectly shaped lips glimmered with moisture. He had the overwhelming urge to trace their shape with his tongue, to see if they tasted as sweet and perfect as they looked.

Thoughts like that had plagued him all evening. Ever since they'd stood under that mistletoe. His body tensed as he thought of how close they'd stood—so close he'd imagined feeling the fibers of her sweater brushing his shirt when she breathed. And that sweet mouth, so close for the taking....

Shoving his hands into his jacket pockets, he searched for a benign topic. Anything to keep his less professional thoughts at bay. "Hope my meter didn't run out while we were eating."

"Do you think we were in the restaurant that long?"

"Hard to say. I can't remember when we walked in."

That was another thing—suggesting dinner. A smart man would have backed away under that mistletoe, called her a cab, and said goodnight. But, no, he'd not only offered her a ride home but suggested dinner as well. What was he thinking? So what if her stomach had growled?

Truth was, he hadn't been thinking at all. The truck had been dark and the interior had smelled like evergreen. It had been as if they were still standing beneath the mistletoe. The words were out before he could stop them.

He unlocked his truck, then held the door for her to hop in, which she did, sliding across the faded leather seat with ease. He hadn't expected her to look as at home as she did in a pickup truck. It surprised him to see how comfortable she looked, with her cashmere coat wrapped around her legs. Her long, slender jean-clad legs.

Quickly he shut the door. No matter. Soon as he slid into the driver's seat, sealing them both into the close dark space, the thoughts returned.

She, on the other hand, was thinking about business. About "getting what she wanted." He could think unseemly thoughts about licking off snowflakes all he liked; she was busy thinking of her next move up the corporate ladder. Guys like him, guys driven by other motivations, didn't register on the upwardly mobile radar of women like her. Or if they did they didn't last long. He'd learned that lesson from Julia.

"Where to?" he asked, starting the car.

"Beacon and River," she replied. "It's across from the Comm—"

"I know the address." The answer came out far more abruptly than he'd intended, causing her to tense in response.

"Is that a problem?" she asked.

"Why would there be a problem?" Just because with those three words life had managed to dump a virtual bucket of cold water on his thoughts. Just in case he didn't remember the lesson, apparently.

"I don't know. You sounded annoyed. If it's the traffic this time of night…"

"It's not the traffic." Nor was it her fault where she lived.

Or how. "I had a friend who lived in that neighborhood, is all."

"Oh." She fell silent, but he could feel her eyes on him. "From the tone, I'm going to guess the friendship changed, not the address."

"You could say that."

They made their way through traffic in awkward silence. Oliver watched as the landscape gradually changed to the business district. That was Boston. Parking lots and neighborhood stores gave way to insurance company high-rises and, eventually, the luxury of Back Bay. The buildings became grander—refurbished rather than old, or sparkling new with historic overtones, since the Back Bay forbade modern-looking construction. Commuters picked their way toward train stations, many carrying shopping bags along with their briefcases.

In the next seat, Gill shifted her weight. She hadn't said a word since they'd discussed her address. His fault, he thought guiltily. His tone hadn't been exactly warm and encouraging.

"Lot of people out shopping," he noted. "Got your Christmas shopping done yet?"

As an attempt at conversation it was lame, but apparently good enough—because Gill jumped at the bait. "Not even close. Fortunately I only have to buy for Gwen and hers."

Oliver noticed her voice changed when she talked about her sister. It grew softer, more indulgent. She'd had a similar tone when talking about the Teaberry trees. He also noticed she didn't mention parents. "I'll probably do what I do every year. Wait till the last minute, then go overboard spoiling everyone. How about you?"

"I've got some stuff for the kids at the center—and Maria, of course."

"Of course." She was looking at him again. "No family? Or have you simply not gotten to them yet?"

"My father and I don't really—we don't celebrate together."

"Sorry."

"Don't be. We're both happier for it. He's free to drink the day away, and I'm free not to watch."

"Ouch."

"Sorry. I'm not sure why I said that." The words had been out before he'd realized what he was saying. He *never* talked about his father. Why he chose to now he had no idea.

"Hey, if it's the truth…"

"Oh, it's the truth all right. If not for the center… I grew up a block away from the place," he elaborated.

He felt as much as saw the understanding cresting on her features. "No wonder you're so dedicated to the place."

Dedicated wasn't a strong enough word. "The place saved my life. Showed me there was more than benders and unemployment in my future. In fact, it was a volunteer at the shelter who convinced me I had what it took to go to Harvard."

"You went to Harvard? As in Harvard University?" Disbelief laced the question, like it did whenever he mentioned his alma mater.

"No, Harvard Junior College," he shot back, the sarcasm a habit.

"Sorry."

"Don't be. You're not the first person to react that way. You going to ask the next question?"

"What next question?"

"What's a guy with an Ivy League education doing running a community center instead of a corporation?"

"The thought did cross my mind."

Of course it did. She was the one who'd left her hometown and never looked back. "I guess I wanted to make sure other kids got the same opportunities I did."

"Admirable." She sounded sincere enough that he believed she meant it. "Is Harvard where you met your friend? The one who lives near me?" She looked away when he tensed—a reaction he always had when Julia came up. "You can tell me to mind my own business if you prefer."

What the hell? He should, but, having already opened the door to his past, he might as well fully cross the threshold. "Julia was my fiancée."

"What happened?"

Oliver shrugged. "She wanted someone different. Someone I wasn't."

"Oh." The sympathetic silence that followed said everything else.

They arrived at Gill's block. Although not the fanciest building in the area, it was still upscale, and it had a great view of the Common. Amazingly, there was a parking spot across from her front door. Oliver grabbed it and shifted into "park."

Suddenly the cab of his truck felt dark and small again. Having bared his past, Oliver felt open and exposed, and Gill's presence was too close for comfort. "Here you go—home sweet home," he said, in a voice that sounded too boisterous.

"So it is," Gill replied. "Thanks for the ride. And for suggesting dinner."

"No problem."

She made no move to leave. Oliver wondered if she expected him to step out and open the door. That would be the gentlemanly thing to do. He was about to when she spoke again. "Frog Pond's crowded tonight."

Following her gaze, he saw the glow coming from the rink. "We're taking the kids there on Sunday," he replied. "Part of our plan to expose them to new experiences. Believe it or not, a lot of them have never been here—despite growing up in the city."

"Then it's good that you're exposing them to new experiences," she replied.

"I wish I could do it more often, but unfortunately—"

"The budget only goes so far?"

"I must sound like a broken record."

"A little, but I understand why." They locked eyes for a second, then she looked away.

Oliver could see her fiddling with the strap on her pocketbook.

After a couple a beats, she added, "This party will bring in a lot of donations."

"I hope you're right."

"I'll talk to Peter McNabb about including a more overt solicitation for donations in the press materials. I'll also recommend he make a sizeable one himself."

"Buy himself some goodwill?" Oliver teased.

"I was thinking more like buying a new van." She smiled, her teeth bright in the dark. "Best way to change his image is to put his money where his mouth is, right?"

"Right." He shifted his weight, wondering if he was the only one dragging this goodbye out, or if she felt the same sense of hesitancy. From the way she fiddled with her purse strap it seemed so. "You never said what it is *you* get out of all this," he said. "Back in the restaurant, we toasted us both getting what we were looking for, but you never said what it was. Don't tell me you're looking for a new van, too?"

In the closeness, her laugh sounded soft, like a sigh. "There's a vice presidency opening at the agency after the first of the new year. I'm one of two candidates up for the position. I do a good enough job, and the job could be mine."

Yup they were, just another rung on her ladder. "That's important to you, isn't it?"

"Absolutely." There was a note of defensiveness to her tone; he'd chipped a nerve. "This has been my plan for as long as I can remember."

"To be vice president of Rosenthal Public Relations?"

"To be a success."

"You're not now?"

"You can always be more." Her voice dropped a notch. "I didn't have a center growing up. I only had myself."

"And your sister."

There was another, even softer laugh. "Gwen is amazing, but she and my mother were more accepting of our circumstances than I was. *I hated them.*" The last three words were said more harshly than he'd ever heard her speak, even when hurling insults at him. "I won't settle. Not ever."

No, Oliver thought to himself, he didn't suppose she would. The realization saddened him. "I hope you get what you want, then."

She leaned forward and looked him square in the eye. "I always do."

"I'm not surprised."

Oliver couldn't help himself. She was so close, so tantalizingly close. The sweet evergreen scent still clung to her. Like Christmas. He slipped a hand into her hair, the strands like damp silk flowing through his fingers. She gasped, her perfect mouth making a perfect O.

It was a bad idea. A very, very bad idea. Because now his palm was caressing her cheek, his thumb tugging her bottom lip.

"I don't think…"

Her protest was breathy, weak, and not very convincing. But it was enough to break the spell. With painful reluctance he pulled away. He turned and gripped the steering wheel with both hands. "Goodnight, Gill."

"Goodnight." She offered him an apologetic smile and slipped out the door.

He waited until she'd climbed her front steps and disappeared through her front door before pulling away. For a crazy second he thought she looked back in his direction—even imagined it was in regret—but knew it merely wishful thinking. In her protest, Gill had voiced what they both knew. Business didn't mesh with pleasure. As she'd said so clearly, Gill McKenzie was all about business and success. He'd made the mistake of asking a woman to choose once before; he'd be a fool to put himself in a position to lose again.

* * *

"Some of the kids have limited family, some have no family at all. More than one have lost brothers or sisters to violence."

As Oliver talked, the TV reporter nodded sympathetically, her heavily lined eyes moist with emotion.

Off camera, in the entrance hall of the community room, Gill was fighting a few tears herself. Oliver was doing magnificently. Handsome and sincere in selling the center's mission. He'd even made sure Peter McNabb received credit for funding their work, painting the tarnished businessman as a friend to the community.

She smiled. He'd done that for her, she was sure.

Since that night in his truck she and Oliver had kept their relationship on the most professional of planes. No touching, no personal conversations. Which was good, because she had no business thinking otherwise. She didn't have time for dating. She wasn't interested in anything but getting that promotion.

She listened as Oliver continued, relaying how they'd created the center's basketball team in response to a drive-by shooting at one of the playgrounds. "It's all about giving kids a home base," he was saying.

His dedication was beyond admirable. He'd built something here. Something he could be truly proud of. A family, almost.

That nagging sensation from before returned. Odd, but she seemed to be feeling it more and more. Though still vague, it was definitely stronger, increasing that restless sensation. Almost as if she'd forgotten something. She'd run down her to-do list at least a dozen times, but nothing glaring popped out at her.

Maybe she was feeling anxious on Stephanie's behalf? Despite the fact the Remaillard launch was next week, her rival didn't seem fazed at all. In fact this morning Gill had overheard her making plans for a ski weekend. Goodness knew if *she* had had that project she wouldn't have taken a weekend off. Not that she took weekends off to begin with.

On the other side of the camera, Oliver and the reporter were wrapping up. "You've given our viewers a lot to think about," the reporter said.

"Hopefully that'll mean donations," Oliver replied.

"Oh, I have no doubt you'll get a few." She nodded toward her camera crew. "Let's get some shots of these trees. This enchanted forest idea is terrific."

"It did turn out pretty good, didn't it?"

He shot a look in Gill's direction. She smiled.

"How do you think the interview went?" he asked, once the reporter and her crew had turned their attention.

"I think Roberta's right; you're going to attract quite a few donations. Your commitment really shines through. The center's lucky to have you fighting its corner." Anyone would be, she caught herself thinking.

He smiled, those eyes of his warm and something more. "You, too. You weren't kidding when you said the center would benefit. I guess I…" he rubbed the back of his neck, a now familiar gesture "…owe you another apology."

"A thank-you will suffice."

"Thank you."

"You're welcome."

The air between them settled. Gill wasn't sure what to say next. She should move, head over to where Roberta was shooting, but she couldn't seem to move. Oliver's close presence had her pinned.

"Good thing Carlos isn't here," he added with a grin. His eyes looked upward.

Following, Gill saw the mistletoe above them. "Think he'd take advantage?"

"A fellow would be foolish if he didn't."

In a flash they were back in Oliver's truck, with the dark, evergreen-scented air swirling around them. Gill swore she could feel him move closer. "I suppose a fellow would." She ran a tongue over her lower lip.

"Oliver? Can we get a couple shots of you moving the kids' trees around?" Roberta called over. "I want to get some B roll footage."

Was that reluctance or relief crossing his face? Relief, she decided. On both their parts. Because business didn't mix with pleasure. It simply didn't.

And yet, as she watched Oliver cross the room, the restless vagueness returned.

"Did I see the *Eyewitness News* truck driving away?" Maria walked into the community room shaking snow from her jacket. "What happened? Something wrong?"

Oliver was in the middle of moving the mini-trees back to their original places. "Nothing's wrong," he replied. "Gill convinced them to do a piece on the party."

"Wow—second reporter in three days. She's good."

"That she is." Very good. Though right now his mind was more on her standing beneath the mistletoe. Since the other night in his truck he hadn't been able to shake her spell. Simple things, like the smell of pine or a piece of stray tinsel, and *boom!* He was thinking of her.

"Gill came with them?"

"She wanted to make sure the reporter got her facts straight."

"Oh."

"What, oh?"

"Nothing," Maria replied, in a voice that said anything but.

Oliver set down the tree he was carrying and looked her straight on, giving her what he hoped was a mirror image of her intimidating stare.

"I can't help noticing she's been here a lot this week. Every day, in fact."

Yes, she had. Which didn't help keep her out of his head.

"The party's only a week away. She wants to make sure things are done right."

The volunteer arched her brow. "Why? Doesn't she trust us?"

"She does. She's just hands-on."

"Hands-on, huh? Is that what we're calling it now?"

Oliver shot her a scowl that had her tossing a fiercer one back.

"Don't give me that look. I've seen you two looking at each other. This party ain't the only thing Ms. McKenzie's interested in."

Trying his best to ignore the way his gut jumped at Maria's pronouncement, Oliver shook his head. "Nice try, Maria."

"You gonna tell me you don't like her?"

"Doesn't matter." One of Becky's decorations fell off its branch. He bent down to retrieve it. "I know her type. Come the day after the party, she'll move on to bigger and better things."

"Wow, you're harsh. She seems really dedicated to helping the center."

She's dedicated to getting a promotion, Oliver thought to himself. He *had* to think that way. He had to remind himself that all her hard work was for personal gain. Otherwise he'd fall more under Gill's spell, and he was already treading a very thin line.

"Not harsh, Maria. Realistic."

His friend folded her coat over her arm, taking a long time to smooth the nylon material. "I think maybe you've been in the neighborhood too long. For a guy who preaches the sky's the limit to his kids, you're pretty jaded."

CHAPTER EIGHT

AFTER a week of off-and-on snow showers, Sunday found itself bright with sunshine. Gill found herself staring at the blue cloudless sky while sitting at her desk. Having spent so much time this week working on the McNabb party, she'd fallen behind with other projects. As a result, she had a small mountain of paperwork to get through—e-mails, client correspondence, and one new client proposal—but she couldn't concentrate. Restlessness had taken hold. All of a sudden her apartment felt too empty. She thought about calling Gwen, but her sister would be busy selling Christmas trees with Drew and their family.

Family. The word unsettled her more, made the apartment feel that much more lacking. She needed to do something, occupy herself somehow, but work didn't appeal to her.

Her gaze drifted across the street, to the public Commons and the crowds making their way to the Frog Pond. Oliver had said he was taking the kids skating today. She wondered if he was there yet.

Why? It's not like you're joining them.

She opened an e-mail from Elliot Rosenthal. He wanted a report on year-end activities. Great, another project.

Her eyes went back to the window. She bet Oliver was a good skater. He looked like an athlete. She could picture him now, leading kids by the hand around the pond. It'd be fun to watch.

What the heck? A short break wouldn't hurt. Might even quell the restlessness.

It wasn't until she reached the rink entrance and her pulse sped up that she admitted her true motive: a chance to see Oliver. Why she'd pretended otherwise was beyond her; she'd been making up excuses to see him all week long. Although during the week she cloaked her motives behind business excuses. What would she say today? Maybe she should go back before Oliver got the wrong idea.

She was just about to turn around when she heard, "Look, it's the tree lady!" Carlos, the mistletoe plotter, stumbled toward her. He wore a protective helmet and gripped the guardrail with both hands. His grin was brighter than the sun. "You ice skating, too?"

"Carlos, her name is Miss McKenzie, not the tree lady," Oliver skated up behind him, wearing a thick coat and a battered ice hockey helmet that covered his sandy brown hair. He managed to look simultaneously dashing and silly.

"Nice helmet," Gill remarked.

"Isn't it, though? It's what all the cool skaters are wearing—right, Carlos?" He knocked playfully on top of the boy's helmet. "Safety first. We don't want anyone cracking their head on the ice."

Watching the exchange, Gill felt her heart flip-flop. His obvious affection for the kids was something she was quickly coming to adore about him.

She realized he'd turned his smile on her. Catching his gaze, she smiled back. The winter air disappeared in a wash of warmth. "I was working and remembered you were taking the kids skating, so I thought I'd take a break and see how things were going."

"The kids are having a blast."

"I can skate backwards," Carlo piped in. "Watch." Still holding on to the railing, the boy took several baby steps to the rear. He looked so ridiculously proud of himself Gill had to laugh.

"Nice job, pal."

"You going to skate, too? You can be my partner."

"That's a nice offer, Carlos, but I—uh…"

"Ms. McKenzie already promised to be *my* partner."

Gill looked to Oliver, whose eyes had taken on an expectant light. He smiled and reached out a hand. "What do you say, angel? If you're worried about falling, I'll catch you."

Too late, Gill thought, her insides tumbling.

Ten minutes later she found herself sitting on a bench while Oliver laced her rented skates. "Do I get a helmet, too?" she teased.

"Do you need one?"

"No, but I wouldn't want to give the kids the wrong impression."

"Don't worry about them. I'm sure they'd prefer you kept the snow bunny look." He grinned and smoothed his palms around her ankle. "I know I do."

Gill's insides tumbled a little more. She reached for the hand he offered. "It's been a while since I've been on skates," she warned him. "I'm going to be a little rusty. You better keep your promise to catch me."

"Believe me, I will. I never break a promise."

No, she thought, from what she'd seen these past couple of weeks, he didn't. The knowledge made her feel safe and protected. Oliver was definitely a man you could count on. A good man. The kind of person a woman would be lucky to have in her life.

Except you're not looking for a relationship, remember? You've got bigger fish to fry.

"You don't look so rusty to me."

Lost in thought as she'd been, she hadn't realized they were already navigating the ice. Oliver still held her hand. His gloved fingers wrapped around hers felt so natural.

"I think I've been misled. You skate better than me."

Doubtful. Just as she'd expected, he moved on the ice with

the natural grace of an athlete. "What can I say? I played a mean game of pond hockey in my day."

"Pond hockey, huh? Somehow I pictured you more the figure skating type."

"Nah, I left that to my stepsisters."

"I thought it was only you and your twin?"

They must have hit a chip in the surface, because she stumbled slightly. Oliver's strong hand steadied her from behind. The comment came out unconsciously. "That's because as far as my father is concerned my sister and I don't exist."

"Sorry."

"Don't be," she said, cutting off his sympathetic expression before it could take hold. "That chapter in my life closed when I left Towering Pines. I'm a different person now." The pronouncement didn't feel as certain as usual. Probably because she was reliving a childhood activity.

"Well," Oliver said, giving her ponytail a playful tug, "he certainly couldn't ignore you today. That ski jacket is the pinkest creation I've ever seen. Is that standard color for pond hockey?"

"Oh, look who's talking, Mr. Fashion Statement." She gave him a nudge with her shoulder.

He pretended to stumble a little, pulling her close. Their bodies slipped together in perfect alignment. "That how they check in pond hockey?" he asked. His breath was warm and moist against her cheek.

She turned, bringing her lips inches from his. "You'd be surprised how tough those games got."

"I like surprises," he replied.

"Miss McKenzie, watch!" Becky came stumbling by, more walking than skating behind a plastic milk crate.

"Looking good!" Gill called out. "Try taking a break between steps and see what happens. Step, step, step, glide."

The little girl followed the directions and glided half a foot before catching her balance. "Hey! I skated! Carlos, look! I can skate."

Suddenly Gill found herself surrounded by kids from the center, all clamoring for instructions. For the next thirty minutes she held an impromptu and not very accurate skating lesson. By the end the kids weren't much better than when they'd started, but they could all chant, "Step, step, step, glide!" and everyone laughed. A lot.

Gill decided she'd laughed the most. If someone had told her last week she'd be having the time of her life ice skating with a bunch of kids, she'd have told them they were crazy. She would have told them she was too busy to waste an afternoon like that. But today…today the decision felt natural. Like holding Oliver's hand.

Speaking of which, while he'd relinquished physical contact, Oliver's presence had stayed with her the entire afternoon. She'd needed only to look up to catch his smile or see his warm expression, and she could feel him.

"You look like you could use a hot cocoa," a familiar voice purred in her ear.

She wished she could relish the warm body behind her, that they were alone so she could lean up against him. "Sounds good to me."

Leaving the kids to practice, they made their way side by side to the concession stand. Gill could feel the back of Oliver's hand brush hers, and she wondered what he'd say if she entwined her fingers with his here, off the ice. She settled for giving his hair a tussle when he removed his helmet. "You better put a hat on that damp hair or you'll catch a chill."

He leaned into her space, coming dangerously close. "Then I'll have to find a way to warm up."

Shivers that had nothing to do with the cold danced down Gill's spine. Lack of personal space wasn't the only danger they were flirting with. Looking into Oliver's eyes, she saw a heat that told her their thoughts were the same.

"Fresh air agrees with you," he said, his eyes dipping to her mouth.

"You, too."

For a moment it looked as if he would lean closer. Instead, he quickly pulled back. "Heads up, we've been spotted."

"Mr. Oliver, can *we* get cocoa?" Carlos burst upon them, nearly falling as he hit the lip of the rink. "I'm thirsty."

Several other kids echoed the request.

"I have to pee, too," Becky added.

After much discussion, begging and disorder, it was decided Gill and another two chaperons would take restroom duty while Oliver and Maria would order the group hot chocolate.

Standing in the crowd at the refreshment stand, Oliver pretended not to notice Maria giving him the eye.

"Someone's having a good time," she said, clearly not deterred.

"Isn't that the point of a field trip?" he replied.

"I'm not talking about the kids. Interesting Gill showed up, don't you think?"

"Not really. She lives across the street. The kids asked her to stay." He didn't want to think about how excited he'd been to see her standing there. Like a teenage kid. She had to be the most beautiful woman at the rink. Even if she hadn't been wearing Day-Glo pink he wouldn't be able to tear his eyes off her. Every smile she shot in his direction went straight to his gut. It was ridiculous, but his insides swelled with pride that this gorgeous creature was looking at *him*.

"We should get chips to go with the drinks," he said to Maria. "The kids have to be hungry."

"Stop dodging the conversation. Why don't you just admit you like her?"

Admitting it wasn't the problem. He *knew* he liked her. Hell, watching her with the kids today, he'd begun to more than like her. "Okay, I like her. You satisfied?"

"From the looks of things she likes you, too."

Yeah, she did. That was the real problem. Every time he looked in her face and saw a desire matching his, the free-fall feeling he got terrified him. Say they gave in to their feelings—what then? A woman like Gill belonged in a world with designer clothes and luxury apartments. How long before she tired of a man whose life was anything but? How long before she dumped him for bigger and better?

Out of the corner of his eye, he saw a flash of pink approaching. "How about we just focus on the kids and leave my personal life for another day?"

"Okay." His friend sighed. "But I think you're missing the boat."

Better to miss then have to disembark, Oliver replied in his head.

There was only one picnic table available, so they did their best to crowd in. Playing the gentleman, Oliver stood to the side, intending to let everyone else rest, but Gill scooted over, making space.

"Here," she said patting the bench, "there's still space. If you don't mind squishing up against me."

With the entire table looking, he had no choice. He perched on the corner. Even then Gill's body nestled next to his cozily. The contact sent his nerve-endings into overdrive. From the look flashing in her eyes, it did hers, too.

God help him, but resisting was getting near impossible.

The group drank their cocoa and enjoyed the warmth. With Christmas around the corner, most of the conversation focused on the upcoming holiday. The younger kids, like Becky, still believed in Santa and looked forward to finding presents under the tree Christmas morning. Fortunately, the older kids were polite enough to keep the secret. One of them asked Gill what she was doing for Christmas.

"Are you going to visit the magic trees?" Becky asked.

"Actually, I am. My sister lives on the farm where they grow."

The word farm started a slew of questions, about chickens and milking cows and other stuff. Oliver watched as Gill answered all of them. She shared what it was like to take a sleigh ride, and cut down your own Christmas tree. By the time she got to Christmas morning and how she and her sister baked apple muffins, Oliver was as enchanted as the kids.

"Sounds like a great time," he said.

"It is," she replied. "Though thanks to work, I probably won't get to stay more than a day, maybe two, before coming back."

"But you're coming to our party, right?" Carlos asked.

"Are you kidding? Wild horses couldn't keep me away. It's going to be the highlight of my holidays. Well, that—" she tugged Becky's ponytail "—and Santa."

"So you'll definitely be there?" the boy prodded.

"I promise," Gill replied.

"Cool." There was a gleam in his charge's eye Oliver recognized all too well. The boy was smitten.

Get in line, Carlos, he thought, stealing a glance at the woman next to him. *Get in line.*

CHAPTER NINE

FOR as long as Gill could remember, one day had been the same as another. But, come Sunday night, she found herself finally understanding the phrase "weekend regret."

The day had flown by. Not in a blurry haze, like when she was engrossed in work, but in a "the hours are too short" kind of way she remembered from childhood. In fact, today she felt like a kid again. Energized and carefree in a way she hadn't felt in a long time.

Skating had brought back memories, too. She couldn't believe the stories she'd shared with the kids. Yet reliving her small-town roots hadn't disturbed her the way it normally did. Maybe because the kids had seemed genuinely interested. They'd listened to her stories as if they meant something. As if *she* meant something.

Huh, imagine that.

And then there was Oliver. Flirty, sexy, amazing Oliver, whose encouraging smile made her feel like the belle of the ball. Who knew one person's expression could make a person feel so special? Closing her eyes, she conjured up his face, enjoying the thrill the image sent through her.

Maybe Gwen's romantic streak had a point after all.

That thought was still rattling around her head when she walked into the office Monday. She was ticking off her day's to-do list, trying to figure out what excuse she could use to stop by the center and see Oliver. She was so engrossed, she failed to notice the chaos whirling around her. That was until Elliot Rosenthal's bellow ripped through the office.

"I'm going to kill her! Who on earth goes skiing four days before a major product launch? Gillian, get in here!"

The center was completely lit up when she stepped from the cab. Community league basketball. Oliver had mentioned something last night. Gill winced. She'd purposely waited until after pick-up time, so she and Oliver would be able to talk in private.

Oh, well, she thought with a sigh. It was the kids she was avoiding anyway. Adults she could handle.

She let herself in, noticing the kids had hung more snowflakes in the entranceway. Her enchanted forest was growing by leaps and bounds. Peter McNabb would have a terrific backdrop for his photographs. She looked forward to reviewing the coverage.

Oliver was in his office, going over paperwork. He must have had a meeting, because instead of his usual sweater and corduroys he wore a black suit and tie, looking every inch the businessman he'd chosen not to be.

She took some hope in seeing him look that way. Maybe she was blowing this out of proportion? After all, Oliver was a professional; he understood the demands of a career. He'd understand her dilemma.

"This a bad time?" she asked.

His face brightened from the inside out the second he saw her. "Never a bad time for you. In fact, I was just thinking about ordering takeout. Feel like a little Chinese? We can test our fortunes again."

Gill could think of nothing she'd rather do than stay—especially with the way Oliver was smiling at her. Her stomach somersaulted at the knowledge she was about to let him down.

"I'm afraid I can't stay. I have to get back to work."

"Oh?" he replied with a frown. "What's up that you had to come by personally? There a problem?"

"A small one. Stephanie DeWitt had a skiing accident. She hit a tree and shattered her pelvis."

"That's terrible. Who's Stephanie DeWitt?"

"A co-worker. Actually…" She toed the floor with her boot. "She's the other woman under consideration for the vice presidency. With her out, I have to handle her project. It's a major aftershave launch for Remaillard Cosmetics. This means I'm pretty much a shoo-in for the promotion."

"That's great. That's what you wanted, right? Congratulations."

"Thanks."

"But you didn't come here just to share good news, did you?" His smile faded and his expression turned wary. The change made Gill uneasy. In that moment she knew her news wouldn't be taken well.

Might as well deliver the blow quickly. "The product launch is Thursday night."

"The same day as the McNabb Christmas party." Wariness gave way to something darker, reminding her of the anger she'd seen the day they met. "You promised the kids you'd be there."

And now she had to break that promise. Something, as he'd pointed out yesterday, he didn't believe in doing. But surely he had to see there were extenuating circumstances?

"Remaillard Cosmetics is our biggest account; a successful launch means a lot of new business."

He turned back to the paperwork on his desk. "What am I supposed to tell the kids? They think you're coming."

"Can't you tell them something came up?"

"You mean like a better offer?"

Gill didn't like where this conversation was headed. Or the coldness in his voice. Surely he had to understand that in the business scheme of things the Remaillard account had to come first? "I didn't choose for the launch to be held the same day as the party."

"No, you're simply choosing the launch over us."

"I have to. It's my job." Why was he making this sound so personal?

Because to him it was. *My kids. My center.* How many times did he use those phrases?

"Oliver, I didn't do this on purpose." She touched his shoulder. "I'll make it up to them."

"Sure you will. Unless another project comes up." Disbelief laced his every word. What hurt most was that he had wouldn't look at her. He simply shuffled the papers on his desk, his spine and his voice stiff and hard. "Look, I have a lot of paperwork to finish up. Do you need me to call you a cab?"

A cab? He was dismissing her? "Oliver—"

"What do you want me to say, Gill?" Finally he turned to face her. The look on his face made her wish he hadn't. "That I understand. Fine. I understand."

No, he didn't. Otherwise he'd see she truly didn't *have* a choice. She had to take this project. "Elliot Rosenthal is counting on me. I've worked too long and too hard to get where I am to mess up now."

"Of course you have."

He sounded so crisp and cold.

"This doesn't mean I don't..." She paused, unsure how to put her thoughts into words.

Before she could continue, Oliver held up his hand. "Don't, Gill. I'll tell the kids you had an emergency and couldn't work on the party anymore. Don't worry, they'll take it fine. They're used to disappointment."

Oliver listened to the angry click of Gill's boots fade in the distance. There was the slam of a car door, and he saw a pair of taillights disappear down the street. She'd asked the cab to wait. For some reason that only made him feel more annoyed. Feel more like a temporary stop.

"One more rung on the ladder of success," he mocked. He should have listened to his gut the day Gill walked in here, all high-heeled and high-powered.

Of course it was the kids he felt bad for. He'd always known she wouldn't stick around. That he and his center wouldn't be enough.

Paperwork had lost what little appeal it held. He needed to go home, crack a beer, and lose himself in a Celtics game. Tomorrow he'd figure out what to tell the kids.

He did his nightly tour, making sure the windows and doors were all locked and bolted. On the way back through the community room he stopped. Over the past two weeks the dingy space had been transformed. Garlands draped the windows. Ribbons and snowflakes hung from the ceiling. Surrounded by mini-trees, the Teaberry tree bathed the rest of the enchanted forest in soft light.

Slowly, he walked over and touched one of its branches. The pine fragrance reminded him of Gill. Longing welled up inside him. Longing stronger than he'd felt in a long time.

It was for the kids, he told himself. He was sad for the kids.

"Magical tree, my ass," he muttered, plucking a handful of needles. "If you're so magical, then make things right."

He let the needles fall on the floor.

The next two days passed in a blur of meetings and last-minute preparations. What Stephanie possessed in confidence and outward bravado, she apparently lacked in organization and follow-up skills. It took Gill half a day alone to figure out who was in charge of what task.

By the time she made it home to her apartment she was beyond exhausted. She crashed on her sofa. Even microwave popcorn was too much trouble tonight.

What she wouldn't give for some Kung Pao Chicken.

No, she wouldn't go there. According to Jeff, her stand-in on the center project, Oliver hadn't so much as mentioned her name during their meetings. He was obviously still upset. Knowing the chip on his shoulder, he'd probably stay that way forever. Just as well. Relationships and career didn't mix. If you could call what they'd had a relationship. What kind of relationship could you form in two weeks?

Gwen and Drew fell in love in four.

She wasn't Gwen. She wasn't in love. The hole in her chest was not a broken heart.

Her cell buzzed. Gill groaned. Not another text message. Couldn't she get five minutes to breathe?

She looked at the screen.

Thought you'd get a kick out of this video. Call when you're not so busy. Love, G.

The video was named "Claire Bear Snowman."

Gill loaded it up, and instantly her mood brightened. Her niece Claire was making a snowman—or, to be more accurate, Drew was making the snowman. Claire was helping by throwing handfuls of snow at him.

"Come on, help Daddy push the snowball," she heard Drew say. He bent over to push, only to have Claire dump a handful of snow on the back of his neck. She could hear Gwen laughing behind the camera as Drew pretended to growl like a bear and chase Claire down. "This," he said, giving his stepdaughter a gigantic bear hug, "this is what it's all about."

Gill clicked off the video. Without the sound of taped laughter her apartment became very quiet and cold. She curled onto her side and stared at her mini-tree, unlit and browning from lack of water.

"I am a success," she said. The mini-tree and the apartment didn't answer.

CHAPTER TEN

THE ballroom of the Fairlane Hotel looked like a Parisian bistro. Gill had taken Stephanie's original idea, run with it, and with some last-minute tweaks turned it into a product launch for the books. The guests—members of the New York and Boston fashion elite—raved left and right. As did the executives from Remaillard.

"Magnificent!" one exclaimed, kissing her on each cheek Parisian-style.

Elliot Rosenthal was suitably blown away as well. "Nice recovery," he said, handing her a glass of champagne. "The kind of results you expect from a top executive."

There it was. He might as well have called her Madam Vice President. Tomorrow she expected he would call her into his office and bestow the title on her officially. Gill saluted his raised glass. She'd done it. She'd reached the next plateau.

The moment wasn't as celebratory as she'd hoped.

Smiling and nodding at the crowd, she walked the perimeter of the room, pausing to adjust a poster that had slipped on its display. *"His Present, Your Treat,"* the ad read. *"Make Every Night Christmas Eve."* Gill had bought a bottle for Drew. Someone might as well have fun.

"He's made me take him to see Santa Claus three times. I swear the boy has the longest Christmas list in America."

"Did you tell him Santa can't fit everything in his sleigh?"

"When I did, he said, 'That's okay, Mommy. I asked for a trailer, too.'"

Behind the poster, two women laughed at the story. Gill tried not to listen in, but the minute she heard the word *Santa* she found herself tuned in. A quick look at her watch told her "Santa" would have just arrived at the center. Peter McNabb probably had his hands full right about now.

Stop, Gillian. You weren't going to think about Oliver or the center tonight.

She continued on her route. Another poster on the other side of the room needed fixing. This time she overheard two couples.

"I try to be a disciplinarian, but one look at those big brown eyes and I melt. I can't help it."

"The way they look when you walk through the door at night. Makes coming home worthwhile."

Coming home worthwhile. The conversation continued—something about puppy school—but Gill was no longer listening. She was replaying Gwen's video in her memory. Drew had said something similar. Her brother-in-law ran a successful worldwide corporation; he was worth millions. Yet she never saw him happier than when he was doting on Gwen and Claire. When was the last time she'd been truly happy, outside of visiting her sister?

Ice skating with the kids. She smiled. Sharing Chinese food. Every time Oliver smiled at her.

Makes coming home worthwhile.

What did she have to come home to? Work and a dying miniature Christmas tree.

All these years trying not to be poor Gillian McKenzie, and her life sounded more pathetic than ever.

A hand tapped her shoulder. "Stéphane Remaillard is about to make his remarks," Ken the intern told her. "Elliot wanted you up on the dais with them."

"Sure. Be right there." Time for her moment of glory.

Worth coming home to.

You always succeed when you put your mind to it.

Gwen was right. Since when did she just let events sweep her along as if she didn't have a choice? If life didn't give you something, you went out and made your own magic.

Maybe it was time she followed her own advice and made herself happy.

Christmas music blasted from the DJ's speakers. The community center had never been fuller or more lively. Kids, both the center's and children of invited guests, ran amok, playing and laughing. Older kids danced. Peter McNabb, in Santa garb, glad-handed and posed for photos in front of the enchanted forest. Adults mingled and read literature on the center's work. More than one had seen the feature on television and had promised a check upon an introduction.

"Mr. Oliver!" Jamarcus ran up, brandishing a candy cane and a stuffed teddy bear. There was chocolate rimming his mouth. "Look what Santa gave me."

Oliver put aside his blues. "Good for you, Jamarcus."

"I also got chocolate from Maria."

"So I see." He barely got the response out before the toddler was off, searching for the next activity.

He had to hand it to her, Gill had pulled together a triumph for McNabb and the center.

Too bad she wasn't here to see her success. Then again, she was basking in another success tonight.

At least a dozen times he'd picked up the phone to call her, only to change his mind at the last minute. The problem was bigger than just her career aspirations. Hell, he understood workaholism better than anyone.

No, it was a matter of priorities. If she chose her career over her promise to the kids this time, who's to say she wouldn't make a similar choice again? Who's to say the next time he wouldn't be the thing that came up short?

Face it, Harrington, you cut bait because you were afraid

she won't think you're good enough for her. Why not? Didn't Julia come to that same conclusion right before she walked out? Right after he refused to give up working at the center?

Only Gill wasn't Julia. She was far, far better.

And Gill didn't ask him to choose anything. He made the choice for her. Without giving her a chance.

For a guy who preaches the sky's the limit, you're pretty jaded. Maria's words came floating back to him. It was true. What kind of example was he for the kids if he was too afraid to take a chance himself?

Or rather, give Gill a chance?

A hand tugged the back of his suit jacket. He turned to see Becky and two other girls. "Carlos keeps dragging us under the mistletoe," they complained. "Can we slap him?"

"No," Oliver replied. He had to fight his chuckle. Carlos had been carrying out his mistletoe mission all night, much to the chagrin of Becky and the other girls. Although they didn't seem all that upset at the moment, despite their complaints. "I'll go talk to him and tell him to knock it off. Where is he?"

A look passed between the girls. "Hanging out in the doorway," one of them finally answered.

The better to catch unsuspecting girls; the kid wasn't stupid. "Don't worry," he told them. "I'll take care of everything."

"We know you will," Becky said, before the trio ran off giggling. Girls. They were a mystical lot.

He wove his way through the crowd to the doorway. The mistletoe had been the one part of the room he'd avoided until now. Looking at it only reminded him of Gill. A fresh bout of chagrin attacked him. As soon as he'd talked to Carlos he was definitely finding a phone. He'd leave a million messages if he had to.

Or maybe not. Halfway across the room, he froze.

There, under the mistletoe, stood Gill.

He recognized her red dress as a designer number from

Newberry Street. Simple, but elegant, it needed no adornment other than her long blond hair. His heart began to race.

She'd changed her choice.

Gill's heart pounded in her chest. It had been ages since she'd sent the girls to get Oliver. What if he didn't believe their ruse? What if he saw her and didn't want to talk with her? Or, worse, what if she'd misread the emotions she'd seen in his eyes?

Suddenly she saw him. Standing stock-still in the crowd. Their eyes locked. Slowly, he began moving forward. Blood pounding in her ears, Gill counted his steps. Five. Six.

At last he reached her. "You came."

Gill nodded. "I made a promise. I had to keep it."

"The kids will be happy."

"Just the kids?"

With a shake of his head, Oliver moved a little closer. "Not just the kids. Me. I owe you an apology."

"You do?"

"For losing my temper. For misjudging you. I always saw this center as a sort of symbol of what I overcame. Except I'm beginning to realize I didn't escape my roots as much as I thought. When you chose your project over the party I felt… I took it personally. I felt like you thought the center wasn't good enough for you."

Rubbing the back of his neck, he dipped his head and toed the doorway threshold with that sheepish expression she adored. "That I wasn't good for you."

Not good enough? A lump rose in Gill's throat. Her handsome, confident Oliver didn't think he was good enough for *her?* He couldn't be more wrong.

"I compared you to Julia and that was wrong. I should have given you a chance. Do you think you can forgive me?"

He looked up, and the emotion she saw brimming in his eyes brought a lump to her throat. The tightness that had been gripping her lungs slowly melted through her, filling her with an emotion too light, too wonderful to describe. Forgive him?

For what? Letting his past color his actions? Hadn't she been doing the very same thing?

"I can forgive you," she said with a smile, "if you can give me another chance."

"Oh, angel, I'll give you all the chances in the world." He paused, his happy expression suddenly growing confused. "What about the big product launch? Aren't you supposed to be there?"

"Uh-huh."

"Then why aren't—?"

Gill pressed her fingers to his lips. He was getting that inner glow she loved, and she was dying to touch him. "Being with you, being with the kids—it made me realize there's a little more to life than working twenty-four-seven. There's something to be said for having more in your life. *I* want more in my life."

"Same here," he replied.

Seeing the expectancy in his eyes, she knew without doubt what she needed to say next. He'd taken a chance and bared his soul. It was time for her to do the same. "I want *you* in my life."

Oliver moved closer. Gill took a deep breath. His eyes shone with emotion as they searched her face. Finally, after what seemed a thousand years, he answered. "Same here." Reaching out, he brushed her lower lip with his thumb. The caress reached to her heart. "I think I might be falling in love with you, angel."

Gill let out her breath. She hadn't misread those emotions after all. "Same here," she whispered.

"You know something else?" Oliver whispered back.

"What?" Gill was on cloud nine. No promotion, no words, nothing could possibly be more wonderful than what she'd just heard. Oliver Harrington was falling for her.

He slipped his arms around her waist and pulled her close. "You're under the mistletoe," he murmured against her lips.

"So I am," Gill responded with a smile. "What should we do about it?"

"I don't know about you, but I'm going to claim my woman before Carlos gets here."

Slanting his mouth over hers, he did just that.

EPILOGUE

One Year Later...

OUTSIDE the snowflakes had begun to fall. It looked as if Towering Pines would get a white Christmas after all. Curled into a corner of the sofa, Gill sipped her ginger tea with a smile. Across from her, this year's Teaberry tree glistened magically.

The sound of slippered footsteps drew her attention. "Took five readings of *Santa Mouse,* but Claire finally fell asleep," Gwen announced. "She wanted to know if Santa would leave the baby in her stocking."

She eased herself onto the sofa, sighing happily. Eight months pregnant, she glowed with maternal expectancy. "I swear she's as eager for the baby to arrive as Drew and I are. Of course part of me thinks she's confusing getting a baby sister with getting a pony."

"Knowing Drew, she'll get both."

"As well as a puppy, a kitten, and half the West Virgina Zoo. I swear that girl has him wrapped around her little finger."

"That a bad thing?" Gill asked.

"No," her twin replied, her eyes filling with love. "He's such a wonderful father. I can't wait to see him hold this baby."

It was true. Since meeting Gwen, Drew had turned into the consummate family man. *Just goes to show what love will do to a person,* Gill thought to herself, absently pressing a palm to her belly. She had her own Christmas secret she was planning to share tonight.

"Where *are* the boys anyway?" Gwen asked. "Still delivering trees?"

"Apparently so."

With Gwen so far along in her pregnancy, Drew had insisted she cut back on her work at the farm this season, so Oliver and Gill had flown down early to help out. True to his nature, Oliver had convinced Drew to have the leftover trees donated to local needy families.

"Shouldn't we spread some of the Teaberry magic around?" he'd teased.

She must have smiled—she'd been doing that a lot lately—because Gwen asked, "Penny for your thoughts?"

"I was thinking about the Teaberry legend. How we used to think the trees were magical."

"Well, they certainly brought *us* magic, didn't they?"

Gill shook her head. Even after four years of marriage, Gwen was still a hopeless, whimsical romantic. Before she could correct her, however, the front door opened and a trio of handsome, snow-covered men tromped in. All three were handsome as sin, but only one made her pulse quicken. She palmed her belly again while she watched Oliver untie his boots.

"Man, but I miss California," Brody said, shaking the snow from his baseball cap. Nearly twenty, he was the spitting image of his father. "You don't have to worry about getting your car stuck in snow out there."

"No, just traffic," Drew teased back.

"Very funny, Dad. I'm going to go call Susan; see if she's more sympathetic."

"You better hurry. Something might have happened since her last text message."

Brody stuck his tongue out before disappearing upstairs.

"I swear," Drew said, joining them in the living room,

"those two are joined at the hip." He sat next to Gwen and gestured for her to raise her feet. "Did I miss storytime?" he asked, slipping off her slippers and massaging her feet.

"'Fraid so, but I won't be surprised if there's a round two."

"I'll take that one. You better get some sleep. She's going to be up at the crack of dawn."

"Urged on, no doubt, by her Christmas-loving daddy."

Gill was watching the exchange when she felt a pair of strong hands rest on her shoulders. "Miss me?" a voice whispered in her ear.

"Always," she whispered back.

Oliver nuzzled the crook of her neck, instantly sending tingles through her. They'd been married eight months now, and his touch still thrilled her as much as it had that first time. She suspected the sensation would never change.

"Did you get all your trees delivered?"

"Every one. Teaberry magic has now been distributed."

"Gill and I just were talking about the Teaberry legend," Gwen said. "She was going to tell me, like she does every year, that there's no such thing as magic trees. Right, sis?"

Looking around the room, Gill saw nothing but love and happiness flowing from the people in it. She looked at Drew and Gwen, expectant parents who'd found love and trust here at Teaberry Farms. Then there was the man standing behind her. Her husband. It was Christmas that had led her to his doorstep. Her life would be so empty had she not met him. She thought of the life they had created together, and how thrilled he would be when she told him he was going to become a father. Tonight, under a Teaberry Christmas tree.

"I don't know," she replied, her gaze traveling to the tree across the room. "Maybe there's some truth to that old legend after all."

* * * * *

Snowbound Cowboy

PATRICIA THAYER

Dear Reader,

Christmas has always been my favourite time of year. I grew up in the Midwest and as a child one of my first wishes for the holidays was to have snow. Another was for a giant tree that smelled of evergreen and reached all the way to the ceiling in our big old house.

I have a large family—four sisters and three brothers—and though my parents never had a lot, they managed to fill up the bottom of the tree with gifts from Santa. It was years until I realised how truly blessed I was because I had family around to share it with.

As I got older my hopes and dreams changed. Now that I have grandkids, I've discovered that the best presents aren't always wrapped up with a pretty bow. The best are part of everyday life. Like seeing my grandsons' smiles as they run through the waves at the beach or point up at the moon in wonder. How they grip your hand with complete confidence that you'll keep them safe. How our oldest grandson, who has autism, smiles so brightly when you read his favourite story or sing his favourite song. And how every word he speaks is like a precious gift. No, you can't buy that in any store.

This is my first Christmas story and I was lucky enough to share it with talented writer Donna Alward. Together we came up with a ranch in Montana, the Rocking H, with two sisters, Kelley and Amelia Hughes.

In my story I created characters who needed to find some holiday joy. When this idea came to me, I kept seeing a five-year-old boy making a Christmas wish. All Jesse Hughes wants is a dad. He even writes it down on a list and every day he believes that his dad will arrive by Christmas morning. It takes a Montana snow blizzard and my hero and heroine getting stranded together just two weeks before Christmas.

Amelia, a single mother, is afraid to trust another man again. Boone Gifford carries a burden with him that makes him think he doesn't deserve a family. Somehow these two begin to believe in a Montana Christmas miracle and never have to unwrap one gift.

In Donna's story, Kelley enlists the help of chef Mack Dennison to help her create the perfect Hughes family Christmas. Somehow they both start to realise that the most perfect gift could very well be each other…if they're willing to open their hearts.

My hope for all of you is to receive the kind of gift that isn't always found under the tree. Just look around and count your blessings.

Happy holidays!

Patricia Thayer

PS Look for Patricia's new novel, *Daddy by Christmas*, out in November 2010, and a fabulous new set of books in the autumn of 2011. –Ed.

CHAPTER ONE

SHE'D DONE IT NOW.

Amelia Hughes stared out the windshield at the blowing snow and thought about her rash decision to drive into town in spite of blizzard warnings. She had thought she could outrun the storm. In her haste to get back to the ranch, she had hit a slick spot, and the truck had slid off the snow-packed road onto the soft shoulder.

"Mom, we got stuck!"

"We don't know that for sure," she said, wondering what her penance should be for lying to a five-year-old boy. In an attempt to right her wrong, she eased her foot onto the gas peddle causing the tires to spin and the back of the truck to slide further off the road.

Great. With a sigh, Amelia stopped her attempt to regain traction, and turned to meet her child's wide brown-eyed gaze. His stocking cap covered a head full of whiskey-colored curls, and light freckles dusted his small nose and rosy cheeks. Jesse Thomas Hughes was her everything.

Somehow she had to get them out of this. After all, she'd lived in rural western Montana all her life. She came from sturdy, frontier stock. Her great-grandparents mined this land, finally turning to ranching. They never gave up, nor would she.

She gripped the wheel and went back to work. Yet, no

matter what direction she turned the wheel, or how gently she worked the gas peddle, she couldn't get the old truck to move forward. She finally stopped to save fuel. They might need heat if they had to spend the night here. No, she refused to think about that. They had hours of daylight left.

"Boy, Aunt Kelley is going to be mad."

"No, Aunt Kelley won't be mad." Another lie just rolled off her tongue. "But maybe we shouldn't tell her. She has a lot to worry about with taking Grandma Ruby to the hospital."

Jesse nodded. "Okay. Maybe if we wish really hard someone will come by and save us."

Amelia wasn't so sure that was going to work, either. There wasn't much reason for anyone to be on this road. Everyone else was at home heeding the storm warning. She'd only gone out to buy supplies before they'd gotten snowbound.

Normally the Hughes household was prepared for bad weather, but the December storm caught them off guard. With Gram's illness, everyone had been distracted getting her into Helena and the hospital.

Jesse turned to her again. "Maybe we should call Aunt Kelley. She'll know what to do."

Amelia didn't doubt it. Her older sister pretty much ran the cattle operation, while Amelia handled the household. It wasn't that she didn't love taking care of the family, but she'd also like her sister to listen to some of her ideas for the ranch. Kelley hadn't even trusted her to handle things while she was in Helena, and made arrangements to hire a ranch hand to help out.

The last thing Amelia wanted was for her sister to know she'd already messed up things in her absence. But what was more important, she needed to get herself and her son out of this weather.

She pulled out her cell phone. "I've got a better idea. I'll call the sheriff."

* * *

Boone Gifford was a Texas boy, born and bred.

He had never been crazy about cold weather or snow. Now he was in the middle of a blizzard outside of Rebel Ridge, Montana. He'd only come here because he'd given his word. And Boone never went back on his word. So the sooner he got to the Rocking H, the sooner he could leave for a warmer climate.

He swiped his gloved hand over the windshield to clear away the condensation. It didn't help. Visibility was nil. Even reducing his speed to a crawl hadn't helped much. He wasn't even sure where he was.

Absently he rubbed his sore shoulder, reminding him of his last job on the off-shore oil rig and the accident that nearly took his life. He'd survived, but he would never forget the men who'd died that day. Especially one.

He shook away the memory to concentrate on his task. Not an easy one, either. The wind gusted again, continuing to make it difficult to keep his vehicle on the road. His grip tightened around the steering wheel. If he had a brain, he'd never have attempted to get to the Hughes ranch today.

No, he needed to finish this, once and for all. He needed to see Amelia Hughes, then he could move on with a clear conscience.

Boone kept his gaze sharp as his new four-wheel-drive truck crept along the dangerous terrain. Lucky for him, his tires could handle mud and snow. Suddenly he saw flashing emergency lights up ahead. As he got closer, he realized it was a truck parked at a funny angle along the shoulder.

So he wasn't the only crazy person out here. He stopped in the middle of the road, then, pulling the collar up on his coat, he climbed out. Fighting the sharp wind, he made his way to the embankment and the truck cab.

"Hey, is there anyone in there?" he called, and banged on the window.

He blinked the snow from his eyes as the window came down and a woman's face appeared. "Oh, thank God you came by. My son and I went off the road and we're stuck. If you could just help us to our ranch? It's just up the road a few miles."

"The Rocking H?" Boone asked.

"Yes." The pretty woman smiled, lighting up her rich green eyes. "Oh, you must be the hand from the Sky High Ranch. I'm Amelia Hughes."

So he'd found her. As Russ had described, she was a pretty brunette. Not wanting to stand here and give her an explanation, he gave her a quick nod. "Boone Gifford. Look, we need to get out of this, and my truck seems to be our best bet." He pulled open the door and helped the woman out of the truck, then behind her he saw the small boy.

"My son, Jesse," Amelia called, fighting the wind.

The boy slid across the seat. His eyes were wide along with his smile. A sudden tightness gripped Boone's chest.

"Hey, kid."

"Hi." The boy cocked his head to the side and grinned. "Are you my Christmas wish?"

The normal ten-minute trip had taken nearly thirty by the time Boone pulled the truck up to the back door. Amelia finally released a breath. She climbed out of the truck and carrying two grocery bags, trudged her way to the porch. Boone Gifford swung Jesse up into his arms and followed her.

"We made it," Amelia cried as she stepped into the big kitchen. She set down her groceries on the long table. She wanted to drop to the floor and kiss it. She didn't want to think about what could have happened if they had been left out there.

"Yeah, we made it," Jesse mimicked as he came into the room.

Boone put her son down, but Jesse wasn't leaving his side. Amelia noticed the child's budding hero worship.

She pulled off her hat and shook out her long hair. "How about some coffee, Mr. Gifford?"

"Please, call me Boone." He took off his cowboy hat and unwrapped the scarf from his neck. "Yes, please, I wouldn't mind a cup to warm up."

"Can I have some hot chocolate, Mom?"

Amelia took her son's coat and hung it on a hook beside the mud room door. "Yes, you can, but I want you to go change out of your jeans into some warm sweats."

He tugged off his cap, revealing his curly dark hair. "Ah, Mom. I want to talk to Boone some more."

That was the problem. She had to nix this before her son drove the ranch hand crazy. "You can when you get back, but right now there's a storm coming and we need to take care of the livestock, too."

"'Kay," he murmured and walked out of the room.

"I apologize for all my son's questions on the way home."

"Not a problem. He seems like a good kid."

"I think so, but I'm a little biased." She smiled and he smiled back before he turned away to the window.

Boone Gifford wasn't what you'd call classically handsome, but you took notice of the man. His ebony eyes were deep set, his jaw was chiseled with a shadow of a beard. His thick hair was coal black with a slight wave and long enough to brush the back of his collar. He was tall, well-over six feet, with shoulders so broad it made the room seem crowded.

Boone turned back toward her, catching her looking at him.

"Looks like this storm is going to be a rough one," he said, his gaze holding hers. "I should get out to the barn while I have a chance."

She cleared her throat, but couldn't remember what she wanted to say. She nodded, then went to the counter and began making coffee. "Good idea."

"Okay, you have anything special you need done?"

"My sister, Kelley, left written instructions in the tack room. And your sleeping quarters are right next door."

He nodded. "I'll go check out things and be back shortly." He started for the door, then stopped. "What did your son mean when he asked if I was his Christmas wish?"

She froze. "Oh, you know how kids are. It's only two weeks before Christmas and he has his list of what he wants. I'm sorry if he bothered you."

"It's not a problem." He paused again. "What exactly is he asking for?"

Jesse walked into the room. "I want a Dad."

Boone hurried into the barn and forced the door shut against the bitter cold wind. He was a coward. He'd had the perfect chance to tell her the real reason he was here. Instead he let her continue to think he was the ranch hand who'd been hired to help out. Why not? Amelia Hughes needed help, and he could at least hang around until the other guy showed up.

Boone walked down the center aisle to find everything neat and orderly. There were nearly a dozen stalls lining the walls, four with horses. He found he was a little envious.

Back in Texas his barn had looked a lot like this one. He'd taken pride in all the work he and his dad had put into the Last Dollar Ranch. The house had been far from a showplace, because they put every penny into the care of the stock. Then, after the bank took over, the ranch fell into total neglect. But not for long. Thanks to the financial settlement from the accident, he had the money and the opportunity to get it back.

Just as soon as he paid his other debt.

Suddenly a big chocolate Labrador appeared and began

barking. "Hey, fella. Where'd you come from?" Boone held out his hand and the animal approached, then began wagging his tail. Once the dog relaxed, Boone petted him. He noticed the animal's full flanks. He grinned after further examination. "So you're a gal and a mother-to-be. And by the looks of it, you don't have long to go."

The dog barked in agreement.

Boone stood. "Come on, show me around?"

They headed toward the immaculate tack room and the dog's bed lined with blankets. He also found the list of boldly printed instructions. The next room was the sleeping quarters for the hired hand. A single bunk and a dresser, plus a wall heater. This wasn't meant for him. And before the real ranch hand showed up, he'd best tell Amelia the truth.

His thoughts turned to the pretty woman with the rich green eyes. She had a full, tempting mouth that caused his body to tighten, making him realize how alone he'd been the past six months.

He shook off the wayward thoughts. What would Amelia Hughes do when she realized he hadn't been exactly truthful? He rubbed the back of his neck. Maybe he should just hand over the envelope addressed to her and head out.

The wind howled outside. He wasn't going anywhere right now, and maybe not for a while.

And there was Jesse. He needed to know about his daddy, especially since Russ Eldon had died before he got the chance to come and meet his son.

Now all Boone had to do was tell a little boy he would never get his Christmas wish.

CHAPTER TWO

AMELIA PACED THE KITCHEN, occasionally glancing out the window at the blowing snow. She couldn't see a thing. And according to the forecast, the weather wasn't going to improve for at least three or four days. How bad was it going to get? She looked toward the barn, barely able to see the red structure. Suddenly, she was happy Boone Gifford had showed up.

The phone rang and she picked it up on the second ring. "Hello."

"Amelia. It's Kelley."

"Kelley, hi. Is Gram okay?"

"Yes. I got her settled in her room and she's resting right now."

"That's good." Amelia knew how hard it had been to convince seventy-five-year-old Ruby Hughes to have this procedure done.

"Well, the doctor had to sedate her so she'd be relaxed." There was a pause. "How are you and Jesse doing? I'm worried about this storm, Amelia. It's going to get bad."

Amelia glanced outside again. The wind was blowing heavy snow. "We'll be fine, Kel."

"But what if you can't get out?"

"I have help."

"Oh, good. So Joe sent over the hand from Sky High Ranch."

She wasn't going to tell her sister that he had already rescued her and Jesse. "Yes, he's moving his things into the barn and checking on the horses."

"I'm glad you're not there alone."

So was she, but she'd never tell Kelley. "I know you don't think so, but I can handle things. I've lived out here as long as you have."

"I know, but I can't help being worried."

"Don't, because then Gram will worry, too. She's got to be your only concern right now. Mine is the ranch and Jesse." She went to the high counter that divided the kitchen from the dining room and glanced further into the great room to find her son sitting in front of the television watching a video.

Kelley still wasn't convinced and rattled off a list of instructions. Amelia heard the back door shut and turned as Boone walked into the kitchen. His dark eyes met hers, and her throat suddenly went dry.

"Amelia...Amelia. Are you there?"

She shook away her wandering thoughts and turned back. "Yes, I'm here. Look, Kel, Jesse needs me so I better go. Call after the surgery tomorrow. Bye."

Amelia hung up the phone before her sister gave her more things to do.

"I came for that coffee." He removed his hat and coat revealing a dark-green flannel shirt.

"Sure." Amelia swung away from the distraction and went to the freshly brewed pot and grabbed two mugs. After filling it, she placed them on the table. "Cream or sugar?"

He shook his head. "No, black's fine, ma'am." The large brown dog lumbered into the room.

"Oh, Izzy. I forgot all about you." She glanced at Boone. "Thanks for bringing her to the house. She's pretty close to her delivery time."

Amelia went over and petted the dog. The animal basked in

the attention, then wandered over to the warm kitchen hearth and lay down on the rug.

"Have a seat," she offered, and sat down across from him. "That was my sister, Kelley, on the phone. She wanted to make sure you got here." Amelia took a sip of coffee. "She was checking up on me, too. To see if I was staying out of trouble."

"She's probably worried."

Amelia nodded. Kelley had watched over her since they were little; since their dad died and their mother left them here for Grandma Ruby to raise. "She'd have a fit if she knew I'd gone out in the storm." She met his dark gaze. "I can't thank you enough for showing up when you did."

Boone knew he should tell her his real reason for being on the road today. But then he saw Amelia's nervousness. "You already have. Besides, you and Jesse are safe now." He set down his mug. "I checked the supply of wood on the porch. There seems to be plenty for a few days. I'll go out before dark and move more from the side of the house."

"That's a good idea since the radio says it's only getting worse. The roads are impassible. Not uncommon for this part of the country."

"Did they say how long the weather system will last?"

"Through Thursday, at least."

Great. He couldn't leave for three days. He took a long drink of coffee. This was a bad idea all around. "I should get settled in." He stood and carried his cup to the sink when Jesse rushed into the kitchen.

The boy smiled. "Oh, Boone, you're back."

"Not for long."

The child frowned. "You can't leave now. Mom's going to fix lunch." The boy turned to his mother. "Mom, will you make egg salad?"

"I can."

"It's the best," the boy bragged. "Everybody says so. I even like it, but not as much as peanut butter and jelly. That's because Mom makes the bread and her special jelly. It's peach. That's my favorite. What's your favorite, Boone?" The kid finally took a breath.

"I'd say peach is probably at the top of my list, too."

The boy grinned. "I bet Mom would fix you peanut butter and jelly if you want."

"Jesse," his mother called, "slow down. We can have both for lunch." Amelia glanced up at the clock over the sink. "Why don't you go and wash your hands?"

Jesse started to argue, but at a look from his mother turned and hurried down the hall.

"I apologize for my son. Outside of seasonal ranch hands, he doesn't have many men around."

Boone had learned as much from the friendly waitress in town at the diner. The Hughes women were well respected and admired around here. "From what I can see, you've done a fine job with him and this place."

She glanced away. "Thank you. My family helps a lot."

He nodded in agreement. "Family is a good thing."

"Do you have family? A wife...children?"

"No," he said, trying not to react. He'd lost any part of that dream two years ago.

She sighed and refilled their coffee mugs. "Since you'll be around for a few days, there's something you should know." She paused. "When Jesse started kindergarten this year, he realized his classmates have dads. Everyone except him. So he came up with this crazy idea that all he had to do was ask for one. So on the top of his Christmas list he has the word *Dad*."

Boone nodded. Great. And here he'd arrived with news that would make it impossible for the boy to get that wish. "And his father?"

She shook her head. "His father has never been involved in Jesse's life, nor at this stage do I want him to be."

Boone couldn't blame her for that. "I guess every boy wants a dad."

"But he can't go around picking one out, either. I'll have a talk with him."

This was getting complicated. "Maybe I should leave now." He stood. "I mean, go to the barn."

"No, you're not going to stay out in a cold barn all day. I'll handle Jesse. I just wanted you to know the situation."

Amelia got up, walked to the refrigerator and took out the ingredients for the salad. When she bent over he caught the appealing shape of her bottom and long legs. His attention was drawn upward as she went to the counter, took a loaf of bread out from under a towel and began slicing it.

"Is there anything I can do?" he asked, knowing he couldn't just sit there and ogle this woman.

"You can get the plates down from the cupboard." She nodded overhead.

Boone walked up behind her. Reaching over her head, he caught a whiff of her shampoo. Something lemony. Something that normally wouldn't be sexy to him. It was now. He gripped the plates and carried them to the table before he got himself into trouble.

Jesse came in. "I'll help you, Boone."

The boy pulled flatware from the drawer and placed it beside the plates.

"Good job," Boone said.

"Gram Ruby says I'm her best helper," Jesse said proudly. "I help Kelley with the horses, too." Those big brown eyes widened. "I can help you, too."

"Jesse Thomas," his mother called. "Don't even think about leaving the house in this storm."

"Ah, Mom. If I get lost, Izzy can find me."

At the mention of her name the dog looked up. "Izzy isn't in any shape to go traipsing around in this weather," Amelia said.

"What if Boone gets lost? Who will find him?"

Amelia swung around to look at Boone. She was asking for help.

"I strung a rope from the barn to here. And believe me, once I get back there I'm staying put."

The wind howled outside, and suddenly the lights flickered, then finally died.

"Oh, no," Amelia said. Although it was afternoon, the room was dim, only illuminated by the fire from the hearth.

"Do you have a generator?" Boone asked.

"Yes, it's in the mud room." She led him out to the enclosed porch and to a closet.

Boone examined the old machinery. "Have you used it recently?"

"Not since last spring. And only for a few hours. Gram had it checked out just last month."

Jesse poked his head in. "And the man said she needed to get a new one," he volunteered. "Gram was looking in the catalog. She showed me a picture of the one she wants." He looked up at both adults. "You want to see it?"

"Not now, honey." She turned to Boone. "Do you think you can start it?"

He threw a switch, then pulled the cord to get the motor running. He stood back. "I'm just not sure how reliable it is. It's best to keep both fireplaces going. You can sleep in front of the living room one tonight."

"Oh, boy. Can you sleep there, too, Boone? Can he, Mom, huh?"

Boone watched the pretty brunette blush. "I don't think Mr. Gifford would be happy to share space with a rambunctious five-year-old."

The boy wrinkled his nose. “That means I jump around too much. But I’ll promise to be quiet.”

“I appreciate the offer, son, but maybe you and your mother should have the sofa space. I’ll make sure you have plenty of firewood to keep you both warm.” He started to walk off.

“Wait, Boone,” Amelia called as he started out. “I have to agree with my son. You can’t sleep in the barn, not without electricity. You’ll move in here.”

CHAPTER THREE

BOONE WASN'T SURE how to react to Amelia's statement. True, he couldn't sleep in the barn, but invading their personal space was a different story. He hadn't signed up for this.

"Maybe the electricity will be back on by then."

Amelia frowned. "I take it you haven't lived in Montana long. This outage could last days."

"I'm originally from West Texas. We don't get many blizzards."

"Well, we do. So unless you want to freeze, you better decide to camp out with us tonight. You can have the small room off the kitchen." She led them back inside and pointed to the eight-paneled door across the room. "One of its walls is the back of the fireplace. It stays pretty warm in there."

He hated doing this. "I don't mean to put you out, ma'am." He had no business being here in the first place.

"You'll only put me out if I have to worry about you sleeping in that cold barn."

He felt a strange feeling in the center of his gut. It'd been a while since a woman had been concerned about him. "I would have been okay. The animals are my responsibility."

"Their stalls are pretty well insulated. And there's another generator out there, but we don't usually use it unless it's absolutely necessary."

He was surprised how well Amelia Hughes handled the

emergency. If she was nervous about the situation, she didn't show it.

"Seems you have everything under control," he told her.

"I'm fine as long as we stay in the house and have enough food. And we do. Since the stove is propane, I'll be able to cook."

Boone stood at the counter, the only thing that separated the kitchen from the dining area, then past it was the living room with two overstuffed sofas angled toward a huge stone fireplace.

He looked up to see the exposed beams, then down at the polished hardwood floors. No doubt the place had probably been remodeled over the years. He found he liked the mixture of both the old and the new.

His attention was drawn back to the woman wandering around turning off unneeded lights. She smiled and he felt a funny tightness in his chest. Her green-eyed gaze locked with his, then quickly she turned away.

"How about I finish making us lunch?"

Boone nodded. "I could eat."

"So could I," Jesse chimed in. "I'm real hungry."

She messed up her son's hair. "You're always hungry."

The boy grinned. "That's cause I'm growing."

The twosome walked into the kitchen, and Boone found he enjoyed listening to the bantering between mother and son.

Something tugged at his heart as his thoughts turned to Russ. His friend would be happy at how well his boy had turned out. Now all Boone had to do was find a way to tell the kid's mother about her son's father.

As Amelia mixed the egg salad, she could feel Boone watching her. It had been a long time since a man had been in the Hughes house. Sad, but true. She hadn't had time, or any desire, to attempt a relationship. Since Russ, she hadn't let anyone get close to her. Not that men had rushed to her door. If one did, Kelley would probably be there to give him the third degree. Her big sister had always been Amelia's protector. She'd also sat with Amelia during the rough times after Jesse's father left. Later she'd coached her through labor and the delivery of her son. And she loved Jesse as much as Amelia did.

What would Kelley think about Boone Gifford? That he was handsome? Her sister didn't get her head turned easily. Not when she worked side by side with ranch hands that drifted from job to job. She couldn't afford to.

Neither could Amelia, but she couldn't deny that she'd taken notice of Boone Gifford. She sighed. She had to keep reminding herself that he was a stranger. Thank goodness Kelley had checked him out.

Amelia handed out the sandwiches and poured the milk.

She sat down and glanced at the smile on her son's face as he chatted with Boone. It was Jesse who'd suffered the most from his father choosing to desert them. With just women around, a boy craved male companionship.

She turned her attention to Boone. He wasn't the kind of man either one of them needed. He wasn't even from Montana, but West Texas, and she had no doubt he would be going back. No way was she getting mixed up again with a guy who was just passing through.

Jesse said something, and Boone managed a smile. Her attention went to his mouth and the tiny lines bracketing it, which only seemed to add to his rugged features.

Suddenly he looked up. She swallowed, feeling the strange tension in her stomach. This was not good.

"Mom!"

"What?" She turned to her son.

"I asked if Boone and me can play cards."

"Honey, Boone isn't here to entertain you."

"It's not a bother," Boone said, then turned to her son. "First, we need to help clean up."

Amelia watched as her son picked up his empty plate and followed Boone to the sink. The big, tall cowboy took up too much space in the kitchen, making her feel crowded and edgy. And a lot more. She stood, too, but kept the needed distance between her and the man. Boone Gifford was a stranger and he would be leaving soon.

She needed to remember that.

The afternoon dragged on as the snow continued to fall. Boone had played card games with Jesse to keep the boy occupied. Amelia kept busy going around the house, closing off rooms to conserve the heat. She'd brought out candles and extra bedding from upstairs. When Boone had offered to help her she put him off. Instead, she began chopping vegetables for supper.

"Jesse. I think it's time to put the cards away."

"Ah, Mom, I'm winning."

"You've been playing for the last hour. I need your help to prepare for tonight."

Boone glanced over. As the afternoon turned toward evening, she seemed to grow nervous. Was it only the threatening storm, or was it him?

"Your mom's right." He got up from the table. "Besides, I need to check the animals." He headed to the coat hook, pulled on his sheepskin-lined jacket and wrapped the scarf around his neck.

"Boone, would you mind bringing up Izzy's food?"

"Sure." He reached down and petted the dog. "You want to go with me, girl?"

The large animal walked to the back door and waited.

Boone tugged his hat low on his head and pulled on his gloves. He went out the back door noticing the snow had slowed but not the wind. He grabbed hold of the anchor rope he'd rigged earlier and began to traipse through the knee-high snow toward the barn.

Inside, he stomped off the clinging snow before he fed and watered the horses, then retrieved the dog's food and headed back.

Izzy finished her business and didn't have any trouble finding her way to the house. Boone set the food in the mud room, then went to his truck and got his duffel bag.

Back on the porch, he found a bundled-up Jesse waiting.

"Mom said I can help you carry in some wood."

"Good. I can use a strong helper." He glanced toward the window, not surprised to see Amelia. He nodded to her and went to load up the boy's small arms with split logs. Once inside, they stacked it neatly beside the fireplaces. After three trips, he decided they had enough to get through until morning.

Amelia had been working, too. She had a pot of homemade stew simmering on the stove, filling the kitchen with a heavenly aroma. He carried his duffel bag into the small room off the kitchen where he found the double bed already made up with snowy white sheets and two heavy blankets.

Amelia appeared at the doorway. "My grandfather stayed in here during his long illness. Gram Ruby never changed the room back to her sewing room."

"I won't disturb anything," Boone told her as he set his bag on the cedar chest at the end of the bed.

"It's okay," Jesse said as he walked in. "'Cause when I'm sick I get to stay here. I even throwed up all over the blankets." He made a face. "It was gross, but Mom didn't even get mad."

Boone hid a smile. "That's good to know."

"Jesse, why don't we let Boone get settled in?" She motioned for her son to come with her.

The boy obeyed, but paused at the doorway. "Can we still play cards later?"

"If it's okay with your mom."

The boy swung around to Amelia, looking for the okay.

"We'll see, Jesse. Come on, you can help me with the bread." She looked at Boone. "Supper will be ready about six, unless you get hungry before that."

"I'll be there at six." He looked at Jesse. "Why don't you come and get me, so I don't miss your mama's stew?"

When the boy smiled he could see a strong resemblance to Russ, but the physical likeness was where it ended. Did he have a right to burst in here and intrude on their lives? Yes, the boy needed to know that his father had cared about him and wanted to come and meet him. He had to at least tell the kid's mother, then she could decide what to do. What would Boone's announcement do to Amelia Hughes?

Amelia tugged her son's arm. "We'll see you at supper." She stepped back, leaving the door open to help circulate the sparse heat.

Boone sat down on the bed and lit the candle on the nightstand. The daylight was quickly fading. He pulled off his boots, rubbing one foot over the other. Once he'd stimulated warmth back into his toes, he lay down and rested his head against the feather pillow.

He couldn't help but think back to six months ago. It had never been his dream to work as a roustabout on an oil rig off the coast of Galveston, Texas. And that was where he'd met Russell Eldon.

Boone hadn't cared much about making friends, only about making money to buy back the ranch he'd lost. Russ wanted to give something to the child he'd abandoned, and he couldn't stop talking about it.

Sharing close quarters, Boone had listened to Russ's story.

How at twenty-one he'd gotten a girl pregnant. In a panic, he'd taken off, even before he knew if she had the baby or not.

About a year ago, Russ had learned that he had a son. For the past months he'd worked on the oil rig to make fast money so he could help with support before he came to meet his child. Jesse Hughes.

It wasn't to be. Last summer they'd been evacuated when a hurricane headed for the platform, but the last helicopter crashed and they all ended up in the gulf.

A shiver went through Boone as he recalled that awful night. The rough waters that kept pulling him under. The excruciating pain in his injured shoulder. His struggle to stay conscious. Through it all, he kept hearing Russ's voice, telling him not to give up. The guy had been there with him, keeping him afloat until help came.

Boone shut his eyes, seeing Russ's face as the rough waters took him down, all the time knowing it should have been him who died that night.

If Russ hadn't had to rescue him, Jesse wouldn't be without a father.

CHAPTER FOUR

THROUGH THE FOG Boone heard a feminine voice whisper his name. A rush of sensations drifted through him, and his body stirred with longing. He groaned, wanting the dream to go on. Then came the gentlest of touches, and warmth shot through him.

She spoke his name again and he blinked, aching to see her, praying reality would be even better. When he opened his eyes, he saw Amelia Hughes's face in the dim candlelight.

She smiled shyly. "Hi."

"Hi," he returned.

Her gaze was guarded and she stepped back from the bedside. "Sorry to wake you, but you said you wanted us to let you know when it's suppertime. Jesse wasn't sure what to do when he found you asleep."

He wiped a hand across his eyes, taking time to ease his racing pulse. "Thanks, I'm glad you woke me." He swung his legs off the bed and sat up. "I don't usually fall asleep on the job." He checked his watch to see that two hours had truly passed.

"It's probably the boredom," she said. "There isn't much to do trapped in the house."

He definitely hadn't been bored since coming here. The brisk chill in the room made him realize he wasn't going anywhere, not for a while, anyway. He noticed Amelia wore a long sweater that covered her all the way down past her shapely hips. On her feet were heavy, wool socks.

"How's the wood holding out?"

"I've been keeping both fireplaces going, but even after closing off the upstairs, it's still chilly. We're managing for now, but tonight the temperature is predicted to drop well below freezing."

Boone pulled on his boots, trying not to think about the intimacy of her watching him. He stood and walked toward her. At six foot three, he towered over most women, but Amelia was also tall. He liked that. She tilted her head back slightly as her emerald eyes met his gaze. Suddenly his mouth went dry. There wasn't much about this woman that he didn't like. She was definitely trouble.

"I'll bring in more wood."

"It can wait until later," she said. "I don't want your supper to get cold."

He wasn't used to anyone worrying about him. "Okay." With a nod he followed her into the warmer kitchen. The table was adorned with candles and three place settings.

"Hi, Boone." Jesse came over and took his hand, leading him to the seat at the table. "Mom made stew for supper. It's my favorite."

Amelia placed her hands on her hips. "Hey, I thought you liked my macaroni and cheese best."

The boy nodded his head. "I like that, too. I like everything you make." He turned to Boone. "Mom's the best cook. She makes pies for the diner in town. Everybody loves them."

"Jesse," she warned. "Stop bragging."

"I'm only saying what's true, Mom. Even Mrs. Hoffman at church said so. She told my teacher, Miss Claire, that Mom's a good catch."

Amelia gasped. "Jesse Thomas Hughes you're not supposed to listen to other people's conversations."

"But I didn't, Mom. They were talking right to me."

Boone tried hard not to smile as a blushing Amelia came to the table. She avoided his gaze as she placed the soup tureen in the center, then went back for the basket of rolls.

She sat across from Boone. "Enjoy this meal, because if this storm keeps up, no one will be eating anything but canned soup."

"Are we going to be snowed in for Christmas?" The boy looked worried. "And what about Izzy's puppies?"

Amelia spooned up a bowl of stew for Boone. "She's not on her own, we're here to help if she needs us."

Boone took the warm bowl. "Thank you." He looked at Jesse. "I think she can handle it."

"Have you ever seen puppies born?" Jesse asked Boone.

"No, but I've helped with calves and foals. Believe me, mamas know what to do."

Jesse gave his mother a curious look. "Mom, did you know what to do when I was born?"

Even in the dim light, Boone watched another blush cover Amelia's face. "Well, not everything, but I had Aunt Kelley and Gram Ruby with me. And the doctor, of course."

Still looking bewildered, the boy picked up his spoon. "Do I get to help Izzy, too?"

Amelia placed a napkin on her lap. "Well, I'm not sure."

"It depends on Izzy," Boone jumped in. "She might just want to do it all by herself."

"Is that why Mom put a big box in the closet?"

Boone nodded. "So Izzy can have some privacy."

Before Jesse could ask another question, Amelia spoke up. "Let's say grace so we can eat."

Jesse took his mother's hand, then held out the other to Boone. It had been a long time since he had much to pray about, but maybe it was time he started. He took the boy's hand, then reached across the table for Amelia's. For a second he allowed himself to think about a home and family.

Amelia liked the feel of Boone's large hand. Too much. The man was little more than a stranger. That alone sent up warning signals. She definitely couldn't let herself romanticize the situation. She let that happen once, not again. She had a lot more at stake this time than to be foolish enough to allow some good-looking cowboy turn her head.

She glanced at her son as he talked with Boone. It didn't take much to get a five-year-old's attention. Especially since all he'd ever wanted was a father.

"Are you going to be here for Christmas, Boone?"

"Not sure, son. I'm hoping to be back in Texas by then."

"What about your job?" Amelia asked.

His gaze shifted to her as he raised his spoon. "It's temporary. I'd always planned to head back home someday."

"Texas," Jesse said. "Do you have kids there?"

Boone shook his head. "No family to speak of. Not anymore."

The boy's eyes rounded. "Then why not stay here? You can work for Mom and Aunt Kelley."

"Jesse," she said in her best warning tone. Her son had to stop this. "You know we only hire hands during calving season."

"But, Mom…"

Boone stepped in. "It's a nice offer, son, but I'm going to buy my own ranch, in Texas."

"Oh…" Jesse didn't hide his disappointment.

Amelia felt a twinge of the same. She glanced at Boone to find him watching her. Her breathing grew heavy as she locked on his mesmerizing gaze. This was crazy. She'd only just met the man and suddenly she was wanting him to stay around.

Boone turned back to her son. "You see, Jesse, I've been

wanting one particular place for a long time, and now I have a chance to buy it."

The boy looked thoughtful. "Hey, you could buy a ranch in Montana." He turned to his mother. "Right, Mom?"

Hours later the house was quiet as Boone stretched out on the double bed, staring out into the darkness, trying to sleep. But the words that Amelia Hughes spoke earlier were still swimming around in his head:

Boone's place is in Texas, and ours is here in Montana.

He knew it shouldn't bother him, but it had. He'd never had much as a kid.

Years ago, Hank and Jolene Gifford hadn't been much more than day laborers until they scraped enough money together to buy some land of their own. With their old truck loaded up, their son and all their worldly belongings, they arrived in West Texas and their first home.

Many nights, he'd slept in the bed of the pickup until the house was built. His mother took a job in town to help them survive as his father ran a small herd. Boone had worked hard as a boy and continued as a man, building the family ranch.

Their hard work finally paid off until the day he lost both his parents in an accident. He couldn't run the place without his dad.

Now at the age of thirty, he was getting a second chance. Nothing was going to keep him from his dreams this time.

He stood, went to his duffel bag and found the manila envelope tucked under a pair of his jeans. He knew what was inside without even looking. All Russ Eldon's personal effects. Everything his friend had wanted to give his son.

Boone sighed. Coming here wasn't supposed to be so complicated. He'd planned to hand over everything to Amelia Hughes and just leave. Instead he was trapped here in her home, and he was feeling things for the woman he had no business feeling.

He needed to get out of here and fast.

That same husky soft voice called his name again. Boone looked toward the doorway and saw Amelia. Holding a hurricane lantern, she stood shadowed in the dim light. Her dark hair was slightly mussed and she had a blanket bundled around her trim body. Her gaze was questioning.

Boone drew another breath, trying to fight the urges she invoked in him. He zipped the bag and went to her.

"Is there a problem?" he asked.

"I think we're going to need more firewood."

He suddenly became aware of the chill. "Maybe you should turn on the heat, too."

She released a breath. "I'm just worried that the generator won't hold out."

He nodded. "How's Jesse? Is he warm enough?"

She smiled. "He's fine and sound asleep. How are you doing in here?"

"It's not bad." Hell, it was cold.

She smiled at his lie. "Okay, we turn on the heat. But I'll need to close the vents upstairs."

"I'll help you."

He followed her through the kitchen, checking on Jesse as they went. The boy was layered with blankets on the sofa. He followed Amelia up the steps to the second floor where she opened the door at the top.

Amelia felt the drop in temperature immediately. "Oh, burr, it's freezing."

"Colder than a witch's…" Boone began. "It's darn cold." He stood behind her and held up the lantern. "Go back downstairs, Amelia. I can handle this."

She turned, nearly bumping into him. "But I know where all the registers are."

With a nod from him, she headed into her grandmother's bedroom. They worked quickly to shut off the vents, then moved on to Jesse's room. Next, they went into hers. This had been her childhood bedroom and not much had changed since then. It seemed strange to have Boone here. There hadn't been a man in here ever, not even Jesse's father.

She knelt down next to her twin bed, and worked the iron grate, but it wouldn't budge. "Stubborn thing."

Boone appeared, shinning more light. "Here, let me try."

Before she could get out of the way, he leaned over her, and his hard chest brushed against her back. She felt his muscles strain as he fought the stubborn lever and won.

He didn't move away, and strangely, Amelia didn't want him to.

"Where to next?" His voice vibrated against her ear. "Your sister's room?"

"Kelley doesn't live in the house anymore. A few years ago she moved into the foreman's cottage." She stopped her rambling and took a breath to relax. It didn't help. Was she so starved for a man that the slightest contact set her off?

With this man, yes.

He finally moved back. "Then I guess we're finished," he said. "We should head downstairs."

Still on her knees, she turned to face him. In the dim shadows, they were close in the confined space. Dangerously close.

Suddenly she heard her name called. "Mom! Mom! Where are you?"

She broke eye contact, got to her feet and hurried into the hallway. "I'm coming, Jesse."

"Hurry, Mom. Izzy's having her puppies."

CHAPTER FIVE

BOONE FOLLOWED AMELIA downstairs to find the mother-to-be in her box in the pantry. Seeing her owner, Izzy whimpered.

"See, Mom?"

Amelia knelt down inside the narrow enclosure next to her son and gently stroked the dog's head. "What's the matter, girl? Are your babies getting impatient to be born?"

In answer, the animal licked her hand and panted heavily.

"Mom, is Izzy having her puppies now?"

Amelia stood and backed out of the small space. "It looks like it, honey. Maybe we should give her some privacy."

The boy didn't like the idea. "But what if she needs us?"

"She might. So we need to get some towels and thread to tie off the puppies' cords in case she needs help."

When the boy started to argue, Boone spoke up, "Come on, Jesse, I'll help you, too. Do you know where the thread is?"

With the boy's nod, the threesome gathered the things needed and returned for the expected delivery. Wrapped in a blanket, with the lantern next to him, Jesse sat in the doorway waiting.

Boone stood holding another light overhead, and watched in awe as Amelia coaxed the Labrador to push out the first tiny puppy. Jesse gasped in delight, and showed even more excitement as the second and third came along.

"You're doing fine, girl," Amelia spoke to her patient as she wiped off each new arrival. "Here comes another," she said, then amended that. "Oh, and another."

Boone handed Jesse the light and instructed him how to hold it. Then he jumped in and assisted Amelia so none of the puppies would be lost.

By the end, the litter count added up to eight healthy puppies. Amelia gently helped clean the last arrival, and gave it to the mother to begin nursing. Then she worked quickly to remove the soiled towels and replace them with fresh bedding.

Boone took the dirty towels and set them aside, then helped Jesse bring some food and water for the new mother.

"Mom, can we keep one this time?" Jesse pointed to the yellow pup that was busy trying to find a vacant nipple to feed on.

"Honey, we talked about this. You know we have to sell them. Besides, Mr. Clevenger might want that one to keep."

The boy hung his head. "What if I don't want to go to college?"

Amelia looked at Boone. "We started breeding Izzy when our neighbor, Ralph Clevenger, approached us because he had a registered Labrador, too. After Ralph takes his pick, I plan to sell the others and put the money in Jesse's college fund."

Boone wanted to tell Amelia that she didn't have to worry about money for college. Russ had left everything to his son, along with a hefty life insurance policy. But that wouldn't mean much to a little boy who wanted a dad. Instead, Boone spoke to Jesse. "Your mom will make sure they all have good homes with other boys and girls."

Amelia glanced down at the new mother. "This is Izzy's

third litter. I usually have the vet come out to check her. That's not going to happen this time."

He could hear the worry in her voice. "They should be fine for a few days."

"I hope so." Amelia walked to the kitchen sink, then turned on the water and washed her hands and forearms. When she turned, Boone held out a clean towel for her. Even in the shadowed light, he could see her fatigue. But nothing took away from her beauty.

"I can keep an eye on Izzy," he said.

She peeked back into the pantry. "I wouldn't want anything to happen to her."

"The sofa isn't that far away. You take Jesse and at least lie down. I'll stay here."

"You need sleep, too," she said.

"Yeah, Boone," Jesse said. "Come sleep with us."

Boone glanced at Amelia and saw her uneasiness. No way was he intruding any more. "How about if I come sit with you until you fall sleep?"

Jesse let out a yelp, ran to the sofa and dove under the blankets.

Boone followed, but added more logs to the dying fire before heading to the opposite sofa. With the heater running, the room was warmer. Boone sat down and looked across the large coffee table as Amelia tucked her son under the covers, then she moved to the opposite end and took off her boots. She lay back, her brown hair spread against the pillow, making him think about anything but sleep.

"Good night, Boone," Jesse said on a yawn.

Boone jerked his gaze away. "'Night, Jesse." He shut off the lantern, leaned his head against the high-backed sofa and closed his eyes. Just for a minute, he told himself.

The wind howled outside, the cracking of the warm fire combined with the boy's soft snores was like a symphony.

The feel of Amelia's presence, so close but so untouchable, made him ache. He shifted, trying to push away any wayward thoughts. He didn't even know this family twelve hours ago. They didn't know him either, but that didn't seem to matter.

Amelia woke up surprised to see it was daylight. Suddenly thoughts of last night ran through her head.

The blizzard. Izzy! Snowed in with a stranger.

She sat up to see she was alone. The scent of coffee teased her nose as muffled voices came from the kitchen. No doubt it was Jesse and Boone. She glanced at the clock on the mantel. Eight-fifteen!

She got up and walked to the window. Looking out at the beautiful winter scene, she tried to gather her thoughts. A mountain of snow covered everything. She could barely see the barn, and Boone's truck was buried up to the bumper. At least it had stopped snowing. She glanced at the threatening gray sky. For now.

How long before it started again? Would they be able to plow the roads? Restore the power? Get her truck?

Suddenly the isolation bothered her even more. She and Jesse were here with a stranger. A man she was drawn to. In the last twenty-four hours, she'd been thinking about Boone Gifford instead of her grandmother's heart procedure. It was today, and she couldn't even find out how Ruby was doing.

Had Kelley tried to call her? With the utilities out, her sister would be worried about not being able to reach them. Had the storm knocked out power in Helena? She shook her head. She had to stop worrying. Kelley could handle Gram.

Laughter came from the kitchen and she smiled. At least Jesse was happy to be snowed in with a stranger.

And so was she.

Boone wasn't much of a cook, but he could whip up some scrambled eggs when he had to. And this morning he had a good reason. Jesse needed to eat, and so did Amelia. She'd already provided him with two meals yesterday. It was his turn. Besides, with the electricity on only periodically, he wasn't sure how long the food would stay fresh.

He set a plate on the table in front of Jesse. "Here you go, bud."

The boy smiled. "Thanks." He took a big bite. "Why did you call me bud?"

"It's just a friendly term. Short for buddy."

Those brown eyes widened. "I like you calling me that." The boy scooped up a forkful and took a big bite. "This is good."

Boone sat down across from Jesse and began his meal. After a minute the boy had more questions. "Boone, do you think it will stop snowing before Christmas?"

"I expect so. I'm not an expert, but it will probably stop in a few days."

"Oh." Jesse looked disappointed.

"You don't want it to stop?"

Jesse shook his head. "I want you to stay here."

The boy climbed off his chair and went to a calendar hanging on the wall that revealed the month of December, with big *X*s marked through half of the days. "See, we have eleven days before Christmas. I don't want you to leave."

"Jesse, I can't stay until Christmas."

"But what about my wish? And I wrote Santa."

Boone had no idea how to answer him. "I just happened along, bud. I have to go back to Texas."

Tears blurred the boy's eyes. "Who's going to help me cut down a tree?"

Lost childhood memories flashed into Boone's head. He and his dad used to do that while his mother was home cooking. He blinked and focused on Jesse. "You cut down your own Christmas tree?"

The boy nodded and wiped his eyes. "Yeah, Gram, Mom and Aunt Kelley and me. This year Mom said I'm old enough to use the saw. What are we going to do if it doesn't stop snowing?"

"It's going to stop." He hoped that was true. "And you'll get your tree."

"Oh, boy, can you help us this year?"

"Can Boone help us do what?"

They both turned to see Amelia stroll into the kitchen. She was wearing the same jeans and sweatshirt, now wrinkled from sleep. Her hair was mussed and hung against her shoulders.

"Hi, Mom." He went flying across the room and hugged her. "Boone said you were tired and we should let you sleep. He fixed me breakfast, and he can help us cut down a tree." The boy finally took a breath.

Her gaze met Boone's and she smiled. He felt it all the way into his gut.

"Looks like you two have been making a lot of plans. Did you also happen to notice all the snow?"

"When it stops we can go," Jesse said hopefully. "Boone said we have plenty of time before Christmas."

Boone couldn't stop the boy's excitement, or his heart racing as Amelia looked at him.

All he managed was a nod at the coffeemaker. "Coffee?"

"Please," she said. "I think I'm going to need it." She followed him to the counter. He filled a mug and handed it to her. Close up her eyes were dark from sleep.

"I brewed some coffee while the generator was on."

She took a sip and sighed. "So worth it." Her gaze met his, then glanced away. "It has stopped snowing, but probably not for long."

He wasn't happy about the forecast. "So there's no hope that it will warm up today and melt the snow?"

She smiled and his heart tripped again. “Getting cabin fever?”

“I did get out to the barn,” he told her. “Had to do a little shoveling to get there.”

Amelia’s son jumped into the conversation. “Boone wouldn’t let me go with him. I had to promise to stay here.” The boy smiled. “I got to watch the puppies, so Izzy could go outside and do her business.”

Amelia tried to keep her focus on Jesse, but having Boone in her kitchen was definitely a distraction. Especially a man who handled chores and could cook breakfast.

“Thanks for your help, honey. Why don’t you finish your breakfast before it gets cold?” She expected an argument, but Jesse only walked back to his seat.

She had no choice but to acknowledge Boone. “Thank you for letting me sleep.”

He shrugged. “I didn’t see any reason to wake you. You were sleeping so soundly.”

She took another sip. “How did the horses do last night?”

“They were fine. Happy for a little attention.”

She leaned against the counter and watched her son eat. “Kelley usually handles their care. But someone had to take Gram for her procedure.” She frowned. “I just wish I knew how the procedure went. If everything went well, they should come home tomorrow.” She glanced out the window. “That isn’t going to happen, either.”

Boone knew that if Kelley Hughes came home, she’d discover he wasn’t the ranch hand she’d hired. He used that rationalization for not telling Amelia the truth. Right now, she needed his help. With another winter storm coming, they seemed destined to stay together. But he still needed to tell her the reason for his visit, and soon.

But he still wanted to ease her mind. "Do you have a cell phone?"

She nodded. "It's funny, but there's poor reception inside the house." She went into the other room then returned with her phone. "No service."

"Your grandmother is in the best place possible. If this storm came any earlier she could have been stranded here and unable to get the care she needed."

Amelia nodded. "I know you're right, but it doesn't stop me from worrying. She's my family. Gram raised Kelley and me. Jesse, too. She's our rock. She wasn't too keen on having the procedure. Somehow Kelley talked her into it." She smiled. "Kelley's a little more forceful than I am."

"So you three run this place?"

"Yes. A mama-and-baby cattle operation, and a yearling herd in the summer. We lease some of the grazing land and rent out three cabins during hunting season."

"That's a lot for three people to handle."

"It didn't start out that way. When we were little, our parents moved here to work in the cattle business. Mom died shortly after I was born, and we were barely settled here when Dad was thrown from his horse. He was in a coma for a while, then he eventually died.

"Grandma Ruby and Granddad Jesse stepped in and raised us. Then about six years ago, Granddad died. Gram said we had no choice but to go on."

Amelia drew a breath and released it, but he could still see her pain as she looked at him. "What about you, Boone Gifford? You said you were buying a place in Texas. Where?"

He drank the rest of his coffee. "Outside of Odessa, Texas. It had been my family's place, but when my parents passed away, I couldn't make a go of it on my own. Now I have a little more capital to carry me through the rough times. I'm hoping to buy the ranch back from the bank."

"There sure are enough foreclosures around here," Amelia added. "Is there anyone else back there to help you?"

He shook his head. There had been someone once, until he lost everything, but he didn't want to talk about the past. "It's just me." He suddenly realized how sad that sounded.

CHAPTER SIX

BOONE STARED OUT the kitchen window as night began to fall on his second day trapped with Amelia Hughes. Again flurries started blowing against the window, letting them know that another storm was brewing. He'd hoped that if the weather held tonight, he could take off tomorrow. Only, that meant he'd be leaving Amelia and Jesse to fend for themselves.

He couldn't do it.

That was the excuse he'd given himself all day to keep from mentioning Russ's name and handing over his friend's personal things. Worse, it would mean spoiling a little boy's Christmas.

Instead he'd kept the fireplaces going, fed the stock just as if he were the hired hand. He also occupied Jesse to keep him from being bored. It wasn't hard. He liked spending time with the boy, even with his endless questions that every kid asked.

He'd also been plagued by a different kind of guilt. If Russ hadn't hung back to save him, he might be here himself to meet his son.

Boone couldn't think about that now. He had to fulfill his promise. Somehow before he left the Rocking H Ranch, he had to find a way to tell Amelia the truth about his connection to Jesse's father.

He glanced at Amelia. Earlier he'd made it out to the barn to check on the animals. The temperature had risen some during the day, but after hearing the forecast on the radio, he had no doubt they were in for more snow. So that meant he had to stay put for now.

He got up from the kitchen table while Jesse set up another game for them and went into the living room to find the beautiful brunette pacing. Tall and graceful, Amelia reminded him of a Thoroughbred with her fine bones and delicate features.

Were the men around here blind? Even after only a few days together, she was going to be hard to leave.

"Amelia," he called to her.

She turned around. "What?"

"Worrying isn't going to help."

She seemed to relax a little and offered him a hint of a smile. "I know." She sighed. "I guess I'm the one with cabin fever now."

"It's understandable."

"We haven't had a bad storm like this for a few years. I guess we're overdue." She looked out the window at the fading light. "I normally love this time of year. It's beautiful here with the mountains covered in snow." She raised her startling green eyes to his. "I guess I miss Kelley and my grandmother, too. What if something has happened to Gram, and Kel can't reach me?"

He shook his head. "You can't think that way. From what you've said about her, she's a strong woman."

A smile appeared on her pretty face. "Yeah, she is. We had to fight to even get her to go to the hospital. And the doctor said she was healthy enough to handle this procedure."

"See. She's strong like I said."

"You have to be when you run a ranch."

Amelia enjoyed talking with Boone. She didn't get much male companionship, and she never realized how much she missed it. And she had to admit, it was nice to lean on someone for a change. Just so she remembered that he was doing a job, and he'd be leaving for Texas soon. If she were looking for something serious, Boone wasn't the man. He wasn't even from around here. And Montana was her home.

Besides, she wasn't sure she could trust a man again. That foolish girl who'd been willing to run off with the first guy who'd given her attention no longer existed. She was a mother now and had to think about her child. No matter how attached Jesse was getting to Boone, she had to make him understand that the ranch hand wasn't staying around.

His voice broke into her thoughts. "It's nice you have your family."

She nodded. "They've both been there for me and my son."

"From what I gather from Jesse, his dad hasn't been in his life."

Amelia never explained her life to strangers. She'd never needed to before. "It's no secret that I never married Jesse's father. When Russ found out I was pregnant, he took off. Never heard from him again."

"You must have been pretty young."

She glanced away. "And naive. It's funny how easy it is to let love cloud your judgment. Yet, at nineteen, I'm not sure we even know what it is."

"Love can do that to you."

Something in his low tone of voice caused her to turn around. "Sounds like you have your own experiences."

He shrugged. "Past history. I found out in time."

Amelia could see a flash of hurt. She wanted to reach out to him, but she held back. "Were you married?"

His dark eyes met hers. "No, but we planned to, before I lost the ranch."

"She left you?"

His jaw tightened. "I don't blame her. I didn't have anything to offer her."

"Don't say that. You had love. She should have stood by you. Together you could have worked to get it back. That's what love is, working for a future." She crossed her arms. "Well, you're lucky to be rid of her."

An easy smile crossed his face. "You are fierce when riled. Remind me never to cross you."

"I'm sorry. It just seems that so many people just walk away when things get too rough. A commitment means sticking it out through the hard times as well as the good times." She blinked at the sudden tears welling in her eyes. "You had to be devastated, losing your home, then someone you love. I'm sorry." She moved away, swiping at the rush of tears. "I don't know what's wrong with me."

He touched her arm. "No, Amelia. Please, you have no reason to be sorry." He came closer. "Besides, it was a long time ago. I don't think about Kendra anymore."

"Good. She doesn't deserve your time."

"God, Amelia. I wish…"

His dark gaze held hers, and Amelia knew it could be trouble. She wanted to blame what she was feeling on the storm and their being thrown together.

"If only I had met someone like you," Boone began.

"Yeah, right. A single mother with a child. Not that I've been pining after Russ after all these years. I haven't. It took a while, but I realized I don't need a man to make me complete. Of course, that doesn't mean men are exactly beating down my door."

"Then, they aren't worth your time. And they sure don't deserve you. If things were different—"

Amelia held up a hand. She didn't need to hear his reasons why he couldn't be that man. "It's okay, Boone."

She started to move away, but he stopped her. "I was about

to say there are things you don't know about me. And there's also the fact that you live in Montana and I live in Texas."

Three hours later Boone was in his room. Restless, he'd done a fifteen-minute workout, hoping exhaustion would help him sleep. He should be used to the confinement after living and working on the oil platform, except there he had television and other guys to talk to.

All he had here was a five-year-old boy and one beautiful woman, making him realize what was missing in his life. And tonight he nearly stepped over the line. Just touching Amelia's softness had him reeling with need. It had taken everything in him to keep from dragging her into his arms and kissing her senseless. Great, he was turning into some sex-starved maniac.

Boone suddenly heard the puppies' cries. He hurried to the pantry, hoping they hadn't woken up anyone else in the house. Amelia was already there. She was leaning over the box. He started to move away, but she turned toward him.

"Seems they want some attention." She stroked the tiny animal in her hands.

Boone couldn't resist and sank down beside her, trying not to notice as his leg rubbed against hers. He scratched Izzy's head, then gently scooped up one of her crying babies. "You know, you're spoiling them," he told her.

"Everyone needs some spoiling. Besides, I don't get to keep them long. All these precious babies will be in other homes soon."

He smiled down at the now-sleeping chocolate-colored pup. He wouldn't mind having one of these himself. He shook away the thought. It would be another connection to Amelia Hughes, and give him a reason to keep in touch. She probably wouldn't want to when she learned the truth about him.

Amelia propped her back against the shelves that stored

canned goods. Boone did the same on the other side. Even though the small closet was cold, it wasn't bad, or was it the fact she warmed his blood whenever she got near him?

"Jesse asleep?" he asked.

She nodded. "He fought it for a long time, but lost in the end. Thank you for helping burn off some of his energy earlier."

"He does seem to have a lot to burn, doesn't he?"

"Always had." Amelia smiled as if she were remembering. "Even as a baby. He crawled at five months, and was walking before he was a year old." She continued to stroke the puppy. "I guess I should say running. He hasn't stopped since."

"He's a fine boy, Amelia. Any man would be proud to have him for a son."

"Thank you." Her smile faded. "There are times when I think I've cheated Jesse, with him not having a father."

This was the time he could tell her. "Earlier you said the boy's father was never in his life. Have you explained why to Jesse?"

She shook her head, but didn't seem angry at the question. "Somewhere around the age of four he began asking about his daddy. I only told him that he lived somewhere else. Then this year he went off to kindergarten and discovered all the other kids had fathers." She glanced at him. "That's how this silly Christmas wish came about. A little girl on the school bus, Emma Clark, told him to make a wish for one. Jesse took it to heart." She released a long breath. "I don't know what's going to happen when Christmas arrives and he has to face reality."

"It's a hard lesson for a little boy. I wish…" He hesitated and looked at her. "I wish things could be different."

She smiled and his gut tightened with longing.

"You know what they say," she began "'If wishes were horses, beggars would ride.'"

He nodded, silently cursing Russ for putting him in this spot, and for waiting so long to contact his son. Now it was too late, and Boone had to bring the bad news to a little boy. "I know I won't be around much longer, but if you ever need anything for the boy, you can call me."

Amelia was shocked by Boone's offer. It also made her look at reality, too. He'd be going back to Texas. "Oh, Boone, that's sweet of you, but we can't intrude on your life. Besides, you'll be so far away."

"Not that far." He put the pup back with its mother.

Amelia couldn't stop looking at his hands. His palms were large and his fingers long and tapered. What would they feel like against her skin? A shiver ran down her spine. She shook away the thought. "But you'll have your own life."

"I doubt I'll have time for a life if I'm busy with a ranch." He shrugged, his gaze focused on her. "A boy needs a man around when he gets to a certain age." Then hurried on to say, "That's not to say you won't find someone, you're very attractive. But if you don't, then you can always call me."

Amelia's heart pounded as she put her pup back with Izzy, then bravely leaned forward and planted a chaste kiss on Boone's cheek. She pulled back slightly and swallowed hard. "You're a sweet man, Boone Gifford."

The look in his eyes quickly changed as the irises darkened to a smoldering black. "You wouldn't say that if you knew what I was thinking right now." His voice was low and husky.

Amelia knew she should get out of there, but it had been so long since she'd been close to a man. A man who stirred her. A man who made her yearn to feel his touch, his kiss.

She threw caution to the wind and said, "Tell me, Boone."

He didn't hide his surprise, as he reached out and cupped

her face. "Can't seem to find the words, darlin'. I'll show you," he breathed as his mouth closed over hers.

The kiss was gentle at first, but it still sent Amelia's heart racing, as she hoped and prayed that he would never stop. Her hopes were answered as he pulled her against him and deepened the connection. His tongue slid along her lips until she opened for him, letting him inside to caress and taste her. With a moan she wrapped her arms around his neck and used her tongue to tease him.

On a groan, his hand moved to her breasts, stroking their fullness. He broke off the kiss, his gaze searching her face. Neither spoke as he dipped his head and kissed her again and again. She'd never known such hunger, such need. She'd kissed men since Russ, but it had never felt like this.

Boone's hand slipped under her sweater, touching her skin, raising goose bumps as he reached her bra and managed to unhook the lacy garment. On a whimper, she arched her back as his masterful hands began to stroke and knead her breasts.

"Oh, Boone," she gasped.

He ran kisses down her neck, his breathing heavy. "You want more?" His fingers toyed with her nipple, causing it to tighten into a hard nub. He quickly moved to the other.

"Please," she said.

Suddenly a whimpering sound broke them apart. Izzy was standing next to them.

Boone released her. "Looks like someone else needs our attention."

"I better let her out," Amelia said as she stood.

"No, I'll do it." Boone was out of the pantry before Amelia could say anything.

Five minutes later Boone cursed at himself while he gathered wood as he waited for Izzy to finish her business. What had he been thinking? Apparently, he hadn't been thinking at all when he'd kissed Amelia Hughes. And the last thing he needed to do was fall for this woman. In the end she was going to hate him.

The chocolate lab was easy to spot in the snow. "You ready to go back inside, girl?" In answer the dog bounded up the steps. Boone wasn't as eager to return, knowing he was lying to a woman he was crazy about. He'd lost her before he'd even had a chance to win her.

CHAPTER SEVEN

THE NEXT DAY it was cold and gloomy. The snow had stopped, and all Amelia wanted to do was get out of the house. She wasn't used to being confined for so long. Maybe it wouldn't be so bad if she could hear from Kelley.

She'd listened to the news on the radio and discovered the storm had crippled the entire area, including Helena. Luckily, the weather system was moving on. Now if it would warm up enough so the snow would melt.

She wanted work crews to restore electricity and phone service. Then Boone Gifford could go back to the Sky High Ranch and things would get back to normal. She glanced at the man seated at the kitchen table with Jesse. The same man she'd kissed last night. The same man whose sure hands had caressed her skin, teasing her with a taste of pleasure she'd never experienced before. She bit back a moan of frustration.

"Mom? Are you okay?"

She fought at hiding a blush. "I'm fine, honey. Just tired of being inside."

The boy's brown eyes widened. "Boone said if it's okay with you, and I dress warm, I can go to the barn with him when he feeds the horses."

Amelia stole a glance at the man she'd been avoiding all

morning. He acted as if she was the last person he wanted to be around.

Before she could respond Boone stood. "If you're worried, you're more than welcome to come, too." His gaze met hers. "I expect we're all a little stir crazy."

She nodded. "Yes, I am. I'd be happy to have the electricity back on, too."

"I like it this way," Jesse said. "I don't have to go to school. I get to stay here with Boone."

Amelia was surprised by his statement. "I thought you liked school."

"I do. But I like staying here, too. I like Boone here, too."

"But I can't stay much longer, bud," Boone told him. "I'd planned to be back in Texas soon."

Jesse's head snapped up. "Before Christmas?"

Boone was caught between a rock and a hard place. No matter how he answered he couldn't make them both happy. "I haven't decided yet."

"We still have a while before the holidays," Amelia said.

"But what about getting a tree? Even Gram said we need to have a tree for Christmas. She promised."

"Jesse, I can't promise anything right now. Not until I hear from Aunt Kelley. Gram may need special attention when she gets home."

Boone couldn't handle the boy's disappointment. "I'll tell you what, Jesse. I won't leave until we cut down the tree."

"You mean it?"

Boone glanced at Amelia, seeing her surprise.

Grinning, Jesse got up and came around the table to hug him. "Thank you, Boone. Can we get one today?"

A funny feeling erupted in Boone's gut as the boy's arms came around him. He looked at Amelia as she folded her arms across her chest, cocked an eyebrow and waited for his answer.

"Not today. If the weather holds up, maybe tomorrow."

"Yippy," the boy cried as he ran out of the room.

Boone finally turned to Amelia. She looked beautiful this morning. Her dark hair was pulled back into a ponytail, and her face was scrubbed clean. She took his breath away. That was the main reason he had to get out of here. She was too tempting. And he'd fallen into that temptation last night.

"You shouldn't make promises you can't keep," she said.

"I'm not. Unless you have a problem with me taking him to cut down a tree?"

"Not if I go with you."

"Of course you're welcome. I just figured it's the least I could do."

She seemed angry. "You don't owe anything to my son or to me."

Yes, he did. "It's hard not to care about the boy." He stood and came toward her. "It was you I didn't expect. I never should have crossed the line last night. I apologize. And I don't want you to feel as if you have to worry about it happening again."

She swallowed. "You have feelings for me?"

He blinked and inhaled her sweet fragrance. "Yeah, if things could be different…" He let the words trail off. "You don't need to worry, though, I'll be gone soon."

She started to say something when Jesse ran into the room. "Mom, I put on my long johns and heavy pants."

"Good," she said, then looked at Boone. "Give me twenty minutes to put on the leftovers from last night."

"We can wait," Boone said, and watched her walk out to the mud room and the freezer.

Luckily, they'd been able to store food out there. And with

a propane stove, Amelia had still been able to cook. Hell, she'd come up with some pretty elaborate meals. Even dessert.

He thought about when he went back to Texas. He'd be fending for himself. And he'd be alone. No child's laughter, no woman's touch. Amelia's softness was part of who she was. It was natural for her to stroke her son's hair, kiss him or laugh easily at something he said.

Thoughts of last night came rushing back with a jolt. Her kisses that had him so turned on he couldn't think, only feel. But there was a big possibility that she wouldn't want anything to do with him when she learned his secret. So he had to keep thinking of her as off-limits.

Amelia came back from the freezer carrying a large plastic container and a pie wrapped in heavy plastic. With a smile, she held up her findings. "I also found a pie. Apple. And I'll make some biscuits."

"Sounds great," he agreed. Everything around here was great. So much so he never wanted to leave. But he had to. He knew he'd never be welcome here once he told her why he'd come.

Amelia followed closely behind Boone, who'd taken charge of Jesse as they trekked through the snow toward the barn. Her son was busy asking a dozen questions.

She wanted to tell him to stop, but knew the child had been so good over the past few days of being stuck indoors. And Boone was the reason for that. The man had the patience of a saint to put up with an inquisitive five-year-old.

They reached the large door, and Boone rolled it back just enough for them to get through. Once inside, he closed it, and they stomped the snow off their boots. Luckily, there was sunlight coming in through a window up in the loft, helping them find their way around. Boone also turned on his large flashlight.

The familiar scent of horses and manure assaulted her nose. She didn't mind it at all. This was her life and she loved living out here.

"I think I better muck out some stalls," she said as she went to turn on a few of the battery lanterns next to the stalls.

"I'll help, Mom."

"No need," Boone said.

"We'll all help." Amelia turned to her son. "Right, Jesse?"

The boy nodded, went to the first stall and climbed up on the slats to pet the red roan gelding. "This is the horse I ride, Spitfire. I call him Fire." He rubbed the horse's nose. "He was grandpa's horse, but he died before I was born."

The boy continued with his introductions. "That's Penny. She's Mom's." He pointed to the stall across from them. "And that's Risky. He's Aunt Kelley's horse. Mom says she's going to break her neck someday because he's crazy."

Boone walked across the aisle to the large chestnut gelding. He had a feeling this horse matched Kelley Hughes perfectly. "He's a good-looking animal." Boone rubbed the horse's muzzle.

Amelia came over, too. "He's got a little too much attitude for me."

"That's what Aunt Kelley likes." Jesse climbed down from the stall railing. "She says Risky keeps her on her toes."

Amelia smiled. "Or her bottom," she murmured. "How many times has this horse bucked her off?"

Jesse laughed. "I'm gonna tell her you said that."

Amelia gave an exaggerated gasp. "You're such a traitor. Okay, what's it gonna cost me to keep you quiet?"

He gave her a sheepish grin. "Chocolate brownies."

Amelia placed her hands on her hips, continuing the game. "My Peppermint Kiss Brownies?"

"Sprinkled with crushed candy canes."

She turned to Boone and cocked an eyebrow. "And will that buy your silence, too?" she asked, including him, too.

"Say yes, Boone," Jesse begged. "They're her special Christmas brownies."

His gaze connected with Amelia's. He wouldn't mind her sweetening the deal with a few kisses. "I can be bought."

Amelia seemed to be just as mesmerized. "I have to check to see if I have all the ingredients. If not, I'll have to wait to make a trip to town."

Boone nodded, knowing he wouldn't be around to sample them, or a lot of other things he'd come to like since he'd been here. "I better get to work."

He turned toward the feed bin, and Jesse followed him. Amelia, on the other hand, went for the wheelbarrow and pitch fork and headed for Penny's stall to clean it.

He wanted to stop her, but he knew that women and men shared the chores on a ranch. Especially women who didn't have a man around. For a second, he let himself think about staying. Then he quickly dismissed the idea. After learning of his deception, Amelia Hughes wouldn't want him here.

"Come on, bud. Let's hurry so we can help your mom."

It took just minutes to feed the animals, but mucking out the stalls took a lot longer. Once fresh straw was spread out and water buckets filled, they were pretty much finished for the day.

Jesse followed Boone outside. After clearing a spot of snow, they dumped the barn waste. But before heading back to the house, the boy pointed to the grove of pine trees about two hundred yards away that covered the hillside.

"See, Boone, that's where we go to get our tree."

"That's not too far, Jesse."

"Then can we go and find a tree?"

"The problem is, bud, we can't get there. The snow is still too deep."

The child jerked his cap-covered head around to his mother. "Mom, can we go on the snowmobile?"

Amelia looked thoughtful, then said, "I guess we could."

"Have you ever driven a snowmobile, Boone?"

He shook his head. "There's no need in Texas."

She turned back to her son. "Let's give the weather one more day, Jesse. Tomorrow if the weather holds. Maybe."

The boy couldn't hide his disappointment as they all trudged back to the house.

"You don't have to do this, Boone," Amelia said softly. "Cutting down a tree wasn't part of your job description."

"It's not a problem, Amelia." The snow crushed under their booted feet as they measured each slippery step. Their bodies brushed in the narrow path.

Amelia spoke first. "There are more immediate things to deal with than a Christmas tree."

"Not to a little boy." He studied her profile, her pert nose and rosy cheeks. Her lips looked a little chapped, and he wondered if it was from the cold, or his kisses. "So, if it isn't a problem for you, I wouldn't mind going out tomorrow."

"It's not a problem." She turned to him, and suddenly lost her balance. He reached out and grabbed her, pulling her against him. Even through their heavy clothing, he felt her warmth, her softness.

"You should be careful," he said. "You could hurt yourself."

Their gazes held for what seemed to be an eternity. He couldn't do anything to stop the urge to lean forward and kiss her. He nearly did, but then they heard Jesse call.

"Mom, the phone rang. It's Aunt Kelley."

"Tell her I'm coming." She scrambled to break away and carefully made her way to the house.

Boone hung back. This could be it if Kelley informed Amelia that he wasn't the man hired to help out. He glanced toward his truck, still half-buried in snow. Even if he dug it out, he doubted he could handle the unplowed roads.

He continued the trip to the house and went inside in time to see Amelia hang up the phone. She turned and he saw the tears in her eyes.

He went to her. "What happened?"

She shook her head. "Nothing. Gram is fine. She just came out of surgery a few hours ago. They held it off until today. Because of the storm, the hospital only took care of emergency cases until electricity was restored." A smile broke out. "She's going to be fine. The angioplasty went great. And obviously the phones are back up."

"That's wonderful. So they'll be coming home soon."

"Kelley said it wouldn't be for a few days."

Jesse stepped in. "Then tomorrow we can get the tree and surprise Gram Ruby."

"It's still up to Boone."

They both looked at him. There had been a lot he couldn't do because of the situation, but he wasn't going to disappoint a boy at Christmas.

"We'll find a way to do it."

CHAPTER EIGHT

LATER THAT NIGHT Boone stood at the window, looking out at the brightly lit yard that allowed him to see all the way to the barn. The electricity had been restored just hours ago. Tomorrow the forecast was for sunny skies and warmer temperatures. That meant roads would soon be cleared and he could leave, but not before he finished his business here.

First, he had to keep a promise to a little boy and cut down a tree. He smiled, realizing he was looking forward to it himself. How long had it been since he'd had a Christmas tree? Since he'd celebrated the holidays, for that matter?

He flashed back to his childhood and his parents' ranch. How his mother had decorated the house for the holidays. They'd never had much money, but she always came up with some kind of special gifts.

Seeing Jesse's enthusiasm reminded him of the things every kid should have. A happy Christmas. The boy had a lot, except for a dad, but that was what he wanted most of all.

For a split second Boone thought about Jesse's Christmas wish. The idea was farfetched, maybe he was even crazy to think he could fill the spot as the five-year-old's dad. Yet he couldn't stop thinking about it. Or about Amelia.

Boone drove his fingers through his hair. She was a beautiful woman who kept him awake at night. It wasn't just her beauty that drew him, she had strength and courage. His gut tightened as he thought about the way she looked at him with those rich-green eyes. He felt his body stir as he recalled her hands on him. Damn, he was halfway in love with her already.

"Boone."

He swung around to see Jesse dressed in pajamas. "Hi, kid. Looks like you're ready for bed."

"Yeah, Mom's making me sleep in my room."

Amelia appeared from the kitchen. "I think we all need a good night's sleep. Besides, you get to watch your favorite video."

"I know," he said. "I want to say good-night to Boone, first." Before Boone realized what the boy intended, he came to him and hugged him around the waist. "'Night, Boone."

Boone placed his hands on the boy's shoulders, and his chest tightened. "'Night, bud, see you in the morning."

Jesse pulled back and looked up at him with big brown eyes. "And we're going to find a tree tomorrow?"

"I'm planning on it."

The boy rewarded him with a big grin. "Okay!" He took off and ran up the stairs.

Boone turned to find Amelia smiling at him. "It's still okay to go, isn't it?"

"Yes." She walked toward him.

His heart raced as she drew closer, then reached up and planted a kiss on his cheek. He wanted to pull her into his arms but resisted and remained still.

She pulled back. "Thank you," she whispered, then turned and followed after her son.

"You're welcome," he breathed as she disappeared upstairs. He blew out a breath. Okay, maybe he was all the way in love with her. What made it worse, he knew she had feelings for him, too. But after tomorrow, when he told her the truth, would she still have those feelings?

* * *

The next morning the weather was brisk but sunny. Bundled up in heavy coats, scarves and gloves, Amelia led the group out to the shed. After clearing away the snow, Boone slid the door open and they went inside. The two brightly painted snowmobiles were fairly new and well cared for, Boone concluded, as he put a small hand saw and some rope into the compartment.

Amelia gave Boone some basic instructions, then went to her sled. Jesse climbed on behind his mother and she looked over her shoulder. "We're not going to cut down a huge tree, Jesse," she said. "Let's keep it between six and seven feet."

"How tall is that?" the boy asked.

"Just a little taller than me," Boone said as he climbed on the other vehicle, started it, then drove out of the shed. He rode around the yard, getting a feel for the machine. Amelia, with Jesse onboard, led the way over the deep-packed snow. The trip didn't take long, as they stopped a few hundred yards from the house.

Boone climbed off, but instead of looking at the trees, he glanced back at the compound. The sprawling green house with white shutters, the red barn with a circle of fencing around the corral. It reminded him of a Christmas card.

"Is something wrong?"

He shook his head. "No. It's just about perfect. This is incredibly beautiful."

Amelia's expression showed her pride. "I've always thought so," she said. "Worth putting up with an occasional blizzard. You should see it in the spring. It's so lush and green."

He could only imagine. "How large is your place?"

She pointed toward the mountain range. "About seven sections. To the foothills in the west, and to the south we border the Sky High Ranch. The Anderson place is to the east. It's been up for sale this past year. Kelley would like to buy it, if only for the water and prime grazing land. The price is a steal, but we don't have the capital right now."

For a brief moment he allowed himself to think about what would happen if he decided to stay here and bought the Anderson place. He quickly shook off the idea. Texas had always been where he'd called home.

"Hey, Mom. Boone."

They both turned to see Jesse already on the search. He was standing beside a huge pine.

"Is this too big?"

Boone marched through the snow. "Let me see, bud." He stood next to the eight-foot-plus tree. "I think we'd have some trouble getting this one into the house."

He glanced at Amelia to see her smiling at him, and he had trouble concentrating on finding a tree. Every time he glanced in her direction, she seemed to be watching him.

When Boone helped Jesse up the steep slope, he suddenly felt a thud against his back. He turned and found Amelia packing another snowball between her hands. Without hesitation she threw it at him. He ducked just in time.

Boone smiled. "Hey, are you trying to start something?"

"Just thought I'd introduce you to a Montana pastime. You don't get any chances like this in Texas. I bet you don't even know how to make a snowball."

Before she had a chance to fire off the next one, Boone took cover behind the tree, and Jesse quickly followed him.

"Your mom's a good shot."

The boy nodded. "She's good with a rifle, too."

"That's nice to know." Boone scooped up a handful of snow and formed a ball. He stepped out to throw it and got hit square in the chest. He shot his off, but it hit the tree.

He heard the feminine laughter and smiled. "Looks like I need to show your mom I know how to play, too."

He glanced around the area. "I need to sneak up behind her. You stay here and keep throwing snowballs."

The boy grinned. "It's the boys against the girls, huh?"

"That's right." Boone took off up the hill, then circled around the trees until he ended up behind Amelia.

"Come on, Boone, come out and face me like a man," she yelled. "You, too, Jesse."

Boone came closer. "Maybe you should come out, too."

With a gasp, Amelia swung around to get off a shot. Boone was quicker, and grabbed her, trapping her loaded hand between them. "You better drop it, Amelia. You've lost."

She squirmed to get out of his hold. "Never."

He sucked in cold air to cool off the blast of heat she caused. "I guess I have to make you surrender."

"You can try, buster."

Her struggle threw them both off balance and they ended up in the snow. He landed on the bottom to cushion her fall, but he quickly reversed their positions. He looked down at the beautiful Amelia. Their eyes locked and he couldn't take his next breath. That wasn't all she caused; she made him forget all about common sense.

He groaned. "You're going to be the death of me, woman." He started to dip his head to hers when he heard Jesse's voice. Damn if he hadn't forgotten about the boy.

Boone glanced up the hill to see Jesse trudging through the snow. "Yeah, Boone, you captured Mom," he said.

He looked down at Amelia, fighting the temptation. "I guess I did, but if we're going to find a tree, I better let her go."

Boone got to his feet, then offered a hand to help her up. Once standing, she quickly turned her attention to her son.

"You know, Jesse," she said. "I saw a tree the other day that was about the right size."

"Aw, Mom. I want to pick it out this year."

She nodded. "Okay, but I thought if we got back in time, we could make a batch of Christmas cookies."

The boy's face lit up. "Well, maybe you can kind of show me where the tree is."

Amelia rubbed her hands together. "All right, let's go get a tree. It's cold out here."

Not to Boone. His body had plenty of heat. "Lead the way."

Together they made their way up the hill through the grove of trees. When Jesse gave his okay on the pine his mother found, Boone went back for the saw and rope.

Twenty minutes later they pulled up at the back door. Boone carried the tree to the porch with Jesse's help and Amelia's direction.

Next, he followed her up to the attic to carry down the tree stand and lights. Within the next hour the tree had been put in the stand and moved in front of the living room windows.

Jesse stood back and inspected the position of the tree. "Now Gram Ruby can see it when she comes home tomorrow."

After Boone had strung the lights and plugged them in, Amelia stood back with her son and admired the job. Watching this man take charge of things and interact with her son so patiently, she found just another thing to admire about him. Not that she needed any more. Even knowing he wasn't staying around, she still couldn't stop the growing attraction. Today in the snow had proved that. She wanted him to kiss her. Even his simple touch left her wanting more. It had been so long since any man made her feel like a woman.

She felt a tugging on her sweater. "Mom, can I start putting on the ornaments?"

"Sure. I'll help."

Boone climbed down from the ladder and started to leave. "I'll go check on the stock."

"No, Boone." Jesse raced to him. "Don't go!"

Boone shot a glance at Amelia. "I think this is a family tradition you should share with your mother."

"But I want you to help, too," Jesse argued.

Amelia realized that she wanted Boone to share this time, too. She held out a shiny ball. "Please, stay and help."

It was after nine o'clock that night when Amelia finally had tucked her son in his bed. For the first time in a long time, she wanted to rush the ritual. Her thoughts were on Boone as they had been every day and night since he'd come here. The man had come into their lives during a crisis, and she was going to do everything she could to get him to stay.

"Mom…"

Amelia stopped at the door. "What, honey?"

"I don't want Boone to go away."

She had expected this. She just didn't know what to do about it. "You know he lives in Texas. It's his home."

In the dimly lit room, she watched her son sit up. "Why can't he live here with us? I know he likes us. Gram Ruby and Aunt Kelley will like him, too."

She knew her sister would have doubts about any man. Amelia walked back in and sat down on the edge of the bed. "Of course he likes us, you especially."

"And he likes you, too."

Amelia felt a blush rising to her cheeks. "Well, I like Boone, too."

"Maybe you can marry Boone so he can be my dad."

She gasped, but secretly wished she could give her son what he wanted. "Jesse, we've talked about this. You can't just wish for a dad and have him appear."

"But I did wish, and Boone did come."

"That's because Aunt Kelley hired him to help us during the storm." She brushed back hair from his forehead. "And when Kelley and Gram get home tomorrow, Boone has to leave."

"Not if you tell him you want him to stay." Big tears ran down his cheeks. "I know you like him. Please, Mom. Don't let him go away."

She pulled her child into a tight embrace as tears flooded her own eyes. "Oh, Jesse. I love you so much, and I wish I could give you what you want, but I can't. I can't give you a dad."

The boy raised his head. "Why don't you ask him?"

Boone rolled over in bed. He heard the clock on the mantel chime twice. Two in the morning. He rolled over trying to erase everything from his mind so he could get some sleep. He tossed and turned, trying to convince himself that not telling Amelia the truth was what he had to do.

He sat up. No, it's wrong. He should have told her before now. Should have told Jesse about his father. Now Kelley and the grandmother were coming home tomorrow and everything was going to blow up in his face.

And Amelia would never forgive him. That meant more to him than anything. He'd come to care for her, and the boy. More than he should, but it was too late to go back. He threw back the covers, got up and slipped on his jeans and flannel shirt. Not bothering with the buttons, he opened the door and went into the kitchen.

After he checked on Izzy and her puppies to see they were okay, he took a glass from the cupboard and got a drink of water. He leaned against the counter and saw the tree silhouetted in the window. He inhaled the evergreen scent. Everything about this place felt like home. A place you could feel as if you belonged.

That yearning had eaten away at his gut. He'd spent years

standing on the outside. Now that he'd gotten a taste of it, he wanted more. Every time he looked at Amelia and Jesse.

There was a creaking sound, and he turned toward the stairs to see Amelia. His heart stopped, then began to pound in his ears. He couldn't take his eyes off her as she walked across the living room. Her long robe was open and flowing around her legs. Her dark hair unbound. His fingers ached to be tangled into the thick strands.

She stopped to glance at the decorated tree, giving him the opportunity to head back to his room, but he was rooted to the spot. She continued on, but when she saw his silhouette she gasped.

"Boone?"

"Sorry, I didn't mean to frighten you."

She shook her head. "It's okay. I'm just distracted tonight." She went to the cupboard. "You're having trouble sleeping, too."

"Seems we both are."

"My reason is Jesse." She filled her glass with water. "Why can't you sleep?"

He paused for a while, then couldn't be anything but honest. "You."

CHAPTER NINE

AMELIA NO LONGER FELT brave. She'd planned to talk to Boone when she came downstairs, even dressed in her best nightgown, in hopes of convincing him to stay. Not just for her son, but herself, too.

She sighed. "If we're going to be honest, you've been keeping me up, too."

Setting down her glass, she took a step closer and reached out to place a hand on his chest. The light atop the stove wasn't bright enough to read his eyes, but she could feel the pounding of his heart under her palm.

"Amelia, we shouldn't be doing this," he breathed.

"It feels right to me, Boone."

"We can't always go with our feelings. We have to use some common sense."

She ran her hands up his well-developed chest, and he sucked in a breath. "Sometimes that's hard to do."

"Amelia..."

She smiled, her own heart racing. "I love it when you say my name."

Boone wanted to run, but mostly he wanted to wrap Amelia Hughes in his arms and never let go. "I'm leaving in the morning."

"You don't have to. Jesse wants you to stay and so do I. There isn't any reason to rush off." She raised up on her toes and kissed the underside of his jaw. "Maybe I can even convince you to stay in Montana."

In a second. Boone clenched his fists to keep from touching her.

"Besides, don't you have to give notice at Sky High?" she asked, her hands moving over him.

Boone couldn't take much more of her torture. His hands gripped her arms, but he couldn't push her away. "I need to talk to you about that." She placed another soft kiss at the base of his throat, and he was losing ground quickly.

"I think we've talked too much already."

Boone looked down at her. Her face was shadowed in the dim light, but he knew her beauty, the mesmerizing green hue of her eyes. He lost it. He pulled her into his arms as his mouth closed over hers. She made a whimpering sound and locked her fingers behind his neck.

He slanted his mouth over hers, deepening the kiss, but it still wasn't enough. He lifted her off the floor, swung around and set her down on the counter. He stepped between her legs and pulled her against him. At the same time he slipped his tongue inside her mouth and tasted her sweetness. Heaven.

He broke off the kiss and traced his lips along her jaw to her ear. "I want you so much, Amelia," he whispered. He'd never ached for a woman like this before.

"Oh, Boone, I want you, too," she cried. "Please, don't leave me. Don't ever leave me."

"Amelia." He stopped his words, not knowing how to answer her. Finally he released her, then turned away, working to regain some composure. He couldn't do this. Not until she knew the truth.

"Boone?"

He turned around. "Amelia, we need to talk." He lifted her from the counter and set her on the floor. "There's something

I need to tell you. Something I should have told you when I first got here."

He led her to the table and pulled out a chair for her to sit down.

"If you don't want to be with me—"

"Don't ever think that," he interrupted, then leaned down and kissed her perfect mouth. "It's because I care about you, and Jesse, that I need to tell you the truth."

He could see her swallow. "The truth?"

Boone nodded and sank down in the other chair. "About the real reason I came here."

She blinked but didn't say a word.

"First, I don't work for the Sky High Ranch."

She stiffened. "Who are you, then, and who do you work for?"

"I am Boone Gifford like I said, and I did work on an offshore rig in Texas. That's all true. Last summer there was an accident and I got hurt." He drew a breath and released it. "That's what delayed my coming to see you and Jesse."

She gripped her hands together but didn't say anything.

"I worked with Russ Eldon."

She jumped up and went to the counter. "Russ? Russ sent you here?"

Boone stood, too. "Yes. Just listen, Amelia."

"No, Russ never wanted to be in his son's life, and he can't come here now. Not when he's denied his son all this time." She shot a hard glare at him. "Oh, God, he sent you here to cozy up to me?"

"No, Amelia, it's not like that. I only knew Russ for a few months. We both worked on the rig together, shared living quarters. He talked about Jesse."

"No, he couldn't! He didn't know about Jesse. He took off before I had my son. And he never once contacted me."

"About six months ago he found out that you had a boy. He

told me he wanted to come here and meet his son. So he was trying to make some fast money to pay you for all the years of missed child support."

"I don't want Russ's money or him in our lives. I won't allow him to come here, get Jesse excited, then take off again." Amelia swiped at her tears. "It's been more than five years and he's never wanted his son before. Why now?"

"The only thing he wanted Jesse to know was that he existed."

Arms folded across her chest, she paced back and forth. "See, he couldn't even come himself. He sent you."

"He couldn't come, Amelia. Russ isn't here because he's dead."

Amelia froze. Russ was dead. She finally looked at Boone. "How?"

"In a hurricane. We were evacuating the oil platform and our helicopter crashed into the ocean. Russ was one of the three who didn't make it out. He drowned."

Amelia remembered hearing about last summer's hurricane that caused massive destruction along the Texas coast.

Boone continued the story. "Russ put Jesse down as next of kin on the insurance policy. But with the boy being a minor, he asked me to be executor if anything happened to him." He shrugged. "I never thought anything about agreeing to it. I never thought this would happen…" He paused, then said, "I would have come sooner, but I spent time in the hospital, then a rehab facility until recently."

"You were injured?"

He nodded. "My back and shoulder. I needed surgery and therapy."

She glanced over his body, remembering earlier how he'd winced when he rolled over in the snow. "Are you okay now?"

"Yeah, thanks to Russ. He kept me afloat and saved my life."

The Russ she remembered had been cocky and self-centered. Tears welled in her eyes as she raised her gaze to Boone and burst into tears. Why did this have to happen now? Why had Boone deceived her?

He led her back to the chair. "I'm sorry, Amelia. I know this is hard for you—"

She pulled away from his touch. "Yes, I'm mourning Russ, but for my son, not because I have any feelings for him. I got over that girlhood crush a long time ago. The tears are for my son. For the father he never got to know. Oh, God," she cried. "How can I tell Jesse?"

"I know my timing sucks, but I came as soon as I could." He went into the bedroom and returned with an envelope. He laid it on the table. "I'm not condoning what Russ did to you and Jesse, but I know he regretted abandoning you and his son." He nodded at the package on the table. "There are a few personal effects, a letter to Jesse and the life insurance policy. I signed it over to you."

She didn't touch any of it. "So I'm supposed to show my son this, as if it could ever make up for all the years Russ was never here?"

"No, of course not." He sighed. "But at least it shows your son that his father planned to be a part of his life. He wasn't perfect, none of us are, but Russ was trying."

She remained silent.

"I'll do anything I can to help, Amelia."

"I think you've helped more than enough. Jesse wants a real dad and he's nominated you for the job."

Boone shifted his feet. "I know I made a mess of this, but I care about Jesse. And I care about you."

She raised her hand. "I can't listen to this now."

"I'd planned to tell you when I arrived, but I didn't want to frighten you when we ended up trapped in the house together. Then I never found the right time."

She glared at him. "How convenient for you."

"I'm sorry, Amelia. I'll leave in the morning."

He stood, went into the bedroom and began to pack up his things. He'd only been here four days, but it seemed like so much longer. Long enough to have feelings for Amelia. And to even think about a future with her and Jessie. Now he wasn't going to get that chance.

Carrying his duffel bag, he returned to the kitchen. Amelia was still sitting at the table.

"If it's okay," he began, "I'll stay in the barn tonight, and after I feed the stock in the morning, I'll leave." He paused at the door, but she didn't turn to look at him.

"No matter what you think, Amelia, just know that I may have come here out of duty because Russ saved my life, but believe me, I've come to care about you and Jesse."

The following morning was bright and sunny, exactly the opposite of how Amelia felt. The pain of Boone's secret and reading Russ's letters had kept her up most of the night. But when Jesse came downstairs, she managed a smile as she cooked his breakfast.

"Where's Boone?" her son asked. "He said I could help him feed the horses if the weather was nice. And it's sunny." He shoved a forkful of eggs into his mouth. "Can I, Mom?"

She sat down at the table with her coffee. "I'm not sure if Boone has the time, honey. He has to go back to Texas soon."

His truck was still here, although it had been moved closer to the barn. So she wasn't sure when he exactly planned to go back to Texas. Suddenly she got a strange ache in her stomach. She didn't want him to leave.

"But, Mom, he can't go back, yet. He promised to stay

until Christmas no matter what. He just has to 'cause I've been wishing really, really hard that he can be my dad."

"Oh, Jesse." She sat down across from him at the table. "We talked about this before. You can't just wish for things and expect them to happen."

"But, Mom, you want Boone to stay here, too."

Before she could answer, the back door opened and Kelley walked into the kitchen. "We're home." She put down her bags and grinned at her sister and nephew.

Both Amelia and Jesse raced to the doorway, in time to see her grandmother Ruby helped in by Boone.

The short, sturdily built woman with steel-gray hair looked up at her escort with soft-green eyes. "What a nice young man you are." She glanced at Amelia. "Wherever did my granddaughter find you?"

Boone smiled. "I just kind of showed up during the blizzard to help out."

Jesse rushed over to hug his grandmother. "No, Gram, Boone is my Christmas wish."

CHAPTER TEN

"ARE YOU GOING TO TELL ME what's been going on?" Kelley Hughes asked as she marched into the kitchen.

Amelia looked over her shoulder at her tall, trim, older sister. Kelley had long, blond hair pulled back in her usual no-nonsense braid. Her pretty face was sprinkled with freckles caused by her time in the sun.

"I've been running the ranch during a blizzard, without electricity or a phone." She smiled, feeling the pride. "And I might add, I handled things just fine."

Kelley crossed her arms over her chest. "That's not what I'm talking about. I'm talking about Boone Gifford. Who is he?"

Amelia turned around, realizing her sister wasn't going to end this discussion. "He's a ranch hand."

"Not from the Sky High Ranch, he isn't. Their foreman called me and apologized for not sending over the help he promised. Gifford was never employed there."

"I know."

Kelley's eyes widened. "Then where did he come from?"

"West Texas."

"You let a stranger stay here in this house? Amelia, you're too trusting."

"First of all, we were in the middle of a blizzard. Secondly, he rescued me and your nephew when we got stranded on the road. Thirdly, by the time we got here, we were all stuck." She waved a hand. "What was I supposed to do? Send him out in the worst storm we've had in years?"

"Of course not." Kelley glanced into the living room at the decorated tree. "But it seems he's made himself at home."

"What was I supposed to do, make him stay on the porch? No matter what you think, Kel, Boone was a perfect gentleman. He worked hard, too. He kept the fire going, fed the stock, even helped deliver Izzy's pups. He did everything a ranch hand would have done, and more."

"My, he sounds like he's too good to be true." Kelley continued to study Amelia, doubt in her hazel eyes.

She hated that her sister treated her as if she couldn't handle things. "Stop it, Kel. I know what you're thinking. What happened with Russ was a long time ago. I've grown up since then."

"Are you trying to tell me that nothing happened between the two of you?"

Amelia felt her cheeks warm. "I'm not a child, so stop treating me like one."

Her sister relented. "I'm sorry. But Boone Gifford is a good-looking man."

Amelia raised an eyebrow. "So you noticed."

Kelley bristled. "I also noticed that the man couldn't look at anyone but you. So why is he leaving?"

"Because he only came to Montana to tell me that Russ died."

"What?"

"That's what Boone was doing in Rebel Ridge. It seems last year Russ finally grew curious about his son." She went on to tell her sister about the accident that took his life and Boone's connection.

"And somehow I have to tell Jesse," Amelia said.

"Why? Russ never was a father to him."

"So I shouldn't tell him? Come on, Kelley, you know how many questions Jesse has asked about his dad. And the older he gets, the more he wants to know. I can't keep the truth from him."

"You can wait until he's a little older," Kelley urged, grabbed her jacket, then headed out the back door.

Amelia wiped her hands with a towel and went into the living room. No matter when she told her son the news about his father, it would hurt him. She stared at the tree and inhaled the fresh evergreen scent that made her think of past holidays in this house. Since the death of their parents, Christmases had been a little lonely for her and Kelley. Maybe that was the reason for her older sister's protectiveness. Even with all the love their grandparents had showered on them, they were never a complete family. Amelia had always wanted something more for Jesse. Had hoped that Russ would come back someday to claim his son. Now that would never happen.

She felt the prickling of tears as she looked outside. Just then Boone walked out of the barn, carrying his bag to his truck. He was leaving. Her chest tightened as her fingers gripped the window curtain. She wanted to stop him, but she knew he'd fulfilled his obligation. Was that all she and Jessie had been to him? An obligation?

"That's one nice young man you've found."

Amelia turned around as her grandmother walked into the room. She was dressed in trousers and a starched print blouse. "Gram, you should be in bed getting your strength back."

Ruby waved a hand. "Bah, I've been in bed far too long. And quit trying to change the subject." The small-framed woman made her way to the window and nodded. "Why aren't you convincing Boone to stay?"

She wanted to, but how could she keep him from his dream? "Because his plan was always to go back to Texas and buy a ranch."

"That's a shame. It sure is nice to have a man around again." Gram sighed and got a faraway look in her eyes. "He reminds me a lot of my Jesse. Big and muscular with those dark roguish eyes and the easy grin. Oh, my, a man like that sure gets your heart apumping."

Amelia knew the feeling. She also knew Boone's touch, his kisses…

Her grandmother turned to her. "Good gracious girl, get to movin'. Or are you just going to let that man walk out of your life?"

Amelia was taken aback by her grandmother's words. "I don't exactly have a choice, Gram. Boone's dream has always been to buy back his parents' ranch. He has to go home."

"No, he can't leave." Jesse hurried downstairs, dressed in his heavy coat and boots.

"Jesse Hughes, where do you think you're going?"

"Out to see Boone." The determined boy started toward the back door.

"Well, at least someone knows their mind," Gram said, then turned to her granddaughter. "Sometimes you have to go after what you want."

"And a mother also has to protect her child." Amelia took off after her son. Right or wrong, she was going to tell him the painful truth.

Although the weather was a lot warmer today, it was still cold. Boone had killed about twenty minutes, and he didn't have an excuse to hang around any longer. He'd checked the road conditions, and the main routes were clear. If he took off now, he could make good headway toward home.

Home? He suddenly wondered where that was. Where was his enthusiasm? Before coming here, all he'd wanted was to buy back the Last Dollar Ranch. He already had a deposit down on the place. All that was left was to sign the papers to finalize the deal. Now he wasn't sure that was what he wanted to do.

He heard his name called, and he looked at the house to see Jesse running toward him. He pushed off from the truck's fender and went to meet the boy on the shoveled path. The kid launched himself, and Boone caught him up in his arms.

Jesse's tiny arms wrapped around the neck. "Boone, you can't leave," he cried. "Please, don't go."

Boone gave the boy one last hug and set him down. That was when he saw the tears. "Aw, Jesse, you shouldn't be out in the cold." He worked the zipper on the child's jacket and wrapped the scarf around his neck. "I was going to come up to the house to say goodbye."

"But I don't want you to leave," Jesse cried.

Boone hated this. "I wish I could stay, bud, but there are things you don't understand."

The boy shook his head. "Mom told me about my real dad." Those questioning brown eyes held his. They were so much like Russ's. "She said you knew him. And that he died in the ocean."

Boone crouched down to be level with the five-year-old. "Your mother told you about your dad?"

Jesse jerked his head up and down. "Yeah, she said he's a hero."

Boone managed a nod. "Yeah, he was. He talked about you all the time, too. And he wanted more than anything to come and see you."

Jesse's eyes widened. "He really wanted to be my dad?"

"Yes, very much."

A smile broke out on Jesse's face as he swiped at his tears. "And he couldn't come to be with me so he sent you to be my dad."

Boone swallowed hard, not even knowing how to respond to that conclusion.

"Jesse Thomas Hughes."

They both looked up to see Amelia. Boone stood as she approached them. "Jesse, I think you need to go back inside. It's too cold out here."

"But, Mom, I had to stop Boone from going away."

Boone ignored Amelia's glare. "Look, Jesse, I might need to leave now for a little while, but I'll be back and we'll talk more about your dad."

"You promise?"

"Yes, I promise."

The boy hugged Boone's neck and whispered, "On Christmas."

"I'll try my hardest," Boone told him, barely holding it together. Suddenly all doubts about what he truly wanted faded, and he found himself adding, "I promise." He finally released Jesse and watched as the boy took off toward the house.

Once Jesse was out of sight, Amelia turned back to Boone. "Oh, Boone, how could you make him that promise?"

"Because I made a promise to his father. I owe Russ a debt." Boone took a step closer to her. "Look, I know Russ did you and Jesse wrong for a lot of years. But I believe he grew up and planned to do right by his son. Jesse needs to know that."

"I know you feel a duty to Jesse, Boone, but he will only be hurt when you finally go away."

Boone froze. "You believe I'm coming back here out of duty?" He searched her pretty face, those green eyes he'd come to love. "You really have no idea what I feel for you *and* your son? Or how hard it is for me to leave you both?"

Her gaze held his. "How do you feel?"

His heart lodged in his throat. "That I'd give anything not to have this between us. What brought us together could tear us apart." He reached out and pulled her into a tight embrace. "I care about you, Amelia."

"Don't, Boone." She closed her eyes momentarily. "Don't make this any harder. You're leaving for Texas."

"What if I came back?" If she just said the word, he would change his plans—his life for her.

She swallowed hard but didn't say anything.

"I'll need a little time, Amelia. There are things in Texas I need to take care of. And I need to give you time, too. Time for you and your son to absorb the news about Russ. All I ask is that you trust me. Can you do that?"

Amelia hesitated, then nodded. "Oh, Boone, I want to."

He smiled. "That's a start," he said right before his mouth closed over hers. He put everything he felt for her into the kiss. And by the time he released her, they were both swaying, and their breathing was labored.

"Give us a chance, Amelia. I'll prove to you that we can work this out."

Over the next week, Amelia found she couldn't pass a window without looking out, hoping to see Boone driving up the road. She'd never missed anyone so much. She tried to think about the way he'd kissed her, the promises he'd made to her, to Jesse. But lingering doubts made her face facts. What if he didn't return? Once back in Texas, he might have second thoughts. He might decide to buy that ranch he'd always wanted. Someplace where they didn't have blizzards.

It was Jesse she worried about most. He had her reread the letter from his dad every night. Russ's picture was in his room. There had been times her son had become sad, but perked up when he talked about Boone coming back.

For the past week the first thing Jesse had done every morning was check another day off the calendar. Not so unusual for a child his age during the holidays, but Amelia knew he wasn't waiting for toys on Christmas morning. He was waiting for Boone.

The oven timer went off, and she went to pull the brownies out of the oven.

"Mom, are they ready?" Jesse asked.

She smiled. "Yes, and you're just in time to do your part. Did you crush the candy canes?"

"Yeah." He climbed up onto the chair at the table and held up the bag of red and white bits.

"Okay, I guess we're ready then." She enjoyed sharing this Christmas tradition with her son.

Jesse's little fingers worked awkwardly, sprinkling just the right amount on each square. "Mom, can you make these brownies every Christmas forever and ever?"

She smiled and thought about future Christmases. There might not be a Boone, but she could give him this. "Yes, we can make them every year." She kissed his cheek. "But only if you help me."

Jesse glanced toward the stove. "Good, you made a whole bunch." He looked up at her with those trusting eyes. "I want there to be enough for Boone tomorrow."

Her heart tightened. "Honey, we talked about this. Boone might not make it back for Christmas."

"But Mom, he's my Christmas wish. And he promised."

Amelia glanced toward the back door. Her sister came in, stripped off her coat and hat and hung them on a hook. "Hey, do I smell brownies?"

Jesse nodded. "Mom and me made them. But no one can have any until tomorrow."

Kelley frowned. "I have to wait that long?"

"We have to wait for Boone to get here." His job completed, Jesse climbed down off the chair. "Mom, can I watch a video?"

At Amelia's nod, the boy ran out of the kitchen. She began to clean up the mess, carrying things to the sink.

Kelley helped her. “Sounds like he’s got his mind made up.”

“Kelley, please. This has been a rough time for him.”

“It hasn’t been exactly easy for you, either.” Her sister touched her arm. “I don’t know Boone very well, but I know how much you and Jesse care about him. I hope it works out.”

Amelia bit down on her lower lip. “I’m afraid to hope, Kel. Boone asked me to have faith that he’d be back, but I’m having trouble. After Russ left…”

Kelley hugged her sister. “Oh, Amelia, one thing is for sure, Boone isn’t Russ. I believe the man is sincere.” Kelley smiled. “Maybe you, too, need to make a Christmas wish.”

CHAPTER ELEVEN

JUST BEFORE DAWN Christmas morning, Amelia shut off her alarm clock and sat up in bed. Sleep had eluded her most of the night because all she could think about was Boone. Since he left a week ago, she hadn't heard a single word from him. Not a phone call. Nothing. The faith she'd managed to carry the past seven days was fading now. How was she supposed to keep believing in him under those circumstances?

Closing her eyes, she released a sigh. If only she could push him out of her head. And her heart. But that wasn't likely, not when she'd managed to fall in love.

In just a matter of days—to a man she barely knew.

She stood and went to the window. The breaking dawn spread a dim light over the scene below. Snow blanketed the land, emphasizing each outbuilding on the ranch.

A perfect Christmas day…almost.

There was a soft knock on the door before it opened and Gram Ruby peered inside. "I heard you," she whispered and stepped inside. "You always were the first up on Christmas."

Amelia smiled. "Well, now I'm trying to get a head start on a certain five-year-old."

The older woman crossed the room to her granddaughter. "Or are you looking for your young man?"

"Gram, he's not my young man," she denied weakly.

"You need to have faith, Amelia. That's what love is. And if Boone says he's coming back, he'll be here."

That was Amelia's problem. "Gram, I'm afraid."

"Do you love him?" her grandmother asked.

Amelia glanced away. "I've only known him four and a half days."

Ruby smiled. "I knew your grandfather all of thirty seconds before I fell hopelessly in love with him. Of course he was handsome and a charmer, too." She took her granddaughter's hand as they walked to the bed and sat down. "Amelia, there isn't a timeline on love."

"But Boone lives so far away. And what about Jesse? He's just lost his biological father. What if Boone just feels obligated to us only because of Russ?" She sighed. "I can't make another mistake."

"Stop it, child. You didn't make any mistake. Russ was the one who chose to leave." She beamed. "And look what we were blessed with, our sweet Jesse. So don't let your past dictate your future. Give Boone a chance."

Amelia nodded. "I guess there isn't anything to worry about if Boone doesn't return."

"Oh, he'll return," Grandma predicted. "Then you'll have a lot to decide. So I should let you get to it." Ruby stood and headed for the door, then paused. "I just want you to be happy, Amelia. So don't give that up to please everyone else." With that said, the older woman left the room.

Amelia had a lot more to worry about than her own feelings. Jesse would always be her first concern. And if Boone didn't return, her son's heart would break. How would they both survive the day if Boone didn't show up?

Amelia couldn't think about that. She needed to make today special for her son. She quickly dressed in a burgundy turtleneck sweater, charcoal wool trousers and black boots. She tied her hair back into a knot, leaving bangs across her forehead. After applying some lip gloss, she headed downstairs.

In the shadowed living room, she turned on the tree lights and smiled at the dozens of wrapped presents piled underneath. Even though Jesse hadn't asked for any toys this year, she'd made sure Santa had left an electric train set.

Amelia went into the kitchen and turned on the coffeemaker. Several freshly baked pies lined the counter for today's holiday dinner. She wasn't even sure of Boone's favorite, so she'd made pumpkin, pecan and apple.

Usually Amelia cooked Christmas dinner, but this year Kelley was cooking, giving Amelia the day off. Could her sister's sudden domestic tendencies have anything to do with Mack Dennison? The restaurant owner of Mack's Kitchen had definitely caught Kelley's attention. Even though her sister had been trying to hide it, Amelia had seen the attraction between the two. Although she was a little envious, she was also happy her sister had found someone.

A sound drew Amelia's attention to the back door, and Kelley walked in. "Merry Christmas, sis." Smiling, she pulled off her gloves and stuffed them in her pockets before hanging her coat on the hook.

"Merry Christmas," Amelia answered.

"What are you doing up so early?" Kelley asked as she walked to the counter and poured a cup of coffee.

"I wanted a minute or two to myself before an excited little boy starts ripping into presents."

Kelley leaned against the counter. "Could it be you're waiting for some good-looking, Texas cowboy?"

Amelia sighed, knowing there was no reason to lie. "I'm probably crazy, but yes. I know he went to Texas, but what if he decided not to come back here?"

"I have a feeling he'll be back," Kelley told her. "Are you ready for that?"

"That's what I'm so torn about. How can Jesse and I leave here? What about Gram?" She looked at her older sister. "And you? You're our family—and this ranch is our home. We run it together." This past week she'd finally gotten up the nerve to tell her sister some of her ideas for the operation. "But I don't see any man around, asking me to go anywhere. So you're stuck with me."

"It's early yet." Kelley glanced out the window. "The sun is barely up."

"Since when have you become a Boone supporter?"

Kelley shrugged. "Maybe since I realized that the right man can change a lot of plans."

Amelia watched her sister closely, but Kelley didn't give anything away. A sudden movement outside the window caught Amelia's attention. In the quiet morning, the leftover snow was practically untouched, except for the cleared paths up the drive and the barn, peaceful and picturesque as a postcard. Then she saw the vehicle. The familiar red truck. A man in a sheepskin jacket climbed out.

Amelia blinked, feeling her heart begin to race. Boone. He came back.

"Looks like your man kept his promise."

Amelia barely heard her sister as she grabbed her coat, then ran for the door.

Boone was nervous, more so than at any time in his life. He wanted so much to be a part of Amelia's life. He wanted to make a family with her and Jesse. Today he had to convince them both how much he cared about them.

He'd contacted Kelley and told her his feelings and future plans, imploring her for help. Once she realized he loved her younger sister, she'd been more than willing to help with his plan.

When he glanced toward the porch and saw Amelia, his

breath caught in his chest. Getting a better grip on the bag of presents, he started up the walk and took the steps two at a time until he stood in front of the woman he'd come to love. "Merry Christmas, Amelia."

"You're back."

His gaze locked with hers. Her green eyes searched his. "I said I would be."

She suddenly straightened. "For how long, Boone? How long before you leave this time? I'm not going to let you break Jesse's heart—"

Boone dropped his bag of gifts, pulled her into his arms and covered her mouth in a hungry kiss. After just a second of hesitation, Amelia wrapped her arms around his neck and kissed him back. Before Boone lost it altogether, he released her.

"That's the welcome I was hoping for. God, I've missed you." He pressed a soft kiss on the end of her nose. "Is Jesse up yet?"

She shook her head.

"Good." He winked. "Can we go inside and I'll tell you everything?"

Without a word Amelia turned and led him inside the kitchen. Once again he was hit with the warmth he'd felt that first time he walked into this house. He followed her into the deserted kitchen. Good. He wanted some alone time with Amelia, before he faced the rest of the family.

Amelia looked around. "Kelley was just here."

"She's probably giving me a chance to stake my claim."

She arched an eyebrow. "You've been in touch with my sister?"

He saw the flash of pain in Amelia's eyes and rushed on to say, "Only since yesterday. Remember, Kelley wasn't exactly happy about my first visit."

"Why didn't you call me?"

"I didn't want to do that until everything was finalized."

"So you bought your ranch?"

"Yes, I did."

Amelia tried to hold it together, but it was hard. "So why even come here, Boone? Just to get Jesse all excited again, then turn around and return to Texas?"

He moved closer. "What about you, Amelia? Are you excited that I came back?"

She pressed her hand against his chest. "Don't, Boone. This isn't about us. Jesse has to come first."

"I disagree. You come first, Amelia. With me, anyway. You are the reason I returned to Montana. Of course I'm crazy about Jesse, but it's you I've fallen in love with."

She gasped. "Boone."

"I hope that makes you happy?"

Yes! No! She nodded.

"Don't I get a little more than that?"

"Oh, Boone, I love you, too." She wanted this so much. "It's just that you live so far away. How can I leave my family?"

"Aw, honey, I would never ask you to leave here. That's the reason the ranch I bought is a lot closer. It's the Anderson place."

She blinked. "You bought the Andersons' ranch?"

"Yeah." He nodded. "Well as soon as escrow closes next week. Seems I can't get enough of Montana's blizzards, especially if I'm going to be snowed in with a certain green-eyed woman."

Amelia's throat suddenly went dry. "But what about your home in Texas?"

"It's just a place. I don't have any family there, just memories of a ranch lost." He took her hand. "I want a new start with you, Amelia, and with Jesse. But I'm going to need your help, too. I want you to be my partner."

Boone felt her stiffen and watched as her smile faded. He

realized he wasn't saying this right. "Come on," he said as he tugged her into the living room and sat her down on the sofa in front of the tree. He took the spot next to her.

"A lot has happened in the past year." He cradled her hand in his. "I'd lost everything when I ended up on an oil rig and met Russ. He was the one who befriended me, not the other way around. Yeah, I listened when he talked about Jesse, because I was bitter over my own problems. Then when he kept me afloat in the water until help came…" He paused. "I realized what I owed him. But it was too late."

"Oh, Boone, you can't blame yourself for what happened that day."

"Why not? He had a son and he wanted to be a part of his life. I was all alone." He raised his gaze to hers. "Then I met you and Jesse. God forgive me, but I was suddenly glad I didn't die that day."

She smiled. "So am I."

"But your son lost his father."

Amelia's touch gave him the love and acceptance he needed. "No, Boone. Russ hadn't been a father to Jesse. I'm sorry he died, and I'm sorry for my son, but Russ had many opportunities to be a part of his life. You're the one who's been here for Jesse."

Boone took a calming breath. "And I want to continue being a part of his life and yours." He stood, then went down on one knee as he pulled a small velvet box out of his coat pocket.

That got Amelia's attention. He opened it, revealing a platinum band, square-cut diamond. "I know this seems fast, but we spent four twenty-four-hour days together. Four wonderful days. Most people who've known each other for months don't spend that much time together." He took the ring out of the box and held it in his hand. "Besides, I fell in love with you by the end of the first day. I want us to be partners in everything, Amelia. I love you and want you to be my wife. Will you marry me?"

"Oh, Boone." Tears flooded her eyes as she touched his cheek.

"Say yes, Mom."

They both turned to see a pajama-clad Jesse standing on the staircase. Then Amelia looked in the other direction to see Kelley and Gram standing at the kitchen entrance. Where had they come from? Even Izzy came out to greet them.

Amelia smiled as she turned back to Boone. "Are you sure you can handle all this family? I'm a package deal."

He grinned. "I'm planning on that. Do you think you can move as far away as the Anderson place?"

She shook her head. "No, but I'll move to the new Gifford Ranch. Oh, yes, Boone, I'll marry you."

He slipped the ring on her finger, pulled her to her feet and into his arms, then kissed her long and thoroughly as her family broke into cheers.

Once they broke apart, Jesse ran to hug them. He looked up at Boone. "See, you are my Christmas wish."

Boone knelt down to the little boy he'd been given the chance to raise. "I want to be more than that, Jesse. I want to marry your mother, but I also want to be your dad."

Those brown eyes widened. "For real?"

"For real," Boone assured him.

Jesse looked at his mother and she nodded.

The boy turned back to Boone. "Yeah, we're going to be a family."

Kelley and Gram rushed in, offering congratulations and hugs all around as they began the day's celebration. Then they tore into the presents and gasped at the gifts that Boone bought for everyone. He was also surprised when he opened the pair of fur-lined gloves that Amelia had given him. The two best gifts were Amelia and Jesse.

About a hour later, Kelley's Mack showed up and they disappeared into the kitchen and began preparing the holiday meal, giving Boone and Amelia time to be together. They bundled up and went outside for another Hughes tradition, to take a ride in the horse-drawn sleigh, giving Boone another look at Montana's winter wonderland. They laughed and made plans for the future. A wedding, a new home and a life together.

That evening Boone sat at the dining table with Jesse on one side and Amelia on the other. He grasped his new family's hands during the blessing. When it concluded, Jesse announced, "This is the best Christmas ever."

Amelia smiled as she continued to hold on to Boone's hand, feeling his ring on her finger. "I think we all got our Christmas wish."

Boone looked at her. "I know I got all mine."

Amelia could only agree as she smiled back. She would always be grateful for the man who came to rescue her and her son. And offered her love for a lifetime.

* * * * *

A Bride for Rocking H Ranch

DONNA ALWARD

Dear Reader,

Christmas has to be my absolute favourite time of year. Being from Canada, I love the snow, the ice-skating, tobogganing, hot chocolate and baking cookies with my children. I love snuggling in with a holiday movie and singing along with Christmas carols. I love how in all the frenzy sometimes miracles happen. People smile when they hear children singing. They let go of differences and forgive the ones who've hurt them. And sometimes they even fall in love—like Mack and Kelley.

I was so thrilled to be asked to participate in this collection with Patricia Thayer, an author whose work I've admired for a long time. We had many interesting (and long!) phone calls between Nova Scotia and California! The experience was truly unforgettable.

I do hope you enjoy these tales of the Hughes sisters. And, from my house to yours, I wish you the merriest of Christmases.

Much love,

Donna

PS Look for a new novel from Donna in early 2011.
–Ed.

To Darrell…you somehow know exactly when
I need a push and when I need a hug.
This one's for you, with love.

CHAPTER ONE

KELLEY HUGHES SNAPPED the cell phone closed as her feet automatically stopped outside the gray brick building. She looked up at the burgundy-colored awning, furrowed her brow. Was it some sort of sign that she stopped, at just this moment, in front of Mack's Kitchen? Because she'd just assured her sister, Amelia, that she would have Christmas dinner under control, when the truth was she'd barely given it a thought.

She'd been so preoccupied thinking about Gram and the ranch that the holidays had crept up on her. She'd also realized lately that Amelia put on a brave face but she was handling a lot on her own. Kelley wanted to help. She thought now she should have volunteered some other service, because she simply didn't cook!

Surely there wasn't much to making a dinner. You put a turkey in the oven and cooked some vegetables, right? She bit down on her lip, staring at the green garland and twinkle lights decorating the iron railings. What had she been thinking? She hadn't even done her shopping yet and she was taking on something more. She looked at her watch; she should get back to the hospital. But there was the small matter of the nonexistent shopping she'd done. A display in the window caught her eye—a cookie-making kit, complete with cookie cutters and bright-red and green sprinkles. It was just the kind of thing Amelia would love to do with Jesse. Already she was mentally crossing the first gift off her list.

Then there would only be the gifts for Gram and Jesse, and she could get back to the hospital. She didn't like leaving Gram alone for long, despite the older woman's insistence she'd be fine.

Gram kept her spirits up, but Kelley had seen fear in Gram's eyes for the first time she could remember. Yes, she would buy her gifts as quickly as possible and hurry back.

She opened the door, surprised by the old-fashioned bell above the door that announced her entrance. The next thing she noticed was the smell, and she paused. It smelled like every holiday rolled into one. Cinnamon and fruit and something else…baked bread? Her house never smelled like this. Ever. Carols played softly over invisible speakers, adding to the homey, holiday warmth.

This was Mack Dennison's latest store in his Mack's Kitchen franchise. After three years of building them from San Diego to Seattle, he'd finally come home to Montana and opened one himself. The Rebel Ridge weekly paper had done a feature on him just last week—the hometown boy who had made his fortune and brought it back to Helena. The sharp, savvy man in the picture hadn't jived with the vague memory she had of him from school. Now instead of the tiny house where he'd grown up in Rebel Ridge, he probably had some fancy condo here in the city. But there was no doubt that his stores were welcoming, homey, and stocked to the teeth with anything a cook could possibly want—and then some.

The walls and shelves were lined with pots, pans and unfathomable utensils with funny names. Another section heralded the latest in spices and gourmet combinations, specialty foods and recipe books. And smack dab in the middle was the counter and cash register, and a tall, good-looking man in jeans and a ribbed sweater. It suddenly dawned on her it was Mack. He was speaking to a middle-aged woman while bagging her items. She hadn't actually expected to see him here. After all, he was head of a successful chain of stores. She'd pictured him in a corporate tower somewhere. The smile she'd worn at the sound of a favorite carol faded away. If she'd known he'd be working the register…well, she might have reconsidered coming in.

When Mack smiled at his customer, Kelley's stomach did a flip. It was a good smile, with an even row of teeth and a half dimple that popped in his cheek. He probably didn't even remember her. Somehow she'd always seemed to fade into the woodwork, and that was fine with her.

"Can I help you?"

She blinked, looked up and tried very hard to make her polite smile more relaxed. "Hello, Mack."

He hadn't changed much. A little older, but still with that tall, lean build, only slightly filled out now that he was past his teenage years. Dark eyes met hers, making something tingle down her spine. And his half-crooked smile was so infectious she smiled back. She couldn't help it.

"I'm sorry, have we met?"

Embarrassment flamed in her cheeks, and her smile faltered. Of course he wouldn't remember her now, if he hadn't even known she'd existed then. "You probably don't remember me. I'm Kelley Hughes. I was in your eleventh-grade math class."

His smile dimmed the slightest bit, and she wondered why, but just like that it was back up to its brilliant wattage and she wondered if it had actually happened at all.

"Of course. I remember now. Kelley Hughes. Your family runs the Rocking H." He held out his hand.

She was sure he was being polite. After a long pause, she held out her hand and let him shake it. The little flutters happened again, quite unexpectedly. He held it a little longer than she'd anticipated, and she pulled her fingers out of his.

"It's been a while," she said quietly. She put her hands in her pockets as she didn't know what else to do with them. Her ability to make small talk seemed to have fled, as well. She'd tried to leave high school behind for the most part, certainly shunning reunions and well-intentioned get togethers. She and Mack had never run in the same circles, anyway. She had been busy with the ranch after Grandpa died, and Mack had disappeared to build his empire, traveling the world. They might both be in Montana again now, but they were miles apart.

He shifted his weight at the long lull in conversation. "So... what are you up to these days? What brings you from Rebel Ridge into Helena?"

He was more adept at chitchat than she was, that much was clear. She chanced a look up into his eyes, and for a moment she was caught there. There was something...a tiny flash.

He put a hand on her arm, and she felt the warmth through her heavy jacket, none of the desire to pull away as she'd expected. But before she could think too much about it, he continued on. "I heard about your grandfather's passing. I'm so sorry. How is Mrs. Hughes?"

His inquiry surprised her. Small towns were just that, and in a place like Rebel Ridge everyone tended to ask after everyone else's family. She was sure he was just being polite again. But the concern touched her nevertheless. Especially now.

Her throat thickened with the emotion she'd held in all day.

She moved away, under the pretext of examining the wares on the shelves nearby. It wasn't that she didn't love the ranch; she did. And right now it was more important to her than ever. But in the back of her mind there was something else that she couldn't shake—there'd never been a question on her part, never been an opportunity to do anything else. She'd worked hard, had looked after things. But there had been places she'd wanted to see, things she'd wanted to do. Mack had left Rebel Ridge behind and had gone on to build his own business. He'd had a choice.

But responsibility weighed even more heavily on her these days. The whole trip to Helena was for Gram's angioplasty at the hospital, and it was a stark reminder that things were changing.

"Gram's doing fine." She felt a slight twinge at glossing over the truth, but what did it matter? It wasn't as if she'd see Mack again. She rarely came into town. She was only here for the week because they hadn't wanted to leave Gram on her own. And Mack was busy, now that he'd become somewhat of a local celebrity. She was sure his life here in Helena was busier than it had ever been when they'd both lived in "the Ridge." She was only here to shop.

A pause settled over the pair once more. As the silence drew out, she tried to ignore the way his jeans hugged his body, the breadth of his shoulders or the fluttering that kept happening in her tummy. It was unfamiliar and she didn't like it. The glimmer of attraction was as foreign to her as the merchandise he carried.

Kelley pasted on another smile for the sake of manners. "I really came in to find a Christmas present for my sister."

Mack's shoulders relaxed. "What did you have in mind?"

"I saw that cookie kit in the window. I'm sure she'd enjoy doing something like that with her son."

He went to a shelf and pulled out one of the kits she'd seen. Cookie cutters in the shapes of snowflakes, trees and snowmen danced beneath the plastic coating. Sprinkles and gumdrops were in tiny packages for decorating.

It was exactly the sort of thing Amelia would love. Kelley could give it to her early, and Amelia and Jesse would mix up dough and have a wonderful time cutting out shapes and decorating them for the holidays. The thought put a little ache in her chest. Jesse was such a blessing and a bright spot in their lives.

Kelley reached out and took the kit from Mack's hands, running a finger down the jar of red crystalized sugar. Amelia was a wonderful mom, but Jesse wanted a dad. He'd started school this year and was suddenly noticing things were different in his friends' homes. And he'd whispered to Kelley the other day that he'd wished for a dad for Christmas. It had touched her, made her wistful. She let him help out on the ranch, showed him things. But she was Aunt Kelley, not a father. It wasn't anywhere near the same.

"It's perfect," she murmured. "Amelia and Jesse will have a wonderful time." Jesse was so worried about his great-grandmother. Maybe this would help fill in the gaps that couldn't truly be filled. Gaps that she herself had been noticing more lately, in herself. Resentments that bubbled up from nowhere. Longings—the female kind—that had no place in the foreman of a ranch. A need to be more than that somehow. And not knowing how—or if—she should begin.

But there was no time for those thoughts now. She had her hands full with the Rocking H and looking after Amelia and Ruby. It had always been that way and wasn't likely to change anytime soon.

She looked up at him, unprepared for the expression mirrored back at her.

His dark eyes were soft with what might have been understanding, his lips unsmiling. "Yes," he said quietly. "Kids like baking and decorating. And Mrs. Hughes, too, I expect."

"She probably won't be up to it after—"

Kelley broke off, realizing that she'd said too much as his brows pulled together.

"After what?" The spell that had been tenuously woven around them dissipated. She averted her eyes.

"Nothing."

But he'd already picked up on the hesitation in her voice. "Is there something wrong? You did say she was fine. But you sound upset."

"She is…she will be. It's nothing."

And yet it was. Somehow talking in riddles to Mack brought emotions to the surface, and she swallowed, trying to beat them back. Gram was the glue. She and Grandpa had raised them after the deaths of their parents, and then Gram had kept the ranch going after Grandpa's death several years ago. Kelley had stepped in as she'd always known she eventually would, but it was Gram that was the heart and soul of the Hughes clan, and her illness made Kelley suddenly realize there might not be that many more Christmases with them all together. She blinked and picked up a package that read Chili Pickled Pears. The label blurred.

"Kelley."

She looked up in alarm. The way he said her name sounded somewhere between a command and an endearment. It was silly considering she hadn't seen him for nearly a decade. He'd been busy making his way in the world and she'd stayed in exactly the same place where they'd grown up. But in his eyes was a gentle invitation and she found herself revealing more than she'd planned.

"I'm in Helena because Gram's in the hospital," she explained, her throat tightening once more.

"Is it serious?"

"She's had some tests, and she's scheduled for an angioplasty tomorrow."

Mack placed a hand on her arm and she felt the warmth soak through her jacket and sleeve, right to her skin. Rather than repelling, it was comforting. "I hadn't heard."

"It isn't exactly community knowledge. She wanted to keep it quiet. The doctors say she'll be fine, but…"

"It's a bit scary," he finished.

"Yes," she admitted. She hadn't spoken to anyone of her fears about Gram. Mack was the very first person who seemed to care about how *she* might be feeling, and for that reason alone, she found herself responding to his gentle comments.

For some strange reason she thought it might be nice to be comforted in his arms. But that was insane. She didn't do physical touches. And she wasn't sure she'd know how to accept comfort, anyway. Her own two feet was how she normally dealt with things. She didn't rely on other people. Perhaps that was why the thought of losing Gram panicked her so much. Gram was the one person Kelley had *always* counted on.

She cleared her throat. "Anyway," she continued, "with my nephew Jesse in school, Amelia couldn't really come, and we didn't want to leave Gram here alone. So I'm staying at a motel near the hospital until it's over and I can take her home."

"I'm sorry, Kelley. This must be difficult, especially so close to the holidays." His fingers squeezed, reassuring. "If there's anything I can do to help…everyone in Rebel Ridge knows and loves Mrs. Hughes."

Yes, everyone loved Ruby. And Amelia. If Kelley didn't hold the family together, who would? But then, what was left for her? It was a heavy load, trying to be all things for all people.

The afternoon was waning and she still had to pick up other gifts. "I should get going," she said, hiding a sigh and taking her purchase up to the cash register. "I need to finish up my shopping and get back to the hospital. And the forecast said there's a storm coming."

"When did you eat last, Kelley?"

She met his gaze, a bit confused at his concern. "Me? Why?"

"Because you look a little pale. And like you could use a bite. Here, try this." He plucked a small square from a silver tray and held it in front of her mouth.

She looked at his hand warily, holding out some sort of sweet. It smelled wonderful, spicy and rich. She swallowed, but her mouth watered, anyway, and her tummy rumbled the slightest bit. She shifted her gaze to his face and he raised one eyebrow.

She opened her mouth, and he popped the morsel into it.

Mmm. Chewy, moist, rich and spicy. She closed her eyes. Just this one bite was far better than anything she'd had at the hospital cafeteria today. Or any day this week, since that was where she'd had most of her meals.

"What *is* that?"

With a self-satisfied smile, he picked up her package of pickled pears. "Fruitcake."

But she hated fruitcake. Normally.

"Try what's on the other tray."

She reached over and picked up an odd-looking packet, golden brown. The cube of fruitcake had only increased her hunger and she took a substantial bite. Flavor exploded on her tongue…pastry and butter and…was that ham? Something tasted like dill. She ate the rest without hesitation. "That's really good, Mack." The compliment didn't hurt as much as she'd expected it would. She offered her first, unfettered, genuine smile. "Not bad for a boy from the Ridge."

"I can share the recipe if you like."

Once again she felt awkward and her smile wavered. She was no domestic goddess and most of the time felt no need to apologize for it. But lately she'd had stirrings…a vague sense of dissatisfaction that while she was great at running the ranch, as a woman she was a bit of a failure. And then a resulting anger at herself because in her heart she knew that not being able to cook and sew and do all those things Amelia was a natural at didn't make her less of a woman.

No, the reasons went far deeper than that, in scars that would never go away.

"I could take it for Amelia." She didn't want to admit she couldn't even make boxed macaroni and cheese. "I'm in charge of the ranch. Amelia runs the house." She smiled politely. "We play to our strengths." The fact that her sister was the nurturer of all of them, including being a fantastic single parent, made Kelley proud.

"So you don't cook…at all?"

The surprised tone of his voice took any shred of femininity she'd had and threw it out the window. She was suddenly aware of what she was wearing—faded jeans and a serviceable, sexless jacket. Even her scarf now seemed a dull shade of brown. Grandpa had often teased that she was his "boy," and at one time it had made her proud. But then she'd had glimpses of her own dreams, which were brought to a sharp end when he was gone and it was up to her to keep things going for Amelia and Grandma Ruby. Lord knew Ruby was still the head of the family, but she wasn't up to the task of the physical running of the ranch. That was left to Kelley. She'd known her duty and had done it.

But his surprise at her lack of culinary skills made her bristle. "Actually, I'm cooking the family Christmas dinner this year." Up went her chin again. She'd be damned if she'd let him know that the extent of her cooking was frying a plain old egg for breakfast or putting together a sandwich. She grew suddenly inspired. "As a matter of fact, while I'm here I can look for some new and interesting ideas to add to the meal."

New and interesting indeed. She knew nothing about putting on a dinner, but she was sure she could do it. She'd never failed at anything she'd tried before. It only took diligence and hard work, like any other difficult task.

"Oh, that's a shame, then. I was thinking you should come take a class. I run them through the week, for all sorts of people. Men and women, young and old. We start with boiling water. It's a bird course—impossible to fail. But if you're interested in ideas..."

A cooking school? She hadn't taken home ec the first time, and she sure didn't want to do it now. Besides, remembering high school was a huge source of pain for her. She'd rather just leave it all behind. She probably wouldn't even have come in today if she'd known he was going to be here. "I don't have the time for anything elaborate."

She set her teeth. Just because she didn't cook didn't mean she couldn't. She could still hear the skepticism in Amelia's voice when she'd offered to do the dinner on Christmas Day. Her laugh had been followed by the suggestion of a caterer. It had been good-natured sisterly teasing, but it had stung just the same. Now, looking up in to Mack's handsome face, she really felt as though she had something to prove.

"Would what I tasted work as an appetizer? For my Christmas dinner? You did say you had the recipe."

Briefly she imagined bringing out a tray with warm, golden-brown parcels, serving perhaps a glass of wine or punch before dinner while Jesse played with his new toys and carols played on the stereo. What would Amelia say then? Amelia had been so determined to look after the ranch work in Kelley's absence. Surely Kelley could prove herself equally adept at Amelia's forte. She was getting so tired of being the sister in jeans and boots. There was more to her than that. Maybe she was finally ready to let someone see it.

"Absolutely. They're easy as anything."

She highly doubted it, but they couldn't be that hard could they? "That would be great, Mack. I appreciate it."

He jotted down the recipe on a card and put it in the bag with the rest of her purchases. "You'll need some of my dill seasoning. The rest of the items you can buy at the grocery store."

He put in a bottle and rang in the pears and cookie kit. At the last moment he took a small bag from beneath the counter and tucked it in with her purchases.

"A little treat for Ruby, if you can sneak it in."

"I'll do that." She paid and put the receipt in her wallet.

"Give my best to your family, Kelley."

"I will."

She was nearly to the door, tugging her mittens back over her hands, when she heard his warm voice once more, sending a delicious shiver down her arms.

"And, Kelley?"

She half turned to look back at him.

"Merry Christmas."

For some inexplicable reason, the simple wish made the backs of her eyes sting. She pulled on her mitten, gripped the door handle and stepped out into the bitter cold.

CHAPTER TWO

"DAMMIT!"

Kelley dropped the pan onto the stovetop, fanning away smoke as she sucked on her burned finger.

The puffs were ruined, completely ruined. She took off the oven mitt and went to the window, pushing it open a crack and letting the cold air in and the acrid smell out. She'd picked up the rest of the ingredients on Mack's list and taken them back to the motel thinking a trial run would help her pass the time while the storm blew outside.

Only, there'd been a flaw in her plan. The one aluminum baking sheet in the kitchenette cupboard now appeared charred beyond repair. The tops of the phyllo puffs were burned. And several of the pastry sheets lay shredded on the small countertop amid a mess of prosciutto, parmesan, asparagus and Mack's dill seasoning. The mess was held together by bits of greasy melted butter that hadn't behaved…perhaps because she hadn't had something the recipe called a pastry brush. She'd tried using the curved end of a fork, but it had made nothing but a mess.

She was in deep, deep trouble. She pushed back a few strands of hair that had escaped her braid. The recipe had sounded simple. If she couldn't even make a simple hors d'oeuvre, how could she expect to pull off a whole dinner without burning down the house?

A knock sounded on the motel door as she dumped the

whole lot of ruined food in the garbage. "Hello? Everyone okay in there?"

And the pan froze in her hand.

Okay, so she was thinking about Mack, and the way he'd held her hand longer than necessary today. That was the only reason it sounded like his voice outside.

She went to the door and looked out the peep hole.

"Oh, no," she breathed, pressing her hands to her cheeks and attempting to smooth her wild hair. She looked a fright. It *was* Mack. His dark eyes were flashing, his jaw taut as he lifted his hand to bang on the door again. She jumped at the harsh contact of fist to wood, her heart taking up a frantic hammering.

"Are you okay? I can smell smoke!" She heard the urgent tone of his voice and had the desperate thought he'd do something stupid like call 911 if she didn't answer.

"Hello? Answer me!"

Oh, hell! What if he broke down the door?

"Just a minute," she called, spinning in a frantic circle.

She opened the door, stood firmly in the breach. Snow swirled around Mack's head as his shoulders hunched against the storm.

"Kelley?"

Busted. "What in the world are you doing here?" she demanded, attempting to look defiant though her pulse was still pounding.

"I could smell smoke and was afraid of a fire." Without a how do you do, he pushed by her and into the room. "Is everything okay?"

"Perfectly fine."

She hated how the words came out with a quaver at the end, or how his bursting past her sent a spiral of fear from her head to the tip of her toes. Alone, in a motel room, with a man she didn't exactly know. Memories rushed back, sharp as knives, and she beat them aside angrily. She was sick to death of them having power over her.

"Is that awful smell asparagus puffs?"

Humiliation made her want to sink through the floor, and she had the thought that at least it would provide an escape route. She instinctively shuffled sideways so that she had the door directly behind her. "It was. Definitely past tense."

He coughed. "What did you cook them with, a blow torch? At least I know you're all right and not setting the entire motel on fire."

His obvious concern alleviated a bit of panic she'd inevitably felt at his bursting in. "What in the world are you doing here?"

He shook his head, sending snowflakes sprinkling off his hair. "I'm staying next door. Until my house is finished."

"Your house?" What was he talking about? He was living here? And building a house?

"You didn't know?"

She shook her head. "No."

"I thought the people in Rebel Ridge kept the grapevine going better. Mabel Reese must be slacking. I'm building a house out on the bluff."

She refused to be charmed by his reference to the town gossip who kept everyone in the know whether they wanted to be or not. "And you're here…" She went to close the window and left the idea hanging, still aware that if it came to it, she could reach the doorway first.

He smiled, popping the one dimple most unfairly. "You mentioned a motel in the shop today. I had no idea it was this one. Small world, huh?"

Too small to her mind.

He wrinkled his nose, raked his gaze over her dough-studded clothing and said, "Oh, boy."

And then it suddenly dawned on her that here stood a man who was capable of helping her with her problem. Just not tonight. Not in a motel room. Her blood momentarily seemed to run cold. If she could just ask him, and get rid of him, it would be fine. If he agreed, they'd meet somewhere she felt safe. A controlled environment, like his cooking school. One with lots of people around.

Mack looked around him at the mess everywhere. The bed was the only untouched area in the room. Kelley Hughes, class wallflower, stood before him in old jeans spotted with what looked like dough and spots of grease. Her hair was coming out of her braid and her cheeks were flushed. She had a hard time meeting his eyes.

Everything about her made his blood leap. She was beautiful this way, less than perfect, without the cool control she had exhibited this afternoon. Though he could tell she was trying hard. He hadn't remembered her at first, not until she'd said her name and he remembered the quiet girl who'd sat at the back of his math class. She'd been the studious type, and he'd been too withdrawn to say anything to her anyway.

The acrid smell was horrible, but his nose detected what was likely pastry and ham. He hid a smile. He'd been correct on the first guess…asparagus puffs. Nothing was burning down. It was just burned.

Her soft voice interrupted his analysis. "I'm afraid the puffs didn't turn out as I expected."

"What happened?"

She looked as if she was about to swallow a canary. Despite her words this afternoon, he'd bet his boots she couldn't cook. Someone who could wouldn't have looked so uncomfortable surrounded by pots and utensils.

She took a deep breath. "I can't cook. Not a bit."

"No kidding." A grin tugged the corner of his mouth as her eyes narrowed.

"Look, save the smart remarks, okay? I promised everyone a Christmas Day dinner…I can't ask my sister to put more on her plate. She's looking after the ranch right now while I'm gone, and there's her son, Jesse, and she's going to have Gram when she comes home—" She broke off, took a breath. "But you have a cooking school. You could help."

Well, well. She was asking for help after all. It surprised him.

"Yes, lessons are once a week, above the store."

Snow melted off his dark hair, trickling in a cold path down the back of his neck. He saw the glimmer of despair in her eyes. His regular cooking classes wouldn't cut it, not with the tight timing, and they both knew it. "But Christmas is in days, not weeks," he added.

"I'm aware of that." She sighed. But there was something else behind it, and he wasn't sure what. She looked, at this moment, as if she'd like to be somewhere else. Anywhere else.

"Do you want *me* to cook dinner for your family?"

It was only dinner. Surely it didn't matter that much *who* cooked it. What mattered was being together, or so he was told.

Kelley folded her hands in front of her, and he saw the red tip on her index finger—she'd burned herself.

"That would be the easy way, I suppose. But, no, thank you. I need to do this myself."

She jutted her chin. "Right now you're the only one I can think of to help me. I want you to show me, Mack. I need to do this. I need to prove to them I can do it." She turned her hazel eyes up to him. "I need to prove it to myself."

He swallowed against the rush of something he didn't want to acknowledge. Someone needed him. And that was a rarity.

"Will you teach me how to make a Christmas dinner for my family?"

Mack fought back the sudden urge to hug her. The woman standing before him now thought she looked tough, he was sure of it. She obviously cared deeply about her family—that scored points with him.

Her imploring eyes were exactly the sort of reason he'd started Mack's Kitchen in the first place. And maybe helping her would make Christmas something to look forward to this year, take away the monotony of the holiday. Help him to forget why he'd never bought in to the whole Christmas magic thing. The one time he had…it had been a disaster.

Holiday cheer wasn't for him, but he understood other people's need for it. "I'll help you."

"You will?"

He chuckled at the astonishment he heard in her voice. "Yes, I will. Teaching is what I do, and from what you've said, no one else in your family is up to it. Besides—" he looked around him at the mess, slid his gaze back to hers "—I do enjoy a challenge."

"Ha-ha."

"And since I can't see us making it out to buy any groceries right now, how much phyllo have you got left? We might as well get started."

"Here?" Kelley's eyes darted from him to the door and back, her jumbled-up nerves suddenly back with a vengeance. She'd meant at his *store*. At his place of business. Not a motel room in the middle of the night! "I don't think that's a good idea."

"Are you expecting someone?" he asked.

The worldly question sent a blush straight up her neck. "No! Of course not!" Her eyes widened further as his dimple flashed again and she realized he was teasing. There wasn't much time before Christmas and she had a lot of work to do. But a motel room?

"Come on, this is much more fun than being stuck with only the television for company. Besides, you fall off the horse, you get right back on. It can't be that bad."

She followed him into the kitchen and realized how it must look to him. It was a complete disaster.

He grinned and that damnable dimple flashed again. "Okay, so I was wrong. It *can* be that bad." A laugh rippled out of his throat. "Sit tight. I'm going to pop back next door for a minute." He got to the door and looked back. "And Kelley? Don't touch *anything*."

Moments later he was back carrying his own kitchenette-stocked cookie sheet, a half head of broccoli, a box of eggs, cheese and a tiny spice bottle.

"What's all that?"

"Dinner."

Kelley hadn't followed his instructions to the letter, but she'd cleaned a tidy space on the counter. He put the sheet on the stovetop and rubbed his hands together. "Okay," he said. "First the pastry."

Kelley stood several feet away as he went to get the phyllo. He had no idea how uncomfortable she was right now, and she'd cut off her own arm before she'd explain. In her head she knew the quiet boy she remembered was harmless. But her subconscious kept shouting something else. She wasn't used to being railroaded, and he'd burst in tonight and taken over. But she was the foreman of a ranch. She could do this.

"Kelley, you can't cook from over there." He beckoned her over. She swallowed and quietly went to his side. Gently he showed her how to separate the sheets and lay them out carefully. "Where's your pastry brush?"

"I haven't got one."

He muttered an exclamation and picked up the bowl of melted butter. "That's why it looks so torn, then. We'll have to improvise."

He turned his head to look at her and she shrugged. "Improvise?"

He laughed at her simple response. "You know."

She still didn't get his meaning. Improvise what?

"Okay, so you don't know. Let's put it in ranch terms. Imagine there's a fence line broken and you left your tools somewhere. What do you do?"

"You're going to equate pastry with fences." The analogy relaxed her in spite of herself and she leaned forward, watching the motion of his hands.

"Don't be so narrow-minded. Look. We use our fingers instead. Come here. Dip and spread." She put her hands on the dough, and he quickly reached out to stop her. "Gently," he said quietly, holding her hand in his and guiding it, smoothing the butter on the phyllo.

Kelley's stomach clenched, full of nerves. His hands were firm and sure on hers, the slick texture of the butter warm beneath their fingertips as they smoothed it over the fragile sheets. His body nestled close behind her; she could feel the strong heat of it against her back as he guided her hands. Never in the last decade had she let a man get this close to her. There'd never been a need at Rocking H for personal contact.

She was sure he couldn't tell the battle waging within her—the thin, sharp thread of fear warring with a shocking need to feel close to him. Or her surprise at realizing she *wanted* to feel close to him. This afternoon his quiet concern had been genuine, and something told her that she was safe.

She chanced a look up at him. Big mistake. For in the moment she turned her head to look up, he looked down, and their gazes caught. His pupils were dark. Not teasing at all, but open and curious, like he was trying to see right down into the core of her. She hadn't expected this at all…not Mack, not cooking, and certainly not the knot of awareness that was settling low within her.

There was something here. She caught her lip between her teeth and worried it. Right now they had their hands in butter and all she could think was how good-looking he was, the way he had tiny crinkles at the corners of his eyes or how broad his shoulders were as she was snuggled between them.

She bit down on her lip, fighting back the instinctive fear that rose up without warning.

"What's next?" She made herself say something to break the silence.

A slow smile formed on his lips and Kelley felt completely out of her depth. She hadn't meant it as an innuendo of any sort, but what else would he think as she stood there staring at him like a lovesick kitten? She had to stop this. She wasn't interested in Mack Dennison, or *any* man for that matter. What she wanted was to bake prosciutto and asparagus puffs.

She held his gaze but stiffened her shoulders. "I meant with the recipe."

To her amazement the smile grew bigger. "I assumed nothing less."

Kelley huffed and turned away. That was enough of being silly and making calf eyes. "You've certainly broken out of your shy shell."

"You can't build a business by hiding away in a closet."

She wanted to reach out and give him a push, but then remembered that her fingers were coated in butter. She moved away to the sink where she rinsed and dried her hands, away from his body, feeling safer with distance. "Are you saying you had to force yourself?"

"That's exactly what I'm saying. I don't know if you noticed, but I wasn't the most personable kid in class. I had to learn to meet people. To like people. So I did."

She wished she could shed her old self so easily. She turned away. "I thought you were going to help."

"And so I am. Just having a little fun. Don't you think this should be fun?"

Kelley remembered holding Gram's hand as she lay in the cardiac care unit. And little Jesse's face as he whispered to her what he'd asked for for Christmas. All the little resentments faded away in those moments; family was everything. She squared her shoulders.

"I need to do this, Mack, and cooking is beyond me."

"Okay."

She paused, surprised at his easy acceptance. "That's it?" He wasn't going to bait her more or tease her or ask her why it was so difficult?

"Don't be so hard on yourself. You run a ranch, for Pete's sake. You can't be expected to do everything well."

"I'm not used to being incapable."

"And I bet it kills you to admit it." He grinned.

She raised an eyebrow and he relented. He touched her again, his hand resting on her shoulder. He'd touched her more today than any man had in a long time. What was odd was that it wasn't accompanied by her usual instinct to run or curl into a ball.

"All teasing aside. Everyone can cook, once they learn how. You've just never learned, that's all." He stepped back and reached for some of the thinly sliced ham. "Then let's cook, Kelley. I promise you, it won't be all that painful."

When she looked at his warm smile, she knew he was wrong. Because already she was feeling a tightness around her chest that had little to do with cooking.

Together they layered on ham, asparagus, fresh parmesan and Mack's dill seasoning. He showed her how to fold the pastry over and slice it, laying each piece on his own baking tray. He slid it into the oven and showed her how to work the timer…all without making her feel stupid or inept. All with little touches, correcting her hand or showing her how to slice the rounds without tearing. Touches that she sensed meant nothing to him. And maybe that was why she seemed to accept them. He was in his role of teacher.

When it was done he found a larger mixing bowl. Kelley stared as he put it on the counter and stepped back. "Now what are you doing?"

"I'm not. You are. You're going to make us dinner. A few appetizers does not a meal make."

"But I can't…"

He merely raised an eyebrow. "You can. This was one of the first things we learned to make in home ec. Mrs. Farber was a strict one, remember her?"

Kelley turned a pot holder over in her fingers. "I never took home ec, remember?"

"Oh, right." He seemed oblivious to her discomfort and continued on. "She had this saying…a place for everything and everything in its place. She was terrifying. But she knew how to cook and she knew how to teach it. So tonight I get to pass the torch."

She angled him a dry look.

"Right, well, maybe no torches."

She couldn't help the smile that trembled on her lips at his joke. "What am I making?"

"Crustless quiche."

She couldn't help it; she rolled her eyes. "Quiche? Seriously?"

"You can scramble the eggs if you want, but this is much better and hardly more work. We don't have proper pastry, so we'll go crustless."

A small search revealed one round baking dish. In no time Kelley had whipped eggs, grated cheese, added in bits of broccoli and some of the leftover ham from the asparagus rolls and a dash of something from a bottle Mack had brought with him. It all poured into the buttered pan, ready to go in the oven the moment the appetizers came out.

"I did that."

"Yep." He leaned back against the counter with a satisfied smile as she slid the oven mitt off her hand. The perfectly browned puffs were on the stove, cooling.

"I have a quiche in the oven."

"Indeed. Usually we don't get to that until lesson two, but you did a great job."

Kelley looked up at him. He'd been a gentleman. He'd been patient and understanding and easy to be around.

"Thank you, Mack."

She didn't know how to put the rest into words without sounding encouraging, so she simply let herself smile, and popped one of the fresh bites in her mouth. Delicious. And not a burn mark on them.

"I forgot. I brought one more thing."

Mack boosted himself away from the counter and went to the fridge. He took out a bottle of white wine and a Swiss

Army knife from his pocket. Within seconds he'd flipped out a corkscrew.

Kelley got two glasses from the cupboard. She could hardly kick him out after he'd helped her…and provided most of the groceries. The hour they'd spent cooking had gone a long way in gaining a simple, yet tentative trust.

"Tumblers?"

She laughed. "What do I look like, the Waterford factory?"

"They'll do, then. Though to be fair…this is more of a whiskey joint sort of place."

He poured the wine into the glasses as lovely smells came out of the oven. Kelley grabbed a plate and put the asparagus rolls on it, moving to the tiny drop-leaf table that was set up in the outer area of the motel room.

"This wasn't the dinner you planned tonight, I bet."

"No."

"How's your grandmother?"

His asking pleased her. "Hanging in there. Her procedure has been postponed, though." She was surprised but touched by the concern in his eyes. "Not because of her condition," she added hastily. "The weather warning. The hospital is postponing nonemergency procedures until after the storm."

"And she's going to be fine?"

"The doctor says so. But…"

She stopped as a lump formed in her throat. Grandma Ruby was everything to her and Amelia. She took a sip of wine, unwilling to put voice to her fears.

At her long silence, Mack leaned forward. "Is it worse than you said? Is there more? What's the *but?*"

"But she has a heart condition, and it has really made us realize that she's getting older. That she won't be around forever. And so maybe part of this whole Christmas thing is just me wondering how many more Christmases we'll all have together. I don't know what I'd do without her, Mack."

It was an intimate confession, especially between the two

of them; two people that had always known *of* each other but had never been friends. She didn't know why she was able to talk to him so easily. Maybe because in many ways he was a stranger, and it was easier to admit things when there was that bit of natural distance between them.

Mack reached across the small table and took her hand in his. All she could do was squeeze back.

Kelley stared down at their joined fingers. Mack's thumb rubbed over the top of her hand, the friction creating a warmth she was unused to. Normally she would have pulled away immediately. But this time she accepted the simple touch.

"I'm sure she's going to be fine. Try not to worry so much."

Kelley pulled her hand away. "I'm just out of sorts. I'm not used to being away from the ranch for so long, the main phone lines are down, and Amelia's not answering her cell phone. She probably forgot to charge it."

"I take it that's happened before."

A smile flirted with the edges of her lips. "A time or two. But the reception at the house isn't always the best, either."

"So why didn't she bring Ruby into town?"

Kelley took a sip of the wine. She licked the remnants off her lips and sighed. "It's harder for her. She has Jesse to worry about now, and he's started school. You've seen my cooking." This got a smile. "We'd all starve if it were left to me. I hired an extra hand to help out while I was gone, but I don't know if he arrived before the storm or not. Amelia insisted she could manage. But I just don't know."

"You really don't have much faith in people, do you?"

The quiet question unsettled her. Maybe what had happened to her made her lose faith. She kept to her inner circle—her family—and today's foray into the cooking world with Mack was definitely an aberration. The ding of the oven timer saved her from answering.

She went to take the quiche out while Mack went to the

window and parted the curtains, looking out. "It's picked up out there. You can't even see across the street."

Kelley looked over at him, feeling the intimacy grow, unsure what to do about it. Here they were, shut up in a small motel room in the middle of the first real storm of the year. She pushed away the nervousness that suddenly popped up again. She didn't do well in closed spaces. At least the lights were on. "Good thing you're just next door. It's a short commute."

He laughed, the sound warm and masculine. "You wouldn't send me away before dinner, would you?"

She suddenly wanted him to go, but somehow wanted him to stay, too. The thought of being here alone in the blizzard seemed so dismal that she nearly welcomed the company. Normally when a storm was coming, she bunked up at the house with Gram and Amelia and Jesse. Amelia looked after everyone and Kelley played board games with her nephew. Being stuck in town at a half-rate motel wasn't quite as heart-warming. Somehow having Mack with her made her feel safer, and that was unexpected.

"You helped me make it. I suppose it's unlikely you'll be poisoned."

Again the laugh…my word, he laughed easily, and it sent ripples of pleasure down her arms. Kelley reached up for plates in the tiny cupboard, ignoring the quiver in her belly that his voice ignited. She handed him a plate, but he paused with it between their hands.

"Would you *like* me to be poisoned?"

She looked up into his eyes, bright with teasing. He was having fun with her. And she liked it. The moment held. Her breath caught as his smile faded and his gaze dropped to her open lips.

Was he considering kissing her?

Breath came back in with a rush of panic on its heels as she thrust the plate in his hand. "Keep it up and I'll find a way."

He reached into a drawer and pulled out a knife for cutting

the quiche. He put it into her hand, his fingers warm over hers as she gripped the handle. He was a touchy one! She shivered as he leaned close to her ear and whispered, "Poison's cleaner, but a knife will do the trick in a pinch."

That was it. She stomped her foot and wheeled. "Stop it, you infernal tease!"

The lights flickered. They looked up at the fixture together, and then everything went dark.

CHAPTER THREE

"POWER'S OUT."

"Thanks, Einstein." She put the knife back on the counter next to the warm quiche and tried to cover her sudden unease. His form was dark, his face shadowed in the dimness. The intimacy of earlier was back, sharp and immediate. She tried to make her heart stop pounding so furiously, make her breaths regular. She put several feet of countertop between them.

Mack was already searching the end table beside the bed for matches, and she watched his shadowed form with her heart in her throat. She tried to push the memories away. He was not Wilcox, and this was not an abandoned cabin in the middle of nowhere.

This was Mack, in a motel room; in the dark; in the middle of the first big blizzard of the year. Her heart pounded against her ribs painfully.

"Any luck with matches?" he asked.

She jumped at the sound of his voice. "Not yet," she croaked, opening a single drawer with shaking fingers. A part of her wanted to reach out and let him shelter her. And yet the thought also scared her to death. She didn't know him well enough. His caring had drawn her to him tonight, but how well did she really know him? She didn't.

"Do you have a flashlight anywhere?"

His voice sounded huskier in the darkness and she swallowed thickly. "I think there's one in the truck. I can go look."

"In this weather?

"But we can't just sit here in the dark!"

She could tell he was grinning, even though she couldn't make out the details of his face.

"Why not? I do some of my best work in the dark."

"Stop smiling. This isn't funny." Indeed it was not. She was torn between fear of being alone and fear of being with him, and she was becoming more tied up in knots by the moment.

"Okay," he relented. "Look, the meal is cooked." He moved to stand beside her and picked up the knife. "Can you see enough to get some forks? We might as well eat while it's warm."

She nodded, but he caught her hesitancy. "Are you scared of the dark, Kelley?"

A tiny thread of hysteria bubbled inside her. The dark? That and then some. "A little."

"I used to be, too. I was hoping if I made light of it… But it didn't work, did it?" He reached out and kneaded her shoulders and she closed her eyes, focusing on the reassuring sound of his voice and not the horrible memories she kept trying to push away.

"How did you stop?" There was no sound in the room beyond their breathing. And then she held her breath and there was just him.

"I don't know. I guess I just stood up to it." His fingers rubbed the tendons on the side of her neck and she exhaled slowly. "It's okay. You're not alone in here. We've got shelter from the storm and we've even got dinner. You don't need to be afraid."

But she was afraid. "The walls feel small," she whispered, and to her surprise, he rested his chin on the top of her head.

"I know," he said, and her heart squeezed.

He gave her shoulders a final rub and backed away. "Let's have something to eat. Maybe after that the power will be back on."

She found utensils with shaky hands, and Mack scooped up servings for both of them. He was taking the plates to the table when a knock sounded at the door, the sharp sound making her jump yet again in the darkness.

"Hello? Miss Hughes?"

Kelley stood and went closer to the door. "Yes?"

"It's Jerry Smith, the owner. I wanted to make sure you're all right."

"I'm fine, thank you," she called through the door, and stepped forward to open it.

"Don't bother opening the door, miss, keep your heat in. There should be an emergency candle in the very bottom drawer beside the stove. Hopefully the power won't be out for long."

"Jerry," Mack called out, "it's Mack. No need to check on me."

Kelley blushed. Smith didn't know her, but Mack was a bit of a celebrity, and here they were in a motel room together. Her cheeks felt like fire and she pressed her cool fingers to them.

"Okay, Mack. I'll carry on. Colder 'n hell out here."

"You know the owner?" Kelley whispered.

"I've been here for two months already, remember?"

The chill was already seeping through the walls. "Come on," she suggested. "Let's eat before it gets cold."

Mack found the candle and a simple holder, put it in the middle of the tiny table and poured more wine. She sat stiffly and picked up her fork, ignoring the way the candlelight highlighted his cheekbones, throwing the hollows into shadow. "Let's just eat, and maybe by the time we're done, the lights will be back on." She let out a shaky breath. "I guess Jesse will get his white Christmas after all."

She took a bite of the quiche, surprised at how good it tasted. "It's not bad!"

"I told you anyone can cook." He took a bite of his own.

The candlelight flickered and she lifted her eyes to meet his. "It's not turkey and trimmings."

"We'll get you there," he smiled, and she smiled back.

For several minutes they made small talk about Rocking H and how he'd spent his time since high school seeking his fortunc. The candle burned lower and the conversation grew lazy. She talked about Ruby and Amelia and mentioned Jesse's Christmas wish for a father and how it had touched her. The smile faded from his lips and his eyes grew serious.

"So if you could havc one Christmas wish, what would it be?"

She opened her mouth to answer but he stopped her, holding up a finger. "Wait. One wish for Kelley. Not for anyone else."

What would she wish for? She had the ranch and Amelia and Gram and Jesse, and she loved them. But lately she had wondered what else was out there, for her. She'd always wanted to travel, see some of the world, meet new people and experience new things. Instead she'd been tied to the Rocking H in so many ways. And Mack had just told her how he'd gone and done all those things and had come back, successful, even rich. It made her wish seem foolish.

"More," she whispered finally. "I want more." She suddenly felt unbearably guilty for saying it, knowing she should be thankful for having so much. She pushed out her chair and went to the sink, holding on to the edge.

She heard Mack's chair scrape away from the tiny table. He stepped forward until he was only a breath away. Close enough she could smell him—soap and some sort of manly aftershave, somehow magnified in the semidarkness.

"Kelley, look at me."

"This is highly unusual." She spoke to the wall behind the sink. "We hardly know each other. I can't imagine why I've said as much as I have. I don't usually…" But she stopped. "Maybe this dinner isn't a good idea. I can have it catered—" she started to babble "—it really doesn't matter. And I need to get back as soon as possible…"

"Stop." Strong hands gripped her arms and turned her around. "Lord, it was a simple question."

She froze at the feeling of his hands on her arms. After a few seconds his fingers relaxed and she let out the breath she'd pulled in. Nothing about this evening was simple. Especially not the way he seemed able to knock down fences she'd erected years ago.

"Kelley," he murmured.

She felt like weeping. She'd tried to hide things tonight but apparently she'd failed. He'd seen clear through her bravado and attempt at coolness. She stared at his chest, focusing on a pewter medal that hung from a chain. "I want to see new places. I want to do things." In the darkness she seemed able to whisper her thoughts like a confession. "I want people to see me as more than the ranch foreman in dusty jeans and dirty boots."

She couldn't look at him, not when she was feeling this selfish. He released one arm, but the touch was immediately back as he put a finger beneath her chin and tipped it upward.

"There is nothing wrong with wanting more, Kelley. Don't think that there is. Wanting more saved my life."

She wanted to ask what that meant, but her heart slammed in her chest. *Mack was more.* The kind of more she'd *never* wanted.

A tip of a finger teased her neck, and she closed her eyes. Never was a long time. And right now she felt completely helpless to do anything but accept his light caress.

His chin dipped the slightest bit so that his lips were close to her temple.

Her chest rose and fell as sensations expanded inside her, shattering the reserve she'd clung to so tightly.

She held her breath, feeling yet again the rise of panic. But he stepped back, looked at her for a long moment.

"God, you're beautiful."

"I'm not."

"Damned near the prettiest thing I've *ever* seen. You look like an angel."

"You're just saying that because of what I just said."

"No, I'm not. I'm telling you what I see. You're just trying to hide her. What I don't understand is why."

She really couldn't breathe now as his low voice seduced her. But the why was stuck in a big painful lump in her chest. It would always be there. He could never know the why.

"Stop hiding. For five minutes stop hiding. I will if you will."

He came forward then, his body barring hers from walking away. Outside, the storm howled, but the warmth of his body cocooned her, solid and warm. Mack raised his hand, grazed her jawline gently.

Everything in her went into a slow meltdown. This gentleness was so foreign, so sensual, she wasn't sure she could bear it. A tiny voice inside of her warned that he'd want more, but she pushed it away with a silent promise to herself of *just this much*. She wanted to see, for once, if she could handle it.

His fingers traced the soft skin, over and over, touching her cheek. Their gazes locked for long moments as she contemplated what would happen next.

"This isn't a good idea," she whispered, hearing the longing in her own voice even as she denied him. And still the tips of his fingers stroked, a tactile kiss against skin. Taking his time.

"I know."

"I think you should go."

"I probably should."

"What do you want from me?" She trembled. She needed different words than she'd heard before. She wanted for once in her adult life to touch and be touched, kiss and be kissed without the mantle of fear cloaking her.

"A kiss," he murmured, his gaze following the path of his fingertips, the whole thing setting her body on fire. "I'd like one kiss."

His fingertips caressed, cupping her cheek as he took the last step in and claimed her mouth.

And oh, he was gentle. Her heart wept with the beauty of it as his soft lips touched hers briefly. Their breaths mingled in the silence as the candle flickered behind them. His lips touched hers again, then moved to graze the crests of her cheekbones. She closed her eyes and sighed. His right hand pulled her closer so that she fit lightly against his body. The sensations were heightened as much by places they didn't touch as the ones where they did.

And still he kissed her, feather-light kisses on her mouth until she finally raised her arms to his shoulders and kissed him back.

Mack closed his eyes against the onslaught of her taste as her fingers dug into his shoulder blades. His blood surged as her mouth opened beneath his, letting him in. He hadn't expected the sweetness, and he hadn't expected the heat. Both hit him like a fist in the gut. And with her small breasts pressed against his chest, he wanted more. One kiss wasn't enough, and the knowledge tore into him, leaving him questioning.

Tonight he'd wanted to kiss her, plain and simple. And not just because she deserved to feel beautiful and have someone mean it, and not because she'd admitted she was afraid of the dark like he was, but because he *wanted* to.

Her body was warm against his and he opened his lips wider, demanding more. A sound growled up from his chest and into her mouth and he took a step forward, backing them against the solid counter.

Kelley felt his body press hers more firmly into the counter. The top dug into her and recalled her to her senses. Not this much. She had to stop it now. She had to keep control of the situation.

She wrenched her lips from his, sliding out from between his body and the Formica countertop.

"We need to stop," she breathed, skittering away to the main part of the room. Once there she realized the only furniture was a bed and she felt the silent scream building. No. She would *not* lose control of the situation. Of herself.

He followed her.

"Kelley."

His tone was placating, but she shook her head. "You've got to go. Now."

"It was just a kiss."

"No, it damn well wasn't," she replied, lifting her head and pinning him with her gaze. "I said no. I meant it."

The words gave her power she hadn't expected. There would be no negotiation. No backing down.

"I don't want to leave you like this."

She fought to keep her voice steady. "I need you to go. Dinner is over."

"All right, if that is what you truly want." He agreed but his tone was harsh and her heart continued to pound away in her chest. He spun on his heel and went to the door, grabbing his jacket on the way.

He was gone with a gust of icy wind and the slam of the door. She rushed behind him and locked it with a click of the dead bolt, adding the chain for good measure.

Then she sat on the bed, touched her lips with shaking fingers. A laugh bubbled up from her belly, high-pitched and disbelieving.

And when it faded away, the only other sound was of her crying.

CHAPTER FOUR

"PULLING OUT?"

Mack was watching her from the doorway to his motel room. At the sound of his voice she closed her eyes, exhaled and pasted a smile on her face as she slammed the passenger door to the truck, wading through several inches of snow to the tailgate. She could handle this. She'd had lots of time to think while the snow had blown and drifted outside. At the end, she'd come to two conclusions. One, she still wanted to make Christmas dinner properly, and for that she needed his help. And two, she had to make it absolutely plain that their relationship was a working one. Cool. Distant. Professional.

"Gram's being released today."

"Oh, that's good news." His words made warmth curl around inside her.

"Yes, it is." She tentatively met his eyes, unable to stop the relief sluicing through her at the good prognosis. "She's doing very well, her doctor says. I think we'll all feel better once she's back home where she belongs."

He leaned against the door frame, looking as if he hadn't a care in the world. His breath made clouds in the cool air, and he had on a jacket but it was unzippered.

"You made it through the storm okay, I see."

Small talk reduced them to redundancies. "Yes," she replied. The word came out softer than she intended as she remembered the long hours she'd sat awake, reliving things she didn't want to again, and finding them all mixed up with how good his kiss had felt. Too good. They'd simply gotten carried away. It was up to her to set things straight. To set the boundaries.

She ran her tongue over her bottom lip as if she could still taste him there. There could be no more kissing if she wanted to achieve her goal. It would only muddy the waters.

"About the dinner..." She leaned against the tailgate and put her hands into her coat pockets. "I want to hire you to teach me to cook Christmas dinner."

She put a slight emphasis on the word *hire*. He had to understand.

"Hire me." He paused. "I already said I'd help you. I don't need your money, Kelley."

"If anyone else hired you, they'd pay you for your time. I am no different." She straightened her spine. This had to be about business only, and he needed to understand that. "Whatever your going rate is, that's fine."

"If this is about the other night..." His shoulder came away from the door frame.

"It's not," she shifted her purse in front of her. He should just stay where he was while she laid out the rules.

"Fair enough. You can hire me to teach you to cook."

She forced herself to lean back against the tailgate of the truck. "Just let me know when I should come to the shop and I'll juggle some things around at home."

He considered for a moment. "It's going to be inconvenient for you, isn't it? Coming into Helena."

She shrugged, though he was right. Driving here and back while trying to keep the Rocking H going and helping out with Gram was going to require some good time management skills. "I'll manage."

"You know, I haven't been out to the Rocking H since I was a kid."

"You want to come to the ranch?" Her back stiffened. In her mind she'd rehearsed this conversation and it had always ended with her in a class at his shop. Not him, in her kitchen. Ever.

"I don't usually do house calls, but it's Christmas." His boyish smile was disarming. He continued on as if she hadn't painted a scowl on her face. "Why not? Save you a drive in. I go out to check on my house at the Ridge several times a week, anyway, it's only a few minutes out of my way."

He made it sound almost like she was doing him the favor. It would make things infinitely easier for her. And Amelia was right next door. She raised one eyebrow. "Are you sure?"

He shifted his weight again, and she was glad he was in his stocking feet, his toes curled over the doorstep.

"You're in a special situation that's all. And you have enough on your plate. Merry Christmas." He sent her a wise-crack smile. "I'm normally a scrooge. You should take advantage of my offer before it disappears."

Her hands fidgeted in the pockets of her coat as she remembered his kiss. It couldn't happen again. She'd thought she could handle it but she couldn't.

"Strictly cooking," she stated baldly, amazed at her own temerity. But they'd danced around it enough. If this were going to happen at her house, it had to be crystal clear.

"Scout's honour." He grinned.

Her shoulders sagged with relief. "I don't know where to start…"

"Leave it to me. I'll come out tomorrow night after my six-o'clock class finishes. We'll tackle your vegetable course."

She paused with her hand on the door handle of the old pickup. Good, safe, vegetables. She'd said what she had to and he'd agreed.

"I live in what used to be the bunkhouse," she explained. "Are you sure this isn't too much of an imposition?"

"I'm sure," he replied. He pushed away from the frame, resting his hand on the edge of the door and looking pleased with himself. "Just be there."

* * *

Kelley saw the headlights turn up the drive and stood, taking a nervous breath.

Yesterday she'd been so aware of how she must appear to Mack. When he'd seen her at her truck, she'd been in her customary jeans and plaid shirt, bundled up in a sheepskin jacket. The uniform of a rancher. And it had served her well for a lot of years. She'd never wanted to draw attention to herself. Keeping herself competent and, well, sexless, had worked.

Right up to the point where Mack had kissed her. And called her beautiful.

Maybe he'd meant it, probably he hadn't, but yesterday morning she'd had a sudden desire to look slightly more feminine than a cowpoke in the middle of a roundup. Which hardly made sense since her sole purpose had been to set boundaries.

The vehicle came to a stop outside her door and she brushed a hand down her sweater, smoothing it down. She hadn't wanted to be too obvious, so she'd chosen her best jeans and a soft, thick-knit sweater in tan with a cowl collar. She'd put in earrings, tiny hoops rather than the plain gold studs she normally wore. She tightened her ponytail and took two complete breaths, trying to settle the nerves skittering around in her stomach.

He was here to show her how to cook. It was certainly *not* a date. There was nothing wrong with wanting to look decent rather than like someone who'd just come in from the barn.

She met him on the porch, leaving the door open behind her. He got out of a sport utility and came around the back bumper. Her heart missed a beat, then caught its normal rhythm somewhat accelerated. Lord, he was handsome. The sheepskin collar of his leather jacket cradled his jaw, his breath forming clouds around his head. His dark hair and eyes stood out in the light from her doorway and he paused at the bottom of her steps, holding grocery bags in his hands.

The pause held for only a few seconds, but it was enough that Kelley felt vibrations humming between them. Maybe it hadn't been all in her head. All she knew for sure was that this was the first time in a long time that she was looking forward to spending time with a man. That in itself was an earth-shaking discovery. Once she'd laid out the rules, something had happened to her fear. It had gone into hiding. She'd actually been anticipating his arrival. Maybe because he'd backed off when she'd asked. Or that he'd agreed to her terms without reservation.

"You made it."

His smile lit up his face. "With time to spare."

She found herself returning the easy smile. "Well, you'd better come in. It's cold out."

Kelley stood back as he entered, the grocery bags dangling from his fingers. She reached out and took two, simply to give her hands something to do. It looked as if he'd thought of everything, and she was momentarily intimidated. She was going to look stupid. She'd always considered herself modern, yet the fact that she couldn't cook was something else that made her feel distinctly unfeminine, whether it was wrong or right. It was just there.

No. She would do this. She just had to trust him to show her how.

"Kitchen's through there," she directed. It wasn't as if he'd get lost. She felt her cheeks flush as she followed him. The house was small—a kitchen and living room downstairs, bathroom and bedroom in a loft upstairs. That was all. Four rooms, and a storeroom off the back. She realized how it must look to him. When she'd mentioned his name on the drive from the hospital, Gram had known all about the big fancy house he was building on the bluff. Kelley had kept her eyes on the road, surprised but simply happy Ruby had the energy to make idle chatter.

She started to see the small house through his eyes. She had the main house's cast-off furniture from several years past, and very little in way of decoration. Amelia seemed to have inherited the decorating gene, and when the family got together it was always at the main house.

"Kelley, are you coming or not?"

"Coming!"

She went into the kitchen. He had started unpacking bags and she reached out to help. "Did you bring the whole store?" She was shocked to see the mass of ingredients accumulating on her table.

"It's not as scary as it looks. It's like anything else. Get started, and finish when you're done. Come on…I'll show you how to peel a carrot."

Kelley was pleased he was taking her seriously and keeping things about work. They sat together at the table, companionably peeling potatoes, carrots and chopping something Mack called pancetta.

"It looks like ham. Or thick bacon."

"It is. Kind of. It's not smoked, though. And we'll use the fat from cooking it to flavor the rest of the dish." He reached out to change how she held her knife and she held her breath. The last time he'd touched her this way she'd ended up in his arms. Her fingers shook and she relinquished the knife, took it back when he'd showed her. No more touching; it was too distracting.

"If you say so."

The potatoes, green beans and carrots were all put to boil while he showed her how to fry the pancetta, adding in sage and little bits of red pimiento. This time he didn't cradle her between his arms like he had with the phyllo; it was as if by unspoken agreement they'd decided to maintain their distance. When the pancetta was done, they removed it and cooked lemon, parsley and thyme in another pan. When everything was drained, Mack watched as she poured the lemon parsley mixture over the carrots, then put the beans to sauté lightly as she mashed the potatoes. With a growing sense of satisfaction, she measured out sour cream, cream cheese, butter and milk and added them to the smooth potatoes, then added the pancetta mixture to the beans all under the tutelage of Mack's keen eye.

"Oh, my word." Kelley looked around at her kitchen. Pots were everywhere. Potato and carrot peelings were still on the table. And she suddenly realized that despite the apparent success of the recipes, she had no serving dishes for anything.

"What's wrong?" He moved to her elbow. "You did wonderfully. Far better than I would have expected, considering the asparagus puffs disaster. We didn't even need a fire extinguisher."

She stared up at him, feeling slightly shell-shocked. "It's not that. I'm not ready for this. Look at my kitchen. If I make a mess like this in Amelia's kitchen, she'll…"

He pushed her into a chair and smiled indulgently. "First, you're going to breathe."

"I've finally bitten off more than I can chew."

"You haven't. You run a ranch nearly single-handedly, in charge of how many men and head of cattle? Come on. A single dinner isn't going to be your downfall."

"Yes, but I know how to do that."

"Well, you weren't born knowing how to run a ranch. You know because you learned. Three days ago you were shredding phyllo. Tonight you've made lemon parsleyed carrots, green beans with pancetta and sage, and delicious mashed potatoes." His hand grazed her knee, leaving a trail of warmth. "You're just overwhelmed, that's all. Now that you're getting the hang of things, you'll be able to tidy as you go. Relax, and let me bring you a plate."

Kelley absently rubbed the spot he'd patted as he removed a pan from the oven and sliced an herb-crusted turkey breast he'd brought with him. When the plate was full, he brought it to her. "Taste that and believe."

Where he got his confidence in her, she had no idea. Tonight was a small battle in a big war in her opinion. She picked up her fork as Mack cleaned the table of their peelings. "Aren't you eating?"

"I'm making room. Go ahead, tell me what you think."

"I don't want to ruin it. It's so pretty." The potatoes were snowy white, contrasted with the vibrant orange and green of the other vegetables. The smell of the turkey breast had her stomach growling. She took her first bite of beans and her eyes widened. "It's good. I mean, really good!"

"Of course it is. And you did it. I just watched and offered guidance."

He sat down with his own plate.

And the room got very quiet.

Kelley suddenly realized that for the second time in a week they were sharing a meal.

"This feels weird."

"You'll get over it." He aimed another winning smile her way. How was it that he was so relaxed when she was completely tied up in knots, just from being near him?

The trouble was, Kelley *was* getting over it. She was starting to like him. Unlike the rough, domineering men she was used to, he didn't judge. Mack's patience and careful guidance gave her confidence. He hadn't questioned her "rules," and his easygoing manner had a way of inspiring her trust. If this was the true Mack, then she also knew he was very good at what he did. No wonder he'd made Mack's Kitchen such a success.

He'd done things that she'd only daydreamed about. She still resented it the tiniest bit, knowing he'd seen so much of the world while she'd been held here by an invisible leash. But it was hard to hate him for it when they were sitting in her kitchen, eating a meal he'd helped her cook. He didn't look like a millionaire. He looked like an ordinary guy in jeans and a sweater who just happened to be, perhaps, the best-looking man she'd ever known.

"Can I ask you a question?"

"Sure." He scooped up potatoes on his fork and took a bite. "You did a really good job with these, you know."

His praised warmed her. "Thank you."

"What's your question?"

She looked up, feeling suddenly shy. "You've traveled so much. I was just wondering…what's Paris like?"

"Paris?"

"I've…I've just never traveled."

He was quiet for a few moments, as if trying to decide.

"Paris is noisy and hectic and smelly. Of course, it's easy to love when it smells of the day's fresh bread, or when you're walking the Left Bank and you're assaulted with exotic scents from the restaurants and cafés. It rains like the devil and then the clouds open up and it's like beams of light from heaven." He grinned. "Of course, no trip is complete without visiting the palace at Versailles. And you can really see why the revolution happened."

"Let them eat cake?"

His low laugh warmed her clear to her toes. "Precisely."

"And you've been to Italy? London?" She was hungry for the information now and leaned forward, encouraging him with a swoop of her fork.

He leaned back in his chair, toying with his glass of water. "Of course. I spent a month eating my way through towns and markets in Tuscany. And London is just…London. I lived in Chelsea for a while. Sunday mornings we…I went walking in Battersea Park and drank cappuccino from a paper cup."

"It sounds wonderful."

"Christmas in London is like nowhere else." He smiled, but his eyes took on a faraway look, and the curve of his lips faltered the smallest bit.

Did the memory hold some sadness for him? She wanted to ask, but it felt presumptuous. Besides, to do so would go against the "rules" she'd set up. Cool. Distant. Professional.

Trouble was, the more they talked, the less distant she became.

"What's it like at Christmas, then?"

He sat back in his chair, his face taking on a faraway look again. "There's skating at Somerset House, the lights in the

West End. Then there's the Christmas tree in Trafalgar Square and carolers…"

"Why did you come back?"

"Because this is home, Kelley." He met her eyes with quiet acceptance.

"But you have no one here."

The moment it was out of her mouth she wished she could take it back. Everyone in town knew that his mother had skipped off right after Mack had finished high school. Even though she'd barely known Mack, the story had caused a sensation in Rebel Ridge. His gaze slid away from hers and he picked up his glass of water. What had possessed her to point out he was alone…a week before Christmas?

She started to reach out but drew her hand back. She still wasn't comfortable touching him. "I'm sorry, Mack," she offered. "That was insensitive."

"It's okay. It's true."

She saw the line of his lips and the set of his jaw and knew she'd touched a nerve.

"How's your grandmother?"

She let him change the subject because clearly he was uncomfortable. The sudden realization he was going to be alone for Christmas settled in an empty place inside her. She had Gram, and Amelia and Jesse. But Mack had no one. For the briefest of moments, "Why don't you join us" hovered on her tongue. But she couldn't bring herself to say the words. Inviting someone for Christmas…well it was a family holiday. After the kiss they'd shared—she really didn't want it to be misconstrued. She wouldn't lead him on when nothing could come of it. And Lord only knew what Amelia and Gram would make of her inviting a man to Christmas dinner. So she kept the words inside and answered his question instead.

"She's doing well, but a bit slower. She tries not to show it, but when she thinks no one is looking…" Kelley wrinkled her brow. She couldn't help the worry. "She's not one to take it easy. I wish she'd be more patient. Let herself heal properly."

"If she's like I remember, she always went a mile a minute."

"Not now. And she's lost weight. She insists it's the hospital food, but I know better. She's getting old, Mack. Nothing we can do to stop it, but it sure doesn't make it any easier. She raised us. And she's the only family we have left."

Mack leaned forward and put a warm hand on her knee beneath the table. "You obviously care for your family deeply. And they love you. I know she's ailing, but I envy you that, Kelley. I envy it very much."

All of her senses were focused on the warm spot his hand made on her leg. Normally she shied away from physical touches.

But normally there was no Mack. And he seemed to touch like it was the most natural thing in the world.

"You do? But you've done so much with your life."

"Yes, I have. And I never had to answer to anyone, either. There's something to be said for that."

"But?"

He smiled. "So you did sense the *but*."

Kelley wasn't sure if he realized it or not, but his thumb was drawing lazy circles on her leg. She should move it away, but it felt good. It didn't feel threatening. It felt right.

Finally his voice came low, and maybe with a trace of anger she hadn't heard before.

"Not everyone grows up that way. In my line of work, I see a lot of families that don't work. For whatever reason. People who are alone. Divorcees. Singles. Widowers. All searching for something. You came to me to help your family. You came to me because you wanted to give something, not to find it. You're the exception, Kelley."

She didn't feel like the exception, and didn't feel like she was much of a giver, either. She was trying to hold things together, that was all. Trying to show she could do it, that there was more to her than what people saw at face value. But she couldn't go into all that with him. She'd feel even more foolish if he knew that one of her reasons was to feel more feminine.

"It's getting late," she murmured, trying hard to slow her heart rate down. His hand was still touching her thigh. It was silly to let a simple touch affect her so much. She pushed away from the table and gathered the plates. "Thank you, Mack. Now I have an appetizer, and I can manage the vegetables. I think. Although I have no idea what to do with what's left over."

"I can take it away if you want. If you have any plastic containers."

What on earth would he want her leftovers for? He was a cook, for goodness' sake! Surely he'd want to cook his own food from fresh ingredients.

"I have a place I donate to regularly. Having a cooking school means sometimes there's a surplus. If it means someone gets a decent meal, or any meal at all..."

Kelley looked up into his eyes. Mack Dennison was turning out to be a continual source of surprise. There was no putting on airs with him, despite the flashy SUV and the brand-name clothing. "You're turning out to be a bit of a saint," she said lightly, while emotions within her churned.

"Hardly a saint," he murmured, taking advantage of her full hands and moving in to kiss her.

CHAPTER FIVE

KELLEY'S FINGERS tightened around the plates as Mack's lips on hers made everything in her body turn to jelly. It was the most delicious thing in the world. Like the perfect ending to a long day.

His fingers were firm on her upper arms and his body warm against hers. He took a step and she danced slowly backward with him until her hips met with the countertop. Then there was no give between their bodies at all. His was firm and strong. And heaven help her, she liked it. It made her feel protected, not in danger.

The kiss broke off, and his forehead rested against hers, his breath fanning her cheeks and doing nothing to relieve the unexpected vibrations humming through her body.

"I told myself I wasn't going to do that." His voice was ragged and rough, sexy enough to make her toes curl.

"It's okay," she whispered, realizing that it truly was. The air still crackled between them; the admission had done nothing to defuse the moment. If anything, she wanted him more. His apology told her he'd respected her boundaries. He'd pulled back rather than pushing for more, and she was just feminine enough to be flattered that he'd wanted to kiss her again despite his good intentions.

She turned to the side and deposited the dishes beside the sink. She had to take a mental step back. She wasn't prepared for him and was even less ready for the feelings that suddenly were cropping up. Anticipation. Desire. She didn't know what to do with that. She was used to being in charge, but that was work. Her personal life…well, she didn't exactly have a personal life, and it shocked her that for the first time in ages she actually wanted one. If she hadn't, then why had she made an effort to dress up tonight? And yet still, deep down, fear tried to claw its way out, along with a certainty that she wasn't ready to take this relationship past friendship.

"I can't," she murmured, attempting to squirm out from between his body and the cupboards. She was fighting a ghost that shouldn't matter anymore, and she resented it. Mack made her not want it to matter at all.

She wished she could read his eyes as he watched her so closely, but she didn't have a clue of what he was thinking. He must think her the most irritating woman; she knew she was blowing hot and cold. She'd get just so close and then push away. She could still feel the heat of his hands on her skin and she swallowed.

She ached to be touched again but something held her back. There was a big gap between moving past fear and into trust territory; too large a gap to leap across. "Could we just be friends, please? I'm not looking to get involved."

"As I recall, you were kissing me, too."

His dark eyes were unwavering. He put his hands in his jeans pockets, and she wanted to wrap her arms around his ribs and snuggle in. Somehow he made her feel safe, and perhaps that was the most dangerous thing of all.

"I know." She could do this; she dealt with stubborn old ranch hands every day. She took a breath. "I need your help. I don't think I can pull a Christmas dinner off without it. But if we get involved…it will make a mess of things." She tried to think of it in terms he could relate to. "We're keeping the dishes I make simple, right? Let's just keep *us* the same way. If we make it too complicated…"

His dark eyes probed hers. "You're scared. Don't be. Kelley, friends can kiss. There are no rules against it. But we can take it slow if you want."

She would get through this, she would, and with some shred of dignity. Her hands were cold and she rubbed the damp palms on her jeans. "We agreed to a professional relationship. I'd rather we stayed just…friends. I like having you as a friend, Mack."

Mack clenched his fingers within the denim pockets of his jeans, simply to keep from reaching out and touching her. He'd already broken his first rule—never get involved with a client. There'd been something about her in the motel room, though, a soft vulnerability he found irresistible. She kissed him as though she meant it but then backed off. She had the other night, too, and he'd known he had to back away. Why was she afraid? And what was it about her that kept drawing him in, making him try again?

"The more I'm with you, the harder it is to be just your friend," he said honestly.

Her eyes widened further, but not with the desire he craved. Once again he saw the flash of fear. Why in the world would she be afraid of him? His hand slid out of his pocket and he took the steps necessary to reach her and take her hand, wanting to reassure her. He lifted it to his cheek and pressed a small kiss to the back. Her hand was cold, and questions popped into his head. "I know something's going on with you. But…everyone has wounds, Kelley."

Kelley flinched, but didn't break eye contact. Pain, humiliation, self-loathing, disgust…she remembered those feelings well enough, and they had crippled her for years. Now, when she really wanted to move past them, she felt angry that they still held her back.

And she sure as hell couldn't tell him why.

"Even you?" She let him keep her fingers within his. The contact was strangely soothing.

"Even me."

He hesitated, and she got the sense he was picking and

choosing what to tell and what not to. She'd done it often enough herself. Measuring words, avoiding eye contact until a decision had been made. She knew he'd chosen his words when he looked fully into her face.

"Let's just say, not everyone has an ideal upbringing. And things happen that color their lives. Things happen that you cannot change or take back."

His words struck a painful chord with her. But she knew he wouldn't understand this. Even after a decade, she found it impossible to understand. "It doesn't matter."

He sighed. "If you ever want to talk about it, let me know. I'm here."

She felt as if his dark eyes could see clear through her and accepted her for who she was. That in itself was a novelty. Somehow they'd ended up not only kissing but, more important, talking.

He stacked the last container of leftovers, preparing to leave. "I just want you to know that I think what you're trying to do for your family is a good thing."

She shook her head. "This is no big sacrifice on my part. I love them."

"You're the glue holding the family together, Kelley. If I can see it, I hope they can, too."

Kelley blinked furiously at the unsolicited praise. It was inconceivable that she was the glue. She was just Kelley who ran the ranch.

He was going to be alone at Christmas. It ceased to matter what Amelia or Gram would say. She would explain. They would understand—no one should spend the holidays alone.

She leaned forward, holding out one hand in invitation. "Why don't you come to Christmas dinner?"

He balanced the containers while shock glimmered on his face. "You're inviting me to your family dinner?"

"Do you have somewhere else you need to be?"

He didn't answer right away, and she suddenly realized

maybe she'd been presumptuous. Maybe he did have someplace special to go.

"I'm not a charity case, Kelley. I don't want you to ask me because I told you I was alone. I'm fine. The last thing I want is for you to feel obligated."

She smiled. Pride, she understood. "Heck, I'm not obligated. I'm paying you for your time. This is off the clock and offered in friendship, Mack. Nothing more. Come to dinner with friends."

He blinked twice. "I'd be honored to come."

"Honored?" It was an unexpected compliment. No one ever seemed "honored" when she did something. She was struck again by the gentleness in his voice.

"Maybe it beats sitting in a motel room by myself watching *It's a Wonderful Life*."

He tried to make light, but she could see through it. "Will you see your mom over the holidays?"

"You know my mom left Rebel Ridge a long time ago." His lips were set in a way that let her know the subject was closed. "I'm spending Christmas Eve at the shelter, serving dinner. And Christmas afternoon—" he paused, his eyes skittered away from hers for a moment "—at a rehab centre in Helena."

He had no one, and spent his holiday with others who had no one, too. The absolute loneliness struck Kelley square in the chest. As long as she could remember, they'd had presents and a special family breakfast, winding up with a traditional Christmas dinner. Stockings were hung and old Bing Crosby carols played. The very thought of someone spending the holiday without any of that was impossible.

"Then I'm very glad you're joining us."

He cleared his throat. "Me, too."

Wordlessly he gathered up his leftovers and went to the door. She followed him and held it open as he shrugged into his jacket. They'd just come to an agreement, so why on earth was he feeling as though everything was suddenly more out of control?

At the bottom of the steps he turned to find her standing in the doorway again, the glow from the porch light shining off her hair. With her soft smile, she reminded him of an angel. His heart skipped as she raised a hand in farewell.

He lifted his own and went to his truck, his breath forming clouds in the chilly air. Maybe he should have told her the whole truth. But they'd forged a friendship tonight, and the last thing he wanted to do was endanger it. In the long run, it wouldn't make any difference.

He started the truck and looked back at the house. She had gone inside out of the cold, and the door was shut. As he put the truck in reverse, he wished for the first time in a long time that it wouldn't make any difference at all.

"Easy. Shhh." Kelley held Risky's halter while Mack stayed outside the stall, quietly watching. "I'm sorry, Dr. Laramie. He's usually not this jumpy." Dr. Cooper, the regular vet, was on holidays. Andrew Laramie was his locum, filling in. Risky could sense a stranger despite Laramie's patient and soothing voice.

It had been three days since the kissing incident in her kitchen. Today Mack had brought the small turkey as promised for a practice run. They had worked companionably, preparing the turkey and stuffing and putting it in the oven. They'd bantered and teased. As friends. And yet…she wished he'd look at her *that* way again.

He was in her thoughts all the time. As she took care of stock, checked fences, supervised the hands, he was there on the fringes of her mind, with his casual touches, ready smile, soft seductive kisses. She didn't want to, and hadn't seen it coming, but she was falling for him.

But all of that had fled her mind with Risky's emergency. She'd had her hands full of soapy water when one of the hands had arrived at the door saying Risky'd been cut. She'd dropped everything in the kitchen and rushed to the barn, Mack right on her heels. She'd had the big bay gelding since she was fifteen. And when she saw the blood seeping from the gash, she knew stitches were the best plan.

Dr. Laramie gritted his teeth. "I'd rather not sedate unless it's necessary. But I think he should be stitched, and for that I'm going to have to."

Risky tossed his head once more. "Risky. Hush now."

Her muscles ached from keeping a firm hold on the halter. Even though Risky was cross-tied in his stall, his agitation meant Laramie couldn't make his sutures. For a moment she considered letting the wound go, letting it heal on its own. She met the vet's eyes and asked the question silently.

"It's up to you. It's deep enough to stitch but you could get away with it. Just."

Kelley turned away. Mack was watching her steadily, yet with a vigilance that made her feel as though he'd be there if she needed him. He didn't step in, didn't offer an opinion. His implied confidence in her was a rarity. Most often the men she knew would either be telling her what they would do or disregarding her altogether. That Mack didn't, said as much about him as it did about her.

She looked back at Risky and gave his neck a reassuring rub. She hated sedation. There was something about making a creature so vulnerable that she resisted.

"No, you're right. If you're going to stitch he needs sedation." A vicious jerk left her shoulder aching.

As the vet prepared the needles required, she tried to calm Risky. But his eyes were wild and she knew he was afraid and everything she did seemed to make it worse.

"He knows you're scared for him." Mack's voice was soft in her ear, but sure. His warm breath sent tingles down her body. "Let me try."

She stood back, relinquishing her hold on the halter. She could use the few moments to rest her arms. "Let me know when you have had enough. He's strong."

He didn't touch the halter at all but held out his hand, palm up. Risky sniffed, nudged. Mack stepped in and stroked the horse's jaw. And Kelley heard him muttering words, words she couldn't make out, but Risky stopped jumping and skittering. The whites of his eyes disappeared and the anxious stamping of hooves gentled. Dr. Laramie waited only a few moments. Standing perfectly still, eyes fastened on Mack, Risky received the medication with merely a twitch of his hide.

Mack placed his hands on Risky's head and rubbed softly, uttering soft words while he blinked rapidly. He hadn't expected such a complete reaction…not within the horse and definitely not within himself. He'd merely wanted to try—he'd seen Kelley's wince of pain as she struggled to hold the horse's head.

She had more on her plate than he'd initially realized, and he also knew there was something holding her back. She'd been so jumpy after a few simple kisses. He wanted her to trust him with more than a dinner. And the simple truth was that the gelding was afraid and in pain. It reminded Mack of the many times he'd been the same way. And how much work it had been to pull himself out. If Risky could trust him, then perhaps Kelley would, too.

"Mack…"

"Shhh," he uttered, ignoring Kelley, softly stroking Risky's muzzle as the drugs took hold. For a moment he felt an undeniable sadness that the animal had to be sedated. Turned into a ghost of itself, numb against the pain. Mack had lived that way far too long, without even the benefit of drugs or alcohol. And as he finally met Kelley's eyes across the stall, he knew it was time to start living again.

"How did you do that?"

The glow of approval on her face made him feel ten feet tall. He looked at Risky and murmured, "He just needed someone to talk to." He paused. "How's the vet doing?"

"I'm halfway there, thanks," came the voice from deeper in the stall. "Won't be long now."

Still Mack stroked softly, murmuring reassurances to the animal as Laramie put in the sutures.

When the stitching was done, Kelley watched as Mack relinquished his hold on Risky and stepped out of the stall, back into the corner once again. She listened with only half an ear as Laramie gave her instructions for caring for the wound—it was all things she knew already. What she really wanted to know was how did Mack know how to calm a frantic horse? And why was she just seeing this side of him now?

Watching him talk to Risky had sent a wave of love over her she could scarcely comprehend. In that moment he'd been different. He'd been tall and strong and capable and a man that she felt somehow she could lean on. He was just Mack. He'd dominated Risky with kindness and not force. Would he be that gentle with her? Her eyes had fixated on his hands, softly stroking, soothing. Would his hands be equally as tender on her skin? It was a revelation to her that she even desired it. That she was considering taking that leap after so many years celibate, and with a man she'd known such a short time. Time had ceased to matter, because in her heart she felt she could trust him. She didn't want to be just friends. Up until this moment it had seemed the only option. But maybe, just maybe, Mack had changed all of that.

She blinked, took a step back, collecting scraps of bandage for the garbage. And then what? Where could they possibly go together? She thought about her sister and how she'd rushed into a relationship, had her heart broken by Jesse's father, and how difficult it had been being a single mother. She'd fallen for this Boone she'd hired and he'd gone, too. She thought of her own history and the weight it would bring to a new relationship. She was being fanciful. And there was no time for that.

Dr. Laramie was shaking Mack's hand when she turned back around.

"Thanks for your help."

"No problem." Mack looked more at home in the barn than

Kelley could have imagined. With his jeans and heavy jacket, he could have been one of the hands helping out.

"Just a question," the vet asked. "How did you learn to do that? He responded very well to you."

Mack laughed. "I used to work at a farm outside Rebel Ridge. I always had a soft spot for the horses. Why?"

Laramie bent to grab his case. "I'm only filling in for Cooper while he has Christmas with his family. After that… well, I'm going home myself. A ranch in Alberta," he continued. "It's going to take a few months to get the details straightened out, but I'm setting up a rescue operation. I spent a lot of time working with Thoroughbreds, and it's really hard watching them be put down when their run is done. Or seeing an animal that's been abused. I had enough and quit. We could use a few guys like you. You have a real way."

"Thoroughbreds…wait, Andrew Laramie. You worked with racehorses, didn't you?"

Laramie nodded. "That's right."

"I remember you…. I think it was the Breeder's Cup last year. I was there watching with several of our investors."

It was a reminder that Mack lived in a world different from the Rocking H. Different from hers. Kelley aimed a bright smile at Laramie. "Mack is more than a ranch hand."

She made the declaration with a certain sense of pride. She wouldn't have done that a few weeks ago. She *was* proud of him, she discovered. He was good at what he did, and successful. It couldn't have been easy, not when he started from nothing, no matter what he said. "He owns the Mack's Kitchen franchises."

Andrew grinned. "I know someone who'd love to do what you do, Mack. Personally, I don't know the right end of a spatula."

"Our newest location is opening up in Washington in January. I'm heading up there for the launch. We're always looking for franchising opportunities."

Kelley looked at her feet as the three of them walked

down the corridor to the doors. He really would be leaving, then. After such a short time, she was getting used to having him around. Mack's arm brushed hers as Laramie laughed lightly.

"Might be difficult. *She* lives north of the border. Owns the bakery in Larch Valley and makes the best brownies I ever tasted." His mouth twisted. "Then there's the tiny problem that she won't speak to me."

Mack's fingers found hers and squeezed. She couldn't look at him. If she did, he'd know how much a simple handclasp affected her. It made her feel part of a couple, and that was a novelty. She'd been on her own so long it was a revelation to be a part of a united front. In the back of her mind she knew he would be going back to his life after Christmas. In her heart, at this moment, it didn't matter.

"Well, good luck with that," Mack offered. "Setting up a ranch can't be anywhere near as hard as thawing a woman's heart."

Laramie sent him a significant look. "Amen, brother."

She bit her lip. Did Mack think she needed thawing? She knew it was true. She knew she'd closed herself off for too long. What he didn't know is that he'd already thawed the ice around her heart. Could she show him that and still have her heart intact when he was gone?

Laramie raised a hand in a wave and strode off to his truck, while Mack and Kelley stood in the frosty air outside the barn.

Kelley sighed, looking up at the crystal-blue sky—a sharp contrast to the pristine snow. Seeing Mack here, comfortable in her world, only made the attraction to him stronger. Was it so wrong to want to grab on to any bit of happiness, even if it was only for now?

"Kel?"

She turned to look up at him, saw his dark eyes twinkling back, saw a hint of stubble on his jaw that made her want to run her fingertips along the roughness.

"Hmm?"

"Has it occurred to you that we left a turkey in the oven?"

"Oh, no!"

Together they sprinted through the snow to the house, and Kelley flung open the door. There was no smoke, but an acrid odour wafted out of the kitchen, and she ran forward with a cry.

"Wait!" Mack commanded. He bustled through, opening the back door and windows first. "Let me."

He reached into the oven as thin tendrils of smoke came out. Kelley pressed her fingers to her lips as she tried not to laugh at the sight. It wasn't all funny. She had a dinner in a few days, and the trial run for the main event was a disaster. But the look on Mack's face…a giggle escaped.

He put the roaster on the stovetop and stared at it. Kelley found him as sexy in a pair of oven mitts as she had when he'd held Risky's halter. Maybe more so.

"If my partners saw this—" he shook his head "—they'd be backing out in a hurry."

"Andrew Laramie would give you a job."

He angled a wry look in her direction. "Ha-ha."

Kelley stepped forward, picked up a fork and poked at the bird. "Yep. Definitely done."

"You're not upset."

She smiled. "Oh, Mack, this is one time I couldn't care less."

"But I thought…"

And as the words hung in the air, something clicked into place. For the first time, she was completely comfortable with a man. She trusted him. The dinner didn't matter. Nothing mattered, except feeling free for the first time. He had done that. Just by being him.

In this moment the past ceased to exist, and as it melted away so did the terror, the uncertainty, all of it. He had been careful with her from the start. She'd seen his hands, his wide, big hands so gentle on Risky's halter today, his voice soft and soothing. He was a man who understood pain and hurt and regret, and she knew without a doubt that she could trust him.

The Christmas CD they'd put in the stereo was still playing, over and over, and it no longer mattered what might happen in the future. She didn't care that they were from different worlds. He was here now. It was almost Christmas. If ever there was a time to take a chance, it was in this moment.

In the space of a heartbeat, she pressed her body against his, her lips on his lips.

She opened her mouth, meeting him equally. For once she felt blessed to be tall as their curves fit together like nesting eggs, his frame only a few inches ahead of hers. His kiss was like all the best things of Christmas—candlelight and gingerbread and the excitement of waking at four in the morning to open presents. She smiled against his mouth and found the hem of his sweater, snuck her hands underneath it and spread them wide over the heated skin of his back, marveling at the smooth strength of it.

He broke off the kiss, breathing heavily. "You said you wanted—"

"I changed my mind."

"Why?"

She leaned back far enough so she could see his face. He meant it. He really meant it. He wasn't pushing, but asking permission in his own way. Her heart soared with the realization.

"Because I want you, all of you." The words came out, filled the room, filled her heart because she meant them.

"You want me."

The indecision in his voice tore at her heart. Had no one ever wanted him before? It was inconceivable. His dark eyes clung to hers, tacitly asking—he was a man who would always ask, never take.

Never before had she felt sexually powerful, but she did now. She ran her tongue over her bottom lip, suddenly so sure that it almost made her laugh with the joy of it. The freedom was energizing. "I want you. I want all of you."

If she thought he'd hesitate further, she was wrong. His hand, his very capable hand, the one that had calmed her horse and made delicate pastry in a dingy motel room, now cupped her neck firmly as he dragged her close again. His fingers deftly slid her buttons through the buttonholes and she held her breath as he pushed the shirt off her shoulders. But none of the gut-knotting fear came. Only intense pleasure and anticipation.

His sweater joined her shirt on the floor and their skin was pressed together, hot and firm and oh, so wonderful without the barrier of fabric between them. She took his hand and led him upstairs to the loft, shaking a little as she realized what she was asking. She was asking him to make love to her, and it was exhilarating and terrifying all at once.

"Do you have protection?"

"You don't?"

He couldn't possibly know how silly that question was. Of course she didn't have anything resembling birth control; there'd never been any need. But rather than say it and ruin what progress they'd made, she answered simply. "No, I don't." And hoped he did.

He slid his wallet from his jeans and withdrew a foil packet. "I have one."

"For emergencies?" She raised an eyebrow, surprised at her own temerity.

His responding grin was dangerously sexy. "Exactly."

She lifted her chin, suddenly realizing she was standing before him in her underwear and that his hungry eyes were taking in every inch of her bare skin. She pushed away the shyness threatening to take over and smiled softly. "And this is an emergency?"

Dark eyes glittered at her. "Oh, honey, you've no idea."

He took a step forward, but she stopped him once more.

In one way she was teasing, but in another found she wanted to know. "How long has that been in there?"

And as he reached for her, he growled, "Long enough."

CHAPTER SIX

MACK CLOSED HIS EYES, savoring the feeling and the taste of her that lingered in his mouth. Right now Kelley's head rested on his chest, her blond hair falling over her face and her arm looped around his midsection. She was sleeping; he could tell by the slow, hot breaths that dampened his chest.

Lord, she'd been sweet. And fairly innocent, he was sure. It was in the way she touched, with a hint of shy hesitancy, like she wanted him to take the lead. It had been fresh, like a spring rain. The women he knew weren't like that. But Kelley…

He sighed, closed his eyes, feeling her warmth curled around him. He hadn't wanted to care about a woman for a very long time. Not since Christmas two years ago. That was when everything had changed. Oh, he'd believed once. But it had been a hard lesson to learn.

Her arm tightened around his ribs and he held his breath, not wanting to disturb her. He'd let things go this far and he shouldn't have. Now he'd gone and spent the night—another rule broken. He rubbed a hand over the stubble on his face. And yet he couldn't find it within himself to regret it. That in itself set off alarm bells in his head. It was well and good for her to need his help. It wasn't good when he started feeling attached.

"Mack?" She said his name in a husky whisper that reached right to the middle of him and grabbed.

"What, Kelley?"

And damned if she didn't laugh, a low, sexy rumble that came right from her toes and out her heart.

"That was good, Mack."

He smiled, lifted his head and kissed her hair, determined not to ruin the morning. "I know."

"No, I mean really good. Better than I expected."

He couldn't stop the smile that spread on to his face. "You gotta stop setting your expectations low…"

She laughed, a sexy little sound that did funny things to his insides. "I'm glad you stayed."

Suddenly he was, too. Even if it did complicate things more than he was strictly comfortable with.

"Do you want coffee?"

"Mmmm. You making it?"

"Sure."

She snuggled into him and he felt other parts of his body wake up. He had to move now, or they'd never get out of bed. And he didn't think a repeat of last night was the best of plans.

"I'll be back in a few minutes."

When he came back, mugs in hand, she'd fallen asleep again, her hair and the sheets a sexy tangle. He wet his lips, wondering what the hell he'd been thinking. It wasn't the sex. It was Kelley, and the fact that he cared about her—too much. Right now he wanted to gather her up in his arms and hold her close—every soft, sweet-scented inch of her.

That hadn't been part of the plan. He should have known better than to spend the night. He cleared his throat. "Your coffee, madam."

Kelley dragged herself out of sleep, propelled by the amazing smell. She blinked, opened her eyes, and saw Mack sitting on the edge of the bed, smiling and holding out a mug of steaming brew.

"Good morning." She moved to sit up and froze.

She was naked! And here was Mack in his jeans and shirt,

partly unbuttoned so she could see a generous slice of the hard chest beneath it. She dimly remembered waking a while ago, snuggling into his body. Her face flamed. In the bright light of morning, the magnitude of what they'd done hit her with full force. She'd had sex. With Mack Dennison. She put her hands to her red face and Mack laughed.

"That's charming," he said. He still held the coffee out and she wanted it…badly. She could hide her blushing face behind the mug. How was a woman supposed to act the morning after? She had no idea. Her sum total experience had been limping home from prom and hiding her soiled dress in the back of the closet until she could burn it.

Holding the quilt to her chest, she wiggled until she was sitting in the bed, and reached for the mug.

She took a hot sip and closed her eyes. Delicious. When she opened them, Mack leaned over and kissed her gently. Chaste, if it came down to it. If it could be chaste, considering what had passed between them last night.

"I'll make us some breakfast." Mack reached for his coffee that he'd put on the dresser. She tried not to be disappointed that he didn't crawl under the covers with her.

"I'm awfully glad you're here." Her heart blossomed as she realized how true it was. "And I'm so pleased you're spending Christmas with us. Amelia has the most beautiful tree. And her pecan pie…you haven't lived until you've had her pie."

A shadow passed over his face and Kelley frowned. What had she said that was wrong? She sensed defiance in the set of his jaw, but more than that. Hurt. Her heart melted just a little bit knowing it.

She held the covers to her chest with her arms and put her free hand on his wrist, feeling the pulse there thrum beneath her fingers. "What is it? What did I say?"

He raised his head and she stared into his eyes. She could so easily get lost in the chocolaty depths of them.

He turned his hand over and twined his fingers with hers. "When you talk about Christmas…"

Her breath held. Was he going to back out? Was it too much too soon? She hadn't planned any of this. And she was pretty sure he hadn't, either.

"I don't really talk about this, but when you speak of the holidays and traditions and that sort of thing…well, you should know I've never had a real Christmas."

"Never?"

"Never."

"No tree, turkey and presents?"

He laughed, a bitter, jerky sound. "Not ever. Not even close. My holidays normally consist of tasteful trees in a hotel lobby and a dinner in a five-star restaurant."

She couldn't imagine December twenty-fifth coming and going without a proper celebration. Her heart ached for the childhood magic he must have missed. "That's the loneliest thing I've ever heard. I don't understand."

Mack knew it was better that she know the truth now. He had no illusions about the so-called magic of the season, didn't go in for the sappy sentimentality of peace on earth and good will toward men. In his house, there'd never been Santa Claus or dinners or magic of any sort. Why start now, only for himself?

There'd always been a little voice in the back of his mind saying he hadn't deserved it. In his head, he knew that wasn't true. But in his heart, where it mattered, he'd never been able to shake the thought completely.

He'd tried once, and had failed utterly. He knew there was always a crash at the end of the buildup. It was better that she know the truth now. He wasn't who she thought he was.

"There was never money for Christmas—or much desire to put in the effort, either. Not when the priority is making sure there's enough vodka in the house to get through the season. That's what happens when you grow up with an alcoholic."

"Your mother?"

He heard the gasp that accompanied the explanation and hated it. "That's right," he confirmed. He hooked his thumbs in the tabs of his pockets. "A drunk who cared more about her next bottle than feeding her kid."

"I never guessed..."

She met his gaze; he challenged her with his eyes. "No one did."

"Oh, Mack, how awful for you." Her eyes softened and he tried very hard to hate her for pitying him. "So you really never had Christmas when you were a boy?"

He looked away, determined not to feel like the little lost boy any longer. He'd grown up. Made a success of himself. "She tried a few times. It just never quite worked out in a *White Christmas* sort of way, you know? And now...there doesn't seem to be a point. It's just me, and with the business, it's our busiest retail season. The closest I get is decking out the stores and bringing in seasonal stock."

"I'm sorry, Mack. About your mom. About all of it."

He hadn't wanted to delve further into his past, but he'd rather she walked away now before either of them got in too deep. "I took home ec so I could learn to feed myself. By the time I was a teenager, I had a teenager's appetite. And boxed mac and cheese can only fill a kid's stomach for so long."

"Oh, Mack." She sighed his name, lifted their joined hands and placed a kiss on the back of his thumb.

He shifted on the covers, pulling his hand out of her grasp. "You see? That's why I didn't tell you before. Now you pity me. And I don't want your pity. I never wanted anyone's pity."

"Can't I feel sorry for the boy?"

His anger flared. "No. That boy doesn't exist anymore. I discovered I liked cooking. I was good at it. I got a job at a farm after school and on weekends and used my wages to put food on my own table. Later I used the money to study. And I got backing to open my first Mack's Kitchen."

"Then why so angry? Why so secretive? No one would think any less of you..."

His teeth clenched almost painfully as he heard sympathy

in her voice. “Don’t you?” he bit out. “Don’t you see me differently now?”

“Yes. I see you as a kid who overcame a lot of odds to make a success of himself.” She readjusted the sheet and leaned close to him, forcing him to look at her. “There’s no shame in that, Mack. It’s admirable.”

“I don’t want the past to define me. I want the present. The future.”

“And it does. Look at how well you’ve done.”

“Stop, please.”

“Did you think people would think less of you if they knew? That I would?”

That’s exactly what he’d thought. Plus he’d started having to deal with publicity because of the success of the stores. The last thing he wanted was to capitalize on his childhood woes. Some things should remain private.

“I didn’t want those days to be used to sell a product. I refuse to let my life be a rags-to-riches sob story.”

Kelley smiled softly. She wasn’t patronizing him, or indulging him in any way. She looked so calm, so beautiful. As though she understood. But how could that be?

“You just want to get on with it, do it on your own. You don’t want to need anyone. Oh, Mack, we’re more alike than you might think.”

She leaned up and kissed his cheek. “Thank you for trusting me,” she whispered. He was surprised to see her eyes mist over, but then she blinked and he wondered if he’d imagined it. He’d meant to tell her as a warning, that was all. A taste of what she was getting herself in for. Giving her the opportunity to back away now. Instead she turned the tables on him and was pleased he’d trusted her, when trust had little to do with it.

He was getting in deeper by the second.

“It occurs to me that we’re both abysmal at holiday traditions.” She sat up on her knees and reached for her bathrobe. “So here’s what we’re going to do. This place is completely devoid of holiday spirit. We're going to get a Christmas tree. Then we're going to go shopping and get decorations."

"Shopping?" He didn't attempt to hide the cynicism in his voice, but she continued undaunted.

"I don't even have a wreath or sprig of mistletoe." She dropped a peck on his lips and they fell open, amazed at this new, bubbly, tactile Kelley.

"The mall opens at noon," she chirped, tying the robe belt around her waist. "That leaves us this morning to find the perfect tree."

He raised his eyebrows. Silence hummed for a few seconds. This wasn't what he'd intended when he'd told her about his past. With one finger he reached over and tipped up her chin. "Maybe I want to spend the day with you. Just you. It's not often I take a day off this time of year, you know."

An adorable blush colored her cheeks. "So spend the day with me. We'll spend ridiculous amounts of money on Christmas kitsch. It'll be new."

She leaned over and kissed him, long and soft and sweet. "I want to do this for you, Mack. For both of us."

He couldn't resist her when she kissed him that way, full of promise and sweetness. He'd do it, but only for her. If she still believed a fairy-tale Christmas existed, he wouldn't be the one to play Scrooge.

"As long as you don't make me sing along with carols on the radio, fine. And when we come back I'll make you the best hot cocoa you've ever tasted." He ran a finger down the column of her throat. "Of course, it does mean you'll have to get dressed, and that's a bit of a shame."

"If we're going searching for a tree, we'd better get started." She blinked innocently.

"You," he said, pointing a finger and getting up off the bed, "are the devil to resist when you act like an angel." He kissed her forehead and then stopped at the bedroom door looking back over his shoulder. "How do you like your eggs?"

Her answer prompted a peal of laughter from him that lasted all the way down the stairs.

Mack tugged the toboggan behind him, making tracks that Kelley stepped in, following him to the edge of the pasture to the tree line. The cloud ceiling was high, and snowflakes fell around them, cocooning them in a shushing sound. For a few precious minutes, it was like they were the only two people in the world. The flakes floated to the ground, lying gently on the white blanket already there from the previous blizzard. He paused for a moment, and Kelley came up beside him, the clouds of their breaths mingling in the cold air. Fat snowflakes landed on her hat and stayed there, while her hazel eyes appeared even more green against the flush of her cheeks. He inhaled, his chest expanding, while the valley lay below them, Christmas-card perfect.

He was tugging a toboggan and carrying an ax to cut down a Christmas tree. It was inconceivable. He turned from the scene and began pulling again.

There had been an awkward moment when they'd gone to the main house to ask to borrow Jesse's sled to haul the tree back with. He'd said hello to Mrs. Hughes—who'd acted like nothing was out of the ordinary and insisted he call her Ruby. But Amelia had given him a speculative look he wasn't sure he'd liked. He'd felt under a microscope, as he had many times as a boy. Like he was being measured and found wanting.

"So who was this Boone guy, anyway?" Mack called back to Kelley, who was clumping along in her boots.

"Some guy who rescued Amelia and Jesse during the blizzard, and stayed on to work. But he's gone now."

"You didn't like him."

When the footsteps stopped behind him, he paused and looked over his shoulder. Kelley had stopped, her hands on her hips.

"I didn't trust him. That's all. He wasn't exactly truthful about his reasons for being here. He pretended to be the hand

I'd hired on. And Amelia hasn't always shown the best judgment."

He bit his tongue. Guilt trickled through him. He hadn't been completely truthful with Kelley this morning, either. But he'd already revealed more than he had planned on telling a woman ever again.

Kelley had stopped, put her mittened hands into the pockets of her gray wool coat. A pink knitted hat covered her ears, but her blond curls cascaded over her shoulders. She looked like a winter angel.

"Maybe you should trust her more. We all made mistakes when we were younger."

"I'm just looking out for her. I'm her big sister. Jesse's father hurt her deeply. Am I wrong for not wanting that to happen again?"

"She's a big girl, Kelley. Old enough to know what she wants. Old enough to live with her own mistakes."

Kelley scowled. "That's more or less what she said."

He laughed, turned around and started pulling again. "So what would she say if she knew about you and me last night?"

He kept his back to her, kept pulling even though he would like to have seen her face. After several more steps in silence, she answered.

"She does know. You were parked in my driveway all night. And she said be careful."

He stopped, dropping the cord to the toboggan and turned. She was only a step and a half away, her eyes gleaming in the brightness of reflected snow. There was a relief in not sneaking around.

"And are you? Careful?"

"It sure doesn't feel that way."

He took the extra step and put his gloved hands on her arms. "Then don't be careful for a little while longer, okay?" He wanted her this free, this unexpected, for a bit longer. Guileless and open. The holiday would be over soon and he didn't want to ruin it for her. Christmas Day was a day to be borne, that was all. Kelley was a balm against all of it.

He dipped his head and kissed her. She was soft and sweet and, yes, even innocent, despite what had transpired between them last night. "We can talk about her later," he murmured, his lips close to her cheek. "Right now, I've found you the perfect tree."

He stepped to the toboggan. He picked up the ax and made a well-aimed cut at the trunk of a fully rounded evergreen.

Kelley stood back and watched as Mack took swing after swing with the ax. A short week ago if someone had told her she'd be cutting a Christmas tree with Mack Dennison after a night of lovemaking, she would have laughed in their face. But here she was. She hadn't thought of him in terms as a lover. *Her lover.* And now whenever he was around, she felt the urge to girlify herself. For the first time ever, she felt feminine…and she liked it.

She wanted Mack for more than Christmas, and yet she wasn't sure how it could work. There'd been a brief idea that Boone would be staying on, and that would have been welcome help to Kelley, despite her reservations about his relationship with Amelia. But now…he was gone. She was tied to the Rocking H. And Mack was definitely tied to his business. She had to be realistic. She kept the thought around her like armor, even as she watched him, legs spread wide, shoulders flexing as he chopped down a perfectly shaped spruce tree. His breath made clouds as he struck the tree and exhaled. With a crack, the trunk gave and toppled over, a white cloud erupting in the snow as the branches splayed out.

She'd started out wanting to make Christmas for the family. Now that included Mack, too. What he'd told her this morning had been such a complete surprise. It was high time he had someone do something for him. It was unfamiliar territory, but one she thought they could enjoy discovering together.

Together they loaded the tree onto the sled and began the journey back to the house. Once back, Mack propped the tree up on the verandah and dusted off his hands. "Where's the stand?"

Kelley pulled off her mittens. "I don't have one."

"You don't?"

She smiled a little. "Don't act so surprised. We always celebrate at the main house. I guess we'll just have to get one in town today. Amelia already has a tree set up. She put it up for Jesse days ago."

"He's a cute kid."

Kelley grinned. "He is, isn't he? He made a wish for a daddy this year. I think being around other kids at school really made him see he was different."

Mack had a strange look on his face, a mix of pity and pain and withdrawal. Kelley wrinkled her brow. After what he'd told her this morning, she should have thought before opening her mouth.

"I didn't think..." she rushed to apologize.

He put his arm around her waist and gave a squeeze. "It's all right. I feel for the kid though. Knowing you're different is a hard thing to get used to. You look for ways to fit in. To hide it."

"Or you bury your nose in a book."

"Voice of experience?"

There was something in his voice that was almost defensive and she wondered at the strange turn of the conversation. "No more than yours. You must have found it so difficult."

"Kelley..."

She raised a hand. "I know. You don't want pity. You don't want to talk about it."

"No, I don't."

It wasn't so much what he said but what he didn't. His voice was completely flat, like he'd shut the door on something unpleasant. Kelley looked up at him, at once afraid and intrigued. She was curious, but to press might push him away and that was the last thing she wanted. Part of her wanted to hold his hand and help him as he'd helped her last night, even without knowing it. He had changed everything with his gentle touches and thorough loving. But another part begged her to leave it alone and not ruin this perfect day.

"Then let's go shopping. I'll spring for Candy Cane Fudge at the Creamery."

The dark cloud of his expression passed as she changed the subject. "That sounds good."

CHAPTER SEVEN

THE LAST OF THE PLASTIC packaging was in the garbage, the smell of cocoa came from the kitchen, and Kelley stood in the doorway to the living room, staring at her transformed house.

Evergreen boughs punctuated by red bows swooped from the loft railing, ending in a trail down the banister. A large bouquet of red poinsettias and white mums in a sleigh made a centerpiece on the pine coffee table. Cinnamon-scented candles glowed from a glass holder atop the mantel. A fire burned briskly in the fireplace, and their newly decorated tree stood proudly in the corner, a mass of twinkling lights and shining ornaments, a glorious white angel gracing the top. Kelley realized that for the first time ever, it looked like a home, not just a house. It was warm and welcoming.

In the kitchen Mack turned from the stove, whisk in hand, completing the festive picture. "Cocoa's nearly done."

Even in here she and Mack had worked magic. Now her table was dressed in a bright-red-and-green-plaid cloth. Green napkins were rolled and arranged in a glass jar, almost like a bouquet. It was all so pretty and perfect, like something out of a magazine.

"It smells wonderful. And the house looks gorgeous. Thank you, Mack, for doing all of this with me. I don't remember the last time I had so much fun..."

She stammered at the end, unsure of how to put her feelings

so that he understood, and yet without frightening him away. There'd been times today he'd been so open, so relaxed. And then other times he'd seemed somehow distant, more like an observer than a participant. She knew which she preferred—how could she make him see it?

He turned off the burner and let the whisk sink into the creamy chocolate. His dark eyes touched on hers, and she wished he'd smile. If he smiled she could tell what he was thinking. Her heart pounded as he crossed the kitchen to where she was standing.

"I did it because I wanted to." He reached out and took one of her hands in his. "Being with you has been fun. I don't remember the last time I enjoyed Christmas. You did that, Kelley. Just you."

He paused, as if he was going to say something more, but the cell phone on his hip rang and he took it out of the holster. He looked at the number. "Do you mind?" he asked.

"No, go ahead." He'd been giving her a lot of his time lately; she understood he also had a business to run. She sipped the cocoa while he disappeared into the living room to talk. His business was in the city. Frequently traveling. And hers was here, at the Rocking H. With times getting tougher, she couldn't afford to hire more help. And she needed to keep the ranch profitable to sustain them all. It seemed unrealistic to be swept away in a flight of fancy. Perhaps they'd both been getting caught up in the magic of Christmas. Maybe she should just tuck the memories of last night away like a Christmas present, something special and surprising and unexpected.

"Did you see what else I bought?" His phone call finished, his smooth voice interrupted her thoughts and she bit her lip. He was smiling but there were new lines of strain around his eyes she hadn't seen before.

"No," she said weakly, and then he pointed up.

A sprig of mistletoe hung from the door frame, tied with red ribbon.

She looked back down and into his eyes. And ceased caring

about what would happen after Christmas Day or all the reasons why she should play it cautious. For once in her life she was going to get caught up in the moment. If ever there were a season for it, it was Christmas. She put her hand on his cheek before standing up on tiptoe and kissing him.

He put his hands on the small of her back and drew her closer as their mouths, tongues meshed. He tasted like mint and chocolate from their fudge earlier. His body was a hard, impenetrable wall as she pressed against it, absorbing its warmth and strength. If she got no other gift for Christmas, having Mack's arms around her was enough. He'd taken her fears of the physical and erased them with his first kiss. He'd made her feel wanted and hadn't run away at the first opportunity. He murmured into her mouth, and her pulse raced, fluttering frantically at her neck, wrist. This, just this, was enough.

"Mmmm," he murmured, pulling back so their lips parted. "Do you know how good you are at that?"

"Me?" She whispered it, their breaths mingling as they hovered at another kiss.

"Yeah, you," he replied.

She looked into his eyes, mesmerized by the tiny gold flecks around his pupils. "I haven't had much practice."

"If you improve, you're going to be the death of me, Miss Hughes." He grinned and a dimple appeared. "Come to think of it, maybe we'd better get started on your education. Practice does make perfect." And his mouth closed over hers again, slow and lingering.

A tiny bit of loneliness crept in even as her arms wrapped around his shoulders. What would happen after the holidays, when everything was put away? Would he disappear along with the bows and ribbons?

No. She refused to think of the new year and all the unknowns. She would not ruin it by thinking of things that hadn't even happened yet.

"As much as I would like to carry on this conversatio

upstairs, I have to go," he murmured, pressing a kiss to the tip of her nose. "Something's come up."

"Let it wait." She smiled up at him. "You deserve a day to yourself."

The lines around his eyes were back. "I wish," he murmured. "But I need to look after this."

"You could come back when you're done," she suggested. "We could watch a movie on TV."

His gaze fell to her mouth again, but then he exhaled. "I need some clean clothes. I wasn't actually expecting to spend the night last night."

Kelley had the silly urge to point out she had a washing machine. And a bathtub. The former he could use and the latter he could share, along with a healthy dose of bubbles. But the words stuck in her throat…they seemed so forward, so uncharacteristic of her. Not something she could blithely suggest or seduce her way into. It just wasn't in her. So she backed off, knowing that to feel she'd been rejected was foolish but feeling it just the same.

"That's okay. I'm sure having your truck parked out front two mornings in a row would raise some eyebrows at the house."

She turned away, pretending to tend the cocoa on the stove. She took a spoon and tried skimming off the thin skin that had formed on the top.

He came over and touched her hand, guiding it and helping scoop the skin on to a saucer. "You should be thankful your family cares."

"I am. But I have a right to my privacy."

"Not everyone has a family like yours, Kelley."

Her lips dropped open at his sharp tone. "I know that, too. Are we starting to argue? It feels like it and I don't know why."

"Don't you?"

The air hummed.

"No, I don't!" She grabbed the nearby ladle and started

pouring the hot drink into mugs. She handed one to him. "Why don't you enlighten me?"

He put down his cup, reached over and took hers and put it down, too. Then he grabbed her upper arms and made her face him.

"You have a family that loves you. That cares for you and wants to protect you. You are moving heaven and earth to make Christmas for them, and I envy that."

Her eyes widened.

"This is the first Christmas I've spent any time with anyone other than a business associate. I've been in many cities around the world, but this is the first time I've cut down a tree and decorated it. Having a family whose opinion matters isn't something you take for granted!"

"I don't!"

"You've got everything here, don't you see that? And still you want more."

His censure stung, and she was done with apologizing for wanting something other than a solitary life on the family ranch. Something for herself. "I suppose you're an open book, right? There are parts of you, Mack Dennison, that are one big question mark."

He backed away as if her arms were suddenly scalding hot and burning his hands. "You don't know what you're talking about."

"I did hit a nerve." She felt herself getting angry now. He'd kissed her and held her and made love to her. He understood everything, and yet nothing. So much of him was a mystery.

"What you told me this morning hardly fills in all the blanks, Mack. And I don't know why you're suddenly so angry at me. You told me in the motel room that wanting more saved your life. I think I understand why you said that now. But why is it okay for *you* and not for *me?*"

"I didn't have what you have," he retorted.

"Your *last* store was the one you set up here, not your first. What were *you* running from?"

Mack decided to pick up his cocoa after all. He took one sip but it tasted bitter. He took the cocoa and dumped it down the sink.

He'd let himself get caught up in the Christmas fervor with her today. But that was just it. It was Christmas, a sentimental holiday illusion. In the bright light of the new year, everything would be much more clear. She was getting caught up in the holiday, that was all. It did funny things to people.

"I wasn't running from anything. I was building a life for myself."

"Then why did you come back?"

The answer was so close to the tip of his tongue it scared him. He'd had no choice. It was why the house on the bluff would now be his home.

Did she truly know what today had meant? What a leap it had been for a man like him? The last time he'd let himself need anyone was with Lissy, in London. He'd damn near bought her a ring. But the moment he'd told her the truth about his upbringing, the reason he was suddenly tied to Montana with invisible strings, he hadn't seemed nearly as attractive. He'd realized the links to his past were a liability. He'd spent that Christmas in a hotel in Los Angeles rather than in Lissy's London flat as planned. And he'd vowed he would never let himself need a woman again.

And as Kelley stared at him, he wanted to take away the hurt in her eyes and make her smile again. He was starting to seek her approval, wanting to please her, and the thought went a long way to cooling his heels.

"Let's just enjoy Christmas, okay? I don't want to argue with you. Not now."

He put a hand along her cheek, trying to soften her mutinous expression and failing. He had to get out of here now before he did something crazy, like tell her how he felt about her. He'd broken rules one and two, but three would stay in force. He couldn't be in love with her.

"I need to go now and look after this. I'll be back on Christmas Eve for final prep."

"That long." Her voice was like acid—he'd made her mad. Why did things have to get so complicated?

He laughed tightly, the sound thick with the undercurrents swirling in the room. "You've got everything you need in your fridge. Amelia's still doing dessert?"

"Yes, she is insistent she does the pies. It wouldn't be Christmas without her pies."

Another tradition he had no point of reference to. He felt as if walls were closing in and he had to get away. But he couldn't. He would go straight from here to the one place he dreaded more than any on earth.

"Right. I'll see you then."

Guilt crawled along his spine. And yet he couldn't bring himself to tell her the truth. He leaned over and kissed her forehead. "Bye, Kelley."

He left her standing there in the kitchen, with a mug full of cold cocoa and a little piece of his heart left behind.

Christmas Eve dawned as all Christmas Eves should: cheerfully bright, white and crisp. When Kelley got out of bed, it was with a sense of excitement she hadn't had since she'd been a small child. Today Mack was coming back. She'd fix what had gone wrong between them. It was Christmas Eve! Anything was possible.

Today they were going to make ahead the orange salad and cranberry sauce. They would forget their harsh words and focus on having a merry Christmas.

She touched a finger to an angel ornament, remembering what he'd said when he'd bought it for her. That it reminded him of her. All she knew was that she wasn't ready for it to be over after tonight. She needed him to know how much he meant to her. And that meant sharing with him, too.

She showered and dressed carefully, in low-slung jeans and a soft sweater than hugged her slim form more than she was used to. She pulled a small amount of hair back from each side of her face, holding it with a small clip, while the rest of her hair fell down her back. The interest in her appearance was a first. She realized that with Mack she didn't want to hide. She wanted him to see her. And she wanted him to like what he saw.

She pressed a hand to her nervous tummy as he arrived, carrying a bag with the fresh ingredients required for the day. "Good morning." He smiled, pushing his boots off with his toes and handing her the groceries, as if their harsh words had never happened. "And Merry Christmas."

The bubbles of excitement fizzed stronger as he dropped a light kiss on her lips. More than ever she was determined to prove to him that she could do this. That his faith in her hadn't been misplaced. But more than that, she wanted to show him how things could be between them. Not just today. Every day.

"Are you ready for your next lesson?"

"I put myself in the hands of the master."

"Well now. That's a dangerous spot to be in." He winked at her and she laughed. Perhaps she'd just imagined his darker mood of Sunday afternoon, for right now it was lighter than it had been all week. More than ever she wanted to tell him everything—about how he'd changed things for her, about how she wanted more time with him. It was a matter of waiting for the right moment. Maybe tonight, when it was just the two of them in front of the tree…

"A dangerous spot for you," she joked. "I know you. You won't be able to keep your hands off my turkey."

She put the bag on the counter, thrilled when his arms snaked around her waist. "I won't be able to keep my hands off something," he agreed.

Kelley turned within the circle of his arms and looked up. He was smiling and teasing but there was something else lurking behind his eyes. She wished she knew what it was. "You're different today."

His arms tightened and his gaze dropped to her lips before moving back up. "I missed you, Kel."

"I missed you, too." Her heartbeat quickened as he dropped a light kiss on her lips, then another. It was the closest he'd gotten to an admission of his feelings. But was it enough? Could they make it work beyond Christmas? She knew she wanted it to.

Mack's heart swelled at her words and he kissed her because he didn't know what to say. He had missed her. And in missing her, he'd discovered something very unpleasant. He needed her. And he didn't like needing anyone. He had to find a way to let her go, for both their sakes. But not today. He wasn't so cruel that he'd do it today.

He touched her nose with a finger. "Today is Christmas Eve. The final countdown to your culinary triumph. Should we get started? If we finish early…"

When everything was ready, Kelley wiped the last dish, looked around the kitchen with the cranberry sauce a ruby-red ribbon in a glass dish, the orange salad arranged prettily on a snowflake-patterned plate. Tomorrow she'd prepare vegetables and turkey at the main house, and they'd all sit down to a holiday meal together. With one extra. She smiled to herself. The phone call from Boone today had been a surprise. It was all going to work out—for all of them. She just knew it.

"Well, let's hope the execution goes as well as the preparation," she said, standing back and brushing her hands down her apron. She untied it from around her waist and hung it over a chair. "Thank you, Mack. For everything. When I walked into your store…"

"I know," he replied. He stood in front of the counter, his hands in his pockets. The afternoon sun bathed him in light through the window above the sink. "I didn't expect you. I sure didn't expect any of this to happen."

How could she ever get through dinner, when she was dying inside, longing to tell him how she felt? She swallowed and gathered up some courage. "I was scared to death. I had to be to ask for help, you realize that, right? But I don't regret it, not for a moment. I hope you don't, either."

He came over to her then, and framed her face with his hands. "Kelley the Stubborn. So determined." His smile was soft. "Is that what you think? That I regret it?"

She couldn't answer, so she shrugged.

"Making love to you had been on my mind for days. Ever since the night in the motel room. Maybe even before then…maybe as far back as seeing you walk into my store, pretending to know what you were about."

She laughed, a soft, almost-sob. A sentimental Mack was a treat she hadn't expected. "I had no idea."

"I'm not sorry for anything that's happened the last week. Not one thing."

She took a deep breath and tilted her chin so she could look up at him. It was a sweet thing to say, so why did she get the feeling it was a first step to goodbye?

She rested her fingers on the waistband of his jeans. "That being the case…I was going to ask you. Do you want to stay tonight?"

She held her breath. *Please say yes.* She wanted to share Christmas with him. All of it. She'd never had a significant other to share holidays with, and it was so much more cozy with two. She wanted his face to be the first one she saw as dawn crept over the white hills. To know that she wasn't alone. To watch him over the rim of a coffee cup with the lit tree behind them. Simple things, but special ones.

"I'd love to, but I'm due at the shelter, remember?" There was a trace of regret in his voice. She grabbed on to it.

"Come back when you're done. I'll leave the tree on and a fire burning."

"Why do you want me to, Kelley?"

"Because…because…" She stammered for a few moments. Why did she want him there? And it wasn't just about the sentimentality of the holiday, or not wanting to be alone. She knew that. It went deeper. So much deeper she could hardly breathe. The words sat on her tongue while she deliberated if she should say them or not. The differences between them, the secrets, vanished when he was like this with her. All that mattered was the way he touched her, spoke to her. And if she didn't say it now, she might not have another chance.

"Because Christmas is meant to be spent with people you love." Her words came out on a quiet whisper, yet they echoed to every corner of the room. "Don't you think, Mack?"

He backed away. "Kelley..."

"You have to know what this week has meant to me. And I need to tell you, Mack, because being with you, it changed *everything*. More than you can imagine."

She sighed, knowing she wanted to do this but finding it unbearably difficult just the same. "I don't think you realize how much," she murmured. Her eyes captured his. "I need to tell you something, Mack, so you'll understand. But please...I need your arms around me when I do."

He hesitated a moment, but then took a step forward, holding out his hands. "Come here," he whispered, and she went into the safe circle of his arms.

He was warm and strong and all those things that had made her trust him in the first place. When she'd gathered strength from his embrace, she pulled back just a little. Close enough to feel the heat from his body, far enough away that she could have the room to speak.

The kitchen smelled of spices and cranberries. Kelley knew she would succeed in making a beautiful family dinner. It had been her goal, and yet it all seemed silly and trivial at this moment. His gaze darkened, held reservations, but she expected that. She felt as though she were standing on the edge of something, and one small slip could ruin it all.

She reached up with trembling fingers and touched his cheek. "Being with you the other night changed something in me. I didn't think I'd ever be able to unfreeze enough to be with a man, Mack. But with you it was different. I saw you with Risky and I wondered if you were the one who would be gentle enough, understanding enough. And you were."

"I don't understand."

"When you told me about your childhood, I knew you'd understand. Oh, Mack, you're not the only one with secrets. I've never told anyone about this. Not Gram, not Amelia… but I want you to know, Mack."

She gripped his hands, a lifeline to get her through it. She'd never once said the words out loud, not even to herself.

"I know you felt unloved and unwanted by your mum. But you're not, not by me. I want you to know how much you've given me. The truth is, when we graduated…"

Her throat closed over as images raced through her mind, followed by crippling fear. She could almost feel his hands again, hear the raspy sound of his mocking voice. Her breath quickened and she closed her eyes.

No. It was over and done. Wilcox had left Rebel Ridge a long time ago, and he no longer held any power over her. She replaced the images with the memory of lying in Mack's arms, feeling loved and cherished. Two solitary tears gathered at the corners of her eyes and squeezed out, rolling silently down her cheeks.

"Kelley." His voice was a hushed whisper, his fingers firm on hers. Reassuring.

"The truth is, on prom night I was raped, and I haven't been with a man since. Until you."

CHAPTER EIGHT

THE WORDS SENT A RUSH of relief flooding through Kelley's body. Saying them out loud was cathartic. Suddenly they didn't have the same power. Being with Mack had made it possible to move on. Just saying the words opened up new vistas for her. She wanted to see places, experience things. No more hiding away.

"What?" Mack's voice was filled with disbelief, and he stepped back, leaving her without the shelter of his arms. She shivered, feeling the sudden cold. She'd thought the hard part was over, but the euphoric release only lasted a minute. Explaining was going to be much more difficult than she imagined.

"It happened after the prom," she began, her voice wobbling a little. "I…I had a date for the dance, and I thought I was ready. So many of the other girls…and he was popular and handsome…looking back now I think I just wanted to feel feminine, and pretty, and wanted. Gram had taken me to buy a new dress and it was so beautiful."

She started to choke on the words and fought to regain control. "I was always the tomboy, you see."

"You hid behind boots and jackets and braids."

She nodded, relieved he understood. "When he asked me out, I went. I didn't know I was being used. But at the last minute…I changed my mind. But he didn't care. We weren't at the party everyone had gone to. Instead we went to a cabin out back of their spread. It was small and dark and I heard the click of the door locking. I…I can still hear it in my nightmares. I asked to leave but then he grabbed me and…"

Her lips quivered uncontrollably now as tears swelled over her bottom lashes. She could still feel the hands that had seemed to be everywhere at once, and her stomach churned. "I should have fought him off, right?" Her voice sounded small and far away. "I didn't fight him and I should have."

"He raped you." The words came out dull, dead. Final.

She shrugged pitifully. "I said no, but he didn't like that. In the end…oh, Mack," she pleaded. "In the end… It was horrible and heartbreaking. Even now, I hate being in dark places. The motel room during the blizzard was awful."

Mack stared at her, tears staining her cheeks and her lips quivering. Never had he expected this. He'd known she was innocent; not a virgin obviously, but her sweetness had said it all. But dammit, what was he supposed to do with *this?* The magnitude of it all crashed down on Mack and he had no idea what to say, how to act. If only she'd said something. Dear Lord, he'd kissed her in that room, sensed she was nervous, but had never imagined something like this. If he'd known, he would never have left her to sit through the storm all alone.

"I'm not sure how…I mean…why me?"

She sent him a tenuous smile. "You're wonderful, that's why. Being with you was…a revelation. I wasn't afraid. I trusted you. I knew after seeing you with Risky that you'd be gentle and kind and…"

Suddenly she broke off and her face flamed.

The magnitude sunk in and Mack knew exactly what he'd done. He'd gone and seduced a woman completely unprepared for it. It hadn't been a level playing field. And he'd stupidly told himself he was in control, but the truth was, *he'd* needed *her.* And he'd taken her without any thought as to what effect it would have. He rubbed a hand over his face.

That made him a selfish bastard. Careless. He'd ignored the

signs. The way she'd been timid, innocent, the way she'd been afraid in the motel room…he'd thought only of himself.

Because he needed her.

And it scared him to death.

"Why now? Why tell me now?"

Tears glimmered on her cheeks and he felt about two inches tall.

"Because I fell in love with you. Because you trusted me and I thought I could trust you."

His breath came out in a whoosh. How could he possibly tell her that he'd only talked about his childhood in an effort to put distance between them? And that it had the opposite effect? He paced to the tree, staring at the lights that all seemed to blur together.

He felt as though he was drowning and needed a life preserver. All he could think about was how she must have been terrified. Thinking about another man's—no, boy's—hands on her skin when she'd said no. It damn near broke his heart. What must it have taken for her to let him…knowing what had come before…

He hung his head, letting out a raw breath. There were things she didn't know. She'd been through enough. How could he possibly burden her any further with his own problems? They certainly weren't going away. She was just embarking on her life, making all these self-discoveries. And he was the one tied down.

"You said love," he whispered hoarsely. "Love is a word that gets thrown around far too often, and when it's convenient."

Her eyes took on a wounded look. "You don't believe me."

He had to turn away. He'd had no agenda. He'd said he'd help her. He'd agreed to let her hire him. He'd even trusted her with the story of his mother. How had it ever come to this?

She was really crying now and it killed him to see her red-rimmed eyes. He'd trusted her. He needed her. He'd fallen in love with her. All three rules broken. It was a complete disaster. She deserved better than him. She was ready to spread her wings. He would only slow her down.

"I can't do this," he said, swallowing thickly against the knot of denial. "There are things..." He stopped just short of saying the words. His jaw tightened. "You don't need me, Kelley. You need someone who can put you first."

"And you can't?"

He closed his eyes. What got him most was that he wanted to believe her, and knowing it caused that slow, sick turning he recognized as dying hope. Just like he'd wanted to believe the others. Like he'd believed his mother every time a promise had been made. Like he'd believed Lissy when she'd said the words. But at the end of the day, none of them stayed.

And then a cowgirl in crisis had shown up at his shop and turned everything upside down. And he knew that to let himself hope with her was different. He'd given her his heart without even realizing it. And if he told her, and then lost her...he was pretty damn sure this time he wouldn't bounce back.

He heard her sniff and was filled with self-loathing. She only thought she felt this way. In time she'd realize he wasn't right for her. And yet somehow the little boy inside still longed to hear the words.

"What do you want, Kelley?" He said the words slowly, testing them out. "Because it's more than a turkey and a Christmas tree. What do you see happening between us?"

Kelley gathered what little bit of courage she had left around her. This wasn't how she'd planned it to go. She'd wanted his arms around her, comforting words of love and support. She'd wanted to tell him how she felt, and she'd hoped he would feel the same way. Instead she was faced with a cold stranger, and she did the only thing she knew how to do. She couldn't let herself fall apart again, even though she was quaking on the edge of it. She'd come too far.

She tried to cover her hurt with ice. "If you think I asked

you to stay out of some misplaced obligation, you're perfectly mistaken. I asked you because I thought we shared something special, and that you might want to share your first 'real' Christmas with me."

"If it's because of what I told you and…"

She couldn't let him finish. She had to press forward. "Did you think what we shared was part of your payment? Or that I did it out of what, misplaced pity? Or worse, that I *used* you?" This wasn't about hiring him, or feeling sorry for a poor misused boy. It was because of the man he'd become. Why couldn't he see that?

At his lack of response, she tilted her chin. "I thought you thought more of me than that. I thought you saw me for *me*."

"I do," he uttered, his deep voice hoarse as he stood before the tree they'd decorated together. "Believe me, Kelley, your feelings now aren't real. One day you'll turn around and I'll just be 'that guy' that helped you get over 'that time.'"

"Do you really think so little of me?" Her mouth dropped open in dismay. "Of yourself?"

"No! And…" He paused. Sighed. "This was never part of the plan. And now you tell me you were…raped…" He seemed to struggle over the word. "And I feel like someone sucker punched me."

His eyes darkened with anguish. "I can't get past the picture of his hands on you." He took a shuddering breath. "I'm angry…and I'm feeling helpless. And those are two emotions I've had to work very hard to overcome."

It was becoming clear he couldn't handle the truth. She'd been a fool to think he could. This was exactly why she hadn't told him before. "Are you saying you don't want to see me again?"

"I got caught up in the moment with you. I wanted a real Christmas and I fell for it all. But that's not what's real. Life isn't this way every day—all perfect and pretty and goodwill toward men. Sometimes it's ugly and lonely."

"You are a coward."

The words came out of her mouth in an impulsive, hurtful rush, and Mack recoiled against the blow. It was as though she'd driven a knife between his ribs, cutting off his air. He'd wanted desperately to be wrong. For her to tell him he'd been wrong. But he deserved it. Every single bit. He could turn it around and around all he wanted, use her eleventh-hour revelation as an excuse, but the truth was he would only hurt her, and ending it now would be doing her a favor. He couldn't ask her to take him on. Not with everything he had to deal with these days.

"You're right. I am a coward."

Her eyes glittered as her back straightened. There was none of the timidity, none of the self-consciousness he'd seen. In its place was a strength that was beautiful to behold, even as her words of truth cut into him like knives.

"You, Mack, are lying to yourself. So what if you helped me move past what was holding me back? That doesn't mean it was meaningless." She went to him and touched his arm. He looked down at her fingers but resisted the urge to cover them with his own. Something was happening here, something bigger than asking him to spend Christmas. Something he couldn't face.

"Kelley," he began, but she cut him off.

"In fact, I think the only reason it did work was because it *wasn't* meaningless. I believe in my heart it could only have been with *you*. And if knowing it makes you scared, well join the club. It frightens the hell out of me. I'll be damned if I'll run away from it. You made me love you. But you go ahead and be a coward."

She went to her purse and took out a check. "Here you go. Paid in full. Just like we agreed."

She opened his palm and put the paper in it, then closed his fingers over top. She turned away and disappeared into the kitchen.

For a few moments he thought about going after her. But

then he remembered the phone call on Sunday, knew where he'd be tomorrow afternoon. This was for the best. He quietly put on his things, tucking the check back into her purse as he went out the door.

Kelley sat at the kitchen table, her hands folded in front of her. He hadn't come back. Hadn't called. She missed him. All week she'd imagined having him beside her tonight. She'd imagined giving him the tiny present she'd picked up on impulse as they sat next to the tree. She had wanted to put on the new dress she'd bought and fix her hair and feel beautiful.

Instead, she'd had a good cry, and then gone upstairs and changed into a pair of soft pyjamas. Tomorrow she'd put on a merry face and do the family Christmas.

For tonight she was just miserable.

She got up and made a pot of coffee. The familiar smell of Mack's special grind reminded her of the morning she'd awakened with him sitting on the side of the bed. She missed him with a loneliness so unfamiliar and sharp that she had a hard time breathing. Now Boone was coming back, and Amelia was going to have her chance at happiness. Kelley had thought it was going to work out for all of them. And while she was happy for her sister, it was a stark reminder of how she'd come so close and lost.

She took her coffee and turned on the television. It was all Christmas programming—the day simply could not be ignored. She left it on *White Christmas,* but only half paid attention to Bing Crosby and Rosemary Clooney crooning at each other. She thought of Mack, earlier tonight, serving dinner to the homeless. Why hadn't she volunteered to go with him when he'd first told her? Would it have made a difference in the end?

In a matter of minutes it would be Christmas Day. And despite all her planning, she was alone.

The lights on the tree glittered, reflecting off the foil-wrapped gift that lay beneath the branches. Inside was a set of ornaments in the shape of kitchen utensils. She'd hoped that tonight they could put them on the tree together. Kneeling down, she picked up the box and ran her hand over the paper, feeling the awful urge to cry. She'd come out from beneath the heavy mantle of her hurts, but he hadn't. Her heart ached for the boy who had been so lonely. A man who wouldn't—couldn't—trust.

A man who didn't love her. Who would rather leave than let himself give in to love—to being loved.

The knock on the door startled her out of her musings. She pressed a hand to her heart, her first thought that it might be Mack. She stood upright and let out a breath, surprised that the hope hit her so hard. It was probably just Amelia with some last-minute thought about tomorrow's dinner.

She opened the door and there he was.

His breath made a cloud in the bitter night as a few flakes of snow fluttered beyond the verandah. His hands were in his jacket pockets, the sheepskin collar turned up against the cold.

The frigid air sneaked into the house through the open door as seconds passed.

"I missed you," he said finally.

A tiny glimmer of hope kindled. He was here. She wouldn't risk him leaving again; tonight there could be nothing but absolute truth.

"I missed you, too."

"And I want to be with you," he said, his dark eyes holding hers captive. "I love you, Kelley."

The glimmer burst into flame as he stepped forward, surrounded her with his arms, kicking the door shut behind him. For the moment nothing else mattered…she was in his arms again. He was there, for her. Everything else melted away.

"I love you, too, Mack."

He put her down, cradled her cheekbones with his thumbs. "You mean it? Even after everything I said today?"

"Yes, I do."

He dipped his head and touched his lips to hers, gently, reverently. "I'm sorry about this afternoon," he whispered, dotting light kisses on her cheeks. "Nothing came out right."

She put her arms around him and rested her head on his wide shoulder. The fabric of his coat was still cold from outside, and she inhaled the leathery scent of winter mixed with the clean cologne she now knew was simply Mack. "Keep going," she said softly. "You're doing okay so far."

He laughed, a low, sexy rumble that somehow turned the world right again. "Look at you," he marveled, standing back and holding her hands out.

She belatedly realized she was in cream-colored flannel pyjamas, and that she'd done nothing with her hair since taking it out of the clip. "Oh, don't look at me! I'm a mess!"

"You're beautiful. All cream and pink and…your hair is down." He let go of her hands and reached out, touching a golden strand. "I love it when your hair is down."

Tears stung her eyelids. "Thank you."

Kelley closed her eyes. He was here. Really here. "I missed you so much. I didn't think you were coming back."

"I didn't, either. Until I realized I wanted to stop running." He led her to the sofa and they sat down. "I've been running for so long I'm not sure I know how to do anything else."

She squeezed his hand. "That's a start."

"Why did you come to *me?*" he said at last. "Why did you ask me for help?"

"I think I was just meant to be there, at that time, in that place. And there you were. The answer to all my problems, and I didn't even know it."

He nodded slowly. Kelley watched him struggle with something, and her heart softened even more. "What about you, then? Why did you agree?"

"I saw you were trying to give. To give something of yourself to make it easier for the family you obviously love. I never had a Christmas with decorated trees or dinners or presents.

I never saw one where a family loved each other enough to go the extra mile. What you were doing—it was selfless."

He looked down at their fingers. "You were like that with me, too. And I pushed you away. You deserve better than me," he whispered hoarsely. "You deserve more than the kid of an alcoholic who couldn't have cared less whether her son lived or died, a child who didn't matter."

"You can't turn back the clock. You can't pretend it didn't happen. You do matter. To so many people. To me. Oh, Mack, I know." Her lip quivered but she pressed on, knowing he had to understand exactly how she felt. "You know why Mack's Kitchen works for you? Because you can still be on the outside looking in. And as scary as that is, it's not nearly as scary as dealing with it. Just like me being with a man was too frightening to think about. Until you. You took my fears away."

Mack turned away first, faced the Christmas tree. She was right; he knew it.

"You give other people what you want for yourself, but are too afraid to believe in." She rubbed a hand between his shoulder blades as he nodded. He could feel the warmth even through his heavy coat. He'd gone to the shelter this afternoon, still angry and confused. But as he'd served a turkey dinner to those without homes, his thoughts were always with Kelley. The pleasure he normally felt in helping out was soured. And he'd realized in a very painful way that the rest of his life was destined to be the same if he didn't stop tap-dancing around the facts and just be honest. He needed her. And it was okay.

"When I was home alone tonight I realized that the work was just a substitute for happiness. I went to the shelter, but the joy of helping was gone from it. Because you are my joy. I had you and I lost you."

He looked into her eyes. They were so beautiful, hazel with the green flecks reflected by the mellow glow from the tree. "And then a couple came in. They had nothing. Their clothes were threadbare, their faces wrinkled. But they were holding hands. Her hands were so shaky." He swallowed as he recalled the way the woman's fingers had trembled as she'd reached for her plate.

"They took their dinner and sat together and he reached over and buttered her roll. Such a small gesture, but she smiled at him and I knew. He will always be there for her, no matter what. It's you, Kelley. It's you I need." He leaned forward, squeezed her hand as he emphasized, *"Just you."*

"Oh, Mack..."

"I was afraid. Afraid to trust in you, believe in you. But more than that...I was afraid to believe in myself. I set up those walls to protect myself because loving you made me vulnerable. Only, it doesn't work without you."

But there was more he needed to say, to explain. He should have been truthful with her all along. He should have trusted her the way she'd trusted him. "So now I have to be completely honest."

He paused, tempted to stare at his hands but knowing he had to face this dead on. He had to trust her. They'd come this far. "Tomorrow at the rehab center..." He swallowed. He could do this. "It's not just volunteering. I go to see my mother."

Kelley gasped, her eyes darting to his. Of all the things he could have said, he knew she hadn't expected this, and guilt snaked through him once more.

"Don't look at me that way," he said. "I know I should have told you."

"I thought you didn't know where your mother was."

"I didn't want to have to explain." He ran his hands through his hair. "And her body *is* there, Kel, but it's broken. And I don't know where her mind is. She left after high school, but I never heard from her again. Until I got a call that she was in hospital, and she'd listed me as her next of kin. She'd been drinking. She'd had an accident. The damage was permanent. She can't tell me from one of the orderlies."

She reached out and covered his hand with hers. "Oh, Mack. How horrible. For both of you."

He blinked against the compassion in her voice. "It's why I finally came back, you know. At least this way I can be closer to her. Someone has to pay her bills. I don't want her in some dingy room without a window."

"I'm so sorry. I can only imagine that growing up, you must have wished for things to change. And that with her accident..."

"Yes. There's no chance of it now. Maybe I should hate her for my childhood, but..."

"But she's your mother." She smiled softly, rubbing her thumb over the top of his hand. "And you still care about her and want to look after her."

He nodded, fighting back emotion. She understood. He wished he'd trusted her enough in the beginning to tell her. "The phone call the other day—that was the nurse on duty. My mother asked for me. That's the first time it's happened since the accident. But by the time I got there, she was gone again. And I was angry. I had let myself hope again."

"Of course you did." Kelley smiled. "A part of you always wanted to believe."

His fingers squeezed hers. "The last woman I told was two years ago. Our relationship ended very abruptly. I was afraid to tell anyone again, afraid to care so much about someone that it mattered."

"What changed your mind?"

He raised his hand and ran it down her hair. The tree lights glimmered off it. She was his angel, he realized. His everyday angel. Not just one for Christmas Eve or bringing out on holidays. She was the kind of woman who was strong enough to be there day in and day out. He twisted a few strands of her hair between his fingers. "You."

"Me?"

He smiled into her surprised face. "Yes, you. The weight's heavy, Kelley. And I realized that you had put your faith in me when you told me about your rape. And if you were willing to trust me with something so painful, then I could trust you. I just needed to admit it to myself."

Kelley looked down at their joined hands. It was like a world opened up to her, one with more colors and facets than she even knew existed. "You don't have to go through it alone, Mack."

His breath came out with a whoosh as he pulled her close. "I spent a lot of Christmases all over the world looking for a miracle," he said into her hair. "And it was right here all along."

Tears clogged her throat as her fingers dug into his back. "Right back at you," she whispered. And when she finally eased her grip on him, he kissed her. Again, and again, and once more, as if he was afraid she would disappear from his embrace.

She got up from the sofa and went to the tree, picking up the present she'd bought for him. "Here," she said, holding it out. "It's not much. But when I saw it…"

He undid the ribbon and wrapping, grinning at the display of miniature utensils inside. "For your tree."

"For our tree," she corrected. He stood, handed her a tiny potato masher sporting holly on the handle and tied with gold ribbon. "Here. You should hang the first one."

Together they hung the ornaments and stood back to admire.

"I realized something tonight," she whispered, leaning back into the shelter of his arms. The fire had burned down, leaving only glowing embers. "The truth is I've hidden behind this ranch for so long I don't think I realized I was even doing it. It was my one thing, you know. And I held on to it tight."

"And now you're letting go?"

"I didn't put enough faith in people, either. Amelia deserved more of it. And now…well, her happy ending is on his way here. Things are going to change around the Rocking H. I don't have to hold on to it with both hands."

"You're giving up the ranch?"

She laughed. “Not completely. Maybe I can hang on with one hand?” She leaned back so she could look up at him. “And hang on to someone else with the other?”

“I like that idea. As long as I’m the someone else.”

“You don’t see any other sexy chefs around here, do you?”

He laughed. “There’d better not be. In any case, I’m glad to hear it. Because I was kind of hoping that I could pull you away for a few days.”

She smiled then, a soft smile filled with sweetness. “Where are we going?”

“How does Washington sound? I have a short trip there for work in the new year. It’s not very glamorous…but it is convenient.”

She slid closer to him, felt his arm tighten around her, warm and secure. “It works for me. As long as you’re there.”

“And after that…I’ll take you anywhere you want to go. London. Paris. Rome.”

The idea was so big she could barely comprehend it. But while she’d always felt the need to see things, there was something that suddenly mattered more.

“I got you something, too,” he said casually.

“You did?”

He went over to his jacket and fumbled in the pocket. When he came back, he held up a sprig of mistletoe.

“It worked once before…”

She stepped forward and placed her hands on his chest. “Powerful stuff, that mistletoe.” And she kissed him as he held the mistletoe above their heads.

When she stepped back, breathless, he smiled, like he had a secret.

“What?”

“It worked. Mistletoe is supposed to be a plant of truce. Even among lovers.”

“You didn’t think you needed reinforcements, did you? Not that I’m complaining.”

"Now, about that travel. Paris. London. Rome," he continued thoughtfully, "any of those places would be wonderful for a honeymoon."

She put a hand to her chest. "A honeymoon!"

"Yes, a honeymoon." He lowered the mistletoe and she saw something dangling from the center of the clump.

"Oh…"

It was a ring. Not a traditional engagement ring encrusted with diamonds, but a wide white-gold band with an inlaid filigree design. Tiny diamonds winked from within the setting. She couldn't have picked anything more beautiful herself.

"I left the shelter and saw it in the store window. They were just closing up, but when I explained…" He unfasted the ring from its anchor. "I thought it would suit you for everyday, even when you were working. I didn't want to get you a ring you could only wear on special occasions." He slid it off the ribbon and poised it at the tip of her finger. "An everyday ring, for my everyday miracle."

She blinked rapidly as he looked down at her, so earnest, his dark eyes so full of love. For her.

"Will you marry me, Kelley? We can live here if you want…. I know you like being close to your family. Although, the house is almost done and would be much bigger for our family…if you want babies. But it's your choice."

The tears that clogged her throat earlier returned, making it impossible to speak. After a life of always doing what was expected, to be given a choice was glorious. The horizons were bright and wide. And Mack would be beside her.

"Yes." She found her voice. "Yes, I will marry you. And we can live anywhere as long as we can fill it with babies. If that's what *you* want."

"I want," he confirmed.

The clock chimed the hour and she sighed. "Merry Christmas, Mack."

"Merry Christmas, sweetheart."

EPILOGUE

KELLEY CARRIED THE TURKEY to the table on Great-Grandma Hughes's ivory platter. Dishes glittered on the pristine white tablecloth. On a side table a tray of asparagus puffs was down to crumbs, and the bottle of champagne Mack had brought was nearly empty. She caught Mack's gaze as he talked with Boone; his eyes twinkled back at her. Jesse knelt on the floor with his new train set while Gram sat in her rocker, overseeing the locomotive's progress on the track. Amelia helped bring out the last of the dishes and for a moment the two sisters looked over their family.

"It's a picture, isn't it?" Kelley spoke softly, looking at her sister's beaming face. She smoothed the red-and-green apron that was protecting her new dress. "Everyone together. Gram hale and hearty, Jesse so happy. And you, too. I'm so happy for you, sis." She reached down and squeezed Amelia's hand.

"It worked out," her sister said simply, but the smile that had been on her face since this morning had yet to fade. "And you look beautiful. A dress, and makeup. And did you blow dry your hair?"

Kelley felt a blush rise to her cheeks. She had put in extra effort this morning. It was an important morning. And she and Mack had decided together to wait for the right time to share their news.

"Let's call them all to the table," Kelley suggested, and left the task to Amelia, watching as her sister rounded up the family with motherly efficiency. She swallowed against the emotion rising in her throat. To think that such a short time ago, things had been so different. Now Boone was here and they were going to join forces with the neighboring ranch he'd bought. As they all took their places around the table, Kelley slid the ring out of her apron pocket and back onto her finger, where it belonged.

"Gram? Will you do the honors?"

Ruby's voice rang out, strong and clear as she gave the simple but heartfelt blessing. "Lord, thank you for this blessed holiday, for health, happiness and bringing all of us together. Amen."

Kelley cleared her throat as the five bowed heads raised. "Well…" She gave a little laugh. "Before our professional carves the turkey, I have an announcement to make."

She got to her feet, feeling five other pairs of eyes on her. "First, my big sister welcome-to-the-family to Boone. I've never seen Jesse so happy or my sister so radiant." Boone and Amelia smiled at each other, and Kelley felt the warmth of their love clear to her toes. "I was pretty happy to hear you were on your way back to these parts, Gifford. Welcome home."

Boone stood and came around the table to give her a hug. As he did, her ring sparkled on her left hand and Amelia gave a gasp.

"Kelley?"

She stepped back from Boone's embrace and reached down to her right to take Mack's hand.

"Oh, yes, I nearly forgot!" She laughed, knowing something so wonderful could never have slipped her mind. She gazed down into Mack's eyes. She would never tire of seeing that look there, just for her. "Mack proposed last night and I accepted."

There was a general scrape of chairs against the floor as they were pushed back, squeals of excitement and congratulations echoing through the room. Amelia rushed forward to hug her sister, Boone and Mack shook hands, and Gram came forward to give each and every one of them a hug while she dabbed at her eyes with a red-and-white handkerchief. "It's about time we had some menfolk around here," she announced.

When the hubbub quieted, Mack presided over the turkey, while bowls were passed and plates filled. Everything had turned out just right. Kelley had cooked a beautiful dinner with only the slightest input from Mack, who seemed reluctant to let her out of his sight. As Kelley ate, she listened to the chatter around her…two more places set this year, twice the happiness. What would next year bring?

But Jesse was being unusually quiet and she wrinkled her brow. He'd wanted a father so desperately. What could be wrong?

"Jesse?"

"Yes, Aunt Kelley?"

"You okay, sweetheart? You're awfully quiet."

He shrugged. "Just thinkin'."

She hid a smile behind her finger. "Thinkin' about what?"

Forks paused as everyone seemed interested in his answer.

"Well," he said, thoughtfully scooping up a helping of potato, "I was just wondering. Does this mean I'm gonna have a daddy *and* an uncle, too?"

Her hand slid away from her mouth and she couldn't hold back the smile at the innocent question.

"Yes, Jesse, that's exactly what it means. Is that okay?"

His eyes widened, a gorgeous picture of boyish wonderment. "Oh, yeah, it's okay."

He leaned over and tugged at Ruby's sleeve. "Hey, Grandma?" he whispered, just loudly enough so everyone could hear.

"Yes, Jesse?"

"You were right, Grandma. About Santa."

Kelley's eyes stung with happy tears as she laughed. It was as though a little miracle had suddenly happened right here at the Rocking H. And as she took Mack's hand under the table, she understood that sometimes all you really needed to do was just believe.

* * * * *

As an early Christmas present, Donna Alward would like to share a little treat with you….

MACK DENNISON'S ASPARAGUS PUFFS

6 tbsp/85g butter
12 asparagus spears
12 sheets phyllo pastry
11/2 cup/120g Parmesan cheese
12 thin slices of prosciutto ham
*Mack's Kitchen dill seasoning**

Preheat the oven to 450°F/230°C

Trim the root ends off the asparagus. On a cutting board, spread out one sheet of phyllo, keeping the remaining sheets under a damp cloth. Using a pastry brush, brush the sheet with butter and fold it over on itself. Sprinkle the surface with dill seasoning and Parmesan.

Lay a slice of ham on top, then an asparagus spear, and roll it up. Brush with butter and cut into 2-inch/5-cm lengths. Lay on a nonstick baking sheet. Repeat with the remainder of the ingredients. Bake for 10 minutes until golden brown. May be served hot or cold!

*To make dill seasoning: Mix 2 tbsp/30mL dried dill weed with 1 tsp/5mL sea salt, 1 tsp/5mL dehydrated garlic, 1 tsp/5mL dehydrated onion, 2 tsp/10mL red pepper flakes.

Mack's kitchen hint: If there is seasoning left over, you can use it to flavor other dishes like grilled salmon!

0/26/MB307

Spend Christmas with NORA ROBERTS

Daniel MacGregor is the clan patriarch. He's powerful, rich – and determined to see his three career-minded granddaughters married. So he chooses three unsuspecting men he considers worthy and sets his plans in motion!

As Christmas approaches, will his independent granddaughters escape his schemes? Or can the magic of the season melt their hearts – and allow Daniel's plans to succeed?

Available 1st October 2010

www.millsandboon.co.uk

/MB321

A Christmas bride for the cowboy

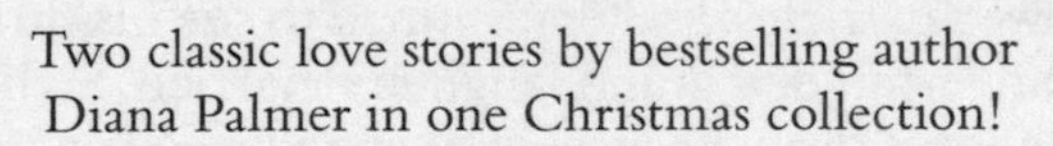

Featuring

Sutton's Way

and

Coltrain's Proposal

Available 3rd December 2010

www.millsandboon.co.uk